MINE UNTIL MORNING

Books by Jasmine Haynes

MINE UNTIL MORNING

HERS FOR THE EVENING

LACED WITH DESIRE

(with Jaci Burton, Joey W. Hill, and Denise Rossetti)

YOURS FOR THE NIGHT

FAIR GAME

UNLACED

(with Jaci Burton, Joey W. Hill, and Denise Rossetti)

SHOW AND TELL

THE FORTUNE HUNTER

OPEN INVITATION

TWIN PEAKS

(with Susan Johnson)

SOMEBODY'S LOVER

MINE UNTIL MORNING

Jasmine Haynes

HEAT
New York

THE BERKLEY PUBLISHING GROUP
Published by the Penguin Group
Penguin Group (USA) Inc.
375 Hudson Street, New York, New York 10014, USA
Penguin Group (Canada), 90 Eglinton Avenue East, Suite 700, Toronto, Ontario M4P 2Y3, Canada
(a division of Pearson Penguin Canada Inc.)
Penguin Books Ltd., 80 Strand, London WC2R 0RL, England
Penguin Group Ireland, 25 St. Stephen's Green, Dublin 2, Ireland (a division of Penguin Books Ltd.)
Penguin Group (Australia), 250 Camberwell Road, Camberwell, Victoria 3124, Australia
(a division of Pearson Australia Group Pty. Ltd.)
Penguin Books India Pvt. Ltd., 11 Community Centre, Panchsheel Park, New Delhi—110 017, India
Penguin Group (NZ), 67 Apollo Drive, Rosedale, North Shore 0632, New Zealand
(a division of Pearson New Zealand Ltd.)
Penguin Books (South Africa) (Pty.) Ltd., 24 Sturdee Avenue, Rosebank, Johannesburg 2196,
South Africa

Penguin Books Ltd., Registered Offices: 80 Strand, London WC2R 0RL, England

This book is an original publication of The Berkley Publishing Group.

ISBN 978-1-61129-007-3

To Rose Lerma, my wonderful friend

ACKNOWLEDGMENTS

Thanks to Kathy Coatney and Rita Hogan for all the encouragement. To my editor, Wendy McCurdy, for giving me the opportunity to write Isabel's story (since I was dying to!). And to Lucienne Diver for all her support.

CONTENTS

THE
ONLY WAY OUT

1

DANI DAWSON WAS DROWNING. EVERY TIME SHE THOUGHT SHE HAD a handle on the bills, she'd find another unexpected statement in the mailbox. The vultures had swooped down on her before Kern was even cold in the ground, and the balance in the checking account was a mere one hundred forty dollars and change.

The walls of her sunflower yellow kitchen closed in on her. The burn in her belly had risen to her chest. If she'd been a crying person, she would have laid her head on the kitchen table littered with unpaid bills and let loose an ocean of tears; for herself, for Kern, for all his pain, his dying, everything they'd lost. She'd scattered Kern's ashes a week ago, on a September day too bright for mourning. Now she missed him like hell.

But Dani was long past the tears. Instead, she picked up her cell phone. Kern would understand what she had to do. She hit a speed dial.

Isabel answered on the second ring. "How are you doing, kiddo?"

"I'm fine, thanks for asking." Dani forced cheer into her voice. "I could really use a date tonight if you can whip up something fast."

Isabel gave a full five-second pause, an eternity. "You know, Dani, you can give it a little bit more time."

Dani swallowed, her eyes aching, but she gritted her teeth. She had to get through this. She'd cried in the early days, when they'd first learned about Kern's cancer. She'd never let him see her tears. She'd been strong and stoic for him in the ensuing year of treatments that didn't work, mounting medical bills, and the rising fear that he might actually die. Six months ago, when the cancer spread to his kidneys, she'd finally broken down, but not in front of him. No, she'd reserved that mortifying moment for Kern's brother, Mac. He'd been kind, comforting, but that was the last time she'd lost a grip on herself. She hadn't cried the day they'd decided to bring hospice into the house—Kern hadn't wanted to die in a hospital—or ten days ago when he passed away. Not even when she and Mac had flown out over the ocean on that bright and sunny day and let Kern's ashes blow to the four winds.

She would not do it now. If she started, she would never stop.

"Isabel, I appreciate your concern. It's very sweet. But I'm fine. The hard part is over. I'm glad he isn't suffering anymore. Kern would want me to move on." God, that seemed pathetically justifying. "And I need the money." Oddly, the truth sounded better.

"Dani, honey, I can help out—"

"Please, Isabel." God, no. She didn't want charity. She'd never lied. Isabel always knew it was about the money. Sure, Dani loved sex, and it was a kick to get paid for it, but she'd only become a courtesan when the money dried up and the medical expenses didn't. When they were doing well financially, they'd occasionally splurged, using Isabel's special agency for a little variety. Dani's sex drive had always burned a few degrees hotter than Kern's, but he loved to watch.

They'd made the decision together that working for Isabel and Courtesans was the perfect solution. Isabel had been more than willing to help, of course.

"Call it a loan, Dani."

Dani snorted. "I owe too much money already." She massaged a temple. "I'm really okay with this. If you can find one of my regulars, great. But someone new, that'll work, too." Yeah, she was getting desperate. She hoped it didn't show in her voice. She would get through this difficult time. And she would do it alone. Kern would have hated anyone knowing how bad things had gotten for them. His biggest fear had been Mac finding out how they'd screwed up. Five years younger than his brother, Kern never felt he measured up.

Aw hell, why not admit the truth? She was not going to lean on Isabel or Mac to get her through. She wouldn't depend on anyone. She'd let Kern make far too many decisions, and look where it had gotten her. She wasn't about to give up her autonomy again.

Besides, this was just sex, and she loved sex. It might be the only way out, but it wasn't such a bad way.

"I don't want to see you push yourself too quickly, sweetie," Isabel said. "You've been through something terribly traumatic."

"I know that." Dani's voice quavered. It was all she could do to stuff the emotion back down. "But I"—suddenly starving for air, she gulped a breath—"I really need this. I—I just need it. Please." It was almost begging. "If it's someone I haven't been with before, could you make sure they're okay with cash?"

Many clients paid in gifts: jewelry, artwork, trips. Dani worked on a strictly cash basis. She had no set price. It depended upon the patron and what they wanted, but Isabel didn't cater to an overly thrifty clientele.

Isabel sighed. "All right, you win. Let me see what we've got going. Will tomorrow night work, too?"

"Yes," Dani answered, feeling a small surge of relief. Tonight, tomorrow night, every night until she could get out from under this weight. "Thanks."

"If you need to talk," Isabel added, "I'm always here for you."

Isabel was one of the few people who knew the true toll Kern's illness had taken on her. "I appreciate it, but I'm fine, honestly. I'll get through this."

"I know you will. You were always the strong one. But you don't have to do it all alone."

Yes, she did. Isabel knew that, too, because she was the same way. "Thanks. I'll wait to hear back."

Hanging up, Dani didn't feel so strong now. In the beginning, getting paid for sex had been a unique thrill. Kern had gotten off on it, too. But the massive financial crisis she found herself in had stolen the fun out of it. Not to mention the fact that she and Kern had always enjoyed talking about it afterward, giving her a second high out of it. It wouldn't be the same doing it all alone, but whatever. Taking care of some of these bills and getting back on her feet was all that mattered for the time being.

She and Kern had made some bad choices. She couldn't blame him; she'd agreed to everything, starting the business, canceling the life insurance, the shitty medical plan. Yeah, when you're in your mid-thirties, healthy and happy, you don't think about dying. You think you've got years to accomplish anything you want. Until the day some doctor says you've got only a few months left to live.

Water under the bridge. Right now, she needed Isabel to find her a date.

AFTER A LONG DAY AT THE OFFICE, MCKINLEY DAWSON PULLED into the circular driveway of his brother's house. His heart hurt simply looking at the familiar wood siding and manicured bushes. He wondered how long it would be before he stopped seeing Kern's emaciated, ravaged body and could remember him the way he used to be. God, he missed him. They'd lost their parents years ago, their dad to a heart attack and Mom to breast cancer. He'd never expected to lose Kern so soon. At thirty-nine, Kern had been five years younger than Mac, for God's sake. It didn't seem possible. Or fair.

Now Kern had tasked him with taking care of his wife. Dani was tough. Amazing, in fact, with the way she'd handled everything. In the eighteen-month battle she and Kern had fought with his cancer, Mac had seen only one crack in her facade. She'd shored it up quickly, and he still saw her as the last woman who would need taking care of. He'd made that deathbed promise, however, and dammit, he was here to make sure she had whatever she needed.

Standing on the pebbled front stoop, he could hear the doorbell echoing through the house. The two weeks before Kern's death, when things got really bad, he and Dani had shared caring for him, with hospice aides coming in twice a day. He hadn't rung the doorbell then. He'd simply walked in. In the evenings, after a grueling day that had seemed to last forever, while Kern slept, Mac and Dani shared a bottle of wine, talk, a movie. They'd watched *Young Frankenstein*, and he remembered laughing hysterically, followed by the stab of guilt at being capable of laughter. The last couple of days, after Kern fell into the coma, he'd spent the night so Dani wouldn't be alone if . . . when . . .

For those two weeks, he'd felt closer to her than to any other human being, even Kern. He couldn't adequately express how much it meant that she hadn't hesitated to allow him those last few precious days with his brother. Some people never got to say goodbye. Then Kern was gone, his ashes scattered, and she'd slammed the metaphorical door in Mac's face.

Inside, he heard her shoes on the tile entry hall. The door swung open.

"You're early. I'm not quite ready." She glanced up, fastening an earring in her lobe, and stopped, her lips parted as if she'd been about to add something.

Holy hell.

She wore a short black cocktail dress, the deep scoop of the neckline barely covering her nipples. In sheer black stockings and fuck-me high heels, her legs were miles long. Statuesque when bare-foot, with the heels and standing a step up from him in the front hall, she was actually taller than his own six-two. Her auburn hair curled about her shoulders like a wave, and her lips were painted a deep, luscious red.

Christ, she smelled good. Something subtly sweet and exotic like the bottled scent of feminine arousal.

The hall clock started to chime. Behind him, a car pulled into the opposite end of the circular drive, a long black sedan.

She had a date. Kern hadn't been dead two weeks, and she had a fucking date.

"Sorry. Didn't know you were going out." He couldn't get the hell away fast enough. What the fuck? He needed time to think before he said something he'd regret.

So he left her with the entry light shining down on her bur-nished hair. She still hadn't said a word. As he pulled away, in his rearview mirror he saw a man climb out of the car, tall, black suit.

Had she been cheating on Kern while he lay dying? Mac's head whirled with a load of shitty thoughts. That bitch. His hands tightened on the steering wheel until his knuckles turned white.

She didn't need him to fucking take care of her. She'd already had someone on the side.

His blood raced in his ears, and he wanted to pound some-thing. Passing through a green light, the bright neon of a bar sign flashed from the street corner, and Mac pulled into the parking lot.

He needed a drink.

It felt as if he had to pry his stiff fingers off the steering wheel. All he could hear was Kern's voice in his head.

I fucked up so bad, man.

In a rare moment of lucidity, before he succumbed to the coma, Kern had gripped Mac's hand. Dani was out getting groceries, and to grab a breath of fresh air away from Kern's sickroom. Mac had thought she needed it. While he spent as much time as he could, she'd borne the brunt of taking care of Kern.

"You didn't fuck up," Mac had told his brother.

Moisture trickled from Kern's left eye, but not his right. Mac's guts twisted as he wiped it away.

"I did, man, screwed up real bad. You don't know. I was a bad husband. I let her down in so many ways. Now I'm dying on her."

They'd had the storybook marriage; they were happy. Until Kern got sick. "It's not your fault. You couldn't help it."

Kern shook his head. "You don't know what she's done for me. You don't know what I've put her through. It's all my fault." He dropped back against the pillow, his face going completely slack, eyelids drooping.

Chest tight, a knot in his throat, Mac put two fingers to Kern's wrist. It seemed like an eternity before he found a pulse.

Kern opened his eyes and spoke as if the moment hadn't happened. "Promise me you'll take care of her."

"Of course." Though Mac knew Dani wouldn't need it. She was strong.

Kern clutched his hand, squeezing with more vigor than Mac would have thought possible.

"Don't tell her I'm saying any of this, okay? She'll kill me if she knew." Kern laughed, then lapsed into a choking cough, his throat rattling. He sucked on the straw Mac held out, his lips dry and cracked despite the Vaseline Mac had rubbed in only a short time ago.

"Joke's on me, I guess." Kern drew in a deep breath. "Where's my cell phone?"

"Right here, buddy." On the bedside table along with Kern's watch, wallet, and keys. As if one of these days he was going to get up out of the hospital bed hospice had brought to the house for him.

"Take it, man. After I'm gone, let her get settled a bit, then call the first number on speed dial."

"Sure. What'll I say?"

"Just say you're my brother, and that you want to help Dani."

"I will." Mac agreed to everything to ease his brother's worry.

"She's gonna hate it when she knows I told you. But don't let that stop you, okay?"

"I won't." Though Kern hadn't told him a damn thing. Mac still didn't know why Kern thought he'd fucked up, what he believed Mac could do for Dani by calling a number, or how the hell long he was supposed to wait to let her "get settled."

That night, Kern lapsed into a coma. He never came out of it. Two days later, he was gone. Dani never asked where his cell phone was.

Sitting in the bar's parking lot, the neon sign flashing on, off, Mac experienced the rush of revelation.

He didn't know where she was going tonight or who the guy driving the car was, but he knew one thing. She'd loved Kern. She'd gone through eighteen months of hell, spent hours at his bedside, soothed his brow, cleaned him, held the tissues as he coughed up phlegm, and so much more. She wouldn't have cheated on him. There had to be another explanation. Something to do with the phone number Kern had wanted Mac to use.

It was time to make that call.

2

KERN'S PHONE WAS BURNING A HOLE IN HIS POCKET. MAC HAD BEEN torn, feeling uncomfortable poking around in something he didn't understand, especially when Kern said Dani would hate it. Now, though, between his promise to Kern and Dani's odd behavior, he didn't have a choice. Or maybe that was justification for satisfying his curiosity.

Pulling Kern's phone from his suit jacket, Mac flipped it on. Hitting the first speed dial, the caller ID read Isabel. Jesus. It couldn't have been Kern having the affair. But wait . . . Isabel. She'd attended Kern's memorial. A good-looking blonde. Dani'd hugged her, but didn't introduce her to Mac, and she hadn't come to the house afterward along with everyone else.

He didn't have time for further analysis as he connected.

"Dani, what are you doing using Kern's phone?" The voice husky, sexy, the woman obviously knew the number on the caller ID.

"This isn't Dani."

She gasped. "Kern? Oh my God. Kern."

His stomach twisted. "No, Kern's dead. You were at his memorial. This is his brother, McKinley Dawson."

"Oh." She paused. "You scared me." She puffed out a breath. "I thought it was one of those phone calls from the hereafter."

"You've gotten calls from the hereafter before?" Damn. Was she some sort of psychic scam artist that Dani and Kern had gotten involved with?

"No, I've never received a call. But it's always within the realm of possibility." She breathed out a long sigh, as if she were trying to get her heart rate under control. "You sound like him, you know."

Mac had never really thought about that. "Look, Kern gave me his cell phone and said to call you so that I could help Dani."

A phone rang in the background, followed by a low voice, so he knew she was still on the line despite her lengthy silence. "Did he say how you were supposed to help Dani?" she finally asked.

"No."

"Did he tell you who I am?"

"No."

"What *did* he say?"

"Just to call this number, tell you I was his brother, and that I wanted to help Dani. That's it." He paused to let it sink in. "So what the hell is this all about?"

She growled. "He said he was going to do this, and I warned him not to."

"Well, he didn't listen. I want to know what I have to be worried about here."

"Nothing. Dani can take care of herself."

He'd have agreed until he saw Dani dressed to kill tonight. "I won't know until I hear the story."

"Look, Mr. Dawson, Kern was a very sweet man, but he didn't have the right to reveal Dani's secrets without her permission. I've already stuck my nose into one friend's business, and I realize now that was wrong. So I'm not telling you anything, and I won't mention to her that you called. This is strictly between you and Dani. You figure out how to bring it up with her. Whatever she decides she wants you to know is her call."

"You sure do know how to pique a man's curiosity." Except that what he felt was more than that.

"I most certainly do."

For the first time, he heard a smile in her voice and suspected a double entendre. "Fair enough," he agreed. "I'll talk to Dani about it."

"If *she* wants your help, feel free to call back. And Mr. Dawson, just so you know, I'm looking out for Dani, too. You really don't have to worry."

Damn. The woman had him going. What the hell was up with Dani? He'd thought he and Kern were so close, yet his brother had been keeping things from him. Mac was beyond being pissed at a possible affair, way past mere curiosity. His need to know was fast becoming obsession.

And it was definitely not good to have any kind of obsessive feelings about your brother's widow.

GOD, WHAT HAD MAC THOUGHT LAST NIGHT WHEN HE'D SEEN HER party dress? She couldn't think about that now. Maybe after a cup of coffee, she'd dream up a reasonable excuse to give him the next time she saw him.

Dani poured herself a mug of the strong brew, grabbed the paper off the front porch, and carried both out to the back patio. The morning sun was already warm and the air still muggy after the storm two days ago. It was the most changeable early-fall weather she'd seen in the Bay Area in quite a few years. She hoped it signaled the end of the drought.

In more ways than one.

She'd stuffed last night's envelope in her purse to take to the bank. She preferred weeknight dates, starting and ending the evening earlier rather than staying out to all hours. The guy had been nice enough, in San Francisco on a business trip from Atlanta. He'd chosen a luxury hotel on Union Square, dinner at a hot spot on Geary, continental cuisine. It had all been so . . . ordinary, lacking the thrill she got when she had Kern to go home to.

In the beginning, Kern had liked to watch her in action, though he never participated. Isabel chose clients who were into that. Kern was always making suggestions on new positions or acts he wanted her to try. There'd been times when he'd gotten so turned on, he needed to relive it all in their own bed when they got home. After he no longer felt well enough to go out with her, he still wanted to know every detail when she arrived home. The naughty recounting made it hot, sexy, and exciting for her all over again.

Last night, she'd had no one to go home to. No one with whom to share the experience. She didn't feel dirty, just tired. And alone.

She'd stopped taking dates a couple of months before Kern died. For the most part, he hadn't been the cancer patient you saw on TV, with tubes and IVs and no hair. Up until the last month, he was just tired, listless, slept a lot, and said he couldn't think properly. That bothered him the most, his inability to process, the things he forgot, how he couldn't come to a logical conclusion. Even his mind was slipping away from him. One night as Mac was leaving, Kern had asked him where he lived. A sickening sense of dread had settled in the pit of her stomach. Mac had simply looked at her, his heart in his eyes.

Dani sighed and picked up her phone. Hopefully soon those niggling memories wouldn't come back to haunt her.

Isabel answered on the fourth ring. They chitchatted a few moments, exchanging pleasantries, while Dani got her emotions under control; then Isabel turned to the real reason for the call. "How did it go last night?"

"He was perfect." Perfect for what she'd needed rather than

what she wanted. But having fun and getting a thrill out of it was, under the circumstances, a luxury.

"Did it help?"

Dani knew she meant the money. "I feel a tremendous sense of relief this morning." It would take care of the mortgage, thank God.

"Now maybe you can stop worrying so much."

"But I'd feel even better with a few more dates scheduled." It might actually take years to get everything in order again.

"Well, I'm sure if your regulars know you're back—"

"Actually, I'd like to do a ménage." For a ménage, she could command a higher price. With Kern gone, this was strictly business.

"What kind? Two men? Man and woman?"

"Which can I get more money for?" It was blunt. She didn't care.

Isabel took it graciously. "That always depends on the clients we choose."

Dani put two fingers to her lips, then blew out a breath. Kern had done all the arranging for her. Often, he went to meet the client or clients on his own first, vetting them. He always had an opinion.

The guy's dog meat—you'll hate him. I told him no.

If he thought she'd like the man, he'd whisper in her ear: *Honey, this one you'll want to swallow. I think I might be jealous.* But he never was.

She'd had a date with a couple once. Kern had watched from a darkened corner so they hardly knew he was there. The wife had wanted to see her husband with another woman. They'd ended up sucking his cock together, and she'd helped the man make love to his wife, holding his cock, guiding it in, showing them new positions.

How she missed having Kern be a part of it. Now it was just a job.

"If it depends on the clients, then I'll do either a couple or two men, whoever would make it more . . . worthwhile." God, now she was going to the highest bidder.

"Then I'll let you know when I have something." Isabel paused. "Need I say again that I think you're rushing things?"

"Yes, you can say it. Thank you for being concerned."

"Is this really what Kern would have wanted?"

Dani rubbed her forehead, squeezing her eyes tightly closed. "Kern was fine with it when he was alive. Now he's gone, and this is the only way out."

"All right. I'll say no more. Call you."

She wouldn't dwell on it, reaching for the paper instead.

And froze when the screen door squeaked on its hinges.

Mac stood in the shadow of the house, the sun pouring over the roof and straight into her eyes. Her heart beat so hard she thought it might pound right out of her chest.

"I rang the bell. You didn't answer."

"So you just walked in?" A slight edge laced her voice.

"Your car was in the driveway. The door was unlocked." He paused. "It never used to be a problem." Unlike hers, his tone was completely flat.

She wished he'd come into the light so she could see his expression. How long had he been there? Stupid question. Even without seeing his face, she knew he'd been there long enough.

"It's not a problem," she said. "There's coffee in the kitchen."

"I don't need coffee."

Then what did he need? For a moment, she had an uncontrollable urge to screech at him. *Get out, get out, get out.* Having his brother find out was the only thing Kern would have hated. Her breath felt shaky in her throat.

Then Mac stepped down onto the sunny patio and stole her breath. He was so like Kern . . . and yet not. He wore his sandy hair slightly shorter than Kern had. His eyes were a darker shade of blue. Kern had been strictly casual while Mac always wore a suit and tie. He was a couple of inches taller and five years older, but the lines at his eyes only seasoned him. His build was huskier with hard muscles, but Kern had lost so much weight the last year of his life. It was his face, though—that struck her, the same firm jaw, same cocky smile, same mannerisms. You saw them together, you knew they were brothers.

Looking at him was a physical ache.

He was all she had left of Kern. She didn't have any family of her own, her parents long gone, a car accident when she was twenty. Mac had been her only friend during the worst of it, the rock she'd clung to in those last days of Kern's life. Maybe he hadn't understood everything she'd said to Isabel. God, she couldn't even remember exactly what had come out of her mouth. She could only hope and pray her end of the conversation had been fairly innocuous.

He stood over her, reaching into his jacket pocket, his eyes an intense blue. Then he laid a cell phone on the wrought-iron table.

Kern's phone.

"He had a woman named Isabel on speed dial."

She blinked, the sun burning her eyes.

"And you were just talking to someone named Isabel." His voice was rough as sandpaper.

Her chest was so tight, she couldn't breathe. He'd heard. He understood.

"What the fuck, Dani?"

And he'd judged.

3

A PULSE BEAT AT HIS TEMPLE, THROBBING SO HARD IT GAVE HIM A headache.

Mac had come to talk. Rationally. He'd rung the bell, checked the door, called out her name, then followed her voice out to the patio.

What the fuck? Dates, clients, a goddamn ménage? She was selling herself? And Kern was *fine* with it? He'd had Isabel on fucking speed dial, for Christ's sake. His brother was more than *fine* with it. Mac felt like his head might explode contemplating it all.

"Why do you have Kern's cell phone?" Her face was blank, eyes unreadable as she squinted against the sun.

"He gave it to me before he died, right before the coma." Then, instead of playing twenty questions, he yanked out a chair, sat so the sun was no longer in her eyes, and gave her virtually the same explanation he'd given Isabel. "He said he'd fucked up, asked me to take care of you, and told me to call Isabel's number after he was gone. That's all."

Her nostrils flared with a deep breath, and a flush rode her cheekbones. "Did you call?" He couldn't tell if her tone was accusatory or merely curt.

"Yes. Isabel referred me back to you without telling me anything. She didn't think it was Kern's right to involve me." He clenched his teeth together, waited. How was she going to answer that one?

"I appreciate that you're trying to do what Kern asked," she said steadily, "but I can take care of myself, Mac."

"If what I overheard is what I think it is, that's not taking great care of yourself."

She pursed her lips. "Then you shouldn't have walked in when I didn't answer the door."

She was fucking calm, cool, and distant. As if they'd never shared those evenings while Kern lay sleeping. There was a closeness, a bond that came from caring for someone you both loved and were terrified of losing. "Talk to me, Dani. If you want me to understand, I'm willing to listen."

She opened her mouth, and her hazel eyes deepened with a glimmer of moisture. Then she rolled her lips, bit down, and stared at her clasped hands a long moment. "You'll need some coffee while we talk." She went inside, the screen door banging.

He ached for her, swear to God. She'd met Kern when she was twenty-nine, dated him for six months, lived with him as man and wife for eight years, and watched him die. She'd lost her parents when she was in college, and Kern always thought that had been part of their connection, being alone in the world, no close relatives except for Mac, no big family.

Perhaps that was the reason Kern had wanted Mac to take care of her. He was all she had left and vice versa. That in itself was why he needed to at least hear her out.

She gave him the coffee the way he liked it, strong and black.

Folding herself into her chair, she curled her feet beneath her. She wore jogging pants that zipped at the ankles and a fleece sweatshirt. Even without makeup, she was a beautiful woman.

"Isabel runs Courtesans," she finally said after a long sip of coffee. She liked hers sweet and creamy. "It's an . . . agency, and I've been working for her for about a year to help make ends meet."

"Working?" The word felt harsh in his throat, his tone ugly.

She bristled, glared at him a moment before settling back again. "You heard enough to know exactly what I mean. Would you prefer I spell it all out detail by dirty detail?"

In his anger, he was also being an asshole. He ratcheted back. "What about Kern's business?"

She waved a dismissive hand. "We got in at the wrong time, with the economy in flux and telecommunications companies struggling. Most firms started doing the work in-house rather than contracting it out."

Kern had been a damn good technical writer for a telecom manufacturer, but he'd wanted to be his own boss. With his contacts in the industry, he'd been sure he could make a go of starting up a freelance business writing technical manuals for the equipment. It was a highly specialized field. The telecommunications industry had taken a big hit, however, and the smaller companies faded away, but Kern had made it sound as if he'd been able to diversify his skills. He hadn't given Mac a single clue they were in desperate straits.

"Things were starting to come back, more contracts," Dani went on. "We weren't running in the red anymore. But then he got sick, and things fell apart." She tapped her finger to her lips, staring into her coffee. "He was the technical expertise. I was just administrative: the billing, purchasing, formatting, editing. The actual writing and meeting with the customers' techs, that was all Kern." She finally looked up. "Even with the customers we did have, he couldn't keep up."

Kern never said a thing. Mac had thought everything was under control, at least until the last few weeks when Kern spiraled down so quickly. "Why didn't he say something? I could have helped somehow."

"He didn't want you to think he was a failure."

So he let his wife prostitute herself? He closed his eyes, reeling in the emotions that threatened to get away from him. "I never thought he was a failure."

She shook her head, then swept out a hand at him. "Look at you. CEO of a highly successful company before you're even forty-five, while his venture simply tanked. Even before he got sick. He didn't live up to your expectations."

"I didn't have any expectations," he said, his gut churning.

"But you were always one step ahead of him financially and professionally."

"I was five years older, too. That made a difference."

She looked him square in the face, and he felt his skin heat under the collar. Had he done that to Kern, made him feel as if he weren't good enough? He'd always tried to give him useful advice. True, he thought Kern was making a mistake going out on his own, especially when he wanted Dani to help run the fledgling company. It was putting all their eggs in one basket. Okay, yeah, he'd tried to talk Kern out of it. For his own good.

Christ. Mac thought they were close, best friends as well as brothers. Yet Kern hadn't confided a damn thing after that, never asked for help or advice. Not until he was dying, and he begged Mac to take care of Dani. When it was too goddamn late.

I fucked up so bad, man.

Jesus. Was this some sort of self-fulfilling prophecy? He'd been dubious about Kern's success, so Kern had stopped asking for anything. His brother had needed someone to believe in him. No, dammit, he'd needed his *brother* to believe in him.

Picking up on his thoughts, Dani touched his hand briefly. "It's not your fault, Mac. That's not what I'm saying at all."

No, he wasn't to blame. But had his lack of confidence in Kern played a role in his so-called fuckup?

Mac might have allowed himself to wallow in the emotion, except for one thing. "Whatever happened with the business doesn't explain letting you work for Courtesans." It was no goddamn excuse for turning Dani into a hooker. "How could Kern allow that? You're his *wife*, for God's sake."

"We were desperate."

He wasn't listening, barely registered the tense lines of her face and the hollowness in her gaze. An even worse thought occurred. Isabel's number had been first on Kern's phone. "Jesus Christ, don't tell me he was fucking pimping for you?"

She was so still, a deep line bisecting her eyebrows, her gaze suddenly bleak, centering on his chest rather than meeting his eyes. "He didn't pimp for me," she said very softly.

Maybe not. But Kern sent her out there knowing what she'd have to do. "God*damn* him." Mac gritted his teeth so hard, he thought they'd snap. He wanted to smash something, anything. He couldn't believe Kern could do it. What kind of man had his brother become? "Tell me how he could fucking do that. Why?" He stopped short of actually shouting at her.

She raised her eyes to his. Something chased away the shadow. Anger. Not just anger, but a deep rage. "Why?" Her lips trembled, she narrowed her eyes, and her fingers clenched. "I'll show you fucking why, Mac."

DANI SHOT TO HER FEET AND YANKED THE SCREEN DOOR SO HARD it slammed back against the wall, the window next to it shuddering in its frame.

How *dare* he judge Kern this way? Mac had no idea how all the bad things had snowballed so quickly. She grabbed the stack of bills, inches thick, and banged back out the door. Slapping the wad of papers down on the table in front of him, she stabbed the pile with her finger so hard it hurt. "That's why."

He picked up the first one, his eyes widening. Then he read another and another, finally looking up at her. "How much?"

Her chest was so tight, she couldn't breathe. Her throat was clogged and her eyes ached from unshed tears. But she would *not* let him see her cry. She'd done that once, never again. "More than a hundred thousand."

He stared at the statement in his hand, a breath in, a breath out. "Holy shit."

Dani collapsed into her chair, grabbed her mug because she had to have something to hold on to or scream. This was exactly what Kern had feared, that Mac would judge them and find them irresponsible and stupid. She'd tried to tell Kern his brother would never do that. Yet Mac had, just as Kern said he would.

"What about medical insurance?" he asked.

"We had a shitty plan that didn't cover a lot of stuff." She covered her mouth. She'd brought hospice in, trying to believe it was because Kern wanted to die at home in his own bedroom with her and Mac to watch over him, but the truth was, she could not pay for a hospital room. She'd cremated him because she couldn't afford a casket or a plot. Oh God, what had she done?

"He should have come to me. I would have given him the money. He shouldn't have made you do this."

She sniffed and told herself it was *not* because she was crying. Then she heard him, actually *heard* what he was saying, felt it deep inside. "Kern never made me do anything. It was my idea to work for Isabel."

He stared at her as if he couldn't even entertain the idea, as if it were easier to think his brother would sell his wife.

She remembered his words. *What the fuck, Dani?* Yeah, what

the fuck. It didn't matter what he thought of her. The truth was better than letting him believe Kern was some sort of sick monster.

"We used Courtesans as clients first. Before everything went to hell." It was almost a relief, to finally tell someone.

"He wanted other women?"

She smiled, really she did. Because he just couldn't seem to fathom it. "I was always more hot-blooded than Kern."

"You?" The word came out of him almost without a sound.

She reveled in shocking him. In making him see her as a person, a woman. A very sexual woman. "Yes," she enunciated. "Me. He couldn't keep up with me." She wanted to laugh when his eyes widened. "I have a very strong sex drive. And Kern liked to watch."

God, yes, it was starting to be fun. She'd never seen McKinley Dawson at a loss for words, and it felt better than anything had in a long time. He was so in control of every situation, always the answer man, always making the right decision. Which was why Kern had never wanted to tell him.

"In fact," she went on, "Kern liked to watch more than actually *do*." Yes, she was being a bitch, but whatever. It was cleansing. "Isabel helped us find men who liked that. It's called the cuckold scenario." She leaned in for emphasis. "And afterward, he and I had the best sex of our marriage."

Mac cleared his throat, then swallowed.

TMI? Oh yeah, way too much information for Mac. He looked shell-shocked. She had the feeling he was as in control in the bedroom as he was in the office. No funny business, strictly by the book.

"It was good for us," she told him. "Perfect for us. Kern always dealt with Isabel, picked the partners, interviewed them beforehand." She laughed a little too harshly, her eyes smarting at the memories of the fun they'd had, the fun they'd never have again. "He had this whole rating system." *Doable, suckable, and oh yeah, baby, you'd swallow for him.* Okay, she wouldn't tell Mac that one. "If he hadn't gotten sick, we'd still be—" She closed her eyes a moment against the deep thrust of pain. Her momentary sense of triumph fled in a flash. "When we couldn't cover all the medical bills and even the mortgage was in danger, I told him I wanted to become a courtesan. It worked exactly the same except that I got paid instead of us doing the paying." Which meant they could indulge far more than occasionally.

For the first time, Mac spoke. "So he arranged everything, went along to watch, right up until he was too sick to get out of bed?" His face lacked expression, his tone even, but his hands on the armrests of the chair flexed, fisted, flexed again.

She felt suddenly sick that she'd said so much. She'd gotten carried away. Her emotions had been bouncing to hell and back for weeks now. That didn't end with Kern's passing. "He stopped before that, when he didn't have the energy to leave the house. He still wanted to speak to the clients on the phone, though, and he and Isabel always talked for a long time. He made me call him before, during, and after to make sure everything was okay." He'd wanted to hear every detail, too, even when he was too tired to do anything about it. It was part of their ritual.

Hands fisted, hands open, a tick along his jaw, then finally Mac spoke. "And he never got jealous?"

"No." Emotionally, they'd seemed closer than ever before.

"At the end, when you went out for groceries or to get a breath of fresh air, were you doing . . . *it*?" His jaw tensed, and she could swear she heard the grinding of his teeth.

He thought she was out fucking other men while her husband lay dying, and that was all he saw. "When Kern started to go downhill fast, a few weeks before we brought in hospice, I stopped doing it. Right then, it was more important to be with him than to pay the bills."

He rose suddenly, the metal feet of the chair screeching across the concrete. Pacing to the edge of the patio, his back to her, he shoved both hands through his hair, and stood that way a long moment, his muscles rigid.

They'd been close for two weeks as Kern drifted nearer to death. She hadn't expected that connection to last. But she hadn't wanted it to end with Mac hating her, either.

4

ANGER, GUILT, DOUBT, AND DESIRE CONSUMED HIM. HE WAS SO goddamned pissed at Kern. His brother had practically shut him out of his life. Mac had known nothing about Kern's business problems. Now that he thought of it, they hadn't even told him Kern was ill until he'd started losing weight with the cancer treatments. Until it was obvious something was wrong.

God, the medical bills. Kern must have been terrified thinking about it all, yet not a word. Mac had to face that he hadn't known his brother at all. Kern hadn't trusted him enough to tell him anything, yet Mac wondered if he'd even earned the trust. Had he always been I-told-you-so and you-shouldn't? Yeah, he had. But Jesus, voyeurism, kinky sex, Courtesans, sending his wife out on dates.

He couldn't comprehend watching your wife with another man.

He couldn't imagine letting someone else touch Dani if she were his.

When he turned to her, God help him, he imagined her naked. On a bed. Her lips around his cock. Try as he might, he couldn't erase the images her confession evoked. She was too hot-blooded for Kern. She loved sex. She loved men, enjoyed having Kern watch, telling him all the naughty details.

Mac wanted her with an intensity that burned. She'd pried open his eyes with her story. He couldn't shut them again. It was like going from zero to a hundred in one second flat. One moment she was Kern's wife; the next, she was a courtesan he'd pay anything to have. Despite his anger and guilt.

With his emotions roiling inside, he suddenly understood Kern's deathbed guilt and mixed feelings. It seemed Kern had thrived on all the kinkiness, yet it had become the rope around his neck choking him. He'd created the financial problems, then sent his wife out to solve them. In dying, he could no longer take care of her, yet he'd known she'd have to continue.

Kern was right—he'd fucked up badly. And he'd wanted Mac to fix it for him.

Mac should have seen it right away, but it was still like a sledgehammer to the chest. "Holy shit, that's what he wanted."

"What are you talking about?"

"Kern wanted me to take care of you. The way he did. To make the arrangements, interview your clients, have you check in, make sure you were safe."

She shook her head, her hair brushing her shoulders, the sun shining through the auburn strands. "He wouldn't do that."

He stood over her. "That's exactly what he did."

She'd been Kern's wife, but the revelations had sexualized her. She was no longer off-limits. By extracting the promise to take care of her, Kern had given permission. As if he were passing the torch.

She gaped at him. "But that's crazy."

He grabbed Kern's phone off the table and damn near shoved it in her face. "He asked me to call Isabel. If that's not what he wanted, you find another explanation that works."

She stared at the phone, swallowed. He knew she didn't have an answer.

But did he have one? Would he actually become a part of this weird, kinky scheme?

"I could give you the money," he said.

She jerked her head up. "I've already got enough debt." She didn't say it, but he understood. She didn't want to be in debt to *him*. "But thanks," she added belatedly.

Still, he pushed. "I didn't say *loan*. I said *give*."

She shook her head, fast, adamant. "No. Absolutely not. This is my problem and I will take care of it."

"So you'd rather sell yourself." His voice was hard.

She glared at him. "Kern was right. You *are* judgmental. He said you wouldn't understand, that you were too high and mighty."

Her words hit him like a jab to his vitals. He'd never wanted to come off that way to his brother. But Christ, the truth was in her anger.

She leaned forward, chin tilted up to him, and slapped her hand to her chest. "I enjoyed it all. Kern loved it. It worked for us."

He turned, threw the phone back on the table, where it skittered to the far edge. He paced like a man who couldn't run away from his own thoughts. Who was he to judge the rules of their marriage right or wrong? It wasn't as if he had some great relationship to hold up as a shining example. He'd never married, never even come close. He'd done some kinky things himself. Some goddamn kinky things, more than one woman, sharing with another man, a sex club. Yeah, he'd mostly watched there, too. A voyeur, just like Kern.

Stopping in front of her again, he shoved his suit jacket aside, planting his hands on his hips. "Maybe it did work for you two," he said. "But at the end, he realized he couldn't leave you unprotected. He wanted someone to take care of you the way he did."

"That's what *he* wanted." She glared at him. "But I never asked for it."

Mac leaned down. "Maybe you don't have a choice anymore." Jesus. He was going to do it.

MAC STRETCHED ACROSS THE TABLE AND GRABBED KERN'S PHONE. "Call Isabel and give her your permission to talk to me."

Dani stared at the phone as if it were a huge hairy spider.

Dammit, Kern hadn't *taken care* of her. All his arranging and checking was part of the kick. Why had he thought he needed to involve Mac? She could manage this herself.

She put her fingers to her temples. "I have to think."

Mac sat. Thank God. She hadn't appreciated him standing over her like some avenging angel. "There's nothing to think about," he said with that arrogant, autocratic tone. "Either call Isabel or take the money I'm offering."

"Don't order me, Mac."

He sat back, tipped his head slightly, regarding her with a slim smile. "I misjudged your entire marriage, didn't I? You wore the pants the whole time."

No, she hadn't. If she'd been completely in charge, she wouldn't have quit her job or bought into Kern's dream. She'd let herself become dependent, and it had all gone wrong. She would not let that happen again. She would not take Mac's money. She would not depend on a man.

"You did misjudge. But not all the mistakes were his." She dipped her head. "Some were mine, too."

"Thanks for your honesty." He waited a beat. "But I'm still going to take over your dating arrangements."

She almost laughed, it was such a diplomatic way of putting it. Typical CEO rhetoric—never call it what it is. "Why?"

"Because I want to."

She had no clue what that meant. Guilt over a deathbed promise? God. She was talking sex with *Mac*. The worst, though, was the hungry voice inside her whispering *yes, yes, yes*.

Her husband wasn't dead a month, but God help her, if she was going to do this, sleep with men for money, she wanted the kick that went with it. She'd always been able to divorce sex from love. She was more like a man in that respect. If she hadn't been, the Courtesans thing with Kern would never have worked. But that didn't mean the connection wasn't important. It was Kern egging her on that made it so hot, gave it that something extra.

It was inconceivable, almost terrifying, but now the primitive, sexual part of her brain wanted that connection with Mac. It was already there emotionally, had been since those terrible weeks when Kern was so ill.

"Call Isabel," Mac urged, as if he could read the desire and indecision on her face.

Slowly, she reached out for Kern's cell. Mac's fingers brushed her skin as he laid it in her palm, and she shivered.

She could only hope Kern would understand. Hell, of course, he would. He'd engineered it. Opening the phone, she hit Isabel's speed dial.

Isabel answered with "Mr. Dawson, I've already told you to talk to Dani. I can't give you any information."

"This is Dani, Isabel."

"And you're using Kern's phone because?" She couldn't read the note in Isabel's voice, not censure, but more than mere curiosity. Which made Dani wonder at the first phone call Isabel had received from *Mr. Dawson*.

Mac stared at her, waiting, almost willing her with his gaze to do what he wanted.

Dani did it. Whether he'd seduced her or she'd seduced herself, she couldn't say. "I've told Mac everything, and I'm giving you permission to talk to him."

"What does that mean, Dani?" She could almost hear Isabel's fingernails tapping on her desk.

She held Mac's gaze. "It means that he's going to take over Kern's role."

Isabel let out a sigh. "I'm glad. That's what you need. You shouldn't go it alone now."

That was it. She wasn't letting Mac take care of her. She was in control, but now she didn't have to do it alone. More than just the titillation, it was having someone to share it with afterward. Well, not that she'd go *home* to Mac.

He waggled his fingers for the cell.

The simple gesture made her feel better than she had in weeks. "He wants to talk to you." Dani gave the phone away.

Mac slouched in his seat, propped his foot on his knee, and put the cell to his ear. "I understand we're doing a ménage." He laughed at whatever Isabel said. "I prefer to have her do a couple rather than two men . . . I'm aware finances are the biggest concern, but I'd be willing to bet you'll find a couple easily." He snorted.

Dani imagined him in his office negotiating a business contract exactly the same way. Authoritative, knowing what he wanted and how far he was willing to go to get it. Her heart beat faster, her skin buzzed, and she was wet.

"When you find them, I want a meet first." He paused, shook his head as if Isabel could see. "If they're not willing, they're not the right couple." Then he smiled with a decidedly wicked cast to it. "I want someone who gets off on having to go through me to get to her." Another pause. "Exactly. It ups the stakes." Then he looked at Dani, held her with a mesmerizing gaze. "They need to understand, too, that I'll be there to watch and protect. She does nothing without me."

Goose bumps raced across her flesh. He was laying down the

law with her as well as with Isabel. His voice did something to her. His attitude. His strength. Her breath felt shallow in her chest, and her fingertips tingled.

How would she feel having him watch?

Terrified. Excited. *Mac.* Oh my God. She was completely enthralled.

"No, I'll drive her," he was saying; then he nodded. "What about remuneration?" He listened.

Isabel was obviously telling him a bit about how Courtesans worked. The agency got a finder's fee. The courtesans didn't charge; they received tips, which could be anything from cash to jewelry and other gifts. The price wasn't set; it was alluded to. Isabel, however, didn't suffer cheapskates for long.

"Fine," he said. "You can call me when you have someone." He rattled off his cell number. "Sure." He held the phone out. "She wants to talk to you."

Laying the cell on the table, he slid it across to her, as if he were afraid he might accidentally touch her again.

She retrieved it, not allowing her eyes to drop as she put it to her ear. "I'm here."

"Honey," Isabel murmured, "this is going to be good for you, I swear it. Just go with it. Don't fight it."

"I don't have much choice," she said, and Mac's mouth curved in a slight smile.

"You have more choice than you know."

Right. Isabel hadn't seen Mac's anger and incredulity, but she wouldn't argue the point in front of him. "I'll keep that in mind."

They ended with polite good-byes. Snapping the cell closed, Dani clasped her hands, holding it against her abdomen. A hiccup of emotion rose up. Kern's phone. They'd done it all as if Mac had stepped right into Kern's shoes, right down to using his cell phone.

"There, it's arranged." Mac tipped his head as if waiting for her reaction.

"Fine," she said. It wouldn't be good to let him think he had the upper hand in any way.

"You'll meet them with me."

She raised a brow.

"We're partners now," he explained.

Her heart tripped. With Kern, she'd led. He might have done the arranging and created the illusion of authority, but she'd made her own choices. Mac was a whole different story. But *she* was in control; she could call a halt to it at any time, and she'd play along only until she didn't like it anymore. Right now, the priority was paying off the debt. Her emotions about how it was done were secondary. "All right, we're partners. We'll meet them together."

"When the date comes off, I go with you. I drive you. I make sure you're safe. I'm there." He drummed his fingers on the table. "Or the deal's off."

Oh yeah. She'd bitten off more than she could chew. Yet her body thrummed to this new development. She felt compelled to see it through, that primeval part of her brain shouting at her, *Yes, yes, yes, anything he wants*. "Fine." She wouldn't, however, completely roll over for him. "But don't push me too far."

He rose, buttoned his suit jacket. "You need to remember one thing."

"What?"

He leaned over her, grabbing the arms of her chair, caging her. God, he smelled good. Yeah, right, she was *so* in control.

"I'm not my brother," he said softly, drawing one finger down her cheek. "And I'm not going to just sit in the corner and watch."

5

SATURDAY NIGHT, SAN FRANCISCO, THE RESTAURANT WAS PACKED and noisy, the menu, Greek food. Which was only natural when you considered the client's name was Spryo Stamos. He'd secured them a secluded booth in the back corner, which, Mac was sure, was due to both his wealth and the fact that he reserved this same booth every time he and his much younger wife visited from New Jersey.

What happens in San Francisco stays in San Francisco, Mac thought.

Like the good little madam Mac assumed she was, Isabel had called him Saturday morning, two days after that heart-to-heart with Dani. She had a suitable couple in mind. Since he was the pimp, he didn't ask for Dani's input, but instead made a date for dinner that evening. If he approved, he would allow her to go to their hotel room. He enjoyed the power of giving the thumbs-up or -down.

Of course, if he decided to say yes, he would accompany her at all times. The couple understood that dinner was the interview.

His blood swooshed through his veins, his heart a steady throb, his senses attuned to Dani's every move, every breath. Next to her, touching her, he felt fucking alive.

"We've never done this before," Jessica Stamos was saying.

The meal plates had been removed, the coffee and baklava ordered, the polite conversation at an end, and now they were down to the details. Mac seriously doubted it was Jessica's first time for a little kink as she fluttered her heavily made-up eyes at him. Obviously she thought he was on the menu, too.

He laid his arm along the back of the booth, twirling his fingers in Dani's hair. She wore it down and curled. It was close to silk against his skin. "Everything is a first with Dani," he said, his voice low enough that Spryo, seated across from him, had to lean in to hear.

The noise level, in effect, cocooned them. Mac had seated the women on the inside, the men on the outside. He didn't want Spryo touching Dani until he, Mac, was ready. *If.* He'd been making up his mind during dinner, assessing, analyzing, and making sure Dani felt his presence every moment. Right now, her body was plastered against his. He could feel each twitch of her body.

"Tell me, Spryo, what do you and Jessica have in mind for the evening?" he asked.

Somewhere in his early fifties, with a large beak of a nose, steel gray hair, and eyes so dark they were almost black, Stamos was a barrel-chested man and no less powerful in spite of his diminutive height. It didn't seem to bother him that his wife wore heels that put her at least five inches taller. The high heels spoke more to his self-confidence than to hers. Spryo Stamos would be hell in a boardroom, Mac was sure. He'd have enjoyed any ensuing battle.

Yet here, Stamos was milquetoast for the little lady. Taking Jessica's hand in his, he turned her wrist to his lips and laid a kiss on her skin. "My Jessica wishes to pleasure me with another woman's help." He spoke with a slight accent. Raising his brows and giving an eloquently European shrug of his shoulders, he added, "Who am I to deny her such a thing?"

Who indeed? Was he doing it for the wife, or she for him? Mac couldn't tell. He trailed a hand down Dani's bare arm. She wore a sexy, strapless evening dress that hugged every curve.

"How do you feel about that, sweetheart? Helping Jessica to pleasure Spryo?"

She was ten of Jessica Stamos. Mac had never been into the buxom redhead type. Dani shivered against him, whether from his caress or the mental image, he couldn't tell. He knew only what it did to him. He couldn't keep his hands off her now if he tried.

Dani batted her eyelashes at Stamos, then smiled sweetly at Jessica. "It would be one of the most exciting things I've done." Her voice was low, husky, seductive, designed to make a man hard in an instant.

Christ, she was good. Mac was totally into the game. It was no mystery now why this had been such a hot scenario for Kern and Dani. But tonight, she wasn't his brother's wife; she was just Dani, and she was his to give away as he wished. Or not. Mac was as hard as ever in his life.

He leaned in for the scent of her hair, laying his hand on her thigh a moment. A tremble only he could feel coursed through her body, and her breasts rose with a deep breath, giving him a magnificent view straight down her cleavage.

Dani touched Jessica's hand, and there wasn't the slightest note of reaction in her voice as she said, "What else would you like to do for your husband?"

Jessica cast her green eyes from Stamos to Mac and finally back to Dani. "I think I'd like to watch him fuck you, help guide his cock inside you, kiss him while he's doing it." She ended with a giggle, a hand over her mouth. "He's very big, you know. I like big men." She wasn't talking about his height.

Giving Mac a long, meaningful look, the woman's scheme became clear. She'd give this to her husband, and it would be her turn next. If not tonight with Mac, then some other night with another man.

Dani made an appreciative sound, then tipped her head to look at him through her lashes. She'd figured out the score, too. Since Stamos was obviously no idiot, Mac decided he'd figured it out, too, and was fine with it. Stamos let his gaze trail Dani's curves above the table, her mouth, her hair, then back to her breasts. The look was a visual licking of his lips.

Something swirled inside Mac. Jealousy. Desire. An image of Stamos's cock driving into Dani. Jessica's greedy eyes. The combination of Dani's body heat along his side, her scent in his head, and his raging emotions thrust him higher, made him harder. This was living on the edge. Where you couldn't decide whether you wanted a thing, yet were almost sure it would be so fucking hot, you'd explode with the first touch.

He rose from the booth. "If you'll excuse us, I believe it's time for my lady and I to confer in private." He held out his hand to Dani. As she laid her fingers across his, a core of heat burst inside him. His suit jacket still buttoned, his erection hidden beneath, he wanted to drill her here and now.

"Back in a moment," she said lightly, fluttering her hand at the Stamoses. The couple bent their heads together the moment he and Dani were swallowed up by the restaurant's cacophony.

"What say you, oh Master?" Dani quipped.

He squeezed her fingers. "Outside." At the front, he pushed through the queue waiting for tables, and once on the sidewalk, he pulled her into the small alcove of a closed shop next door. The street teemed with people, cars, and noise, but here in the dim entry, they were all but invisible.

"So?" Dani's gaze darted over his face.

He shoved her up against the wall, pressed his body into hers, bracketing her throat with his hand. She was close enough to eat. "I never thought I'd say it," he murmured, his mouth within striking distance, "but fuck, I want this."

MAC'S BREATH PUFFED IN, OUT, CARESSED HER LIPS. AS BAD AS HE wanted it, Dani wanted it more. She'd always thought him so staid and vanilla. He was anything but. He'd teased her mercilessly during dinner, touching, caressing, drawing in the scent of her hair and her skin as if he were stating his ownership to the Stamoses. If he lifted her dress, she'd let him fuck her right up against the wall.

Her chest ached with need. It had to be the newness with Mac, the sense of the unknown. Yet even in the beginning, Kern had never vibrated with such intensity. Nor had she. Her heart ached with the knowledge.

"We're going to tell them yes," Mac went on, his body setting her on fire.

"Yes," she whispered as if he'd hypnotized her. Maybe he had.

Kern's emotions had always been so muted. If he hadn't told her things, she'd never have known. Mac's body radiated everything he felt, from his hard cock to the rise and fall of his chest to the burn in his eyes.

"Tell me what you want," he demanded, his voice diamond hard, his eyes glittering.

Fuck me now. She didn't want to go back inside, didn't care about the money, didn't give a damn about the Stamoses. She'd do anything Mac wanted.

God, this was the kick she loved. Feeling it with Mac was so good yet so damn bad. She swallowed, her throat rippling against the hand that imprisoned her. "I want—" She couldn't find the air she needed to finish. She gulped, swallowing his breath along with hers, and started again. "I want you to watch me do whatever you tell me to do."

"Anything?" he snapped out.

She nodded. "Anything." It gave him carte blanche to take her if he wanted.

His chest rose against her; then slowly, as if prying himself off her, he used one hand to push from the wall. Cool night air blew between them.

He dropped his hold on her throat. "I'll tell them you'll do what *I* say." He jutted his chin down, his face in hers. "And they'll give me the money."

She felt like his woman, not his whore. Spryo was handsome. She could do him for Mac. She could love having Mac watch, savor the blaze in his eyes, the heated looks they would share. Oh God, yes, for tonight, she wanted it exactly this way. Where she was dying for his kiss, his touch, his cock, while another man took her.

If he wasn't her husband's brother, the moment would have been perfect.

He pulled her inside, and she thrilled to his power, his strength. At the table, the Stamoses sat much more closely than before. Spryo's eyes sparked with heat, and Jessica's cheeks were flushed, her lipstick slightly smudged.

Mac ushered Dani into the booth. "Here's how it's going to work," he said. "I will be there to watch. I will take all gifts on Dani's behalf. You will ask me for what you want, and I will make the decision as to whether you may have it. I will direct her and tell her when she's gone too far and when she hasn't gone far enough." He passed his gaze over the two of them. "Is that all clear?"

Jessica was breathing hard, faster than when they'd sat down.

She liked it, Mac's stern voice, his power. Dani felt a surge of possessiveness. *He's mine, bitch, hands off.*

Spryo smiled. "Fuck, that's hot." He grabbed his wife's hand, held it to his chest. "Perhaps we need to think about adding their kind of scenario to our repertoire, my sweet." He tipped her chin to him. "What do you think?"

His voice a whisper, Dani read his lips. Jessica nodded as if words escaped her.

Slipping his fingers between Dani's thighs, Mac spoke to Spryo. "I trust we have an agreement, then."

If he'd touched her pussy, even through her panties, she'd have come.

"We're in complete agreement."

Two powerful men making a deal over their women. Yes, by God, it was hot.

One more thing," Mac said. "If I see fit, I will join in." He turned his head, looking pointedly at her. "But I will touch only Dani."

Heat raced across her skin, just as it had the moment he'd told her that he would never just sit in the corner and watch as Kern had done. She'd tried to tell herself then it wasn't what she wanted.

She knew herself for a liar now. God yes, she needed it.

"We have a deal," Spryo said. "Now let us drink coffee and eat baklava." He smiled. "The sweets will give us a much-needed energy boost."

Mac laughed. "I agree." He chose a piece of the confection from the plate in the center and fed it to Dani. Instead of letting him go, she sucked the stickiness from his fingers.

His gaze heated. He got the message. Two could play at this game. There'd be no *if* about it; she would make sure he couldn't help but join in.

6

STAMOS HAD BOOKED A SUITE IN A UNION SQUARE HOTEL, A LONG room with a king-size bed on one end, faux fireplace, sofa, and chairs on the other. The perfect setup for the show the ladies had already begun. Seated on the sofa, Mac put his feet up, crossing his ankles. He'd removed only his suit jacket and tie.

While the ladies were powdering their noses or whatever the hell women did when they went to the restroom together, Stamos had handed Mac an envelope thick with cash. He took it with a momentary hiccup in his pulse. He'd truly become Dani's pimp. Without counting or checking inside, he'd shoved the packet in his inner suit pocket right next to his heart.

Now, fully dressed, Stamos sat on the end of the bed, his wife and Dani on either side of him.

God, she was gorgeous, enough to stop a man's heart midbeat. Mac had no clear memory of how he'd stopped himself from looking at her for all the years Dani had been with Kern.

Her skin was golden with two sets of lines, bikini and her jogging clothes. High, firm breasts smaller than Jessica's—who had the overstated curves of Jessica Rabbit in *Who Framed Roger Rabbit*—they were no less suckable. Mac ached for a taste of Dani's nipples.

"Master"—Jessica giggled—"may Dani and I undress Spryo?" Arms akimbo, hands on her hips, she was definitely a natural redhead and proud enough to display her body without any simpering or false modesty.

"Strip him down, ladies."

Jessica loved it, asking permission for each article of clothing she removed. But it was Dani Mac loved watching. Her hair tumbling in sexy disarray, she showed no self-consciousness, either. Despite how often she must have done this, he'd assumed it would be different with him in the room, but she'd bared all as quickly as Jessica, damn near giving him heart failure. Now she shot him a sly smile as she helped Stamos to stand and went for his belt while Jessica unbuttoned his shirt.

Flanked by the two women, Stamos was shorter than both by inches. But damn if he seemed to mind.

"Oh my," Dani murmured as his chest was bared. "Look at all that lovely hair."

"He's hairy all over," Jessica whispered loud enough for Mac to hear.

Mac himself had a minimum of chest hair. He wondered which Dani would prefer.

"Good Lord," Dani said on a breathy note as she revealed the man's cock. Already wicked hard, it sprang from his slacks.

"I told you he was big," Jessica said, almost as if she were shining up her nails on her sleeve.

Dani laughed. "You weren't lying." Then she glanced down. "I guess we should have undone his shoes first." Together, they went to their knees and took care of one shoe each.

They talked about him, around him, over him, never to him. Stamos merely grinned as they *ooh*ed and *aah*ed with every bit of clothing they removed and each inch of skin they revealed. Mac had figured him to be overweight, but beneath the shirt and trousers, he was mostly muscle. Dani pinched his nipple, and Stamos tipped his head back, groaning.

"Hey." Mac snapped his fingers. "I didn't say you could touch him yet."

She batted her eyelashes. "So sorry."

Jessica giggled. "Master, may we touch?" All three naked now, Jessica rubbed herself against Stamos like a cat. "I want to kiss him while Dani pinches and licks his nipples."

"You have my permission," Mac said solemnly.

The ladies went for the gusto. It was a sexy sight, and he was fine with Dani sucking on the man's turgid nipples, making him moan loudly into his wife's mouth. Mac just didn't want Dani kissing him.

"Make him sit," Mac ordered.

They pushed him down onto the edge of the bed. His cock rose straight up, the crown plum-colored.

"May I touch his cock, Master?" Jessica no longer giggled, her voice breathless, her nipples hard. She hung on to her husband's thigh, squeezing, her nails bright red against his swarthy Mediterranean flesh tones.

"Stroke him."

As she wrapped her fingers around him, a drop of pre-come oozed from the tip. Stamos closed his eyes and braced his hands on the bed, spreading his legs. His hips pumped slowly.

They didn't need Dani at all right then. Mac started to believe he'd misjudged their relationship, not your basic younger-woman-using-older-rich-dude gig. They were into each other as much as the kink.

Dani rose, crossing the room. Mac's heart rolled over at her long-legged glide, muscles defined, graceful, like a pedigreed mare. Grabbing her purse, she extracted a bottle and some packets. Tossing the condoms on the coffee table in front of him like a challenge, she winked. He almost reached out to haul her down on the couch beside him, but he was enjoying the sexy tease too much to stop it.

He wasn't sure how he'd feel when they got down to the actual sex. Maybe he wouldn't give his permission. The thought of Dani's lips sliding over Spryo's cock . . . It roused things in him, equal parts jealousy and desire, triumph and need.

He wanted to see how it all played out. How much he could take. How much he could give.

"I think we need this," Dani said, dropping fluidly to her knees beside the couple. Opening the bottle, she poured lube over the head of Stamos's cock. "It tastes good, too."

"Do not taste until I say so," Mac commanded.

Jessica made an affirming noise as she spread the lube over her husband's shaft and balls, stroking, squeezing, rubbing. The guy was hairy between the legs, too; they both were. Only Dani was trimmed, the lips of her pussy plump.

"You love the way your wife strokes you, don't you, Spryo?" Dani murmured, her tone so hot, sexy, seductive, it burrowed beneath Mac's skin.

"Holy mother, yes." Stamos gave a deep laugh and cracked one eye open. "Sometimes we play Daddy and his naughty little girl."

Jessica laughed, her eyes sparkling, and she leaned in to kiss the prominent bump of his big nose. "I know how to jerk off my daddy better than anyone."

Now, that was kinky. Different strokes. Mac had to admit, though, just watching them had him hard in his pants. It had something to do with how good they were together.

"May Dani try?" Jessica asked in a high, childlike voice.

Then there was the Dani effect on him, of course.

Mac blinked, and, behind his lids, he saw her between his legs, taking his cock in her mouth. His hips almost surged.

He wasn't like Kern, not a true voyeur, getting off only on the watching, but he needed to see her lips devouring hard, male flesh. He wanted to see a man's face as she took his cock deep down her throat, hear the groans Stamos would make. Almost as a prelude to things Mac would make her do to him.

"Suck him, Dani." His voice came out low, harsh, needy.

Dani looked at him, one second, two; then a smile grew on her luscious lips. She knew what he really wanted.

What he would have before the night was over.

"Is that all right with you, Jessica?" she asked. Mac realized there was an etiquette to doing another woman's husband.

Jessica's breath puffed, her eyes wide; then she bit her lip. "Yes. Please. I want to hold him while you suck him."

Mac could understand men sharing. But women? He hadn't thought they were built like that. Obviously, he was wrong.

A light glowed in Jessica's eyes as she fisted her husband's penis in her hand, and Dani bent to take the plum of his cock between her lips. She tongued the slit at the tip, and Mac could swear his own dick jerked as if she'd licked him.

"How does that feel, Big Daddy?" Jessica whispered.

"Oh baby, that's so good. Not as good as you, though."

"Suck hard on his crown," Jessica directed. "He loves that."

Dani enveloped Stamos. His face tensed. He sucked in a breath. Christ, it was hot, watching her cheeks flex, the bob of her head. Mac could actually feel it.

Stamos moaned. Still holding his cock in a tight grip, Jessica gathered Dani's thick, curling hair in her other hand and pulled it to one side for Stamos to see his own cock disappearing between Dani's lips.

Mac could see, too. His sight narrowed to that big cock in her mouth, and his heart pumped hard in his chest.

* * *

"DADDY, YOUR COCK IS SO BEAUTIFUL IN HER MOUTH. SHE CAN hardly take it all, you're so thick and magnificent."

Jessica talked, crooned, enthused, egged her husband on.

Dani slid Spryo deep into her mouth until she left lipstick prints on Jessica's fingers where she gripped him. He was big, thick, and tasted good. Some men didn't. Spryo was sweet, as if he'd been eating fruit.

Dani tipped her head slightly. Just enough to see Mac. Her heart clamored against her ribs. He slouched on the couch, eyelids at half-mast, hands clasped over his abdomen, eyes meeting hers in a blaze of heat.

Despite his seemingly relaxed posture, his cock tented his trousers, his gaze avid as she glided slowly back up Spryo's thick penis to circle the tip with her tongue.

Her breath felt shallow, her blood hot. Jessica's flow of dirty talk and admiration, the vibrations in Spryo's belly as he moaned, and Mac's hot gaze set her skin on fire.

This was what she needed, her man—even if he was hers only until the morning—watching her perform, getting hard, wanting her.

God, yes, Mac wanted her. His heat sizzled across the brief distance between them.

She sucked Spryo harder for good measure, showing Mac exactly what she could do for him. What she was dying to do for him. Every lick of her tongue was a promise.

All he had to do was ask for it.

"Take your hand away, baby." Spryo grunted, surged, drove himself deeper into Dani's mouth. "Make her deep-throat me."

Jessica pushed on the back of Dani's head. She took him to the back of her throat, relaxed her muscles, and he slid deeper.

Spryo arched. "Shit, shit, baby, have her teach you how to do that."

Jessica held her down a moment longer, then gently pulled on her hair. "Show me," she begged, her voice rough, unlike the little-girl tones she'd been using.

Stroking Spryo's cock with one hand, Dani tipped her head back, running her fingers down her throat. "When he's deep, relax the muscles along here and slip him a little farther."

"Oh yes, Daddy, I can do it."

The daddy-daughter scenario was common, especially with their age difference. It excited them both, and in Dani's line of work, that was what counted. Whatever it took to get them hot and bothered. It was no kinkier than playing exhibitionist to Kern's voyeur and taking money for sex.

This time, she held Jessica's hair out of the way as the woman went down on her husband.

They'd stopped asking Mac for permission, and he hadn't complained. Dani crooked her finger at him. He rose, stalked slowly to stand in front of them, towering above, hands on hips.

His sex perfumed the air.

Gazing up at him, holding him captive with just a look, she whispered to Jessica, "Suck his crown hard, stroking your fingers just below the ridge."

She didn't care if Jessica followed instructions or not. Mac would know that was how she'd do him. His pulse beat fast at his throat.

"Slide down," she murmured, "all the way. Then back up, your teeth grazing his flesh."

"Baby, baby, baby," Spryo muttered.

Mac put his hand to the front of his slacks. Beneath the material, she was sure he rivaled Spryo's size.

"Now take him again," she told Jessica. "As far as you can without gagging, and stop."

Spryo made a guttural sound. "Ahhh."

Dani never looked, concentrating on Mac. His chest rose and fell with deep breaths, as if he barely held on to his control.

"Now, relax, honey," Dani cajoled. "Relax and ease him a little deeper. Take a bit more. Until you feel the pulse in his cock at the back of your throat."

"Baby, oh baby." Spryo's hand joined hers on the back of Jessica's head. "You're my only baby."

Mac slowly reached out to push his fingers through Dani's hair. "Put your hand on me."

It wasn't a demand. His eyes burned, his skin flushed, and the muscles of his thighs flexed and bunched. He begged.

Dani cupped him through his pants. With the sound of Jessica's mouth slip-sliding over her husband's cock and Spryo's moans filling the hotel room, Dani savored Mac's girth against her palm.

She closed her eyes and imagined him in her mouth, driving deep inside her, then opened her eyes to find her thoughts mirrored in his gaze.

Spryo flopped back on the bed. "Don't make me come yet, baby doll, please, please."

Dani had forgotten her job, lost herself in the moment. "Stop, Jessica." Her voice cracked on the woman's name.

Jessica raised her head, her lipstick gone, her mouth moist with Spryo's pre-come. "Oh, that was so good. He's never made noises like that before. I could even hear them deep in his belly."

Most women would have found it unsettling. They wanted to think they were perfect. Dani actually admired Jessica for wanting to do something better for her husband. Or for at least making *lessons* out of their play.

Kneeling beside him, his thick thighs separating them, Spryo's wife reached out to cup Dani's breast, flicking the nipple with her thumbnail.

A jolt of sensation shot down between Dani's legs. She didn't do women, but the unexpectedness of it was shockingly good.

"Teach me," Jessica said, low and husky, "to fuck Big Daddy the way a courtesan would." She glanced up at Mac. "Please, Master, may Daddy fuck Dani so I can watch and learn?"

Dani met Mac's eyes and lost her breath. A rush of moisture creamed her. The scent of her own arousal rose up.

"Yeah," he whispered, his gaze dark, hot, intense, "I want to watch that big cock fuck you." He grabbed her chin. "And then you're mine."

7

JESSICA'S RED NAILS AGAINST THE CREAMINESS OF DANI'S BREAST was like a work of art. Mac's blood rushed to both heads at once, his cock throbbing, his brain on sensory overload.

Yeah, Mac was thinking totally with his dick now, and he wanted, needed, everything, whether Dani was doing it to him, Stamos, or even Jessica. He didn't merely understand what Kern must have felt all the times he'd watched. Capturing her chin, feeling her skin, holding her gaze, Mac lived it, breathed it, had to have what Kern had had.

"Fuck him for me," he whispered to her.

She parted her lips, but only nodded.

Jessica bounced to her feet, breasts bobbing. "Oh, Daddy, this is going to be so fun." She grabbed a condom from the table where Dani had thrown several packets. "How will we do her?"

Mac knew exactly what *he* wanted. "Dani will ride."

"Ooh," Jessica enthused.

Stamos grinned. "I like a decisive man. I'm at your disposal for however you wish your lady to take advantage of my body."

"May I put on the condom, Master?" Jessica held it up, fluttering her eyelashes.

She was definitely into authority figures: Big Daddy, Master.

Whatever. "Yes, you may." He helped Dani to her feet. Without shoes, she felt petite next to him, her scent rising to tantalize: apples, powder, and arousal.

Jessica clambered onto the bed beside Stamos, positioning him, pushing him flat. "Oh Daddy," she murmured, stroking a finger across the tip of his cock, then carrying the bead of pre-come to her lips. She sucked her finger clean. "I love how you taste, Big Daddy." Then she leaned down and Mac thought he heard her whisper, "You need to taste it, too."

The kiss she gave him was extraordinarily sweet. It wasn't a married couple's kiss, but a long, luscious melding of lips, sharing the taste, from her tongue to his, savoring. Now, this was voyeuristic, stepping into a moment that was between only them. The sight started a burn in his chest.

Jessica pulled back, rubbed her nose along his cheek. "I love you, Daddy." The gentle look, the tender sound, it couldn't be faked. By God, she really loved him. She could watch him fuck another woman, beg for it, yet somehow make it all about the two of them. Like a present she was giving him.

He looked down to find Dani staring at the couple. That was how it had been with Kern. It didn't matter who was fucking whom; it was all about the unspoken connection.

He was so damn envious, his guts ached.

He had to make this about *him*, with Dani. Cupping her cheek, he wanted to kiss her, badly, yet the moment wasn't right. He would *feel* when it was right, when he would touch her in a way she'd never forget. When she would be marked like a wild animal marks his mate.

Jessica huddled over Spryo's cock, caressing as she rolled on the condom.

Mac lifted Dani beneath the armpits and set her on the bed. She came down on her knees.

"Straddle him," he told her. "I want to see his cock slide inside you."

He did not remove his clothes or shoes. He didn't even unbutton his shirt. Instead, he sat on the edge of the bed, crossing an ankle over his knee, and leaned back against the headboard to watch. Dani spread her legs over Spryo's hips as Jessica held her husband's cock.

"Pour some lube over the condom," Mac instructed Jessica.

Moisture already glistened on Dani's pussy, but he wanted more. To see as well as hear the slide of that big cock inside her.

Jessica rubbed Spryo's coated penis along Dani's cleft, back and forth, wetting her with the lube as well. No, Jessica did not need lessons. She knew exactly how to please her man. Mac would love to be there as a fly on the wall for their next adventure. He was definitely getting into the voyeurism thing.

"Now take him," he ordered.

Her sweet, pink pussy, the fullness of her lips, and the sight of that impressive cock breaching her trapped Mac's breath halfway down his throat.

"How does it feel?" he murmured, without even meaning to speak.

"It stretches her," Jessica answered, "fills her up. All that hard meat"—she speared Mac with her gaze—"a man can never know how good it feels." She released her grip on Stamos's cock, then laid her hand on Dani's shoulder and pushed her down until her spread legs encompassed his hips and his cock was buried to the hilt.

Mac leaned closer, balancing on a knee, one hand supporting him. Good God, it was gorgeous. He'd always enjoyed looking down, watching his cock fill a woman, but this was more than double the pleasure.

"How does it feel?" he asked again.

This time Dani answered. "Like he's all the way to my throat." She rolled her hips, rocked, leaning back slightly and rising on her thighs. Her sweet ass flexed, and Stamos moaned.

"Sweet Mary, she's squeezing me on the inside." He groaned and grabbed his wife's hand.

Between the lips of her sex, Dani's clit burgeoned. Mac's mouth watered for a taste of her pussy. She did Stamos with short jerks of her body and the flexing of her ass, a sensation Mac knew drove Stamos mad on the inside.

Jessica lay down beside Spryo, crooning. "Oh Big Daddy, that's so hot. Look at you, how big you are inside her, how she's stretched to take you." She raised one leg, planting her foot on the bed, and stroked herself.

Dani looked at Mac. He was so fucking hard, he could have pushed her forward and done her from behind with Stamos still inside her. She bit her lip, watching him, knowing how badly he wanted it, that he hung by a thread.

Maybe that was what she'd always wanted from Kern. To get him so hot, he had to bully his way in.

The perfect moment for that first touch was almost upon him. It built behind his eyes. "Face the wall and straddle Big Daddy's mouth," he told Jessica, his tone harsh with need. "I want to watch him lick you."

He wanted her occupied.

She made an excited little noise and scrambled to do his bidding, planting herself over her husband's face, her feet alongside Dani's knees.

Lifting his head, Jessica put his mouth to her pussy and tipped her head back, eyes closed. "Oh Daddy, lick me, lick me." Her red hair swayed across her back.

Together, she and Dani rocked almost in time, one fucking his cock, the other fucking his mouth. The sounds, the scents, the heat in the room, it was like being caught in a crashing ocean wave where all you could do was feel. Thinking was impossible. Without conscious movement, he found himself on his knees beside Dani, his palm cupping her nape, her hair caressing the back of his hand.

Her lips were a wet, luscious, cock-sucking red, her naturally hazel eyes a deep olive, her cheeks flushed with desire and exertion. The rise and fall of her body mesmerized him, her mouth called to him, and Mac took that first taste of her, the one he'd craved, dreamed about.

She was like expensive sweet wine, filling him up, going to his head, turning his world topsy-turvy. She moaned into his mouth, and he wished to God he'd gotten naked so they were flesh to flesh.

He took her with a kiss as deep as the cock buried inside her. He made love to her mouth, his kiss saying everything he couldn't utter aloud.

The sounds of Stamos, his groans, Jessica's moans, the rhythm of their bodies, the hot scent of salty come and sweet feminine cream, the whisper of her moans on her lips—it all made Dani's kiss hotter, Mac's need greater. Despite another man's cock inside her, for this one moment, this first taste, there was just the two of them and no one else.

He was going to hell for how badly he wanted his brother's wife.

But he wasn't about to let her go.

Sliding a hand down Dani's throat, to her breast, Mac stroked her nipple, then pinched just as Jessica had.

Oh God. Dani flexed on the inside, squeezing Spryo's cock. His hips jerked, drove deep. It was so sweet, Mac's tongue in her mouth, his lips taking her, his fingers shooting bolts of lightning straight from her nipple to her clit, and a hard cock deep inside her.

She'd dreamed of this. She'd just never thought the man would be Mac.

More, more, more, she chanted in her mind. She couldn't let go of that kiss, his mouth, his sugary taste as sweet as the baklava. His fingers brushed the underside of her breast, her abdomen, played with her belly button, then finally tunneled into her sex, finding that hot, hard, needy button.

Her breath puffed. Oh God, so good. *Mac.* He couldn't know how good. She rode his touch as much as she rode Spryo's cock. She was close, so close, driven even higher by Jessica's rising voice as she neared her own climax.

Then Mac tore his lips from hers, pushing her back slightly in the saddle, and put his mouth to her clit, sucking, licking, circling. The sensations were so intense, colors burst before her eyes. She keened, threading her fingers through his hair, holding his head to her, riding his tongue. Spryo's cock pulsed and throbbed, and he pushed deep as much as she drove down on him, but when orgasm broke free inside her, it was not the cock inside her, but Mac's sweet caress that sent her over the edge.

THEY LEFT THE STAMOSES COLLAPSED IN EACH OTHER'S ARMS, EXhausted, sated, delirious. Dani had lightly kissed both Stamos and Jessica on the lips. Mac had kissed only Jessica. He turned the light out, leaving them in the sweetly scented darkness before closing the door behind them.

He hadn't known sex could be like that when you didn't even have an orgasm. He hadn't known he could feel such involvement when he'd never even removed his clothes or touched his cock. Dani's taste lingered on his lips, her scent all over him, his hands, his hair, his clothes.

She'd marked him. Now he needed to mark her.

Instead of hitting the elevator button, he pushed through the door opposite, pulling Dani into the stairwell with him.

"What are you doing?" she whispered. It was late. The fire door clicked shut. They couldn't get back out without walking all the way to the bottom.

She was his captive.

"This," was all he said as he pushed her up against the wall and took her mouth, feasting on her.

She moaned and opened, wrapping her arms around his neck, pulling him tight against her. The kiss was deeper, longer, stealing his breath, his soul. He needed her to taste herself on his lips, to remember how he'd made her come. He shoved his knee between her thighs, parted her legs, tugging her dress higher to rub her pussy. Her heat seeped through his slacks, his cock hard against her.

Then she was pushing at him. "Wait, wait—stop." Breathing hard, nostrils flared as if she could get more air that way. "The night's over." She searched his face.

"It's not fucking over." He tangled his fingers in her hair, pulled her head back. "I said I wouldn't sit in the corner and just watch. I *had* you in there, my mouth on you." He bent, bit her neck, not hard, just enough to leave a red mark. "But I never said I'd fuck you in front of them." He shoved her dress all the way to her waist. "Fucking is just for us."

He pushed a hand between them and unzipped, the sound echoing in the stairwell. Her eyes wide, lips parted, she stared at his mouth. Christ, he knew she wanted it. She just didn't want to say how badly. She wanted to make him take instead of her giving. In that moment, fuck if he cared how it went down.

"I will have you. You are mine tonight." He pulled his cock out, rubbed his crown over her silk panties. "Say yes."

She swallowed. Then nodded.

He simply raised a brow.

"Yes," she whispered, then added, "please." Almost a whimper, as if she couldn't help begging.

He reached in his jacket pocket, having grabbed a condom off the table while she was dressing. He hadn't known exactly when or where, but he knew he'd take her before the night was over. Hell, he hadn't even made it to the elevator.

Keeping her pinned to the wall with his legs, he leaned back to roll on the condom. Tossing aside the wrapper, he shoved his hands beneath her armpits and lifted.

"Wrap your legs around my waist," he demanded.

She was so damn good at following orders, legs at his waist, arms around his shoulders. Her thong and the condom were the only things that lay between them.

"I'm going to fuck you," he murmured, his mouth only a breath away from her lips. "Tell me you want it."

"Yes, I want it."

He pulled aside the thin, silky crotch of her panty. "Say my name. Say, 'Please fuck me, Mac.'"

"Please fuck me, Mac, fuck me hard." She gave him what he wanted and three words more.

She was already wet, already stretched, already open and waiting for him. Mac slammed home. She cried out, eyes closed, wrapped him tight in her embrace, and squeezed his cock, drawing him deeper, closer, higher.

Nothing had ever felt as good or right as being buried to the hilt in his brother's wife.

8

WITH THE DELICIOUS FEEL OF MAC INSIDE HER, COHERENT THOUGHT wasn't possible. There was only sensation. So closely on the heels of Spryo, she could feel the tighter, longer fit of Mac inside her. His kiss hot, his taste sweet, his hair caressing her arms as she clung to him, the deep sounds in his throat as he plunged; it was too much, and not enough.

"Oh God, oh God," she panted against his lips as heat built in her clitoris, along the bump of her G-spot. She needed to come that way. It was so rare for her, yet with each thrust, Mac rode her as no man ever had.

"Fuck me, Mac," she breathed against his hair, needing to say his name, needing to hear it echo in the stairwell. "Oh God, Mac, please."

A hand beneath her butt holding her against the wall, with the other, he pinned her chin and took her mouth in a kiss that was as deep and ravishing as his cock inside her. She clamped around him, her body squeezing. His cock pulsed, then he swore against her lips, pumping fast and hard. It was all her body needed, shooting her to the roof. He took her cries into his mouth, the throb of his climax filling her.

For long moments after, she clung to him, her face buried in his hair, his lips against her neck, aftershocks flowing between them, their breath harsh, calming, finally returning to normal.

He pulled out slowly, let her slide down the wall until her shoes hit the concrete. There was a trash can right by the door for the condom. Dani wriggled her panties back into place and straightened her dress as she watched him right his clothing.

His sandy hair was mussed, his cheeks ruddy, pupils wide, his jacket wrinkled. He buckled his belt.

This was what she'd always needed. A man so hot watching her, that the moment they were alone, he had to take her against a wall, couldn't even wait for home or a bed.

She couldn't think Kern's name without a wince, but what Mac gave her had answered a deep craving. His tongue on her as she rode Spryo's cock had been like nothing else she'd ever had. A delicious prelude to what he'd done to her in the stairwell.

He put a finger to the corner of her mouth. "I messed up your lipstick." He leaned in for a quick, sweet kiss.

Her body started to vibrate all over again with the brief touch. "I'll fix it in the lobby restroom."

"That was fucking hot," he said, his eyes dark in the hall lighting.

"Yes," she agreed. He could never know how incredibly hot it had been for her.

She could never tell him. It hadn't been part of the deathbed promise he'd made to Kern to take care of her.

He pointed to the door. "Fire door. We can't get back in." He glanced at her shoes. "You okay to walk down?"

They were on the twentieth floor. She held on to his arm, as much for balance as a need for connection, and removed the high heels. "Yes, I can walk." The concrete was cold against her soles.

He took her hand, leading her, holding her in case she fell. There was a whole lot of metaphor in that.

Would Kern really mind? He'd watched her so many times, gotten off on it. This was just sex, even if it was spectacular and with Mac. She'd actually done more with Spryo. Sucked his cock, fucked him for longer. But she hadn't gotten this feeling from Spryo. Hadn't felt it until Mac looked at her, touched her, wanted her. The same emotion had flowed between Spryo and Jessica. Dani had wanted it for herself, with Mac.

She held tight to his hand as if she'd tumble headlong down the stairs without him.

Kern couldn't mind because Kern was dead. She was on her own and doing the best she could.

"You okay?" Mac asked as they hit the tenth floor.

"I'm fine."

"You're quiet."

"Just tired."

He wrapped an arm around her, hugged her close a moment. "I'll have you home in no time." Then he took her hand once more, continuing on.

His consideration felt so . . . nice. So comfortable. She could start to need it.

The main-level door let them out into the lobby, the ladies' room just by the elevators.

She slipped on her shoes, then he held her fingers to his mouth, gazed at her over them, a smile playing on his lips. "Powder your nose. I'll be here waiting."

Again, it felt like a metaphor for something more. It might actually be her own wishful thinking. Which was a very scary thought. If she'd thought she'd lost her independence to Kern, how would it be with Mac? The man who didn't take no for answer, who'd dictated to the Stamoses exactly how the evening would go. Come to think of it, Mac had even dictated to Isabel.

No. What they'd done was good. Great. But it was *just* sex.

With that thought, she pulled the ladies' room door closed behind her. The night was over; now he was just her chauffeur.

DESPITE THE LATE HOUR, THE LOBBY BORDERED ON BEDLAM. CONversation and laughter spilled from the bar filled with out-of-town conventioneers. Loud groups queued for taxis and waited outside the hotel restaurant.

The moment the restroom door closed, Mac turned to the wall and pulled the envelope from his jacket pocket. He did not count how much money Spryo had given her; he simply pulled a wad from his wallet and added that to it. When he'd arranged the date, Isabel had said they didn't talk money, per se, though there was a threshold expectation she communicated to the client. If a courtesan felt underappreciated after the fact—he'd almost laughed when she'd used that euphemism—the client was not matched with her again. Consistent underappreciation and the client was dropped. In other words, a courtesan got stiffed, so to speak, only once. But they also didn't have an up-front certainty. Dani would never know he'd added to the stack.

She wouldn't take his money. This way, she wouldn't know it came from him. The debts would be paid down faster. No harm done.

He closed his eyes a moment. God, he could see why men paid for her. His body still thrummed. Her scent still enveloped him. He wasn't done. He needed more. She was not the kind of woman you did once and walked away from. The kicker was the connection, the hours they'd spent together, the things they'd helped each other through. The sex didn't simply burn hotter, it ran deeper, curling around his mind, his body, his heart. For God's sake, he could still feel the heat of her hand on his arm as she'd balanced herself to put her shoes back on.

On the stairs, he'd lost himself inside her, and that had never happened before. Sure, it was the heat of the moment, the hot fucking with Stamos and his wife, need driving him. But it was also Dani. A woman he'd known for eight years and never allowed himself to see.

She left the ladies' room with every hair in place, every smudge erased. Heads turned as she sashayed to his side. Beautiful, sexy, confident, she could hold the world in her palm.

He took her hand. They'd parked in a garage a block away. In the car, she snapped in her seat belt, then curled into her seat to watch him drive. The Saturday-night city traffic was stop and go. He tightened his grip on the wheel so he wouldn't be tempted to take her hand. Fiddling with the radio, she found a news talk station. He felt tongue-tied, another new experience. She chattered and scoffed at the radio host, a liberal. Dani was decidedly conservative, at least on the political spectrum.

By the time he pulled into her driveway, his head ached from thinking instead of doing. He shut off the engine, and the car fell into silence.

She smiled. "Thanks."

He'd expected her to jump out and run for the door. "You're welcome." Fuck, he wanted to kiss her. He wanted to follow her inside the house like a lovesick puppy and beg her to do him in her bed.

The bed she'd shared with Kern before he got so sick.

"Is Isabel going to call you the next time? Or me?"

It hit him why she hadn't scrambled from the car. The envelope in his pocket. He'd forgotten. Though God knew how.

"She'll call me," he said. "What nights are you available?" It sounded like a goddamn business deal. Which it was.

"I'm wide-open."

"I'll let you know when she has something." Finally he reached into his pocket. The envelope singed his fingers. The night had been so fucking hot, more than he'd ever expected it to be.

Now he couldn't even goddamn kiss her.

Fuck that. Laying the envelope in her lap, he wrapped his hand around her nape and pulled her close, stopping short of touching his lips to hers. "Kiss me good night," he demanded.

He felt the puff of her breath against his mouth. Then she closed her eyes and licked the seam of his lips. It wasn't a peck; it was a tease.

He opened. She pressed her mouth to his, forayed inside with her tongue. And moaned. The car's interior heated. Her breasts caressed his chest, and he wanted to crawl across the seat and take her. His fingers flexed along the back of her neck as her taste filled his mouth.

Then she slipped away, leaving him utterly bewitched. "Call me when Isabel calls you," she said.

The door opened, closed; she unlocked the house, disappeared inside while he watched. His limbs wouldn't move. He should have followed.

Closing his eyes, he leaned his head back. No. Wrong. They had only this. The nights of her dates when he took care of her, made sure she was safe. The nights were all Kern had given him. He hadn't given Mac his wife.

Christ, he needed that next date like he needed a breath.

DANI CLOSED THE DOOR AND SLID DOWN UNTIL HER BUTT HIT THE tile floor.

Oh God. She'd wanted to beg him to come in. *Stay with me.* The words had hovered on her lips. He would have come if she'd asked.

The man could own her if she let him.

"You're in control," she whispered to the empty house. She thought she heard the echo of a laugh. It sounded like Kern.

Stabbing her hand in her purse, she yanked out her cell. It didn't seem to matter how late, Isabel usually answered.

"Did it go well?" Isabel wanted to know.

That was code for the money. She'd almost forgotten the envelope in her hand. It wasn't even why she'd called. "Very well," Dani said, though she hadn't checked. Sticking the phone between her shoulder and ear, she opened the envelope. Oh. My. God. She could barely breathe. "They were *very* appreciative." And rich. She'd never expected that much. Damn if it wasn't heaven-sent, though. She laughed, overcome. "I think I need some more dates like *that* one."

"Generous, I take it?"

"Above and beyond," she admitted. "I'm almost shocked." Though she'd also say that she and Mac had shown the Stamoses an extraordinary time, a date they'd never forget, and one she was sure they would try to duplicate.

Okay, there was a reason she'd called Isabel. She needed another date as soon as possible, and it wasn't all about the money. A date was her excuse to have Mac again. She craved what he'd given her tonight.

She was in danger of losing control all over again. With Kern, it was the money. With Mac, it was her body. Or more.

9

"THAT WASN'T THE DEAL," MAC SAID THREE DAYS LATER.

Though it would have been simple enough to make the arrangements over the phone, Dani had dropped by his Silicon Valley office two hours after Isabel had called him with the lowdown on a date. Mac damn well knew why Dani had come, and it wasn't the afternoon coffee break she claimed. To make it look good, she'd brought him a stout cup of his favorite brew from the coffee bar across the street. He wasn't fooled.

Her real mission? She wanted to bat her eyelashes at him, tie his guts in knots, and get him to do anything she wanted. He was in danger of falling for it, too, sucker that he was. At this point, though, he was still maintaining a hard line. Damn difficult with her dressed in tight, sexy jeans and a low-cut formfitting white T-shirt with a black bra beneath it. There was something about seeing a woman's lingerie through her clothes that set his motor rumbling. It was goddamn slutty, and he loved it.

"This is how Kern did it," she replied evenly.

He wanted to smack a fist on his desk. "I don't care how Kern did it. We had a deal. I can only look out for you if I'm there to watch."

She snorted.

Damn if she didn't see right through him.

Three days had passed since their *date* with Stamos. Mac's skin felt stretched too tight for his body, and the sun falling through his office window turned him hot under the collar. The closed door was too much of a temptation. He wanted to grab her up out of the chair, bend her over his desk, and make her cry out the way she had in the stairwell on Saturday night. He didn't go in for high jinks in the workplace, but for her, he'd make an exception.

"Mac," she said, overly patient, as if she were talking to a child, "he's a regular I've dated for six months."

Dated? She meant fucked, but he wasn't about to say it.

"Isabel already spoke with him," she went on, "and he does not agree to be watched."

He held up his hands in mock surrender. "Look, you said you wanted *ménages* because they were more lucrative"—yeah, he'd thought about how to phrase that one—"so deviating from that plan doesn't make sense."

She pursed her lips primly and sighed at him. "The kind of thing we had with Jessica and Spryo doesn't come along often. I've got to supplement with my regulars."

He knew nights like that didn't fall out of the sky, but he wanted it again, needed it, was close to begging for it.

It was fucking unmanly to beg. He was used to negotiating.

"The priority is paying off the medical bills." She was so irritatingly matter-of-fact. "To do that, I have to see my regulars." Why did her simple statement make him see red? "And we'll handle it the way Kern did." She smiled pleasantly. "You drive me, meet him with me, wait for me, I complete my business, and you drive me home." She spread her hands, tipped her head, waiting for his agreement.

She was offering him a goddamn bone. One that had already

been chewed, buried, and dug up again. No fucking way. "Here's how it's going to work." He gave her a smile equally as pleasant, like a shark, perhaps. "I drive you, we meet him in the bar, we all three go up to the room, I watch you complete your *business*"—drooling like a mad dog every moment—"we leave, I drive you home"—then fuck like rabbits all night long—"or we cancel the date."

Her gaze didn't waver, yet her chest rose with a mesmerizing breath, her eyes narrowing as she exhaled. "Excuse me?"

"I promised your husband I would take care of you. This is how I've determined I will do it, choosing your dates appropriately."

She uncrossed and recrossed her legs. Slow and deliberate. "Kern never chose *for* me," she said with heavy emphasis.

"Maybe he should have."

She stood, magnificent in her anger, cheeks stained with red, eyes the shade of leaves just as the colors start to turn in fall. "Is this an ultimatum? Either I let you watch, cancel my date, or"—she jutted her chin—"or *what*, Mac?"

He'd seen it as a battle of wills. He was used to winning. If he didn't get what he wanted, it had never really mattered if his opponent walked away.

It mattered if she did. It mattered if he lost her. Their so-called deal had moved from being a deathbed promise he'd made Kern to being all about her. What he needed from her.

He didn't want to be her protector or her pimp. His skin hummed as if an electrical current raced through him. He wanted to be the man in her life. Fuck. It was too new and terrifying to acknowledge aloud.

For the first time in his adult life, Mac backed down before he actually dared her to step over the line he'd drawn between them. "I'll allow it, but only with a time limit, one hour, and only if you call my cell to give me the room number when you get up there, then again before you fuck him, and finally when you're done."

She laughed, the tension easing. "You're such a freak. He's harmless. I don't know what you're so worried about."

Neither did he, except that the thought of her alone in a hotel room with another man made him insane. "I'll pick you up at seven."

She smiled, shaking her head, sashayed to the door, then turned with her hand on the knob. "He only takes half an hour."

Getting in the last word, she shut the door behind her, her perfume lingering.

Only half an hour with her? The guy was crazier than Mac was.

But it did mean the rest of the night was his.

LEAVING MAC'S OFFICE BUILDING, DANI WANTED TO JUMP UP AND down and punch her fists in the air like a football player who'd made the winning touchdown. Of course, that would have been an unsportsmanlike display.

She'd won. Over herself. No begging, no compromising. Yeah, sure, she planned to have sex with Mac after her date with Sheldon, but on her terms. She'd bested *Mac*. Unbelievable. Inconceivable. He hadn't exactly backed down; he'd given her a time limit and ordered her to call, yeah, yeah, but he had to sit down in the bar and wait.

All right, it was a small triumph, but it was like telling herself she had to wait, proving she *could* wait. That gave her back the power.

Okay, it was odd. One would think getting paid for sex made a woman powerless. Not so. She could turn a man down. She could get him blacklisted. It was when you *needed* what he could give you. Yes, she needed the *money*—and she was the first to admit how marvelous it had felt paying bills on Monday with what she'd received on Saturday—but she didn't need payment from any particular man. The loss of power came when you needed the man himself.

Saturday, Mac had overwhelmed her. Three days later, she'd gotten that in perspective.

Back home after leaving his office, perusing her closet, running her bath, soaking, shaving, rubbing lotion into her skin, painting her nails, curling her hair, well, all that was for herself, not Sheldon. And certainly not Mac.

It took three hours to prepare. A man would marvel at that. Dani savored every pampered moment. If she did say so herself, in a short red dress that hugged her breasts and flirted with her bare thighs, she'd knock Sheldon's socks off. She'd paired the dress with four-inch spiked heels, which would put her at precisely three inches taller than him. He loved feeling dominated by a woman who dragged him by his tie into the room, pushed him down on the bed, and had her wicked way with him despite his feeble protests.

The side benefit to all the prep time was knocking Mac's socks off, too.

He stared for a full ten seconds without a word when she opened the front door. Helping her into the car, he trailed a hand down her arm as if he couldn't help the brief touch. As he drove them to the downtown San Jose hotel, his glance kept falling to the bare skin of her thighs.

It felt deliciously good. Maybe too good.

They were early, Sheldon hadn't arrived, and Mac ordered her a white Russian as they waited. It was a convention hotel, and the lobby bar was packed. Rather than tables and chairs, the seating arrangements were sofas and chairs with coffee tables in the middle. Every nook was filled, but Mac managed to snag one more chair for her *date*. Voices and laughter echoed off the high ceiling. Dani scooted closer on their little couch to hear Mac better.

And because she loved the way he smelled.

"Where's your cell?" he asked.

Dani smiled and patted her purse. "Right here. Yes, I remember I'm to call you with the room number when we get in, before we go all the way, and when we leave." She smiled, saccharine sweet. What she hadn't told Mac was that Sheldon never had intercourse with her, so technically, she wouldn't need to call Mac in the middle. God, Mac had breathed life back into sex, and he didn't even know it. This was how it used to be with Kern, before—

She stopped right there, closing her eyes for only the briefest moment as pain and guilt spiked right up into her heart. She couldn't think about Kern now. If she had to do this, she'd have the fun, too. It was the only way to get through.

She poked at Mac to push herself back into the mood. "Oh, and I'll tell him only the usual half hour, no matter how much he begs for more."

He smirked. "You're getting cocky."

Dani grinned. Yes, she was. She needed to. Then she pinched Mac's hand. "Shh. Here he comes."

Sheldon O'Dell shuffled into the hotel lobby, his suit rumpled, his hair windblown. A short, thin man in his late fifties, he wore wire-rimmed glasses and looked like the quintessential hen-pecked accountant. He was actually chairman of a Silicon Valley–based Fortune 500 and on the boards of several influential charities. He'd never given her his last name, but she'd seen his photo in the paper. The hotel he chose was decent but not extravagant, he drove a five-year-old American-made car, and his suits were purchased off the rack from a fine department store.

All of that was why Sheldon O'Dell was a very rich man. He paid her well. He was also masterful at oral sex. Especially when she ordered him to pleasure her. Sheldon loved to be ordered about. That was when he performed the best, and he certainly didn't have any trouble on that end.

She'd always wondered what his wife was like.

He slid into the chair beside her. "How do you do? I'm Sheldon." He held out his hand. Mac shook.

Dani would love to see Sheldon in the boardroom. She couldn't imagine he would sound as meek.

Clearly, Mac hadn't been expecting Sheldon's type. The way his gaze danced from her to Sheldon and back again amused her. He'd been ready to play the enforcer as he had with Spryo, laying down the rules, demanding. He didn't know what to do with Sheldon. Dani loved throwing him off-kilter. It shifted the balance of power to her, right where she needed it.

"This is Mac," she said, "my muscle."

Sheldon did have a sense of humor, and he smiled shyly, his eyes reaching the knot in Mac's tie and no higher. "Mac the Muscle. I like it. Very appropriate."

Kern had met Sheldon in the beginning and deemed him harmless. He was actually a very nice man. She'd seen him a couple of times a month until she'd needed to stay home with Kern. He'd been solicitous, generous, and understanding.

Mac finally seemed to decide on the tack he'd take. Crossing his legs, he folded his arms and stared Sheldon down. Even if Sheldon wasn't quite looking him in the eye. "I trust you'll take good care of Dani."

"Of course," Sheldon agreed, removing his glasses to wipe them with a cloth he pulled from his pocket.

"I've instructed her to call me during the evening so that I know she's all right."

"Your concern is commendable." Sheldon pushed his glasses back up the bridge of his nose.

Mac raised one brow. "She tells me you require only half an hour."

It could have been a slam, but Sheldon didn't react. His only reactions took place during their session when he begged her not to make him do all those naughty things. Other than that, he showed no emotion whatsoever.

Now he simply said, "Half an hour is the perfect amount of time."

Mac glanced at her, a curve to his lips that only she would recognize as a smile. "Shall we transact our business, then?"

"Of course." Sheldon slid his eyes to Dani. She opened her purse, pulling out a small tin box, and handed it to him. Wedging it between his thigh and the padded arm of the chair, he surreptitiously removed a wad of bills from his pants pocket, laid them inside, snapped the lid shut, then slid the box across the coffee table toward Mac. Square and bright blue with a field of tiny forget-me-nots, it was well used, scratched, and dented. Filled with her payment, he'd given it to Dani the first time they'd met and told her to bring it back the next time.

Her clients often had rituals they needed to perform in order to get off on the experience, things they couldn't ask of their spouses. Part of Sheldon's ritual was that tin box. Sometimes she thought he left it with her for safekeeping. If there was ever a time their relationship were to end, she would give it to Isabel to return to him.

Mac stared at the tin, then lifted his gaze to hers. She didn't expect him to understand, but courtesans played into their client's fantasy. Sheldon never told her what the box meant; she never asked. Though she had her suspicions, especially based on the nature of his sexual preferences.

With the passing of the tin, she was now in charge. "Sheldon, it's time," she said sternly. "You know what to do."

His breath quickened as he rose. Dani followed.

"Sheldon," Mac said.

Sheldon's head jerked up.

"Half an hour. That's all you've got. One second more, and I'm coming up to get her. And you won't like what I do."

Sheldon shuddered. Dani knew that shudder. Excitement. Anticipation. Mac had upped the stakes in the fantasy. Sheldon might actually take thirty-one minutes tonight.

Hopefully the extra minute would drive Mac crazy.

10

AFTER DANI CALLED WITH THE ROOM NUMBER, MAC STEWED. HIS imagination ran away with him, and the heat of his blood rose with his ire. Sheldon might be meek, mild-mannered, and odd, but Mac hated the idea that he was up there touching Dani as much as he would were Sheldon some handsome, young stud who'd stolen his girl.

How had he managed to get himself into this position? A god-damn cuckold—wasn't that what she'd called it?

He closed his eyes, and he could *see* that little man touching her, and it made him crazy.

The waitress was busy with a group of businessmen. A gaggle of office workers gossiped. There were couples, heads together, talking intimately, and men trying to do the pickup thing, their glances darting about the bar, landing on a quarry momentarily, then a flurry of discussion between them as they set up the game plan. No one paid Mac much attention. He flipped open the tin box, hitched his hip to pull out his wallet, and wrapped his own set of bills around the wad already in the box. Did Sheldon always pay the same? Would Dani notice? Mac didn't give a damn. Let her fight him on it. He was spoiling for a fight.

The guy was weird. He'd liked Mac's he-man act. To each his

own. Mac glanced at his watch. He'd been brooding for more than fifteen minutes. His phone hadn't rung. If Sheldon intended to finish in his requisite half hour, he'd better get started soon.

How could a man take *only* half an hour? It wasn't possible. Well, it was, but not with a woman like Dani.

Mac had never been a jealous man. True, he'd never imagined giving a girlfriend to another man, but he also hadn't watched a lover for any telltale signs of too much interest in someone else.

Jealousy over Dani had, quite simply, slammed into him like a Mack truck going a hundred miles an hour.

He sipped the remainder of her white Russian. Sweet and creamy with an afterkick. Just like Dani. Everything came back to Dani. Would Kern understand how the feelings had gotten away from him? When he asked Mac to take care of her, had he thought it might become more? Had he intended it?

With a raucous burst of laughter from the male businessmen who had now combined their sofa and chairs with that of the female office workers, Mac realized he'd lost another five minutes.

Dani still hadn't called. Dammit, she was leading him on, teasing him, testing him. Would he follow through on his threat to come looking for them if they were one minute late? Or would he sit and take it like a cuckold?

The white Russian was down to ice cubes. He threw a bill on the coffee table, shoved the tin in one pocket and his cell in the other. When you make a threat, you have to follow through. Even if he'd done it partly because he got the impression a little hardball was Sheldon's preference.

In the elevator, he stabbed the button. The evening with the Stamoses had been hot for more than just watching Dani. He'd gotten her off, not Spryo. Stamos and his wife were peripherals. It had been about Dani and him. Tonight with Sheldon was different. He'd never had his control stripped from him like this. Dani had a whole host of reasons for doing this that had nothing to do with Mac.

That was what fucking pissed him off and made him nuts.

He exited the elevator with three minutes to spare. Stalking the hall, he felt like a grizzly bear just out of hibernation and Sheldon was in the way of his first meal. A passing woman gave him a wide berth. He admitted he probably looked a little crazed.

He found the room number and raised his hand to knock. And . . . Jesus. That was a moan. A sweet, feminine voice moaning in ecstasy. Goddammit. He put his head to the door because, really, he'd lost complete control of his faculties, acting like a jealous idiot . . .

The door gave an inch. It hadn't been latched. The goddamn door was unlocked. He should have been angry, but the faint moans were higher now, louder, calling to him. He looked up and down the hall. No one else, no one heard. Two fingers to the door, his heart pounding, Mac pushed it open.

The room was standard, bathroom and closet as you walked in, desk and TV cabinet straight ahead. And a man's feet hanging off the end of the bed. Mac closed the door as softly as he'd opened it.

His heart stuttered to a stop as he took the two steps necessary for a full view of the room. And the bed. And Dani.

Auburn hair strewn across the white pillow, her eyes were closed, luscious red lips parted. Sight, sound, scent overwhelmed his senses; long, smooth expanses of creamy skin, the room perfumed with her citrusy lotion and sexual musk, Sheldon's head between her legs as she moaned and writhed. Her hips rose, wordlessly begging for more. He'd never beheld a more gorgeous woman or a more beautiful sight. All woman, taking her due, savoring it to the fullest. Nipples pebble hard, skin flushed as climax drew closer, her legs began to tremble.

"Filthy man, you love being so naughty, don't you," she murmured in a husky, sultry voice that strummed Mac's cock. Sheldon seemed to go at her with renewed gusto.

"Don't stop, dirty man, don't stop," she chanted, "or you'll be punished." With one last arch of her hips, she cried out, then her body shook and shivered. Her beauty in orgasm mesmerized him, each aftershock a little lighter, less intense, as she drifted back down from the pinnacle. She was never more desirable to him than she was in a state of orgasmic bliss.

Mac was so fucking jealous he couldn't see straight, think straight. He went with his gut and all the emotion roiling there.

"What the *fuck* are you two doing?" he barked into the near silence as her moans faded away.

Dani shrieked and shimmied up to the headboard, closing her legs, her cheeks a brilliant red. Sheldon scuttled backward off the bed, his tumescent cock bobbing, the crown purple with need before he covered it with his hands in terror.

His pulse throbbing in his ears, Mac grabbed Dani's hand and yanked her across the bed. "Get your clothes on, you little tramp."

"Please don't be mad," Sheldon stuttered. "It was all my fault."

Mac speared him with a look as Dani tugged her dress over her hips. "Shut"—he enunciated slowly, sharply—"up."

Dani barely had her shoes on when he hauled her toward the door. At the last moment, almost as an afterthought, he turned, pointed at the cowering Sheldon. "You're in so much fucking trouble. Get dressed, go home." He narrowed his eyes. "And be prepared to pay big-time for what you've just done."

Closing the door behind him, he made sure it was locked, then dragged Dani all the way down the hall to the bank of elevators, where he stabbed the button. It dinged almost immediately, the doors opened, he yanked her inside.

The moment the elevator moved, Dani threw her arms around him. "Oh my God, that was perfect. You were magnificent."

She grabbed his face between her hands and kissed him, smacking her lips so hard to his he had to brace himself against the wall.

He knew he was lost when he pulled her tight to his chest and kissed her back.

DANI'S LIPS STILL TINGLED FROM THAT BONE-MELTING KISS IN THE elevator. "How did you know exactly what to do?" Her seat belt secured, she pulled her feet beneath her and turned to him.

She enjoyed watching his capable hands on the wheel. They were equally as capable on her body. His sandy hair was dark amber in the shadowed confines of the car, the lines of his face almost harsh along his handsome features.

"It was a predictable assumption." His tone was flat. "Who left the door unlocked?"

"It must have been Sheldon." So yes, Sheldon had wanted Mac to find them. He had taken a bit longer than usual tonight, too, stretching it out.

"That was stupid," he said. "What if someone else walked in?"

"But they didn't. And," she purred, "if it hadn't been unlocked, you wouldn't have been able to watch. You know you loved watching."

He reached out, tweaked her chin. "Smug, aren't you?"

She stared at him as he negotiated the freeway on-ramp. "You're really pissed." After his acting job, she'd thought he'd had fun. Now she could see she'd been wrong. The air heated and sizzled around him.

"You didn't call," he said, teeth gritted.

"I phoned with the room number."

"In the middle." He paused. "There was no call."

She laughed. "I followed your instructions to the letter. Sheldon doesn't actually *do* me. We just play orally the way you saw." She raised a brow and smiled smugly for him. "So I had no reason to call." It had been so good; her body was still humming. She'd heard the door—yes, for a moment, she had a teeny-tiny spark of panic it might be someone else—but then she'd seen Mac, the dazed, glazed expression on his face. Watching him through mere slits, she'd given him the performance of her life. Swear it, with Mac watching, it had ceased to be a performance. His fists clenching, unclenching, the rise and fall of his chest as he took in every inch of her naked body—oh yeah, when she'd come, she'd come hard for Mac.

But he was stuck on technicalities.

"The rules are for your safety."

She wanted to climb across the seat into his lap. She was high, drunk on power and sex, and she'd wanted him to repeat Saturday night; drag her into the stairwell and do her fast and hard. The elevator wall would have been fine, too.

"Screw the rules," she said, her voice low and seductive in the heat of the car.

"Kern tasked me with protecting you. I can't do that if you take unnecessary risks."

With his mention of Kern's name, Dani suddenly heard herself, her thoughts. Kern hadn't been gone a month and she was panting after Mac.

She closed her eyes, leaning her head against the seat's rest. She shouldn't want Mac this way. Shouldn't play with him. He was Kern's brother. She was trying to turn him into Kern. No. Worse. She wanted to turn him into her lover. Anyone but Mac. She was a fool, a tramp, a shameless hussy, a bitch in heat.

They completed the rest of the drive in near silence. "You don't need to walk me in."

He popped his door anyway. "It's my job." His voice oozed sarcasm.

When she pulled her keys from her purse, he took them from her hand and unlocked the door. He didn't give them back until he was inside with her, the door closed behind them.

"So I suppose this is when you'd tell Kern everything you did, all the dirty little details." His eyes glittered.

Oh yeah, he was pissed. She just wasn't sure why. "Yes, this is when I told him."

She reached for the hall light. He pulled her hand away before she flipped it on. "So tell *me*." His voice was dark, dangerous, sensuous.

"You already saw."

"You had half an hour before I walked in." He advanced a step. "Tell me everything else you did."

She backed up. "What's wrong? Why are you so angry?"

Without a word, he opened his jacket, pulled out Sheldon's tin box, and set it on the hall table, either as a reminder, or to divest himself of the remnants of another man. "I'm not pissed," he murmured.

She'd grown used to the dark and saw some inner light sparking in his eyes. "Then what are you?" she whispered.

"So fucking turned on that I'm close to tearing your clothes off and taking you right here on the tile."

This was what she needed. She'd loved Kern, but he'd never made her feel this way. He'd never wanted her this way. Not with such intensity. It rose off Mac like ozone off concrete. She could see it shimmer, smell it, feel it like a touch along her skin.

"Or maybe I'm just going to pick you up and fuck you in my brother's bed."

Yes, he was pissed, too, turning desire into a potent combination that set her blood racing through her veins. He'd been grabbing, dragging, hauling her all night—God, she'd loved it—and he did it again, hands under her armpits, lifting her high, until she was forced to wrap her legs around his waist.

It was wrong. The bedroom should be off-limits. Yet when she opened her mouth to say it, he put his hand to the back of her head and took her with a fierce kiss that melted her resistance.

He had cat's eyes in the dark, heading straight down the hall to the master bedroom. Moonlight streamed across the bed. He stopped for one long moment, his cock riding her between the thighs, eyes burning. Then he tossed her on the bed.

"I'm going to fuck you. Then I'm spending the night in that bed." He stabbed a finger at the mattress.

That was too much, almost like a punishment. "Oh no, you're not." Maybe he was doing it for Kern. Because he considered her faithless.

"Fuck yes, I am." He tossed his jacket, yanked off his tie, threw it, then literally popped the buttons on his shirt. "And you want it."

She should have crawled off the bed and run, but the sight of his chest mesmerized her, all that muscle, the dusky nipples, the thin line of hair arrowing down to his slacks. Then it was too late. He came down on top of her, straddling her, his hands pinning her shoulders, and put his face right down in hers, his breath sweet with Kahlua.

"I'm spending the night tonight, and a helluva lot of nights after this. I told Kern I'd take care of you, and I will the only way I know how. By making you all mine in every way."

Oh God. He wanted to control her, steal her independence.

"So don't fight me on this, Dani."

Her independence was the only thing she had left that was her own. She wasn't giving it up without a fight.

11

MOONLIGHT KISSED HER CHEEKS, AND EVERY EMOTION PLAYED across her face. His cock was hard, his lungs aching with each breath. The feel of her beneath him stoked the fire burning in his belly. He knew she would fight. As much as she wanted the sex—oh yeah, heaving bosom, tight nipples, soaked pussy; she wanted that—she'd fight against every inroad he made into her life.

He put his lips to her throat and bit her. "I always win every battle. Didn't Kern tell you that?" he whispered, taunting. He wanted the war out of the way, over and done, victor taking the spoils.

She thrust her hips, trying to shove him off, and pushed on his shoulders. "Get off me."

"Make me," he muttered.

She heaved, twisted, wriggled, pummeled. Not his face, but everything else she could reach. He'd never manhandled a woman, and he didn't now, but her efforts turned his cock to pure steel.

"If you do this, I'll never forgive you." She glared, an inferno in her gaze.

"Maybe you won't." He reached down, grabbed the bottom of her dress where it had ridden up past her hips with all her squirming, and yanked. The seams gave, the threads popping. "I'm willing to take the chance."

"It'll be rape," she hissed.

He held her chin in his hand. "Will it?"

Her gaze flicked across him, from one eye to the other, and he wondered if she'd lie.

"It'll just be fucking." She said the word with all the distaste she could muster, but he knew she wanted it. As badly as he did.

Her panties went the way of her dress, in tatters and tossed to the carpet. She wasn't wearing a bra. He bent to a beaded nipple, sucking it into his mouth, and pinched the other hard.

She moaned, arched, her pussy riding the outline of his cock in his pants. He fucked her through the material, grinding his hips against her. Her sweet, hot scent rose around them.

He tipped her head, thumb beneath her chin. "Ready?"

"Whatever."

"Undo my belt."

"Do it yourself."

He reached between them. Her pussy was slick, sweet, hot. He circled her clit, dipped inside, back out, rubbed slowly. She shuddered beneath him, her lids falling closed, lips parting.

"Tell me you want it," he whispered.

"I hate it." But she gasped, rolled with his rhythm, getting wetter, hotter.

"You need it as much as I do."

She didn't say a word, but raised her legs to his hips, locked her ankles across his ass.

He kept it slow and sweet, taking her closer, but not giving her the ultimate, keeping her on the edge, but not pushing her over.

"Oh God" slipped from her lips.

"Undo my belt," he said again, this time on a whisper of breath.

She fumbled, finally got the job done. He backed off to let her pull the zipper, his fingers maintaining the slow, steady, mind-altering rhythm on her clit.

Being naked would have been the best, but he didn't dare leave her for the amount of time it would take. "Back pocket, there's a condom."

She lifted her lids and smirked. "Aren't we prepared?"

He bent his head, his lips to hers. "You damn well know how much I want you. You've teased me all night. Now it's time to pay the piper, baby."

"You're so full of yourself." Then she jerked as he found a particularly sweet spot.

"*You're* going to be full of me," he muttered.

He took her lips, hot, fast, sweet, while she dug in his back pocket. Finding the package, she shoved his slacks over his hips.

He pulled away long enough to roll on the condom. Coming back down, he braced on both arms and rolled his hips against her, his cock sliding in the heat and dampness of her cleft, grazing her clit.

"Now tell me you don't want it," he challenged.

She looked at him, then drawled, "It's just sex. I'll take it. Because I like my orgasms however I can get them."

She wouldn't give an inch, not even in the heat of the moment. Mac didn't care. Even fighting her was goddamn hot. He'd take her anyway he could have her, and he'd meant every word. He was staying. "Take me inside you."

She arched, opened, wrapped her fingers around him, and guided him inside, just the crown. He covered her with his body, chest to breasts, sliding half a glorious inch deeper. Burying his face in her hair, he crooned, "Say it, say it."

He didn't expect her to cave in. Yet she dug her nails into his butt and whispered, "Do me, Mac. Please."

He drove home, deep inside her. She moaned, wrapping him in her arms, her legs, her heat, exactly where he wanted to be. Then there was just the sound of her breath, her cries, the scent of her skin, her sex. He lost himself in sensation, pumping harder, faster, deeper, until she gripped him on the inside, his cock, his heart. He didn't reach release; he reached fulfillment, shattering inside her, calling out her name, taking her with him into the sweet oblivion.

SHE DIDN'T QUITE REMEMBER MAC REMOVING THE CONDOM OR undressing or climbing into the bed to wrap her in his heat.

Dani remembered only the contentment.

God, how she'd missed falling asleep with a man's arms enveloping her. What he'd done to her had been hot, sexy, intense, with an edge. She wanted it, needed it, hated his tone, his dictatorial attitude, and succumbed because she couldn't help herself. Sex was best when it was edgy, straddling the line between emotions, when you couldn't decide whether you were pissed or delirious.

Damn, it was good with Mac. If she wasn't careful, she'd become addicted.

When she woke again, the night was deep pitch, the crescent moon having trekked beyond the window. Without even a moment of disorientation, she knew another man's arms held her in the bed she'd shared with her husband. Not just any man, but Mac. Her husband's brother. Yet neither the guilt she'd expected nor the fear of losing her independence materialized. Maybe it was the darkness keeping it at bay. Maybe it was the need still trilling in her blood.

"I haven't tasted you yet," she whispered, despite his even breathing at her nape. He was still asleep.

She didn't want the guilt or the morning light until she'd had that, his taste in her mouth, the musk of his come in her nose, the caress of his pubic hair against her cheeks.

She shifted as he rolled to his back, flinging an arm over his head. Pushing the sheet down, she revealed him inch by inch until she'd uncovered his cock. Her eyes adjusting to the gloom, she could just make out the proud jut of his erection. As if he were dreaming about her.

Her body hummed with last night's intensity. He'd demanded, ordered; she'd fought and made light of him. She'd needed it, wanted him, frighteningly so, yet now, in the quiet, she wasn't scared. Did he truly mean he intended to stay with her, or was that part of the hot game they played? It didn't matter. Whatever came between them tomorrow, right now, there was this. His beautiful cock, her mouth.

Sliding down, she rested on an elbow and stroked a fingernail from his balls to his tip. His cock flexed, but she detected no change in his breathing. Lifting him, holding him as if he were fragile, she rubbed him against her mouth, smoothing a drop of his essence over her closed lips.

He was the perfect combination of sweet and salty. Sliding down over him slowly, she savored his thickness, the pulse beating through his cock. She stopped, relaxed, took him farther. Until he groaned, the sound vibrating against her. She backed off even as he arched, his body striving for a deeper penetration of her mouth.

"Christ, what are you doing to me?" His breath, his sounds, his words filled the night.

Wrapping her hand around him, she sucked hard and fast, suctioned his crown, then caressed his balls.

"Holy hell, where'd you learn that?"

Everywhere, nowhere. She loved the male body. She loved the taste of come and the feel of a cock between her lips. No tricks of the trade; she excelled at what she loved.

Dani didn't know how long she sucked, how long she worked him. His taste was so good, his words so sweet, the writhing of his body so perfect.

"Hell, fuck." His fingers fisted in her hair, his body rose, fell, out of control. The first hot spurt of come filled her mouth, overwhelmed her senses, flooded her mind. She stroked, sucked, licked, soothed, caressed, until the spasms subsided and his breathing returned to normal.

Then he hauled her up his body, held her so tight she thought she'd squeak. They didn't speak. She wondered if he was as afraid to say anything as she was. Tomorrow would come and things would be said, demands made, orders refused. But for now, there was only this moment, and she wanted to hang on to it at least until dawn.

HE SHOWERED, SHAVED, USING A RAZOR OF KERN'S SHE HADN'T gotten rid of. Kern's things littered the bathroom, meds in the cabinet, out-of-date contact lenses, male deodorant. Reminders were everywhere. He was sure if he opened the closet and bureau drawers, he'd find Kern's clothing.

He had a vivid memory of him and Kern packing up his mom's things for Goodwill, touching personal items he'd never been meant to touch, learning secrets she never would have shared.

Death stripped away so many layers people hid themselves behind.

Now he knew too many of Kern's secrets, too many of Dani's. She was still asleep, her hair strewn across the pillow, curled into a childlike ball. He dressed in relative darkness, the sun starting to come up. He didn't disturb her, wanting instead for her to wake remembering what she'd done to him in the night. Without him there, she would think only of how good it had been. Of the times he'd been with her, that moment had been the best. He didn't take; she gave. Though she couldn't know, when he came in her mouth, he gave her everything.

There was time enough to talk tonight, to say what he needed to say, to fight or beg or whatever it took. For now, he just wanted to savor the sigh of pleasure she'd made as he came for her.

THE BED STILL SMELLED LIKE HIM, AND THE BATHROOM TOWELS were scented with Kern's shaving cream. Mac had left a pot of coffee brewing for her, a slice of bread ready in the toaster.

God, yes, there were things she missed about having a man around. She missed cooking for someone other than herself. Toward the end, Kern had subsisted on protein drinks and what amounted to baby food. That wasn't cooking.

She missed Kern the way he used to be. The way he laughed and teased, the sparkle of good humor in his eye. Dani squeezed the coffee mug so hard she thought it might crack. The things she'd done with Mac didn't mean she'd loved Kern less, but Mac rejuvenated her. She'd been so worried for so long, she'd forgotten what it felt like to let herself go, even if it was only for a little while. The things she did with Mac gave her courtesan dates the *extra* she used to feel with Kern. Last night, when she'd taken him in her mouth . . .

How would it be if there weren't Courtesans and the money between them? Would it really be so bad to let him in?

It didn't bear thinking about now. She couldn't plan or move forward with the bills hanging over her.

Mac had left the morning paper for her on the kitchen table. The phone rang just as she turned the first page. Isabel's number. Dani stabbed the speaker button. "Hey, there, you usually call the cell."

"You didn't answer it, and I wanted to talk to you ASAP."

"Oops, sorry." Right. The cell phone was in her purse, which was in the hall where she'd dropped it when Mac picked her up. Last night there'd been only Mac and how badly he'd wanted her.

"Darling," Isabel drawled, "Sheldon was ecstatic. He's never had a better time. And you know"—she paused for effect—"he's *neh-ver* called after a date."

True. The only way one really knew with Sheldon was if he called back for another date. "I'm glad he was pleased."

"He said you and Mac were an unbeatable combination. What did you *do*? Tell all."

Isabel wasn't generally so effusive. It *had* been totally hot when Mac stormed in. As if he'd actually caught them at something. As if he were pissed as all get-out and there'd be hell to pay. "Mac played the angry cuckold. Sheldon must have left the door slightly unlatched hoping he'd come up and 'catch' us. Mac did"—she laughed—"and dragged me out, threatening Sheldon."

"My, my."

"I didn't have a thing to do with engineering it. Mac figured it out all on his own."

Isabel chuckled. "Well, you need to keep him around, that's for sure."

Her stomach pitched. She liked having him around too much. She could start to depend on him. "For right now, the bills are my top priority." Speaking of which, she needed to take Sheldon's money to the bank. "So if you've got anything else brewing for me, give me a shout."

Isabel promised and rang off. Dani wandered into the hallway. Her purse lay on the carpet just beyond the tile entry, Sheldon's tin box sat on the hall table, and Mac's words echoed in her mind.

So fucking turned on that I'm close to tearing your clothes off and taking you right here on the tile.

She hadn't cared about the money or Sheldon or Kern or the bills or anything else. In that way, Mac was dangerous. He could make her forget everything.

At the kitchen table, she upended the box and scattered the bills. There were tens, twenties, and hundreds. Hundreds weren't Sheldon's usual style. She stacked, counted. It wasn't his usual amount, either. By a lot. Wow, he really had been pleased last night.

Wait, wait, wait. Sheldon gave Mac the box *before* they went upstairs, before Mac became so forceful. Yeah, he gave the tin to *Mac*. Now it contained more cash than usual.

Just as there'd been far more than she'd expected in the envelope from Spryo. Goddammit. Mac had stacked the deck. He'd bullied his way into arranging her dates, dictated that he'd be spending the night, and now this. She'd told him she didn't want his money, so he'd tricked her.

Oh yeah, Mac was dangerous. He was a corporate raider stepping in for a hostile takeover of *her*.

12

OUTSIDE HIS OFFICE BUILDING, DANI WAS DRESSED TO KILL AND leaning against his car.

"Why didn't you come in?" Mac asked as he approached.

"I was enjoying the sun, and I knew you'd be out eventually."

It was a little after five, and he'd had work that would carry him at least until six. "I saw you through the window." He had no idea how long she'd been in the parking lot. Or why. The roiling in his gut told him it wasn't good.

"I have a date tonight," she said without smiling.

Hence the mouthwatering sweater dress that molded to her breasts, clung to every curve, and made his heart race. "Isabel didn't call me."

"I told her not to."

"Why?" He knew why. Because he'd *told* Dani, in no uncertain terms, that he intended to make her his. No matter how she felt about it. It took her less than a day to balk, and they hadn't even fought about it yet.

She surprised him by removing an envelope from her purse. "This is why."

He took it, opened it, found the hundred-dollar bills. Yeah, he clearly remembered thinking he was spoiling for a fight. Now he'd gotten it. "Busted," was all he said.

"You broke the terms of the deal. So now the deal is *off*."

A couple of girls left the building, laughter, chatter. It died the moment they saw him. "Why don't we discuss this inside?" he said, taking Dani's arm. "Or elsewhere."

She pulled away. "No," she said, her gaze following the girls. "That's exactly why I stayed out here. So you couldn't cause a scene."

He smiled, feeling anything but happy, but the way she'd reversed roles on him was amusing. "I don't intend to make a scene. But this"—he waved the envelope—"doesn't change a thing. I still have that promise I made to Kern."

"Kern's dead," she said far too harshly, her nostrils flaring. Then she stopped, took a breath.

He remembered his brother's things all over the bathroom. "I don't want to replace Kern. I just want to take care of you."

She rolled her lips between her teeth a moment. "I know you mean well. But I can't let you do this."

He opened his mouth. She put a hand up, almost touching his lips. The heat of her fingers arced across the brief space.

"Let me finish," she said.

The lobby doors opened again, more voices, the click of high heels, a car door, then an engine. Moments ticked by. He didn't want her to finish. He knew what she'd say, and he damn well didn't want to hear it.

But he chose to let her say her piece. "Go on."

"I loved Kern very much. But"—a deep breath—"I should never have let him talk me into quitting my job." She held his gaze. "Yes, you thought that was stupid, too, and it was, but he wanted it, and I did it. Running the business together wasn't working even before he got sick. He made all the decisions, and he didn't want my advice, and instead of fighting about it, I let him do what he wanted. Everything snowballed on us. Then he got sick, and the bills"—she threw up her hands—"so we went for the quick cash instead of having me return to work. We weren't sure he'd be covered by whatever medical plan I got anyway, because of the preexisting condition."

His breath chafed in his lungs, struck again by how little Kern had confided in him.

"I let him make the decisions. So I'm not saying I have anyone else to blame." She held his gaze for a long moment. "But I'm not doing it all over again. I will solve my own problem my way. I will not let you help me. Because if I do, I stand to let you take over like I did with Kern."

"I'm not my brother. I wouldn't allow you to be overwhelmed with bills you couldn't pay and things you couldn't control." He'd make mistakes, too, sure, but he wouldn't let her get flushed down the toilet by a mountain of debt. He was prudent.

"You're not getting it. This isn't about what you would or wouldn't allow." She put her hand to her chest. "I am not going to let myself be dependent. I'm going to pay off my bills, and when that's done I'm going to find a real job, and start my life over. Rebuild. You have to let me do that." Her eyes were intent, her features earnest. She truly believed he would stand in her way.

Perhaps he would. He'd pushed and shoved his way in. It had been about him fulfilling his promise to Kern, not about what Dani needed. He couldn't deny a thing she'd said, and he felt his heart cracking in two.

"One more thing," she said softly. "I never thanked you for all you did to help me take care of Kern." Her eyes misted, lips trembling. "I couldn't have coped without you. I would have fallen apart."

He'd never met a stronger woman. "No, you wouldn't."

She shook her head abruptly. "You don't know how close I was. But you saved me. Now let me do the rest myself, Mac, please."

If she'd gotten angry, yelled at him, fought him, dictated to him, he would have ridden right over her because he knew what was best for her. *He* was best for her.

But he couldn't force her to see things his way. He couldn't fight this. He couldn't override her desire to take care of herself.

He trailed a finger down her cheek for the last time. "Call me if you need me."

As she climbed into her car, he knew she wouldn't call. A piece of him died thinking of her touching other men, taking them in her mouth the way she had him. He wasn't sure he could survive this. His brother hadn't.

He withdrew Kern's cell phone from his suit pocket and punched a speed dial. Isabel answered. He didn't give her a chance to speak. "You damn well better make sure she's safe. Because she won't let me do it."

"All my courtesans are safe, Mac." He heard her breathe, knew she wasn't gone, then she murmured, "She'll be back, I promise."

He no longer believed in promises. Some shouldn't even be made in the first place.

MAC HADN'T CALLED HER IN A COUPLE OF WEEKS. ALL SORTS OF adjectives describing how much she missed him flitted through Dani's mind. None of them expressed the depth of her emotion. She'd had six dates and made inroads into the medical bills.

She'd faked every orgasm. At least when she had to. Some men didn't really care.

Sex without Mac was . . . rote.

The mail had arrived with all the monthly bills. October rain arrived as well. She lit a fire to keep out the damp and curled up on the couch to open each envelope. With the start of the cold season, the heating costs would rise. Her life was about money these days. She opened the phone bill, and there was Kern's cell number. She'd forgotten about it, especially since Mac had the phone itself.

When Kern had become too ill to go out with her, she'd used the cell phone to check in with him. Until she'd stopped accepting dates. And then . . . well . . . she hadn't cut it off because . . . she couldn't.

Now he was gone.

Dani held the bill to her chest as if it were a pair of his favorite pajamas. Which, incidentally, were still in the dresser, along with his clothes in the closet, his home office, and his computer. His toothbrush in the bathroom. She didn't notice it because it was there. She'd notice more when it was gone. Someday she would have to clean out.

She'd have to start with the phone because it was costing money.

Oh yeah, Dani was all about the money. If her dead husband was costing her, well, hell, out he'd go. She felt sick. Tired. Lonely. She wished Mac was there to share a glass of wine with her as he had during the evenings after those long, long days of Kern dying.

But he wasn't. She'd banished him, too. She could have called him, but instead, she dialed the phone company and shut down Kern's cell.

MAC WASN'T SURE EXACTLY WHEN IT HAPPENED. KERN'S PHONE didn't work. He'd been keeping it charged, God knew why; it was just this thing he couldn't let go of. As if, like Isabel, he thought Kern might call him from the other side. Or perhaps he was hoping Isabel would call and tell him Dani had changed her mind. It had been two weeks; the phone hadn't rung.

Then tonight, there was no service.

Dani had canceled it. For a moment he couldn't breathe. His eyes ached. Kern was dead. As dead as his phone. He couldn't say why it hit him then, but the pain was so goddamn intense, he doubled over. Men don't cry, but his cheeks were wet. He wiped away the moisture, but more trickled.

"I failed you, man," he said to the empty house. "I should have had more faith in you." People lived up to expectations. If you thought they'd fail, they usually did. With someone to believe in them, they could perform miracles. To his brother, Mac had always been a *but* man. *But what about this and what about that? You're not thinking everything through.* No wonder Kern had stopped confiding in him.

"I'm so sorry. I miss you. I'd change everything if it would bring you back." His temples throbbed. "I wish I'd told you that before you died." He'd have changed how he'd handled Dani, too.

Fuck, that was the problem. *Handling* Dani. She didn't need handling or taking care of. All she needed was to share the load the way they had those last two weeks with Kern. Someone to help her do the heavy lifting. Instead, he'd bulldozed.

He stared at the dead phone a moment longer. Until he realized exactly what it meant. She was cleaning out.

He could not let her face it alone.

The drive took fifteen minutes, and it was a little past nine when he pushed her doorbell. He half feared she'd be out on a date, but a few seconds later, the porch light flipped on.

Her eyes were reddened. She wore an old pair of sweats too

big for her and her hair knotted on the top of her head with one of those scrunchy things. She looked more beautiful than in the sexy dress he'd last seen her in.

A pulse beat at her throat, then she sighed. "I'm glad you came." She backed up, held the door open. "I was packing up some of Kern's things." She met his eyes. "I thought I'd donate the computer to a school."

He followed her inside. "I could drive it over."

"Thank you."

They were both so polite, so careful, as if nothing had happened between them.

She led him down the hall to Kern's office, which was filled with open boxes. Computer components, unidentifiable electronics equipment, books on car mechanics, Kern's ham radio equipment.

"Maybe you can sell some of that on eBay."

She grimaced. "I don't really know what all this stuff is."

"I do. I can help."

"Do you want any of it?"

They'd learned ham from their dad. Kern had still enjoyed a good field day. Mac had long since given it up. "No. Thanks."

She tipped her head. "You should take something, though. Maybe his watch. It's a Rolex." She'd given it to Kern as a wedding present.

"Yeah. I'd like that."

She stared hard at the half-filled boxes, the gaps in the bookshelves. "How did you know I was doing this?"

He dug the cell phone out, held it up. Slowly, she raised a hand, took it, considered it. "I got the bill this morning." She glanced up, her eyes misty. "I knew it was time. I think you can give working cell phones to battered women's shelters."

"I'm sure you can."

She pursed her lips, sniffed, composed herself. "Thank you. I appreciate that you came. I was going to start on his clothes and stuff, but then I couldn't seem to do it. That part was too hard."

He laid a hand on her arm, the only touch he dared. "I can do it if you want. Whatever you need me to do, just tell me."

Her lip trembled, her jaw tensed, she sniffed, then whispered, "I need you to hold me."

He didn't know who moved first, but she was suddenly tight in his arms and no woman had ever felt as right. She didn't give in to tears, but her grip on him was fierce.

"I was wrong," he said gently.

"About what?" she asked, her breath caressing his ear.

"About how I treated Kern. The way I ordered you to let me help you, to let me into your life."

She wrapped her arms tighter, her heartbeat so close it was almost his own.

"What I should have said was that I fell in love with you while Kern was dying. I couldn't help myself; it happened. I didn't even recognize it at first. But instead of admitting it to myself, I blackmailed my way into your life with Kern's dying wishes."

Her body trembled. She sniffed. He knew she was fighting the tears. He wanted to tell her to give in to them; it was okay. But lately, he'd been telling her far too many things she should do.

"I don't want to control you or force you to take my money to pay your bills. I don't want you to be dependent on me." He stroked her hair, soothed as she quivered against him. "But I don't want to walk out, either. I don't believe Kern would be upset about the way I feel for you. He would have understood because he loved you so goddamn much, and he hated leaving you."

She sobbed, once, hiccupped.

"I want to share with you, not overpower you." He took a chance, putting his hands to her shoulders and holding her away.

Her nose was red, her cheeks wet. "I'm not telling; I'm asking. Please let me stay, Dani."

He ran a thumb under first one eye, then the other, wiping away her tears.

Finally she spoke. "I missed you."

He smiled slightly, his heart aching. "Not as much as I missed you."

"Kern loved you." Dani sniffed. "He always admired you. He was proud of everything you did, and he wanted to be exactly like you."

Mac cupped her cheek. "I know. But I still know I made a lot of mistakes with him."

His touch was so good after two weeks without him. God, how she'd missed him. Dani sniffed again, glanced around. "Doesn't he even have any tissues in here?" Then she smiled tremulously, her heart wanting to burst wide-open. "How you make me feel scares me. But this is what Kern wanted when he asked you to take care of me. He wanted me to fall in love with you." She stroked the nine-o'clock shadow along Mac's jaw. "You're so beautiful." She could love them both. What she felt for Mac didn't lessen her love for Kern. She just had to allow herself to accept instead of fight.

Mac trailed his hand down her arm, then pulled her to the corner workstation and the box of tissues stuffed next to a dying philodendron. She needed to water it. She didn't want it to die.

"Here." He handed her a tissue. "Dry your eyes. Blow your nose."

She did. "I must look awful."

"You look gorgeous." He put her hand to his chest where she could feel his heart beat. "Here's what we're going to do. We're going to pay off Kern's medical bills together."

"How?"

His eyes danced. "By doing exactly what we did with Spryo

and Sheldon—play the game: me, jealous enforcer; you, sexy babe. It was so fucking hot, people will be lining up begging to play."

Her heart swelled. "You're not just saying that because I'm an oversexed slut you have to appease, are you?"

He drew her closer, until his body was pressed to hers, his cock hard at her belly. "Baby, it was so good, so hot, and yes, I was crazy jealous, which made it even better." He rubbed noses. "What I really wanted to do was toss Sheldon across the room and take you myself right in front of him."

Her bones melted just thinking about it. The idea made her crazy hot, too. Rising on her toes, wrapping her arms around Mac, she whispered, "You don't think I'm a freak because I like it kinky?"

"If you are, then so am I, because now that I've gotten used to the idea, I want it." He pulled back. "It'll be the spice, but you better be prepared for a lot of making love in our own bed, too. Because I do want you, and I'm not like my brother; watching will never be enough." He held her chin, kissed the tip of her nose. "Let Isabel know we're a team, baby."

Her heart filled her chest. Kern couldn't stay with her, but he'd left something miraculous behind. Mac.

THE
WRONG KIND
OF MAN

1

CLEO CARPENTER RUBBED HER TEMPLE. HER HEAD THROBBED WITH an ache that hadn't gone away since Heidi had turned fourteen. Was that some magical age where all mothers and daughters went from being BFFs to mortal enemies overnight?

Heidi's room looked like a hurricane had blown through, tossing clothes, shoes, purses, books, makeup, and school papers over every surface. Cleo wasn't *even* going to tackle that messy subject.

"You don't trust me," Heidi said, eyes narrowed, hands militantly on her hips.

That was true. She'd caught her daughter in more than one lie. But say that aloud? Not. "I still want to check with Cat's mom to make sure the sleepover is convenient."

She so did not have time for this. With exactly one and a half hours between her day job as a receptionist and her evening gig as a waitress, Cleo barely had time to eat, change, brush her teeth, put her hair up, and make the half hour drive from Palo Alto to the restaurant up on Skyline overlooking Silicon Valley. God, she was tired. But dammit, she needed to make sure there really was a Halloween slumber party.

"Fine." Heidi thrust the cell phone at her. "Call her."

Cleo couldn't afford the extra cell phone for Heidi, but she'd found her daughter had gotten into all sorts of trouble when she could use the well-if-I'd-had-a-cell-phone-to-let-you-know excuse. Now Heidi had a cell phone, and she still got into trouble.

Cleo prayed for patience. Actually, she wished she'd never let Heidi go to public high school in the first place. Heidi had fallen in with the wrong crowd, fast boys and loose girls, and after the first six months of her freshman year, Cleo yanked her back to the private Christian school she'd attended through eighth grade. Heidi absolutely hated her for it.

"I want her mother's number," Cleo enunciated, her teeth gritted, "not Cat's number."

"Oh, fine." There was such derision in the word. Heidi stomped to the computer to check her online address book. Cleo had purchased the used PC when she realized that sending Heidi to the library to do her Internet research for this anthropology essay or that history paper meant all sorts of excuses for staying out past her curfew.

Booting up was slow as molasses, or that was how it felt. Cleo couldn't keep up, couldn't make ends meet. Private school was killing her. They lived with her mother in the three-bedroom, two-and-a-half-bath house Cleo had grown up in, which, thank God, was paid off. Cleo, however, took care of the maintenance since her mom was on a fixed income. The house was more than fifty years old. Everything was breaking down. She'd wanted her mother to sell. In Palo Alto, it was worth a fortune, but Ma claimed she wasn't leaving until they carried her out in a box.

Heidi finally came up with the phone number. "Here."

"Thank you." Cleo took the scrap of paper and punched in the call. "Hi, yes, it's Cleo Carpenter. Heidi told me about the party." Heidi glared at her, daring her to say she was checking up. "Well, good, I'm so glad." Yes, Cat's mom had agreed, this was a *supervised* sleepover. "Would you like me to send her over with some snacks or something?" Cleo offered. Listening, Heidi rolled her eyes. "All right, well, I'll drop her off in a few minutes. What time shall I collect her in the morning?" Heidi glared at the timetable. "Yes, wonderful, thanks. Bye-bye."

Cleo rang off and snapped the phone closed.

Heidi held out her hand. "Satisfied?"

"Excuse me, but I don't like that tone." Her daughter had never been a rude child. But over the last few months, she'd picked up the nasty habit from somewhere.

"I'm so sorry, Mother," Heidi said sweetly. "I'm very happy that you checked up on me so now you know I'm not lying or making up stories or sneaking out with boys." Then she turned on her heel and stomped to her vanity to trowel on more eyeliner.

Heidi would be such a pretty girl without all that black make-up. A couple of inches taller than Cleo's five foot six, she was statuesque but waiflike. Cleo worried about what she was eating. She had Cleo's black hair, but hers was silky, falling to her waist. Yet more often than not, Heidi wore it pulled back in a messy, unkempt, and unattractive ponytail.

Cleo had never felt so helpless in her life. Nothing she said or did was right. "Be ready in ten minutes. I'll drop you off on my way to work." She'd probably end up being ten minutes late at the restaurant, but it couldn't be helped.

"Was I that bad?" she muttered to herself once she was in her own bedroom. The answer was probably yes. She remembered a lot of the same fights, not to mention when she told her mother she was pregnant. Barely out of high school, she'd had dreams of college. That was all they were now—dreams. But she had Heidi, and Heidi was the absolute most important thing in the world.

Cleo didn't want Heidi to make her same mistakes. She wanted her to have good grades in high school so she could get a scholarship. The meager amount Cleo managed to save in the college fund probably wouldn't last more than two quarters.

Cleo closed her eyes, put her hand over her mouth. She was so tired, and the worry was murder on her. But dammit, she'd made her bed more than sixteen years ago, and, as tough as it was right now, she would not let Heidi down. She would work two jobs, do whatever it took to make sure Heidi had the life she deserved. They'd just hit a rough patch, that was all. She would make things better.

WALKER RANDALL FLIPPED HIS WRIST TO GLANCE AT HIS WATCH. His date was half an hour late. At seven thirty on Friday night, Bella's was full and buzzing with conversation. Flower boxes of bright fuchsias separated the two halves of the restaurant's large dining room. The floors were hardwood, the ceiling raftered, and a fire blazed in the hearth. In the fall and winter, Walker requested a table with the fireplace as a backdrop. He liked the warmth and the cheery crackle. Being a regular at Bella's, he always got what he requested.

This was a first. He'd never had a Courtesans' date do a no-show on him. Isabel prided herself on making the perfect match, with everyone going away satisfied. Perhaps Estelle, his date, had gotten cold feet. Walker signaled the busboy for more water. He didn't want to drink too much champagne before Estelle actually arrived.

It was Cleo who returned with the pitcher. She was a large part of the attraction of Bella's. The continental cuisine was superb and the drive up through Woodside along Kings Mountain Road relaxing though winding, but Cleo was the icing on top of his cake. He felt very proprietary about her, in fact. He always made sure he was given one of her tables.

"Have you been stood up, Walker?" With a barely there teasing smile, she tipped her chin down, gazing at him through long, lush lashes.

Her startlingly blue eyes reminded him of a mountain lake, though tonight he noticed a slight shadow in them and dark circles beneath. Tired? Worried? Both? He didn't like his Cleo being sad, but at least she could still manage a smile for him. She'd pulled her long black hair into its usual neat bun at the back of her neck. Her black pants hugged her behind, and she had one too many buttons undone on her white blouse. Perhaps it was an oversight, but it afforded Walker a view of her magnificent cleavage. Cleo was deliciously curvy.

"I've called her twice," he admitted. "Perhaps she got lost on the way up." The mountain road was tricky. He'd offered to pick Estelle up. She'd wanted to make her own way.

Estelle typified most of his clients, women who wanted to prove how independent and capable they were. Beneath the bravado, their self-confidence needed shoring up. That was Walker's specialty. He loved women, loved pleasuring them and empowering them. Every woman needed to believe she was a goddess.

But Cleo Carpenter actually was. It would be so much better, though, if he could banish that shadow from her eyes. A fight with her daughter? She didn't dump her problems on him, but sometimes a detail or two slipped through in their brief conversations. If Cleo was wearing a shadow, it usually had something to do with Heidi.

"Wishful thinking," she mocked sweetly, waggling her fingers as she moved on to another table.

He knew she referred to his date being directionally challenged, but Walker had certainly done his fair share of wishful thinking where Cleo was concerned. He'd never asked her out, though. He was extremely content with his life as it was. Most women, Cleo included, wouldn't understand what he did for a living.

Three years ago he'd been a stockbroker, and well on his way to a hardening of the arteries, both medically and figuratively. So instead of cashing in his life's chips, he'd converted his stock portfolio to gold and struck a deal with Isabel of Courtesans. She set up his dates, and he made the women happy.

He didn't take money—or the expensive gifts—from women because he needed or wanted it. He took it because *they* needed to give it. Money was power, and when they paid him, they reveled in their own supremacy. The amount didn't matter. The transaction was more about how much a woman needed to pay to get the most bang for her buck, so to speak. In other words, what was the price that made *her* feel the most powerful?

His cell phone vibrated in his pocket. Surreptitiously, Walker popped his Bluetooth in his ear and answered quietly so as to cause the least disturbance to the other diners around him. "Hello."

"I can't do this."

"You don't have to do anything you don't wish to, Estelle. But I have the champagne iced, and we can enjoy a quiet dinner. No strings attached, nothing required. My treat, no obligations."

While ultimately, he was the one who received payment, Walker usually took care of the incidental bills such as drinks, dinner, cab fare, et cetera. While he provided women empowerment, he also provided pampering. Though some ladies did prefer the power play of paying for everything. When that was the case, of course, he obliged them. Whatever the lady wanted.

"No, no, I can't do that, either." Estelle's voice wobbled.

"Did something happen?"

She sniffed. "I can't talk about it."

He didn't know her circumstances, whether she was married, partnered, or single. He'd noted a certain hesitancy on her part, but this felt like far more than mere cold feet. "Where are you? I can come there and make sure you get safely home."

"I'm *at* home."

Well. That could be bad. "Shall I ask Isabel to give you a call?" Perhaps she needed a woman's shoulder.

Isabel was particular. She didn't match women who were not fairly comfortable with what they were doing.

"No, no, I'll call her." Estelle sniffled.

"Good. But if you need me, you have my number. Please call anytime."

Estelle didn't even say good-bye. He immediately called Isabel, got her voice mail. Unusual, too; if Isabel was unavailable, she had a receptionist. He wondered if Estelle had immediately dialed in. He left a message, gave Isabelle fair warning about the alteration in plans and Estelle's flighty manner.

Damn. He had tickets to Fright Fest, an outdoor showing of three cult classic flicks over at the local community college. It was an unusual date venue, to be sure, but it was Halloween, and he'd planned something different, exciting even. Estelle was supposedly partial to the unexpected.

Well, hell, he'd go on his own. But first, he'd enjoy a glass of champagne and a fine meal.

As if she were a genie he'd summoned, Cleo suddenly stood before his table, a hand on one hip. "So?"

He realized she'd been watching him. It gave him a bit of a kick start. "I'll be eating alone."

"Poor Walker," she sympathized, shaking her head sadly.

"I had a special event planned, too." He had the glimmer of an idea. Something that might very well make Cleo smile for real, no shadows lurking behind it. But really, he shouldn't. There could be complications.

She tipped her head, raised one brow. "But you still want to order dinner, right?"

He wanted more than dinner. The glimmer was growing brighter.

He wanted it. To hell with complications. "Do you like classic movies?"

Her eyes slid left to right, as if she thought she'd actually see the ball flying at her from out of left field. "I guess."

"I have tickets to an outdoor movie marathon and no one to go with now."

She swallowed. "I'm working."

"They don't start the first movie until eleven."

He detected a pulse beating at her throat. She blinked before she spoke. "It's probably not a good idea."

No, it wasn't. But the idea had planted itself firmly, and Walker wasn't about to uproot it. It was just a movie—well, three movies that would play well into the early-morning hours. He had blankets and wine and cheese.

Now all he needed was Cleo. "Say yes," he said softly.

Cleo tapped her pen on her pad. "I don't get off till ten."

"Ten's fine."

"I'll have to go home and change." She pointed vaguely behind her as if her house were that way . . . somewhere.

"Where do you live?"

"Palo Alto," she said slowly.

"We can still make it in time from there."

She huffed out a breath.

Walker let women make their own decisions. He asked instead of ordered. He cajoled instead of demanded. With her, he nudged hard. "Say yes, Cleo."

Finally, after forever, she whispered, "Yes," then held her pen poised. "Now, what do you want for dinner?"

He ordered the duck in alalaberry-bordeaux sauce. Cleo would be his midnight treat.

2

WALKER RANDALL WAS A GREAT TIPPER. HE'D BEEN A REGULAR AT Bella's for three years, almost since Cleo had started working there. He treated her with respect, whether he was with a woman or dining on his own. Perhaps ten years older than her, forty-five or so, his bald head and buff body were a turn-on, especially with that cheeky smile of his. It was sexy and sweet all rolled into one. Coupled with milk-chocolate eyes, he was a hit with the ladies. And he was a nice guy.

She'd always had a bit of a wistful feeling about him, a *what-if*, maybe even an idle fantasy or two, because Walker was definitely attractive. Okay, let's be completely honest here. Walker was hot as hell, and she'd given herself many a devastating orgasm in the privacy of her room while imagining him taking her in various positions. Her favorite was Walker with his bald head between her legs. It made her purr thinking about touching all that bare skin while he licked her. But, still being honest, she couldn't compete with the women he dated. And he had a *lot* of dates. Some real hotties. Sometimes they paid. Sometimes he did. She liked it a whole lot better when Walker took care of the tab because women were terrible tippers. There were times she recognized the women from a previous date, or two or three, but for the most part, Walker played the field. He'd just never played in *her* field.

Until he asked her to the movies.

Call her needy, but for tonight, after that altercation with Heidi, she didn't care how late it was or how her feet ached or how tired she was; she needed a little TLC, and TLC was what Walker dished out in spades. You could see it on the faces of the women he wined and dined. Bliss. Cleo wanted her share.

She was glad for the sweater she'd worn as she climbed out of her car. The day had been in the seventies—not so unusual in the Bay Area even for the end of October—but the night was chilly. Leaving the restaurant, she'd rushed home to change into a wool skirt and her fur-lined boots, then hightailed it over to the community college where they were holding this Fright Fest. Walker had offered to drive her, but she didn't want him to know where she lived. In case things got messy somewhere down the road.

The lot was full, people heading up the walkways, couples, groups, college-age and older, some with lawn chairs and picnic baskets, blankets, flashlights. Laughter rose into the night.

At the end of the row of parked cars, Walker appeared under a light, the beam shining on his bare head, giving him the look of a guardian or something. Watching out for her. It felt extraordinarily good. Like that old show from the eighties, *Beauty and the Beast*, where Vincent was always there when Catherine needed him. Okay, she was a sucker for a good romance when she was a kid. Yeah, then she grew up.

"Hey, you." He smiled that sweet, sexy smile as she came abreast of him. A quilt was tucked under his arm and a basket dangled from his fingers. Wearing black jeans and a cable-knit sweater, he looked thick and powerful and oh so sexy.

"Hi," she said, almost shyly.

He held out his hand. Cleo stared. She didn't go in for hand-holding, too much like a boyfriend/girlfriend thing. She'd stopped bringing boyfriends home for Heidi to get attached to because she sucked at picking the right men. Case in point, Heidi's father left before she'd even been born. There'd been Greg when Heidi was seven. He'd cheated on Cleo, but in many ways, he'd cheated on Heidi, too. Then she'd met Phil. She'd thought he was permanent, but in the end, he wanted a family of his own. He didn't like the word *step* in stepdaughter. If she'd known that in the beginning, she'd never have let Heidi meet him, and though she hadn't said why he left—Cleo didn't even tell Ma—Heidi took his defection hard. She'd been only eleven, and she didn't understand why Phil was suddenly gone. She'd blamed Cleo. To avoid the issue altogether, Cleo didn't have boyfriends anymore. Sometimes she had friends who took care of needs, but even that had been ages ago. Damn if loneliness, physical and mental, wasn't starting to wear on her.

"I won't bite," Walker said.

Screw all his other women, and her bad judgment. This was one night, that was all, and Cleo wanted to be touched. She took his hand. He wasn't extremely tall, but his body was stocky enough to make her feel petite.

"I'm glad you decided to come." He squeezed her fingers.

"You thought I'd stand you up?"

He smiled, his teeth gleaming in the lamplight. "It's already happened once tonight." He didn't seem terribly broken up about it. But then, he was always good-natured whenever he came to Bella's.

He led her up the incline, walking faster than most, winding through openings in the crowd. "I have a special spot in mind for us."

Passing through a gate, Walker handed over the tickets. They picked their way up a grassy slope dotted with partygoers. Some wore costumes—Dracula, aliens, killer clowns from outer space, a big silver robot.

"Gort," Walker said, following her line of sight.

"Huh?"

"The robot. His name is Gort."

"Oh." All she was really thinking about was how big and warm Walker's hand felt engulfing hers.

He chuckled. "You'll see."

He took her to the top of the incline, tossing down the quilt in a small clearing nestled amid a ring of bushes. He'd actually had more than one blanket secured beneath his arm. Setting aside the basket, he flipped out the quilt to cover the grass, then swept out his hand.

"Have a seat." He hunkered down beside her after she sat, wrapping one of the other blankets over her shoulders. "This will keep you warm."

The way he looked at her, she had visions of other ways to keep warm.

Sitting beside her, he opened the basket, pulling out a bottle of wine, glasses, cheese, crackers.

"Wow, you think of everything." He certainly knew how to treat a woman well. Then she remembered that none of this had been for her. "No wonder the ladies flock to you."

In the midst of uncorking the wine, he tipped her chin. "I'm with you tonight, Cleo, because I want to be with you. And only you."

God, she'd sounded jealous. To hide it, she picked up a glass. "I'd like to toast you for being such a nice guy and inviting me to the movies."

"I'm not so nice." As he poured, he gave her a wicked grin.

"So where do we see this movie?" She pointed out over the throng sloping down the hill.

"The gymnasium wall."

She laughed. "They play them on the wall?"

"Yeah. I come every year. It's great." He handed her a cracker topped with deliciously fragrant cheese.

"What silly classic are you going to make me watch?" she teased.

He put his hand to his heart. "You wound me with your sarcasm."

"Yeah, right." She'd never seen anything bother him. Walker was a man with an even keel if ever there was one. "Now, what are we going to watch?" She'd never been to an outdoor movie before.

"*The Day the Earth Stood Still*, *Psycho*, and *Black Christmas*."

"Oh, I love Keanu Reeves and Vince Vaughn."

Walker shivered dramatically. "We're talking *classics*. Classic sci-fi, Hitchcock horror, and campy slasher. Originals, no bad remakes. Keanu Reeves is in no way classic yet." He pulled more stuff from the basket. Squishy down pillows that filled out when he drew them from their cloth bags. The man did indeed think of everything.

"I like my creature comforts," he said as she eyed his setup. "And Vince Vaughn has nothing on Anthony Perkins." He leaned closer and lowered his voice. "Not to mention the luscious Janet Leigh in the shower."

"You like blondes?" Although she wasn't quite sure if Janet Leigh had been blonde in *Psycho*.

"Hah, you've seen it!"

She sniffed snootily. "*Everyone's* seen the shower scene."

The wall suddenly lit up, and the audience hushed. Walker pulled her down beside him, shoved a pillow beneath her head and the blanket up to her chin. Beneath her, the grass was soft, and, so close, Walker smelled good, something outdoorsy. As if he'd just been walking in the woods.

"Now, shush," he whispered as the opening credits rolled.

Well, the actor certainly wasn't Keanu Reeves, but she had to admit the big tall guy playing the alien was handsome. When he spoke to Gort (yes, the robot) in his alien language, the audience yelled out the words just before he said them.

Walker murmured them into her ear. "See, I'm bilingual."

Ooh. Lingual. *That* made her think of certain things, but she elbowed him. "Shh," she said, then muttered, "Klaatu the alien's kinda hot."

Propped on his elbow behind her, Walker wrapped his arm across her abdomen beneath the blanket and snuggled her closer. "I think Patricia Neal should dump her loser fiancé and do Klaatu."

She laughed. "How about a threesome with Gort?"

"Oh baby," he cooed at her ear, chuckling. "I like the way you think."

With his body pressed along her back, Cleo shivered. She liked the way he felt.

He misinterpreted. "Cold?"

She was about to say no. She had the blanket, his body heat. But now . . . she wanted more. "Yeah, I'm cold."

He muffled around behind her, pulling both blankets on top, adjusting the pillows; then he was flush against her, back, knees, powerful thighs. And everything in between.

Oh man. That was some *everything* nestled along the crease of her butt.

"Better?" he murmured.

He simply couldn't know. She hadn't been with a man in months. Though a vibrator could be a girl's best friend in a pinch, especially when she was fantasizing about Walker, there was just nothing like the feel of a real, hard, flesh-and-blood cock. "Oh yeah," she murmured. "Much better."

While the crowd repeated damn near every line of the movie

before it was spoken, Walker teased her with seductive one-liners. They bantered and laughed, and, hell, she hadn't enjoyed herself this much in . . . forever. She had to admit that while Keanu Reeves was cute, the original version of the movie won hands down. Later, when Janet Leigh stepped into the *Psycho* shower, Walker put his lips to her hair. "What I wouldn't give to see you stepping into that shower."

She laughed. "Sorry, dude, but I've seen what happens, and I would never get into that shower."

"Naked," he went on, "all slippery."

God, he was good. The feel of him was decadent. She pressed closer, if that were even possible. With his body surrounding her, his voice at her ear, breath in her hair, she felt like a woman instead of a waitress or a receptionist or a mom. Lying there, the movie images flickering on the wall, the after-midnight moon high in the nighttime sky, the voices and laughter and Walker, she was no longer tired after the long day and an even longer week. Energy coursed through her. Sexual energy. It had been much too long.

Beneath the warmth of blankets and body heat, Cleo covered Walker's hand and drew it to her breast.

WALKER'S HEART BEAT SLOW AND STEADY IN HIS CHEST. HE NEVER rushed, never pushed. In his mind, the timing had to be right for the lady, and Christ, yes, *her* timing was so damn perfect. He'd been salivating over her all night, crushed up against her as Patricia Neal and Klaatu battled to save the world and Janet Leigh screamed in the shower. Cleo's breast was firm and full, filling his hand, the bead of her nipple discernible through the soft sweater. Her simple, sweet vanilla scent fogged his mind; the silk of her hair caressed his face.

With his head propped on his hand so he could see the movie over her, they were nestled together by the bushes, behind everyone else. Blankets covering them, their embrace was practically invisible.

"Cleo?"

"Hmm?"

"You have the most perfect breasts."

She laughed. "Thank you."

"Tell me how sensitive your nipples are." He could have tested for himself, but he loved having a woman tell him what she liked. He'd always been verbal. Phone sex was a favorite pastime.

"Pretty sensitive."

Some women needed to be enticed into opening up. "Do you like them licked or sucked?" He circled her nipple and felt her sigh against him.

"Both." Her voice grew huskier.

"Do you like a little pinching?" He demonstrated with a gentle tweak.

She gasped—"Oh"—as if the pleasure was totally unexpected.

"Like?"

She nodded, her hair brushing his cheek.

"Harder?" he enticed.

"Yes."

Harder, longer, he gave it to her. She rewarded him with a low, breathy moan. He could almost scent her panties dampening. Her body strained against him, and his cock surged along the base of her spine.

He licked her earlobe. "It would feel so much better skin to skin."

She huffed. "What are you waiting for?" She lifted her sweater and pulled his hand beneath the soft wool. "That was so good, it makes me want to come."

Okay, so she didn't need a lot of cajoling. He liked that she showed no fear or maidenly hesitancy. He liked equally as much that she hadn't experienced everything: case in point, a hot little pinch.

Her bra was front-clasping, and he popped it with minimum effort. Her breast fell into his hand. He rubbed one nipple with his palm, circling the other with his thumb. "Better?"

"Pinch them like you did before."

He took turns with each bead. She squirmed and moaned. "Oh man." Her ass rolled over his cock, massaged him; she revved his motor.

"I didn't think I'd like"—she gasped—"that BDSM stuff."

Walker laughed. "This is not BDSM."

"Whatever. Just don't stop, okay?"

He favored both equally, and this time he was sure her hot, sweet, aroused scent perfumed the air. Christ, he wanted her nipple in his mouth, the salty-sweet taste of her skin on his tongue. Getting arrested for lewd behavior in public, though, wasn't an option. He was only allowed things he could accomplish under the blankets with no one being the wiser.

Walker was an expert at finding all the right spots without getting caught.

3

JEEZ, THE GUY HAD MAGIC IN HIS FINGERS. HER SKIN WAS HOT, HER body wet, her nipples tingling, aching, and pure heat streaked straight down to her clit. Man, oh man, how had she missed out on this? Just for a little jealousy about his number of women?

Cleo tightened her grip on his forearm beneath her breasts, holding him close, her head back against his shoulder. "That is so good."

"I thought you'd like it."

She'd always found his voice deep and sexy, but now it was a husky rasp at her ear that seemed to shimmy down every nerve ending. "What else can you do?" she asked from some dreamy near-orgasmic state.

Walker chuckled, and the warmth of his breath was like pure sex drizzled on and licked off. She didn't want a kiss; she didn't need warm fuzzies. She just wanted hot sensation all over her body.

"My trick is to find out what a woman really wants, then give it to her." He leaned over her, trailing his lips across her cheek. "Tell me what you need right this minute." He licked the rim of her ear, eliciting a shiver. "Better yet, show me."

Oh, this man really did have a way with women. She was willing to show him anything. Turning her head and putting an arm back, she pulled his lips down to hers just short of touching. "I didn't have this in mind when I put on a skirt, but . . ." She trailed off, letting him get the message.

"And?"

She huffed. He wanted her to say it. "I think you should take advantage of me."

"You do?" Her breath brushed her mouth.

Now he was teasing her. "I'm not going to beg." But she swept her tongue across his lips.

"Mmm," he murmured. "That feels like begging." His chest rose and fell against her back, a little faster now.

"If you want to think so, go ahead. Just put your hand up my skirt."

"Whatever my lady wants."

The skirt was long. Walker trailed his hand down her abdomen, to the waistband, then over her hip. Her skin hummed. He traced the edge of her sex, along her thigh, until he curled his fingers in the material and tugged the skirt higher.

"What do you want me to do once I'm there?" he whispered.

She burned. *Make me come.* But that was not what he asked for. He wanted the means to the end. "Stroke my thighs just along the edge of my pussy."

He breathed deeply, shot it out. At her back, his cock pulsed, hard, hot, as he laid his hand on her bare knee. "Your skin is so soft and smooth. Did you shave just for me?"

"I shaved this morning for me."

He nipped her neck. "I love feisty."

Well, hell, she was that. At least where men were concerned. You get dumped on enough, you learn not to take a lot of crap. "You're taking a long time to get there."

He chuckled, the vibration rippling through her. "We have half of *Psycho* and all of *Black Christmas* to get through. I don't want to rush." He followed the line of her thigh, leaving tingles in his wake.

"I might fall asleep before you get around to it."

"I'll be sure to wake you up when I finally make it all the way there."

Man, he was fun. She'd always appreciated his sense of humor. He teased and flirted when he was alone, polite and sweet when he was with a woman, but always quick to smile and laugh. Then his touch made her gasp, his fingers tracing the seam of her pussy through her cotton panties.

He growled like a jungle cat. "I knew you were already wet. I could smell how sweet you are."

She trembled, sliding one leg down his until she rested her boot on his ankle, parting her thighs. "You are a sweet talker." She lowered her voice, purred to match his growl. "But let's see some action. I don't want to miss the climax of the movie." She'd forgotten all about Norman Bates, but she loved the word *climax*.

"I need direction."

Hmm, dirty, classy, or euphemistic? "Rip off my panties."

"You naughty woman." Laughter edged his voice as he slid his fingers beneath the elastic and yanked her cotton panties over her hips. She wriggled, helping him pull them down her legs.

It was so wonderfully decadent, to be naked beneath the skirt, the blankets, the heat.

"If I was sure I wouldn't be seen, I'd hold your sweet cotton crotch to my nose and breathe in your scent."

"Pervert," she whispered, but he was deliciously sensual. In her experience, men were wham-bam. If you wanted more, you had to forcibly slow them down. She'd never felt quite the thrill to a man's touch, never been so drawn in by the banter, the sex talk, the sensuality of a mere caress. She'd never become creamy before a man even put his hands between her legs. She'd certainly never had to speed a man up.

"Now touch me, Walker. Put your fingers in me. Make them wet with me." She closed her eyes, turning her head to rub her cheek against his shoulder. "Stroke me. I like it slow and gentle. Not too hard or forceful. Then when I tell you, I want it fast."

Cleo's words heated him straight through. Walker's pulse pounded in his ears. She was so wet, her skin hot, and he slipped inside her with two fingers. She moaned and rocked on him, deepening the penetration.

"Man, oh man," she said on a breath. "You are so good."

Sliding out, he circled her clit, spreading her moisture, caressing as she started to shudder. "Is this what you want?"

"Yes, just like that." She moved with his hand, rolling her hips in counterpoint.

He gazed over the crowd, noisy and excited as Norman donned his mother's frock. No one cared what Walker was doing to Cleo beneath the blankets. No one heard the sweetness of her moans or her soft cries. He enjoyed the noises a woman made. He loved hers. He liked the way women smelled, their perfume, their sweet scent of arousal. He savored hers.

With her arm once again around his neck, she pulled him down, licked his cheek, bit his jaw, her breath fanning across his skin.

"Come on, baby." He circled her faster, but not harder, remembering what she said, everything she wanted. Her body quaked, her breath puffing. She arched, letting out a gentle growl before biting her lip to keep in her cries. Christ, it was good. Cleo. Coming apart in his arms. He hadn't quite understood how badly he'd wanted it until he felt her shudder against him, his fantasies of her come to life. It was sweeter than any of the women he'd pleased in the last three years.

She came down from her peak, snuggling back into him, her ass cupping his cock.

"You better take me now, Walker," she whispered. "I'm gonna go crazy if you don't."

Her voice hummed along his cock. "We'll miss Norman."

She laughed, choking it off. "I'll rent it and we'll watch it again."

"My kind of woman."

"Now, put on a condom because I know you've got one somewhere in your little bag of tricks."

Like a Boy Scout, he was always prepared, condom in his back pocket. Yet for a moment, a hiccup of something blocked his throat. She wasn't the woman who was supposed to be here. He didn't have much of a conscience, but it seemed a little off to be subjecting her to another woman's condoms.

Walker hesitated. "Cleo, I—"

Cleo had no idea why—maybe it was some orgasmic connection—but she could read him like a book. Or maybe it was that she'd seen him with so many women, and she knew she was a fill-in date. Or she was just punch-drunk with lack of sleep. Whatever. He'd hesitated, and *something* suddenly bothered him. She didn't roll into his arms or kiss him or beg him. Cleo was a straight shooter. "Do it, Walker, because it'll be hot and sexy and I really, really need hot and sexy tonight. I had a bad day and right now I don't care about anything else." She pushed a hand between them, squeezed his hard cock, and lowered her voice to a whisper. "So make me feel a whole lot better."

His chest rumbled against her back. "You really are my kind of woman." He pulled her head back by the hair, all he-man-like. Her nipples ached with how hot and desperate he made her. "Tell me how you want it," he murmured on a needy growl.

"Just like this." Back to front. She hooked her foot behind his calf.

He shoved her skirt high over her hip. "Oh baby, I'm going to fuck you. You don't know how bad I want it."

Oh yes, she did. She wanted it just as badly. He shifted and rustled behind her, then his fingers brushed her butt as he popped his button fly. She wanted to touch and suck and taste, and yet she wanted him inside her more.

"Hurry." Her desperation laced her voice and drove her even higher. The orgasm had been good. She wanted more; she needed hotter. "Touch me."

She heard the tear and crinkle of the wrapping, felt the brush of his knuckles as he rolled on the condom. Then he pressed close, slid his hand along her hip, and ran his fingers over her pussy, her clit. "Put me inside you."

Her heart fluttered as if this were some sacred ritual. Walker made it special. She hadn't felt special since Phil left. Why Walker of all people? Who cared? Maybe it was his slow lovemaking, the way he made it all about her. She rubbed him between her legs, wetting the condom with her own juice, then he wrapped an arm across her abdomen and pulled her down.

"Oh God." She barely breathed as he gave her an inch, then another.

She knew she wasn't tight—she'd had a child—but he groaned as he filled her. "You have such a sweet pussy," he whispered into her hair.

She'd been fucked. It wasn't a bad thing. Walker made it more than mere fucking.

Beneath the blankets, he pinned her hip, and pumped, slowly, deeper with each thrust. And he talked. Walker loved to talk. "Je-sus, you feel so damn good. I knew it would be like this. I've dreamed about it."

Words were as important as touch. She soared higher.

"I've dreamed of tasting your pussy." He put his fingers to her clit. "Your mouth on my cock." Stroking, circling, driving her to the edge. "Tasting my come on your lips." He thrust high, forcing a gasp from her. "I want it all."

Cleo hung on as he rode her, filled her, touched her everywhere, not just her pussy or her clit, but deep inside. Stars burst behind her closed lids.

"Wanna fuck you," he whispered. "Wanna have you."

He pulsed inside her, throbbed, flexed, and, despite the condom, she felt the hot explosion of his climax. Groaning, he buried his face at her neck, held her with his teeth like a lion pinning his mate. He slammed home, grunting against her skin, and dragged her into orgasmic heaven right along with him.

4

HIS COCK BURIED INSIDE HER, WALKER FELT CLEO'S BREATHING even out, slowing as she succumbed to the late hour. He tucked her close, wrapped the blankets around them, and relished the feel of her.

Psycho had ended and *Black Christmas* had begun. A few movie-goers had given up the ghost, but most were still rocking out, flashing lighters, talking over the character lines.

He hadn't kissed her fully, hadn't even faced her, yet Walker hadn't experienced an orgasm like that in years. Hard to pinpoint the last time. Certainly not with any of his dates. There was always mutual attraction. He didn't expect a woman to have sex with him if she found he wasn't her type, and vice versa. He'd never been married, though he'd always planned on it. He'd bought his house with that in mind, a family. However, he'd hit the rat race running, and when he looked up, suddenly he was in his forties with no wife and no kids and no plans for it on the horizon. So, in all his loveless life—which wasn't the negative it sounded, merely the truth—as of right now, he couldn't remember anything that quite measured up to tonight.

He wasn't romantic enough to believe that love made sex better or that sex couldn't be fucking fantastic without love. All he knew was that Cleo had fulfilled many of his fantasies. The reality had been better than anything he'd dreamed about her. His blood still simmered, and his body trembled with lingering orgasmic shocks.

Another shock wave rolled through his mind. He needed more of this. He wanted to explore, learn more about her, *know* her, about her life, her daughter, her dreams. More than the bare minimum that acquaintances know.

How long should he let her sleep? She'd been working. She was tired. It was late. Yet she was so peaceful. She brought him a sense of peace, too.

He liked his life, but he'd been living on the surface. Tonight gave him a taste of what living deeper could be like. The sex itself had been vanilla compared to many of the things he'd done in the last three years. Not all the women he'd dated were nervous fillies like Estelle. There'd been a tigress or two or several who'd requested threesomes, foursomes, parties, girl-girl with him as voyeur. But sex with Cleo had touched him on the inside, more than the physical, perhaps because she was fantasy turned reality. He couldn't be sure of the reason; it just was.

Though it felt like losing something essential, he pulled free of her. She muttered and mumbled at his movements as he disposed of the condom and fastened his jeans. Then he kissed her temple. "Wake up, sleepyhead. Time to go home."

She rubbed her eyes, rolled to her back. "How long have I been asleep?"

"Not long. But I'll take you home."

She nodded, breathed deeply. "It's been a long day." Beneath the blankets, she wriggled her skirt and bra back into place. "Ooh, my panties," she whispered, feeling around.

Coming down over her, arms bracketing her body, he put his lips to her ear. "I'm taking them home with me." They were already in his back pocket.

He laid the wine, cheese, crackers, and glasses back in the basket as she stuffed the down pillows into their bags. Then he folded the blankets, shoved them under his arm to carry, and held out a hand.

She slipped her palm into his, her touch warm. He led them, picking their way through the audience. With the crowd's collective gasp, a college coed died some horrible death up on the gym wall.

"Ooh, it's cold now." Cleo clung to his arm for warmth.

"Want the blanket around you?"

"No, thanks, I'll turn the heater on in the car."

The top of his head chilled in the very early morning. Down in the parking lot, he walked her to her car. "I'll follow you home."

She hesitated. "You don't need to do that. I'll be fine."

"I don't let a lady go home by herself this late at night."

She unlocked her door. The car was clean, but vintage, without even a remote alarm. "Honestly, Walker, I'm fine."

He held her arm. "Cleo."

She pursed her lips, shuffled her feet. "Look, it was great tonight. But I have a teenage daughter, and I really don't like men knowing where I live."

It felt like a slap in the face. He was just some guy she'd fucked, and she wasn't bringing him home to meet her mom and kid.

Okay. Readjust. Good to know where the starting line was. He had a long way to go to get her to trust him. "I still need to know you get home safely. Here's my cell number." He wrote it down on the back of the ticket stub. "Call me."

"Sure." She didn't meet his eye, though.

He wanted to kiss her, but what they'd shared up on the knoll had vanished with the straightening of their clothes. Instead, he let her climb into her car, made sure the engine turned over, and stood watching her taillights disappear as she turned at the end of the row of parked cars.

He was used to being a woman's interlude. He'd chosen it. He liked the freedom of it. He just hadn't realized he would want to be more than an interlude for Cleo.

SWEAR TO GOD, HE'D LOOKED AS IF SHE'D HURT HIM, HIS JAW TENS-ing. She had Heidi to think about, though, and she couldn't let a virtual stranger know where she lived.

Oh, but she could let him fuck her. Jeez. Didn't that make a whole lot of sense? Cleo shook her head.

All right, he wasn't a stranger, either. Nevertheless, she'd watched for headlights, and no one followed her. He might be kind to animals and babies, but he was totally the wrong kind of guy to depend on.

She shivered.

Still, it had been *so* good. He hadn't rushed her. He'd teased her for more than two hours before . . . and really, would he have taken advantage of her if she hadn't told him to?

The lights were on when she pulled into the drive, and her heart started to beat faster in her chest.

It was almost three in the morning. Oh God. Something had happened to Heidi. She patted her pocket; her cell phone was still there. Pulling it out, she checked the charge. Okay, no calls. Her mom would have called if it was really bad.

The car rumbled for long moments after she shut it off. Not good. It was ancient, but well maintained. It used to be her dad's car before he passed away. Heidi hadn't even been born yet. Really, there was only so much maintaining one could do before the thing croaked. At the front door, her hand trembled fitting the key to the lock. She found her mother in the kitchen.

"What are you doing up, Ma? Is Heidi okay?"

"Fine as far as I know." Her voice gravelly with years of smoking, she stubbed out her cigarette. Her skin was like leather, her steel gray hair permed, and where once she'd been five foot two, she was now slightly under five.

"I thought you were smoking outside, Ma."

"Not when it's three in the morning, colder than a witch's tit, and no one but me is inhaling." She rose, leaning heavily on the table. Cleo could almost hear her bones creak.

At the sink, her mom filled the kettle, setting it on the stove. The range was harvest gold from the seventies with four burners, a griddle, and two ovens, the smaller one for warming. It was scratched, the clock didn't always turn over, the self-cleaning no longer worked, but heck, everything else did. The imitation-brick linoleum was also seventies vintage, but it was clean and unmarked. Cleo had regrouted the yellow tile counter herself and repainted the white cabinets.

"Got a problem in the bathroom." Her mom hooked a thumb over her shoulder.

There was a small half bath off the back hallway. Cleo got a sick feeling in the pit of her stomach. Her steps slow, her boots seemed to echo on the hall's hardwood floor. She shoved open the door.

Oh shit.

Plaster had fallen from the ceiling, revealing bare pipes and floorboards above. The second bathroom, the one Cleo shared with Heidi, was situated right overhead. Water beaded, then dripped to the sodden plaster below. Good Lord, how long had that drip been going on? She couldn't tell exactly where the water was coming from. It didn't look as if the pipes had actually burst.

The kettle whistled as she climbed the second-floor stairs. In the main bathroom, she knelt between the tub and toilet. She didn't see any water, but when she pressed on the linoleum, the floorboards felt squishy underneath, worsening the closer she got to the toilet. She turned the water off at the wall valve, then went in to check Ma's bathroom, which was on the other side of the wall. The flooring felt fine, thank God. But the three of them would have to share it until she could get the other two fixed.

God, she couldn't afford this. Maybe the house insurance would cover the repairs.

Back downstairs, she checked the half bath again and found the drips had slowed. Maybe it was just the toilet and not the pipes themselves. The leak had probably been going on for a while and soaked through the plaster. How could she have missed that there was a problem like *this*? There must have been a mark on the ceiling, but she hadn't paid much attention. What a freaking mess. Plaster covered the sink and stand, the floor, the toilet lid.

"Ma, I need the mop," she called.

"It's in the cupboard," her mother yelled back.

Cleo closed her eyes and sighed. Her mom had helped raise Heidi, cleaned more scraped knees and elbows than Cleo, wiped away more childhood tears. Ma married later in life than most women of her generation, and after Cleo, she couldn't have any more children. Then Dad died of a heart attack when Cleo was in high school. Now Ma cooked and cleaned for Cleo and Heidi, did the laundry, the marketing, swept the leaves off the walkways, and weeded the garden. But she was slowing down and she refused to quit smoking. She said if she was going to get cancer, she damn well already had it. Her mom could be aggravatingly stubborn and obstreperous when she wanted to be, but she'd never let Cleo down when she needed her.

So Cleo got the bucket and mop herself while her mom filled two mugs from the kettle.

Her tea was cooling by the time she'd finished cleaning up the mess. The water had stopped dripping. Turning off the toilet had fixed that part of the problem, at least temporarily.

She pulled out a chair. "I'll call a plumber on Monday. I think it's the upstairs toilet leaking."

"The ceiling made an awful racket when it fell, woke me up." Her mom toyed with her cigarette pack, but didn't light up. "Where were ya? You didn't tell me you'd be out so late."

She hadn't told Ma much of anything when she'd dashed in earlier to change. "I went to the movies." She'd forgotten she needed to call Walker and let him know she was home.

Her mom snorted.

"Really." Cleo smiled. "We saw *The Day the Earth Stood Still*, the old version."

"Och." Her mom waggled her eyebrows. "Michael Rennie was hot."

"Ma." Cleo sounded scandalized.

She shrugged. "Well, he was. And so tall."

"Hmm, Keanu Reeves"—Cleo flipped over one hand, then the other—"or Michael Rennie?"

"Definitely Rennie. Keanu is a pansy. I mean, honestly, his name says it all."

Cleo laughed. "I love you, Ma. Now I gotta go to bed." She rose, brushed a kiss across the top of her mom's gray hair.

"What'll we do about the toilet and the ceiling?" She held tight to Cleo's hand a moment.

"I'm up for that promotion at work. We'll manage." She'd applied for an accounts payable position. It was a pay increase over receptionist. She wasn't holding her breath, though, in case she turned blue and died. Luck didn't come Cleo's way.

But she wouldn't tell her mom that.

"Okay, sweetie. Sleep tight."

Climbing the stairs once more, she puffed out a breath. She could handle this; she could handle anything. Except the look of anger in Heidi's eyes. It was so close to hate.

She slept in the same room she'd used all her life. Once upon a time, there had been a lavender bedspread with purple shag carpet and lots of frills. After Heidi was born, she'd ripped out the carpet, refinished the hardwood, and stitched together two sheets for a duvet over the comforter.

She was suddenly so tired all she could do was toe out of her boots and let her skirt and sweater drop on the floor.

Jeez.

She'd forgotten about her panties. Having tea with Ma, and she hadn't even been wearing her panties. How was it possible to forget? Funny. Being with Walker seemed more like a dream. *This* was her real life, broken toilets and the ceiling caving in. It reminded her of *Chicken Little*. After brushing her teeth, she crawled beneath the comforter.

It had been well over an hour. He'd have turned his phone off, but she called so she could say she had.

"Hello."

Shit. He wasn't supposed to answer. "Hi, it's Cleo. I'm home safe and sound—thanks for a lovely evening." She said it all in one breath.

"It was my pleasure. I'd like to see you again."

"That's not possible." He was a dream. Expecting or even wanting anything more was stupid. She had too many obligations. The house was falling down, her car was on its last legs, and she needed every spare moment with Heidi to repair the damage to their relationship. Now was not the time to bring a new friend with benefits into her life.

"Anything is possible, Cleo."

She snuggled under the covers. His voice. Over the phone, it was deeper. Though he was far away, it was as potent as the moment he'd buried himself inside her.

"I'm not ready for this right now, Walker." But she wanted it.

"You're a sweet man." Hot, sexy, hard, delicious, and she wished she'd tasted him. "But tonight was a mistake." A mistake she could make over and over if she let herself. Suddenly, after one evening with Walker, she wasn't exhausted anymore. He made her feel alive again. He made life fun.

"Cleo."

God, the way he said her name, just that, nothing else, she was wet, burning up. "What?"

"We will fuck again, you know."

She wanted to say he was wrong—she couldn't afford him—but he wasn't.

5

"THANKS FOR EMBARRASSING ME BY BEING LATE." HEIDI SLAMMED the car door, slouched down in her seat, and crossed her arms.

"Please don't be rude." Dammit, Cleo had overslept, a bad combination of a late night and good sex. See, you let a man step into your zone and things got all screwed up. Not to mention waking up at five a.m. worrying about the ceiling. Somewhere around the time the sun began to rise, Cleo had slept like the dead, having forgotten to set the alarm because it was Saturday morning. Thus she was late picking Heidi up from the sleepover at Cat's.

"I'm not being rude," Heidi snapped. "I'm trying to teach you about being punctual."

If it wasn't another one of those fights and another one of those mornings, Cleo would have laughed. As a child, Heidi had been precocious. Cleo remembered picking her up after school—Heidi would have been seven or so—and she was babbling a mile a minute about the bunny that a girl had brought to class. One of the teachers stopped to speak to Cleo. After a few seconds, Heidi piped up, "Excuse me, but you interrupted. I haven't finished yet." It had been amusing, the teacher apologized, and Heidi finished her story.

It was Heidi's tone that had changed over the last year, the snappishness. Cleo had already apologized to Cat's mom, and to Heidi, too. But Heidi kept on riding her.

"We had a problem with the upstairs toilet in the middle of the night."

"I told you there was something wrong in there."

For the life of her, Cleo couldn't remember Heidi saying any such thing. But honestly, she couldn't be sure. She had so much on her mind, and Heidi had taken up the habit of mumbling something, then walking away.

I just can't talk to you right now. Cleo wanted to say the words so badly, but they would only make things worse. She kept her mouth shut because anything she said would be wrong.

Back at the house, Heidi stomped up to her room. Fifteen minutes later she stomped back downstairs. "Misha asked if I could go to the mall with her. Can I go to the mall?"

Cleo was folding clothes in the laundry room. "Is your homework done?"

Heidi rolled her eyes. "Yes. Would you like to check it?"

Part of her wanted to say yes. But while Heidi was sullen and uncommunicative, her grades were good. "Please be home at least half an hour before dinner."

Please and *thank you* and *I'm sorry*. She said that a lot, whereas before it had always been implicit.

Heidi stomped out. She was home by four thirty, right when she was supposed to be. Yet everything was done with a sneer and a roll of her eyes.

Cleo left the house early for her shift at the restaurant before she actually called her own daughter a bitch. With every altercation, the ache in Cleo's heart grew larger.

God, she wished she had someone to talk with about it. Ma didn't count. They had their own issues that would get in the way. Maybe another single mom. Someone to tell her she wasn't just a bad mother who was too busy with her own life to give her daughter what she really needed. But Cleo didn't have a lot of friends. At work, the receptionist was always someone you passed by on the way in or out, so she hadn't managed to make friends. Despite three years at the restaurant, she'd failed to find a common ground there, too.

Except for Walker.

For the first time on a Saturday night, Walker wasn't at Bella's.

She had sex with him, then poof, just like that, he was gone. Despite what he'd said to her on the phone in the wee hours of the morning. Okay, she'd told him she didn't have time for a man, and honestly, she didn't. Bad timing all around.

Contrary to all that, she hadn't expected him to vanish so quickly.

MONDAY, MIDMORNING, AFTER AN INTERESTING RIDE ON BART INTO the city, Walker sprawled in the chair and put his booted feet on Isabel's desk. Mostly because he knew she'd hate it.

"Walker, you have your boots on my desk." She didn't smile, her gaze ice blue.

"Yes, Isabel, I know." He suppressed a smile.

Her office was like the woman, elegant but with many facets. A grandfather clock in the corner, a pair of Cloisonné plates on the wall, an ornate Satsuma vase on a long cherrywood sideboard, a Meissen figurine, an eclectic mix that somehow went together seamlessly. There seemed to be no rhyme or reason, as if she'd seen each piece at one time or another, fell in love with it, had to add it to the beauty she'd placed around her.

"You like pushing my buttons, don't you," she said evenly.

"Yeah." Walker nodded. "I love it."

He'd always found her attractive. Yet even when he was a client, he'd never slept with her, never asked. There was something about Isabel, polished and professional yet somehow aloof. He could have had sex with her, and it would have been great, just as it was with his clients. But she would be holding back. Walker didn't want his women holding back. He enjoyed women who needed him. Isabel didn't need anyone.

So he'd never asked.

He, did, however, enjoy putting his boots on her desk because she gave him that look, part blonde ice queen, part neat freak, part sexy, disapproving schoolteacher. He'd had a crush on Mrs. Winters in the fifth grade.

He knew something else about Isabel. While she could admit she was wrong and apologize for it, she never backed down when she was pushed.

"I suppose," he drawled, "that if I don't get my feet off your desk, you won't tell me why Estelle canceled on Friday."

"Exactly."

It was an odd face-saver. They both won because they both got what they wanted. Walker removed his feet, crossing one boot over his knee. "So tell me."

Isabel grimaced and blew the dust off the edge of her desk. "Her cat died."

He steepled his fingers beneath his chin. Speaking of school analogies . . . "Is this like the dog-ate-my-homework excuse?"

Isabel's lips twitched. "Some people become very attached to their pets."

"I'm not dissing pets. I just believe she was more nervous about our meeting than she told you. Was she married?"

"That's something I can't discuss."

There were things her clients told Isabel in confidence. In that case, he gleaned all he could from a woman's actions, what she *didn't* say. After three years of giving women what they wanted, he considered himself an expert on figuring out what they needed even if they couldn't articulate it. Lonely ladies who needed to be wanted, he made them feel desired. Women who felt impotent in their real lives, he gave them power. Women too busy to take time for themselves, he pampered them for a night. Suddenly *my cat died* wasn't so amusing. It sounded like a woman on the precipice between asking for what she wanted and being terrified of it. That was the only thing Walker couldn't do: *make* her take what he offered.

What did Cleo need?

Isabel tapped the capped tip of her pen on the desk. "So, you could have called me to find out all about the demise of your client's cat. To what do I truly owe the pleasure of a visit?" She smiled big. Like a jungle feline.

Cleo was the reason he'd come to Isabel's office. "I'm considering a hiatus."

Isabel stared.

"You're catching flies, Isabel."

"I thought I'd heard that incorrectly."

"You didn't."

"Because of the cat woman?" she said, aghast.

He snorted. "Don't be ridiculous."

"Then why?"

"I've met somebody."

He wasn't clear on exactly what he wanted from Cleo. Sex, yeah. To learn more about her. Oh yeah. To become a part of her life? Maybe. He couldn't do it while he was fucking other women for money. No matter his reasons for being a courtesan.

Now Isabel really was catching flies for several seconds. "Oh my God, do *not* tell me you're in love."

He hadn't quite thought of it like that. Cleo was a mystery in so many ways. She had a daughter. She'd never been married.

She worked her ass off to take care of her kid, loved her to death, but things were not so sweet right now. The rest was a mystery he wanted to solve. But the fact remained: you could lust after a mystery woman, obsess about her, but if you loved her, you loved a fantasy you'd created in your own mind.

"Not yet." Then he gave Isabel a look. "But if I was, why would you be so shocked?"

"Because . . ." She paused, as if suddenly realizing she'd said too much.

"Because?"

She put her elbows on the desk, laced her fingers. "I don't mean this with a negative connotation. In fact I consider myself to be like you in a lot of ways. And we're not people for deep relationships."

He wasn't easily offended. He liked living without a lot of entanglement and mess. On Saturday night, for the first time, he hadn't been thinking about the client he was with. He hadn't been trying to figure out what she needed to feel important or worthy. That wasn't like him, either. He'd changed his reservation from Bella's to a fancy fondue place in Saratoga. He hadn't wanted to entertain in front of Cleo. The way he ran his chosen profession had changed because of Cleo and Friday night, because of a no-show and a split-second decision.

"My mind wasn't in it on Saturday," he told Isabel.

"I didn't receive any complaints."

"I didn't let her know."

"Who is this woman who's captured your attention?"

"No one you know."

"Does she know about . . ." Isabel waved her hand expressively, encompassing his body.

"No."

"Are you going to tell her?"

There were few people he would allow this third degree. He did so only for Isabel because she knew him well and liked him anyway. He was also sure she was headed toward a point.

"I haven't made that decision yet," he said.

Isabel leaned back in her chair, laying her hands flat on the armrests. "You should make that decision right now."

He eased his head to the side, regarded her. And waited.

"Whatever you decide now is what you'll be stuck with. Whether it's the lie or it's the truth."

Now, didn't *that* sound like the voice of experience. Another of Isabel's many facets.

"I appreciate your concern—"

She didn't let him finish. "She'll either accept you the way you are, or she'll hate you for the lie when it comes out."

Cleo wasn't like that. She wasn't judgmental. She'd seen him with women. A lot of women. She wouldn't have any illusions about him. Then again, he'd already admitted to himself that he didn't believe *any* woman, even Cleo, could accept what he did.

"I'll keep that in mind, Isabel."

She smiled, then shook her head. "You're not going to listen to me, are you?"

"I'm one of those people who has to make my own mistakes in order to learn from them."

"I like you, Walker."

"The feeling is mutual."

"You enjoy women. Most men think of us as tools. But you, you like us. I think you'd like us even without sex." She smiled, and any shadow he might have seen—or imagined—was gone. "You can come back anytime."

"I appreciate that, Isabel." He rose.

"And you don't need to be a stranger, either."

He nodded slowly, letting an answering smile rise to his lips. "I'll be around."

He was almost to the door when she said his name. She waited until he'd turned before she spoke.

"Whoever she is, she'll be lucky to have you in her life."

Once outside her door, he laughed. Cleo had already told him to get out of her life. He just had no intention of listening to her.

6

MONDAY HAD BEEN A DISASTER. THE INSURANCE COMPANY CLAIMED the leaking toilet was a replacement issue that wasn't covered by the policy, and they wouldn't even send someone out to assess it. The plumber came in to look at the toilet. If she'd noticed in time—dammit, dammit—the fix would have been easy, but the toilet, which was wall-mounted, had been leaking just behind the wall, into the floorboards and the plaster below. The damages were astronomical.

In desperation, Cleo met with the accounting manager at work only to be told they were hiring an applicant from outside the company who had better accounts payable qualifications.

She wanted to stab her eyes out with a rusty fork.

Okay, bit of an exaggeration. Not *everything* was bad.

Bella's was closed Sunday, and she'd spent some quality time with Heidi and her mom, even if it was in front of the TV watching *Lost in Austen*. Not her cup of tea, but Heidi, for whatever reason, was into the whole Jane Austen craze. She'd even signed out *Pride and Prejudice* from the school library.

Then tonight, Monday, Walker was back at Bella's. He arrived late, and he was alone. Cleo hated to admit how relieved she'd felt, experiencing heart palpations and mixed emotions, happy to

see him, worried he'd ask her out again, afraid he wouldn't, unde-
cided what she would say if he did.

He'd acted as if they'd never had sex, and she had mixed emotions about that, too.

She brought back his credit card slip. Her feet ached, but she
was done for the night after she handled one other customer's
check.

"I'd like to talk to you when you're off work," Walker said.

Her pulse raced. She should say no, but she didn't want to argue with people watching. "I'll be done in five minutes," she said.
But warned, "It's late, though, and I have to get home."

He smiled, his eyes a gentle brown. "I won't keep you long."

When she left the back entrance, he was waiting by her car,
leaning against the passenger side in a pool of lamplight.

Oh man, he looked good. Beneath a skintight black-and-white
sweater, his biceps bulged, and the ripple of his pecs as he pushed
away from the car mesmerized her. She adored bald, and she
itched to feel the smooth skin against her fingertips.

The night air was cold. Cleo pulled her jacket tighter.

There were so many things she hadn't tried with him. A long
kiss. A sip of his come. Burying her face against his skin and
drinking in his scent. God, what she wouldn't give for this to have
happened six months ago. Or even six months from now when
she'd had time to fix things between her and Heidi.

She didn't have the six months to wait.

He didn't touch her, but he was so close his body heat jumped
across the brief distance. An answering fire spontaneously com-
busted inside her, but she backed up slightly in case anyone was
watching through the back windows.

"I want to see you." Walker's low voice was like a stroke along
her skin. "I'm willing to do it on your terms."

Have sex with me now. Those could easily be her terms. But not her priority. "I wish we could, but it's not good timing for me, Walker." Oh, the truth hurt. Friday night he'd given her something just for *her*. She wanted it again. Even if she couldn't have it. "My daughter, a bunch of other stuff going on now." She spread her hands, trying to encompass everything with the gesture.

"I don't want to take away. Only add to."

She didn't have time, needing every extra hour for Heidi. But oh how she wanted.

He cupped her cheek, sending shock waves through her. Remembering Friday night, how good it had been, she closed her eyes, wanting to lean in to his touch.

"Poor Cleo. No time for yourself."

Her rule for Heidi was bed by ten on a school night. Cleo didn't get home until ten thirty, sometimes later, and Heidi was already asleep. Would it matter if once in a while Cleo came home half an hour later?

That would be little more than a wham-bam-thank-you-ma'am. No holding, no talking, no cuddling.

He smiled gently. "I can see you wavering."

Yeah. Then she shook her head. "Things are tough with Heidi right now." She didn't get terribly personal with Walker but he knew she'd transferred Heidi between schools.

"The offer stands. I'd like to spend time with you." He backed away. "Enough said. You have my number."

It was on the tip of her tongue to say, *Maybe we could just talk for a little bit.* She knew herself. She'd want more than talk. With talk *and* sex, you had a relationship, and really, that was a no-go.

"I've got your number," she said, then unlocked her car, climbed in, part of her screaming that she was an idiot.

Walker was parked four spaces over, and he leaned on his car watching her as she started the engine. It turned over, but didn't catch. She tried again. Same thing. It wasn't the battery; she knew *that* sound. She tried several more times. Nothing.

Walker tapped on the driver's window. She rolled it down. "I don't know what's wrong," she said.

"Has it done this before?"

She thought about it. "A couple of times, when the car was cold. But it started on the third or fourth try." Yep, truly an idiot. She should have taken the car to Jimmy, her regular mechanic.

"It could be the starter solenoid."

She climbed out of the car, then stood staring at it as if the problem would fix itself if she glared hard enough.

"Want me to try?"

What the hell? Why not? He had a magic touch. "Sure."

He turned the key. Nadda, zip. Same noise, no result. His touch wasn't magic after all. At least not on cars.

Goddammit. This was not fair. She wanted to scream. Instead she kicked the tire and growled. Then she calmed. Okay. What next? "Do you have any jumper cables?"

"No, sorry. But it doesn't sound like your battery."

She breathed deeply. She had a road service card. Her mom had insisted since the car was old and she was out late. "Can you hand me my purse?"

Walker climbed out, bringing her purse with him. Cleo dug in it for her wallet and cell phone, pulled out her roadside assistance card, then tipped it to the light to read the number.

Walker covered the card with his hand. "It'll take them forever to get here." He was not going to let her hang around all night waiting for some tow truck guy. "I'll drive you home and come back for your car tomorrow."

She looked at him as if he'd fallen out of a spaceship and landed right in front of her. "I have to work tomorrow."

"I'll take you."

"You can't do that."

"Why not?" He did that kind of shit for friends when they were in a bind.

"Because." She opened her mouth, closed it on whatever else she was going to say. "I need to take care of this tonight."

He was pretty damn sure there was nothing a road service guy could do tonight. He'd worked cars with his dad when he was a kid, and that sound was not the battery; it was the solenoid, and she was gonna be shit out of luck getting anything more than a tow tonight.

She was a stubborn little thing.

"Call them. I'll wait with you. If he can't do anything, I'll take you home."

Dialing the number, she shook her head. "You don't need to do that. I can wait in the restaurant and the tow truck driver can take me home if he can't start it."

He did *not* leave a woman alone late at night. "It's not a bother. I'll wait."

"Honestly, Walker, I'm fine." She held up a finger before he could reply and gave her info over the phone, nodded her head, and finally hung up. "The girl said about half an hour."

Translation: an hour and a half. "We can wait in my car with the heater on." He'd noticed her shiver.

"Don't worry. I'll wait inside."

He sighed. "I'll still wait and drive you home."

She pursed her lips. "Hopefully the car will work, but if not, the tow truck driver can take me."

He breathed deep, his nostrils flaring. "Fine. I get it. You don't want me to know where you live."

She didn't say a word.

Suddenly, despite his usual equanimity, her attitude pissed him off royally. "You feel more comfortable with a stranger you've never met who just happens to work for a towing service." He leaned in close. "Are you fucking crazy? A beautiful woman alone in the middle of the night, any goddamn thing could happen." His stomach churned with some really bad images.

He turned, paced a couple of steps, rubbed his hand over the top of his head. She didn't trust him; he got that. Fine. But that she'd trust some *stranger* over him? Goddammit.

When he came back to her, she'd covered her mouth with her hand and stared at him. Then finally she lowered it. "My daughter hates me right now. I'm not sure why. Bringing a man home"— she shrugged—"I don't want her to think she's not my priority." She covered her mouth again, and he thought he detected a giggle. "Not to mention that my mother was waiting up for me on Friday night and the ceiling caved in because the toilet upstairs was leaking and plaster was all over the place and now there's just bare pipes and . . ." She leaned over, hands on her knees, and yeah, she was laughing. "Now this, the car. I mean really, you've gotta admit, it's pretty funny."

He went down on his haunches in front of her. "Cleo."

She tipped her head to him. There were tears in her eyes, whether laughing or real, he wasn't sure. "I'm sorry," she whispered, "for maligning your character."

"Apology accepted."

"I would also appreciate having you take me home."

He wanted to touch her so badly, his fingers ached. He'd asked her out; she'd turned him down. He didn't give up easily, but he also didn't believe in harassing a woman to death. No meant no. If her car hadn't broken down, he'd have let it end there.

But just maybe, Cleo needed him more than she thought.

* * *

CLEO HAD CALLED MA, LET HER KNOW SHE'D BE LATE. WALKER AND the service guy—who had looked like Tim Allen from *Galaxy Quest*, more dorky and harmless than maniacal and dangerous— had stood over the open hood of her car and talked manly mechanic stuff, tried to jump-start the car just in case, though they both agreed that probably wouldn't work, then proclaimed the issue to most likely be the solenoid. Whatever the hell that was. They were extremely proud of themselves. She was allowed one free tow with her card and gave him Jimmy's shop address.

Then Walker had bundled her into his luxury car and turned on the seat warmers.

"God, that's amazing." Close to nirvana. Walker provided all, even something to warm her frozen butt.

She'd gone overboard with the protectionist attitude even to the exclusion of common sense. Walker had been nothing but good to her, yet she'd been ready to hitch a ride with a stranger just so Walker wouldn't know where she lived. She admitted it was stupid.

Yet in the close confines of his car, he smelled a little too good. He was a little too big. His body heat played havoc with her pulse.

She turned in her seat. "Thanks."

He smiled. Even his quirky smile made her heart beat faster. "Better than the tow truck?" he asked.

"Bet it doesn't have seat warmers." Should she apologize again for being a jerk?

He didn't touch her, yet her skin was sensitized to him. She could feel every breath, into her lungs, out again. Her fingers tingled. "My hands are still cold, though." Leaning over the console, she put the backs of her fingers to his cheek, more because she needed an excuse to touch him than anything else. Yeah, bad idea, but she'd always been full of bad ideas. Why grow up now?

He laid his fingers over the tops of hers. "Mine are a lot warmer."

His skin was smooth from a fresh shave, his scent something light and woodsy.

"Let me warm them up for you." He pulled her hand down between his legs, clasping his thighs around her fingers.

It was warm. It was sexy. She swayed with the car as he took another corner on the winding mountain road. "I suppose I could sit on my hands and warm them both at the same time."

He grinned, glancing briefly in the rearview mirror. "Yeah, you could." He slid her hand higher until her pinkie brushed the crotch of his jeans. "But this is way more fun."

God, yes. One more time. She'd already told her mom she was going to be late. Just this once, when she already had the built-in excuse. One could even consider it payment for driving her home. Ah hell, they were excuses and justifications. She wanted him tonight, and she intended to have him.

Turning her hand, she cupped his balls, squeezed lightly. "I know something even more fun."

7

"WOMAN, YOU'LL MAKE US HAVE AN ACCIDENT." YET HE PRESSED her hand close, his cock hard.

"Hands on the wheel," she murmured. "I'll do the rest." She rubbed him reverently.

Negotiating the road carefully, he let her bring him alive with a burning need. "Do you want to jerk me off, make me come?"

She popped the button fly of his jeans. "I haven't decided yet." She looked up to meet his gaze and, despite the darkness of the road, her eyes danced. No shadows.

"You're a tease."

"Does this feel like a tease?" She ran a finger down his bare cock. He hadn't worn briefs.

He shivered from the tip of his cock to his toes. "Yes, that's a tease. It'll be better if you take it out. Hold it."

"Suck it?"

"Everything." It was almost begging.

"We'll see." She laughed at him, but she pulled his cock from his jeans, wrapped her hand around him, all heat and soft skin. "There, now, is that better?"

"Yes," he whispered. But not enough. Nowhere near enough.

She stroked. His balls contracted, filled, ached. A drop of come seeped from his slit.

"Oh baby, look at that." She smiled up at him, hypnotizing him until he forced his gaze back to the road.

She grazed his skin, slid over his crown, then put her moist fingertip to her lips and licked off the drop of pre-come. "Mmm."

"Woman, you make me crazy. I know a place."

"What place?" she whispered.

A place where he could lay her down, taste her, ease inside her. He'd taken other women there. He heard Isabel's warning, but he ignored it. "A glade off the road."

She slid her hand lightly up and down. "Oh, I like that. I can have my wicked way with this big, beautiful cock." She squeezed him hard, and he felt like his head might explode with need.

The turnoff wasn't far, barely more than a dirt track. He'd done a lot of scouting to find it. Women loved a little earthy nookie. He didn't like the fact that she wasn't the first, or even the tenth. But this was the closest place.

He bumped onto the little lane, holding the wheel hard as she wrapped her hand tighter around his cock. "We'll see who's going to have whose wicked way."

"Ooh, promises, promises," she cooed.

He liked the playfulness. He wanted more of it. The car rolled to a stop, the headlights cutting through the night to reveal a small grassy glade surrounded by scrub and trees. He shut off the engine, the lights, plunged them into darkness, nothing more than a sliver of moonlight illuminating her face.

"I haven't kissed you," he said.

She bent to his cock and kissed the crown, sending a jolt of fire through him. "Now *I've* kissed *you*." She licked her lips. "You're delicious."

"I like when you make up your mind that you're going to do something. And you do it with gusto." He laid his hand along the back of her neck. "Kiss me the same way."

His heart throbbed in his ears, he wanted it so bad.

Trailing her thumb over his bottom lip, she leaned in, tracing the path with her tongue. She teased, he loved it, but he was done playing and trapped her face between his hands. "Fucking kiss me."

She threw herself into it, winding her arms around his neck, invading his mouth with her tongue, taking him. It was the sweetest incursion he'd ever experienced.

"For tonight," she whispered, peppering his mouth with brief kisses, "you are mine." She caressed his scalp, licked his lips, rubbed her nose to his. "I'm going to do the naughtiest things to you."

"Woman, you talk too much." This time he took her mouth.

She laughed, the joyous sound rippling through him. Christ, this was how he always wanted her to be. He buried himself against her, kissing deep, savoring the lush sweetness of her mouth, the crush of her breasts against his chest.

Then she cheated and went for his cock.

"Wench." She stole his breath.

"Your cock is mine," she murmured, "and I want it." She licked his mouth. "To taste it." She punctuated with a slow pump of his erection designed to drive a man mad. "Suck it." She forced her tongue between his lips. "Swallow it."

"You really do talk too much." He crushed her mouth beneath his in a long, deep kiss that left him wanting more. "I've got blankets in the trunk."

"You're such a Boy Scout, always prepared."

"I'm always ready for the spur of the moment." A momentary blip of conscience pricked him, but the blankets were from Friday night, the night he'd had with her, which made it a guilt-free zone.

Though why he needed to think of it in terms of guilt, he

couldn't say, other than Isabel's dire warning. That was his life yesterday. Today, he was on hiatus.

"We don't need to go outside," she cajoled. "We can do it right here." She slipped her hand deeper, stroking his balls inside his jeans.

He let his guilt fly out the window as a flush stole across his skin. Right now, he was giving in to pressure. By the morning light, she could very well change her mind and he'd never have another chance. Tonight, he would have everything.

"Yeah, we can do *me* easily enough in here, but I don't want to fumble around with your pants." He caressed her mouth with a quick kiss. "I want skin to skin, all over."

"Brrrr," she whispered, shooting him to madness with her touch.

Sure, it was cold, but he had lots of ideas on how to keep her warm once he got her naked. With every touch, she gave him more ideas.

"Come on." He pried her hand loose as she laughed, fastened a couple of buttons on his fly, then yanked the door open. She tumbled out beside him.

Grabbing the blankets from the trunk, he edged her toward the dew-covered grass in the clearing. They spread the quilt together, flapping open the two blankets and letting them fall where they might.

She went to her knees in the center and curled her index finger at him. "Come here."

He stood in front of her. She tugged on the button fly, popping it open. Then he was in her hands, and he let his head fall back to savor her touch and her warm breath across his bare flesh.

"You have the most beautiful cock, Walker."

Walker laughed. "It's dark—you can't see."

"Yes, I can," Cleo whispered, brushing a finger over his crown. His cock jerked. "You're thick and hard and meaty." She drew a deep breath, hummed her pleasure. "And you smell good, like soap laced with salty come."

"Kiss me." Walker's voice was nothing more than a rasp of sound across the night.

CLEO'S HEART BEAT TIME WITH THE PULSE OF A THICK VEIN RUNning the length of his cock. She didn't know what kind of kiss he wanted and didn't care. There was only what *she* wanted. Dipping her head, she kissed his tip, tasting a drop of pre-come on her lips. She grazed him with her teeth, caressed with her tongue, then she needed it all. She plunged to his root. He touched the back of her throat before she got there. Thick and long. Walker groaned, played with her hair.

The cool night air didn't bother her. Heat rose off him in waves. Only her fingers were cold, and she shoved them up under his sweater to the warmth of his skin.

He shivered. "Christ."

She glided all the way back up to his crown, as his fingers raked through her hair. Then she clung to his waist and sucked him hard and fast.

"God, you're so sweet. Fuck. Baby." Words fell from his lips, praise, worship, endearments. "Jesus, I've dreamed about this. Hell. Every damn fucking night. Nobody, baby, never, not like this."

She loved his scent of piney soap, his salty taste, the musk of his skin, and the sounds he made, even the light pleasure-pain of his fingers in her hair.

She loved sex and banter and teasing and foreplay. All men loved a blow job, but Walker turned it into more. He made her the only woman in the world who could give him this feeling.

It was heady. Powerful.

His legs began to shake; his body shuddered. He held her tight against him, deep in her mouth. "Fuck, baby," he murmured into the dark, then long moments later, he pushed her gently, falling to his knees beside her. His breath was harsh, his eyes deep and dark.

"Didn't want to come, not yet, too good." Short, clipped words as if he couldn't manage complete sentences. "Couldn't stop it, though." He collapsed against the quilt, pulling her with him. "Next time I come, I'll be inside you."

She tipped back to look at him. "No way. I didn't even taste your come."

He grinned, a Cheshire Cat smile, all teeth in a dark face. "I can come without ejaculating."

"That's not possible." Yet she'd felt the quaking of his body, the throb of his cock. He'd had *something*, that was for sure.

"Takes practice," he said smugly. Then the Cheshire Cat disappeared. "It's different, but it feels fucking good." He rolled, pinning her beneath him. "You took the edge off"—his cold hands wormed up beneath her shirt, making her shiver and gasp—"now I can spend hours pleasuring you." He put his lips to hers. "Tasting you, licking you, sucking you, fucking you."

The man was so deliciously intense about sex, yet so easygoing about everything else. Except when he'd gotten upset about the tow truck. She couldn't blame him, though. She'd never met anyone like him. He could eclipse her troubles, her responsibilities, make her think of only the moment, only the physical, only the pleasure.

"Tell me what you want first." He seduced her with her own fantasies.

"Get me naked and kiss every inch of my back. It's very sensitive." She could damn near come that way.

He made quick, expert work of her shirt, bra, pants, and thong. Practice makes perfect. She wouldn't think about all the women he'd brought to the restaurant or what he did with them afterward, or how *much* practice he'd had. It wasn't her business anyway.

"Stomach," he ordered, and when she complied, he pulled the blankets over them, covered her with his body, then his lips.

"Oh." She moaned as he licked. "Ah," she murmured as he nipped. "Holy Moly." He stroked, sucked her skin into his mouth, probably giving her hickeys, and she groaned. God, yes, she could come like this. He made her wet and ready. "That is so perfect. I'm almost glad you've had a lot of practice."

He pinched her ass, and she squealed, laughing, then flipped to her back. "You have too many clothes on."

"I'm not done kissing your back yet."

"Strip, Walker. Now. You don't want to make me unhappy."

He shook his head, wriggling and rustling beneath the blankets. The top of her head was cold, but beneath the soft wool, she was burning up.

"I love this," she whispered. She loved how special he made her feel. Her life moved so fast, rushing from home to school to work to home to the restaurant and finally back home, where the most she could manage was brushing her teeth and hanging her clothes up. At least most of the time. He made the world stop spinning.

His head poked up above the blanket. "I love it more."

She hadn't meant for him to hear, but the man was a tease, and he didn't miss a thing.

"I'm naked"—he rubbed all that hard muscle and skin against her—"so now what do you want?" He waggled his eyebrows.

"You should make me come."

He stroked down her abdomen, to her navel, then between her legs. "Christ, you're wet." He blazed a trail all the way back up, circling her nipple with her own moisture, then pinching hard.

"Oh my God." Her body arched, almost rising right off the quilt. The man was capable of simple yet amazing things.

"Don't come yet," he told her.

"Not yet," she promised before he sent her blood humming through her veins and set her skin buzzing.

Disappearing beneath the blanket, he kissed and licked his way from her breasts to her belly to her sex. She spread her legs with a sigh of pleasure and a moan of anticipation.

"God, you're pretty." He was barely discernible under all that wool.

She laughed. "You can't even see."

"I see, woman, I see, and you're gorgeous." He plied her with a finger, teasing her clit, sliding knuckle-deep inside her, then out, circling, stroking, charging all her little electrons.

"Lick me," she begged.

He would not be rushed, blowing on her clit, a warm caress, stroking her thighs, then finally, finally licking the lips of her pussy, so close, closer, until he sucked her clit between his lips and teased with his tongue.

"Oh God." Surely this was heaven.

His chuckle vibrated against her, through her. She ran her hands over his bald crown. Nothing had ever felt so delicious or erotic as all that bare skin beneath her fingertips.

She was cold and hot. She was right there in the moment yet soaring in the sky above. The chirp of crickets surrounded them, everywhere, and an owl hooted, his mate answering in the distance. The stars sparkled through the trees, one shooting across the sky. She didn't wish on it. For this moment, she had everything she could ask for.

Then he made her scream.

8

CHRIST, IT WAS THE SWEETEST SOUND. HER CRY, HER PLEASURE.

Walker crawled up her body, planting himself on top of her. She still trembled, breathing hard.

He nuzzled her ear. "Was it good?"

She harrumphed. "You know it was."

Her taste had flooded his mouth, her cries filling the night, her thighs tight around him. He enjoyed making a woman give in to her pleasure.

But he'd lost himself in making Cleo come. The act was unique— he couldn't say why, or rather it was a myriad of reasons. Because she wasn't paying him to give her power. Because he gave himself with full expectation of getting something in return, and he needed that something badly. Because he would have her even if she said no. Because he knew she couldn't say no.

Braced on his elbows above her, he held her face between his hands. "I'm going to fuck you, Cleo."

"Yes." She didn't even open her eyes.

"Look at me."

Starlight sparkled in her pupils. "Yes, please, Walker, I want it." Then she pulled his head down, taking his lips, whispering, "Thank you," as she kissed him.

He'd laid out a condom strategically, and he slipped down to lay by her side as he rolled it on. She nuzzled and kissed him, her hair brushing his face.

Touching her breast, her nipple, he leaned in. "You wanna ride?"

She shook her head, wafting her sweet scent all over him. "I'm a missionary girl. Hold my buns in your hands and drive deep."

"I like a woman who knows exactly what she wants."

Blanketing her body with his, he pulled the covers tight around their shoulders to keep her warm. She opened her legs, and he filled the vee, his cock brushing her. She cupped his head in both hands, stroked her fingers across his bare scalp. "I need you inside me. Hard, fast, and deep."

He plunged, and she cried out. "Oh God, that's good." She breathed deep, settled, laid her head back, and sighed deliciously. "It's been soooo long since I've had a man on top of me."

She'd had a child, yet her body welcomed him, tightened around him, milked him as she squirmed.

"How long?" He nuzzled her hair, taking her with just a flex of his ass.

"Months. Last year sometime." She opened her eyes wide. "Oh my God, more than a year. Heidi was in middle school."

A freaking year. She was too hot and gorgeous to go without sex for a year. "I've got a lot to make up for, then."

"You're going to spoil me."

"Never." But he would if she let him. Grabbing her butt, he hauled her higher, the way she'd told him to. "I'm going to fuck you so good, baby."

He stroked deep and slow, riding her G-spot. She moaned for him, and he knew he'd hit it just right.

"Oh, Walker, yeah, that's perfect."

The slow and steady slide did it. Her body trembled beneath his. She moaned, then, losing her voice, she simply clung to him.

Her body clenched and rippled around him as she came, shooting him closer to the edge.

"Don't stop, don't stop," she chanted. She'd come down off the high, but needed more.

So did Walker.

With the night sounds all around them, the caress of cold air, her body's heat and softness, her sweet scent, he steeped himself in her essence. When he felt her rise once more, he pumped faster, harder, and this time her climax wrenched the orgasm from him. He added his shout to the night.

HIS BODY WAS SO WARM, HIS COCK PULSING INSIDE HER. CLEO didn't want to move. She didn't want him to leave. She loved the weight of his body on her.

She hadn't had this since Phil dumped her, the long moments after sex where you felt like you were one with him. In the four years since, she'd chosen purely for the physical. Good sex. Nothing emotional. No attachment. God, she'd missed this. You don't realize until suddenly it whomps you upside the head; *this* was what made good sex great. His warmth, that uniquely woodsy scent of his. More than just an aftershave, it was innate. The taste of his pre-come still lingered, accompanied by the utterly sublime sense of being filled.

She'd never spent a full night with a man, always dragging herself home. She didn't want Heidi missing her or waking up to find a man in the house. Cleo had been fine with that.

Walker, she wanted to wake up beside him. Just once. Make love to him again.

He shifted on top of her, easing his weight but not letting her go altogether. Layering tiny kisses along her jawline, he settled again as if he planned to fall asleep where they were.

Who could say why? What specifically did he do for her?

Some men were just ho-hum, part of the landscape. Sometimes you looked at a man, and your heart pitter-pattered and some reptilian part of your brain just went gaga, repeating *I want* over and over again. That was Walker. He'd teased and flirted for three years. If he'd asked her out, she'd have been a goner. But things went south with Heidi and her libido had gone with it.

Until Walker turned everything back on again.

He was dangerous. She didn't know how she'd be able to turn it all off in the morning.

God help her, she didn't want to. If you didn't have it, you didn't miss it. But once you had it, man, you were hooked.

SHE LIVED IN A TIDY LITTLE NEIGHBORHOOD. YEARS AGO, THESE houses were modest, middle-class, single-family homes. Now they were worth upward of a million. Or more. Walker knew her mom didn't want to sell. Cleo drove what was basically a clunker from the late eighties, and she worked two jobs to make ends meet. Everything could be solved if they sold and moved to Fremont across the bay.

He stopped in front of the two-story, and shut off the engine. He'd felt her withdrawal with every scrap of clothing she'd put on. They'd been close, connected. Until he pulled out.

Everything good had to end.

"Does your mom have a car you can borrow to get to work in the morning?"

She rubbed her forehead with the flat of her hand. "I'll take the bus. It stops out on the El Camino. One of the other mothers is carpooling the girls to school this week."

"I'll pick you up."

She snorted and gave him a didn't-we-already-go-over-this look. "Don't be silly."

"I can help, Cleo. I'd like to." He touched her cheek. "I want to. No obligation."

There wasn't enough light in the car to read her expression. "Don't you ever work?"

"Flexible hours." He grinned.

She didn't ask what he did, and he dodged the bullet yet again. Holding her gaze, he willed her to accept his offer. He could do this. It was so easy for him. Such a small act in the scheme of things. Small steps led to bigger steps. He'd be good for her. He knew he would. She'd be good for him, too.

"I hate the bus," she said, and he knew he'd won.

He shouldn't feel such a surge of triumph, yet it swamped him. "What time shall I pick you up?"

"Ten to eight would be good." She put a hand on the door as if she was suddenly nervous of how much she'd given away.

"Kiss me good night, Cleo."

She shuddered.

He couldn't let her out of the car without a kiss or an intimate touch. He couldn't let the distance grow, or by the morning it would be a chasm he couldn't cross.

"Just one," she whispered.

One was all he needed. For now. Her lips were still plump and well kissed. As he drew her close, the sweet scent of sex rose off her. He opened his mouth, drew her in. Her sigh rippled through him. He could have her again, here and now.

It struck him how sweetly odd that was for him. He loved pleasuring women, showing them their potential, helping them appreciate their beauty and unique qualities. Which was why he staved off ejaculation until he sensed a woman had surpassed herself, her threshold reached, and gone a tiny bit beyond. Then he released.

With Cleo, he was a double dipper.

"Sleep well," he whispered against her lips, and she climbed from the car as if sleepwalking. He would have walked her to the door, but that felt like pushing his advantage.

Especially since she'd agreed to let him drive her to work. There were so many things he wanted to do for Cleo.

After tonight, she was on the verge of letting him.

WALKER HAD ARRIVED EARLY TO PICK HER UP. THANK GOD HEIDI had already left. Cleo hadn't wanted to explain. So he'd sat in the kitchen drinking coffee and charming her mother while Cleo raced around with those last-minute things. She couldn't hear every word, but her mother did a lot of cackling punctuated by the low rumble of Walker's laughter.

Oh yeah, Ma had definitely been charmed. Walker could beguile a lady of any age right out of her panties. Having been charmed out of hers, Cleo knew all about that, not to mention the quantity and variety of women he'd entertained at the restaurant.

She wouldn't think about that now since she'd been feeling pretty darn chipper all day despite the car and the ceiling. A couple of minutes before five, she switched the messaging system to auto, turned off her computer, straightened the magazines in the lobby, and waved good night as several of the office workers trundled out.

Walker had said he'd pick her up at five. The thought gave her heart a kick. She'd always done everything, shuttling here, there, and everywhere, rushing, rushing, rushing. She did the carpool thing in the morning when it was her turn, but Heidi took the school bus home in the afternoon. If there was a doctor's appointment, she had to take time off work. Ma had given up her license a couple of years ago after a couple of incidents.

So it was nice to have someone do this for her. Just this once.

She hadn't thought about how she'd pay for the car. She'd worry about it when she knew what was wrong. She'd called Jimmy early. He said he'd try his best to at least take a look today. She'd gone to high school with him, and he knew the car inside and out. She'd call him again when she got home to see what he'd found. Until then, she wasn't going to worry.

Walker's blue luxury sedan rolled into the lot. Her heart gave a happy little jolt. It was scary, but oh so sweet. She'd have ten minutes to enjoy it. Dammit, she would take those ten minutes before she went home, faced Heidi, another fight, maybe, maybe not, then rushed off to the restaurant with a stone in her stomach.

She gathered her coat and purse as Walker pulled to the front. She'd pushed open the lobby door, an idiotic smile on her face. Then she realized he wasn't alone in the car.

Oh shit.

Heidi sat beside him in the passenger seat.

9

CLEO OPENED THE FRONT PASSENGER DOOR. HER HEART BEAT HARD against her ribs. What had they been talking about? What had Walker said to her daughter? A whisper of fear spread through her womb. She didn't need any more problems with Heidi, especially not over a man.

"Hope you don't mind," Walker said, leaning down a little to talk to her through the open car door. "Your mother got busy with dinner and sent Heidi and me to pick you up."

Cleo didn't know what to say. All she could do was nod.

Walker waved a hand. "Hop out and let your mom have the front seat, Heidi."

"Sure, Walker." And Heidi did.

It was amazing. She even smiled at Cleo, though she didn't say hello or kiss her cheek the way she used to. Too old for that. Too angry.

But Walker had . . . done something, created magic. Sure, he put women at ease, made them feel special, appreciated. But charm a teenager, least of all Heidi?

Guess the problem really was big, bad *MOM*, with capital letters.

Walker smiled at Cleo as she climbed in and buckled up. "Have a good day?"

She half expected him to kiss her hello, but he kept his lips to himself. "It was good, thank you."

"Walker helped me with my algebra for a couple of hours after school." Heidi leaned between the two front seats.

Cleo opened her mouth, but Walker beat her to it. "Belt in, hon, would ya?" He winked in the rearview mirror. "Safety first."

"Sure, Walker."

Cleo slapped her mouth shut before her jaw dropped. Okay. This was most definitely not normal. It was downright frightening. Had her daughter turned into a zombie, a pod person? Walker waited until Heidi was secured before he eased around the parking lot and out onto the road.

"Thanks for helping on the homework," Cleo said, trying to regain her equilibrium. What else was there to say, especially since Cleo hated algebra. "I suck at math." Walker had saved her from being inadequate again. In school, she'd loved anthropology. If she'd finished college, she would have been a forensic anthropologist.

"My pleasure." He smiled, glancing in the mirror again, then his gaze slid back to Cleo. "I was just taking a look at the toilet and the ceiling and pondering what needed to be done when Heidi got home from school."

Another jaw-dropping moment. "You were looking at the toilet?"

"While I was waiting for you this morning, Ma told me about the ceiling falling in. So I went back to look over things after lunch. Hope that was okay."

He was calling her *Ma* now? "Um, yeah." But was it?

"Walker says fixing it will be easy-peasy," Heidi piped up from the backseat.

He thrust a thumb over his shoulder. "Well, not easy. I'll need some help, but I've got a contractor friend." He shrugged.

"Gran invited Walker for dinner since he's going to be working for us."

Cleo turned in her seat and stared at Heidi. Walker this, Walker that, and Walker was now *working* for them?

"I told Ma we needed to check about dinner with you first." Walker took a turn, his line of sight following her for a moment.

"Well, sure. Of course." She wouldn't undo Ma's invitation, but she wasn't sure how she felt about all of this, either. He was bulldozing his way into her life. Heidi was being human, but only because of Walker. Somehow it didn't seem fair.

How did Walker reach her daughter when Cleo herself was such a miserable failure?

"I called your mechanic to find out about the car," he said when they'd stopped at a light.

"Oh?" She recognized the edge in her voice. So Jimmy had talked to Walker but hadn't called *her* back?

"It was the solenoid. He didn't have one in stock, so he ordered one, but it'll be a couple of weeks. I've been searching the Internet to see if we can get one here sooner."

We? She glanced back at Heidi, who watched the exchange with rapt attention.

Traffic flowed. She didn't want to sound ungrateful or bitchy. Yet she was taken aback. It was too fast, too *much*. But with Heidi in the car, she really had to think hard before she said anything. "Uh, thanks for doing all that checking." Then she winced, remembering the paramount issue. "Did he happen to say how much he thought the whole job would cost?"

"Well, you practically have to take the engine out to get to the solenoid." He glanced at her as he took the turn onto her street. "Five hundred. And another hundred for the part. But I think I can get it down to more like fifty if I find it on the Internet."

Her stomach sank. "I . . . Well . . . thank you for looking for the part."

Okay, step back a minute. Don't panic. She had the fifty bucks to pay Walker for the part, and Jimmy would let her pay on installment. Things could be a lot worse. But how was she supposed to get up to the restaurant if it took two weeks to get the part? She'd have to rent a car. Another expense.

Walker pulled up in front of the house. "Not a problem."

He was invading her life, taking over. She wanted to resent it. She could take care of herself and Heidi and her mom. She might be having a few money problems, but she wasn't a complete failure.

Yet she felt herself blowing in the wind because it felt so damn good to have a little help. Jimmy, while he'd been great to her, didn't have time to search out a cheaper price. If Walker and his contractor friend could fix the ceiling? She didn't want to even think about how much it would cost to find her own contractor, and in the end, how would she know she wasn't being ripped off?

Oh man, she could get used to this. Scary thought. The men she picked had a tendency to walk out just when she started depending on them.

IT WAS EVEN SCARIER HOW WALKER STEPPED RIGHT INTO HER little family as if he belonged. He'd driven Cleo back and forth to work like a regular soccer mom. Ma invited him for dinner four nights in a row, and tonight, Friday, she'd cooked a feast.

Ma had seated him at the head of the table as if he were the man of the house. "Ma, this is the best roast beef and Yorkshire pudding I've ever had," Walker enthused.

It wasn't. Ma had used a lower grade of meat because they couldn't afford the good stuff. The homemade gravy and Yorkshire pudding, however, went a long way to improving it. Ma glowed beneath the praise. Walker drove a nice car, dressed well, had good manners, teased her, complimented her cooking, and that was enough for Ma to grant acceptance.

"Gran makes the best Yorkshire pudding." Heidi beamed, getting her two cents in as if afraid she'd been forgotten.

Her mother and daughter had been taken over by aliens. That had to be the explanation. Or Walker was a magician with hypnotic powers. Moms, daughters, and animals adored him. In less than a full workweek, Walker had captivated her family, tracked down her solenoid, made measurements, written lists, and gotten deals on the materials for the bathroom repair which he and his friend Barry would start tomorrow morning. Walker also made delicious sex with her every night in out-of-the-way nooks on the way home from the restaurant.

She wanted to resent how easily Ma and Heidi accepted him, how inadequate she felt because it seemed as if she were a total screwup, yet Cleo experienced the same mesmerizing tug herself. Between the hot sex, the sense of being important, cared for, and special, she was hook, line, and sinker for the guy. It was all too good to be true, but oh man, she wanted more of him.

He winked at her across the dinner table. "Pass the salt, please, honey?"

Honey? "Sure, *sweetheart*." She gave him both the salt *and* the pepper. Too good to be true? She didn't even know if he was for real.

Cleo was waiting for it all to bite her in the ass. She knew it was coming, because her life was not this easy and simple.

The worst thing, though: when Walker left, what would that do to Heidi?

* * *

WALKER WAS PUSHING TOO HARD, TOO FAST, AND HE KNEW IT. CLEO had been pensive all the way to the restaurant. He'd half expected her to say she'd find another way home, but she'd pecked his cheek and climbed from the car almost in a daze, nodding her head when he said he'd be back for her at ten.

He was a sucker for a damsel in distress, and though Cleo would rather die than admit it, she was in distress. Walker had a habit of assessing a situation, determining what was needed, and moving forward to solve the problem. Things were black and white: Her car needed fixing; he made sure it was repaired ASAP. Ma groused about the ceiling; he offered a solution, especially since Barry owed him a favor. Walker had warned him to liquidate his stock portfolio before the market meltdown. The bathroom job would cost barely more than the materials. As for Heidi, well, she was as pretty and fragile as a porcelain doll and starved for a father figure.

He felt at home in the worn-out kitchen, as if he were part of the small family. Walker had never belonged to anyone or anything, but he'd found he liked the feeling.

He was overstepping bounds with Cleo big-time. If he wasn't careful, it would blow up in his face as Isabel had warned. Yet, like a smitten puppy with his tongue hanging out and his tail wagging, he hit the restaurant at exactly five to ten.

Igor the maitre d' wagged a finger toward the back. "She's in the locker room, down the hall, door on the right. I'm pretty sure she's alone in there, but knock."

A locker room for employees. He'd known Bella's was posh, but wow. He tapped on the door. A moment later, Cleo stuck her head out. "Oh, it's you. Come on in. I'm the only female working tonight. Almost ready."

The place was compact, two rows of lockers one above the

other, a wooden bench, a makeup mirror and vanity with sink, a door beside it that was probably the lavatory. Sweet setup.

Her purse open on the bench and a small cosmetics bag on the vanity, Cleo repaired her lipstick in the mirror. She rolled her lips to smooth it in place, then puckered. After applying a slash of blush to her cheeks, she pulled her hair loose of its bun and fluffed it.

He felt the irresistible urge to bite the tender skin of her neck just above her collar. To mark her. The slow, steady pump of his heart beat against his chest wall. His blood shushed through his veins. His cock stirred to life. He wanted her now, couldn't wait for one of their little secluded spots on the way home. His body clamored for her.

WALKER WATCHED HER IN THE MIRROR, EVERY MOVE SHE MADE.

Cleo's skin heated.

She'd gone over and over it in her mind. Between orders, on her break, as she waited at the bar for a tray of drinks.

Could it be so bad to let him help her? Heidi seemed better. After what happened with Phil, Cleo had been terrified of Heidi's resentment, but maybe she'd worried for nothing. After all, her daughter couldn't get *that* attached in just a matter of weeks. Maybe Cleo was due for some good luck, even if it only got her past fixing the car and the bathroom. She was so used to worrying about the future that she forgot about being grateful for today. It was so good to see Heidi smiling instead of grousing. All because of Walker.

"I'm not sure how I'll pay you back for all your help."

He was on her in a moment, his muscled body molded to her backside, his face next to hers in the mirror. The move was so fast it made her breathless. That was Walker, driving her a hundred miles an hour, the scenery flashing by so quickly she couldn't stop to think, only react. She was reacting, all right, her skin on fire, her nipples taut, her pussy wet for him.

"Pay me in sexual favors." His voice was husky, deeper than normal. His heart beat against her shoulder blade, cock throbbing along her spine.

"Sexual favors, yeah," she whispered. Later, when he'd slowed down enough for her to think, she might regret it, but now it seemed like a hell of an idea.

He slid his arms around her waist, bending to her neck, nipping her throat. "You're salty," he murmured against her skin. "I like it." He licked her clean in that one spot.

She felt it all the way to her toes as if it were an erogenous zone.

"So. You're the only woman working tonight?" He raised his eyes to catch hers in the mirror.

"Yeah."

He popped two buttons on her blouse, opening her cleavage, and delved inside. Her nipples were already beaded, and Walker pinched. "Anyone going to check on you in here?"

Her knees weakened. She shook her head, her hair brushing his cheek.

He went for the button on her slacks, tugged the zipper down, all done slowly, gently. She could think now if she wanted to, stop him. Cleo didn't. The risk was low, but she wouldn't have cared if it were greater.

"Do me, Walker," she whispered as if it were more than a mere sex act. "Do me really good."

"Oh baby, you need to ask for more than that." He slipped into her panties, nudging her legs apart from behind with his knee and sliding into her cleft.

Her body sizzled at the touch.

"You're wet. You been thinking about this all night?"

She nodded.

"Say it," he seduced, his gaze on her in the mirror as he circled her clit.

"Yes, Walker, I thought about this all night." Between all the doubts and fears, shoulds and shouldn'ts, there'd been this, his touch, his kiss, his cock. She was a slut; this would always be what she came back for.

10

"I LOVE SEX," CLEO WHISPERED FOR HIM, AND HIS BLOOD RUSHED past his eardrums.

Her body was slick, sweetly fragrant, hot to the touch. Walker would make her come first before he gave in to his own need. He burrowed deep, filling her with two fingers, then pulling out to circle her clit. Her ass twitched and shimmied against him, caressing his cock. Eyes closed, she bit her lip, moaned, and he loved watching her pleasure in the mirror. He enjoyed taking a woman this way, but taking Cleo was unique for the emotions that simmered in him.

Her skin flushed pink against her white work blouse; her nipples pearled beneath the material. She parted her lips to draw in air as if she couldn't get enough and rocked against his fingers, creating her own rhythm and taking him with it.

"Oh man." Planting her hands flat on the vanity, she pumped her hips as if his cock was buried deep inside her, then her body stiffened, her face tensed. She scrunched her eyebrows together and squeezed her lids tight as she trembled and quaked, but didn't cry out. The sight was magnificent, the play of ecstasy across her features shooting a thrill through him.

Yet it seemed that one small part of her mind knew where she was and held back.

She allowed herself only one brief gasp. "Oh God, Walker."

He didn't let her come down off the high, pushing her slacks and panties over her hips. He shucked his jeans to his thighs, sheathed his cock with a condom, and leaned over her. Pressing her breasts to the counter, he drove deep, forcing a moan from her.

Holy hell. Nothing had ever felt quite this extraordinary nor touched him in quite this way. As if his cock had become a part of her.

"Please," she said on a sigh, opening her eyes to impale him in the blue ocean depths. "I need it, Walker."

He tangled his fingers with hers. Leaning his elbows on the vanity, his forearms snug against hers, Walker fucked her hard, his body pounding hard into hers, her pussy squeezing him rhythmically. The position had never been more perfect, allowing him the sight of her face, highlighting her concentration as he transported her out of herself, her scent rising to intoxicate him, her neck bared for his predatorial bite, a claiming. As he sucked her flesh into his mouth, she moaned, pushed back, cried out the way she wouldn't let herself before.

As her pussy contracted around him, Walker poured all he had, all he was, deep inside her, losing sense of everything around him except the slickness of her flesh, her scent, her taste.

He came back to himself to find her brilliant blue eyes on him in the mirror. Sharp, they saw everything.

"That was good," she whispered, as if the noises they'd made had drawn someone to the door.

It was better than fucking good. He wanted to stay like this, but he knew it couldn't last. With his arms around her, he rose, pulling her with him. His cock barely managed to stay inside her, yet he wasn't ready to let go.

"That was one sexual favor," he said to her reflection. "It'll cover the solenoid." He'd found the part yesterday, had it overnighted to Jimmy. He wouldn't tell her about the express charge.

She laughed, and God, the sound touched him deep, at the very heart. Bending slightly to rotate her hips, she sent a surge through his cock. "I should be the one paying you. You'd be worth beaucoup bucks." She laughed once more. "Ooh, I could be your pimp, and we'd be rich."

Her words hit like a wrestler's body slam, his gut tensing for the blow as he suddenly thought of all the women who had paid beaucoup bucks for him.

What if she found out? Isabel was right. He'd needed to tell Cleo in the beginning. It was too late now. He couldn't risk it.

"What's wrong, Walker?"

He was standing there like an idiot. "Just thinking how good that was." But his smile cracked his lips as if they were made of stone. He would simply give up the life, and there would be no reason for her to know.

Walker bent at the knees and pulled free of her. It was like pulling loose from his mooring.

CLEO COULD ONLY STARE AT HIM AS SHE TUGGED UP HER PANTIES and slacks, zipping them. The lines of his face grim, Walker cleaned up silently, tossing the condom in the trash can beneath the vanity. She had the sudden need to throw a tissue on top so no one would see it. Her heart beat too quickly, out of control. Something was wrong. She'd done something to lose him. Said something. But what? She couldn't remember. In the throes of orgasm, had she stupidly said how much she wanted him, needed him, please don't ever leave, that kind of garbage? Men freaked at that needy stuff.

Oh man. She glanced at her watch. They'd been in here twenty minutes. Igor would be suspicious. She buttoned her blouse.

Walker watched, his gaze unsettling her.

"What?" Okay, she'd mentioned something about women paying beaucoup bucks for him. Maybe he was pissed that she would be willing to share. "I was just joking about the pimp thing."

He busied himself fastening his jeans. "I know." But now he was avoiding her gaze.

Okay, fine. Men were touchy. They always said women were, but a lot of times, men were worse. She shoved her lipstick and blush back in her cosmetics bag, returned it to her purse.

"Cleo, it's not you," he said behind her.

Hah. That was what men said when they were getting ready to do the brush-off. *This* was why she didn't let men into her life anymore. Heidi was enamored with him, and Ma was getting out the good china. How was she supposed to tell them Walker had suddenly gotten cold feet? It would crush Heidi all over again. Stupid, stupid.

"Cleo."

She dropped her purse on the bench, turned, and jammed a fist on her hip. "What? I'm not asking for anything." All right, she wanted more, but she sure as hell wasn't going to admit it. "I know you like to play the field, you've got a lot of women, and I'm not expecting you to suddenly drop them and—" She stopped. He had a look in his eye. Wary. Uncertain. Nervous?

Cleo thought about all those women. He seemed to have regulars that he dated, but many came and went. *Regulars.* What about those times he let his dates pay for dinner? Such a ladies' man, wining, dining, and then he let them lay out their credit cards? She'd never thought that fit his personality. There was his missed date the night he took Cleo to Fright Fest. It hadn't bothered him one whit that he'd been stood up. He always had condoms. He knew all the naughty pull-outs along the road, had the blankets in his trunk. As if he left them there for any opportune moment . . .

I should be the one paying you. You'd be worth beaucoup bucks.

No. It couldn't be. Ridiculous. But that was what she'd said, and he'd gone all weird and serious on her. Oh my God. The canceled date, the blankets, the wine, the cheese, the movies, the perfect little spot hidden from everyone and condoms in his pocket. He'd switched her out for another woman, but he'd fully intended to have sex with whoever it was. It wasn't as if Cleo didn't know that, but something suddenly seemed staged about it all. "Please don't tell me that's what it really is. All those women."

She'd have felt better if he'd cocked his head and said, "Huh?" But Walker didn't say anything, not a word. He who was never without words, always charming, always with the right thing to say to make women feel good. The perfect date.

Because women paid him beaucoup bucks?

Cleo stared him down just as she did Heidi when she thought her daughter was hiding something. No one could withstand a mother's glare.

"Yes."

She swallowed, her heart skipping so many beats, she thought she might be having an angina attack. "Yes what?"

"I sleep with women for money." Not a muscle in his face twitched as he said it.

She stared at Walker. Her eardrums and her brain didn't quite connect. His mouth moved, but she couldn't hear what he said. There was just a roar, like the pounding of a million feet stomping over her body.

"I let you meet my daughter. I let my mother cook you dinner."

She let him make love to her. She'd called it sex, but it had been so much more. She'd let him *in*.

He slept with women for money. She'd meant nothing to him. He did this all the time with so many women. She wasn't special. She just hadn't paid for it. That was the only thing that made her different.

"Cleo."

Just the sound of her name on his lips pushed her over the edge. She didn't feel her hand move or see it connect, but her palm stung, and a flaming red imprint suddenly blossomed like a scar on his cheek.

WALKER DIDN'T MOVE. THERE WERE MOMENTS THAT DEFINED A man. This was one of them. He wasn't ashamed of what he did with women or that he took their money. But most people weren't like him or Isabel. They didn't view sex in the same way. They didn't see that many times the transaction had merit, that it provided something vital that a person could get in no other way. He was not ashamed of the things he'd done or the man he was. He was ashamed that he'd slept with Cleo before he told her, that he'd taken away her choice in the matter.

"I apologize. I should have told you." He didn't offer an explanation. You couldn't explain away something you knew was wrong.

She covered her mouth with both hands, staring at the mark she'd left on his face. She couldn't know the mark she'd left on his heart.

Her eyes were bright, with unshed tears or anger, he couldn't tell. She backed up, her legs hitting the bench, then suddenly she turned and grabbed her purse. "I've got enough money for the car part."

Her words were a knife blade down the center of his chest. "I don't need it."

She counted out the bills from a wad. Her tip money, he was sure. She shoved them at him. "Here."

If he took the money, everything was over. If he didn't, she'd probably throw it at him. Walker folded the cash and stuffed it in his back pocket, but he couldn't stuff down the pain stretching across his chest like a rubber band about to snap.

"I care about you, Cleo."

She jammed her wallet back in her purse. "Isn't that what you say to all of them?"

"No. Only to you. Whatever else you want to think, I do care about you and you are special."

She laughed. Earlier her laughter had been sweet, sexy; now it was just a harsh sound like nails on a chalkboard. She held her purse to her chest like a shield. "Whatever. I need to get home. You're my ride. But I can take the bus to work if Jimmy doesn't finish the car this weekend." She puffed out a breath. "I'll pay you for the stuff you bought for the bathroom, but you don't need to finish it. I can find someone."

She froze him out, wouldn't even accept his help.

The end of the brief affair. He'd never been in love, hadn't known what he was missing. Now he knew all the potential, what he could have felt, what he could have had. A piece of him howled that he'd thrown it away so quickly.

They were halfway down the hill when he couldn't take the silence anymore. "Would it make a difference if I told you I'm not doing that anymore?" It was pathetic groveling, but he couldn't help himself. The thought of losing her was worse. It had taken three years for his feelings to grow, less than a week for him to acknowledge them for what they were. It wasn't in him to let go.

"No." Unequivocal. She didn't even turn to look at him.

It hurt to breathe. The silence killed another piece of him.

Then she finally gave him a crumb. "If I didn't have Heidi, I don't know." She sighed. "But I do have her. And there's no way I can let your kind of man into her life. It's just totally wrong."

Those were the nails in his coffin. He was not good enough. He would never be worthy.

This time the silence never broke.

11

SHE HURT. AS IF A GAPING WOUND EXPOSED HER HEART. IF SHE
didn't have Heidi to worry about, or her mom to take care of,
maybe everything would have been different. Maybe it all would
have been intriguing.

Except that she could never compete with all those women.
She'd thought that from the beginning, but ignored it when her
defenses were down and she was needy.

Cleo arrived home to find her mother still up and in the
kitchen baking. Thank God Heidi, always wanting to get out of
the house, was at another slumber party. Cleo didn't think she
could handle them both.

"What on earth are you doing, Ma?"

"Baking chocolate chip cookies." She held up a beater. In house
slippers, she barely came to Cleo's shoulder. "Wanna lick?"

Cleo succumbed to the lure of cookie dough. "What I meant
was why are you baking after eleven at night?" God, had Cleo
forgotten some bake sale Heidi was involved in?

"They're for Walker and his friend when they work on the
bathroom tomorrow." She winked. "A little-old-lady trick for getting the most out of a man."

Cleo winced. She didn't want to think about Walker or what they'd said to each other or how she'd cut him off. She didn't want to think about him with all those other women. Was it the money or the quantity that bothered her the most?

It was driving her nuts wondering how much they paid him. She could never afford someone like Walker.

What the hell was she supposed to tell Ma? Or worse, what would she say to Heidi tomorrow when she got home from her slumber party? Certainly not that Walker was a gigolo. That he used women. Cleo winced again. He'd never used her. He'd only been good to her. She couldn't put the two things together.

She sighed. "Look, Ma, I have to tell you something."

Her mother shook a dough-laden spoon at her. "Do not tell me you screwed this up, Cleo." Her mom's voice was raspy with cigarettes and annoyance. "I'm going to be really pissed at you if you've scared him off."

"Me?"

Ma went back to spooning dough onto the cookie sheet. "Since Phil, you haven't lasted more than a few weeks with a man, not even long enough to have him meet your family."

She never intended to bring her male friends home to meet her family. But Ma was no dummy; she knew that Cleo's occasional late homecomings weren't for a girl's night out. It pricked her, though, that Ma put the blame on her, as if she'd screwed up all her relationships. She'd been protecting Heidi.

The past, however, was a whole different issue, and she decided not to debate whether or not she and Walker had a *relationship*. "I did not screw up anything. We just agreed that it would be better to nip this thing in the bud. We're too different."

Ma snorted. "Are you crazy?"

Cleo grabbed a yogurt from the fridge. "No, Ma, I am not

crazy. He's just not the man we thought he was." Pain wedged beneath her rib cage. Why did it have to be that way? Why did he have to do what he did for a living?

Why had he lied for three years? Well, it wasn't exactly a lie. It was not telling something really freaking important.

Ma slid two cookie sheets into the oven and set the timer, then glared at Cleo. "He was perfect. Smart. I'd be willing to bet he's college educated. He had money. He treated me and Heidi with respect. He took care of getting the part for your car. And he was going to fix the bathroom."

Cleo pressed her lips together. "So this is all about getting the bathroom done for cheap."

"No, it is not." Stabbing the lump of dough in the bowl with a spoon, Ma began doling out another cookie sheet's worth. "It's about missed opportunities. There aren't a whole lot of men who'll take on the responsibility of someone else's teenage kid. They want to start fresh, build their own family. And your kid needs a dad."

Now, that really pricked a nerve. It was Phil to a fucking T. Yet she hadn't even told Ma why he really left. "You're kidding, right? A couple of dates, some algebra homework, compliments on your roast beef, and now you've got him playing Daddy to Heidi?" Cleo considered senility.

"I've never been more serious. For fifteen years I've watched you run away from men because you found one bad apple in the barrel."

"I have not been running away." She'd tried with Greg and Phil. In trying to protect Heidi, she'd taken the blame for the breakups and let Ma think *she'd* ended the relationships. Okay, she'd been hiding her own bad judgment, too. Her choice in men sucked.

Ma rolled her eyes just like Heidi. "I might be older than dirt, but I'm not the village idiot. You're scared of getting hurt. I get that. But you and Heidi are all alone, and I'm not getting any younger, and when I'm gone, then what are you going to do?" She tipped her head, her white hair gleaming in the overhead light, all trace of annoyance vanished. Concern furrowed deeper lines into her face. "Not all men are assholes, Cleo. Your dad, he was a good man. You should have a good man in your life. Heidi should, too."

"You've never said this before." Cleo wagged her head in disbelief. "I don't understand where this is all coming from."

"You're stubborn. You don't listen. What was the point of saying it?" Ma went back to her dough. "But I liked Walker a lot. He was nice to me. He made me laugh. He let me crab and he didn't even mind. I love to crab. And he was good to Heidi, didn't get impatient or huffy." She heaved a great sigh. "I miss having a man around the house. All estrogen and no testosterone isn't good for a body."

Oh man, didn't she know it. "Ma," Cleo said, then had no clue what to add. She missed a man around the house, too.

"You can tell when a man's genuine, and he was."

Now, that was the lie. Walker wasn't genuine at all. There was no way Ma would change her mind, though, once she'd made it up. After all, Cleo had inherited her stubborn streak from her mother.

The only thing that would change her mind was the truth. Cleo just couldn't tell her. She couldn't answer the inevitable questions, couldn't say she'd seen him with all those women and still let him into her life. It was better to let Ma think Cleo was the one in the wrong. Just like she'd done all the other times.

"I JUST GOT OFF THE BUS AT THE CORNER OF SAN ANTONIO ROAD and Foothill Expressway."

Walker didn't recognize the number on his Caller ID, but he recognized the raspy voice. "What are you doing there, Ma?" It was just short of nine o'clock on Saturday morning. She couldn't be out shopping yet, especially not such a long way from home.

"Waiting for you to come pick me up. Do you know how hard it is to find a pay phone these days?" she groused. "It's like they expect seniors to figure out how to work those little itty-bitty cell phones so we don't need pay phones anymore."

"I can show you how to use one, Ma."

"Don't want to know," she grumbled.

"Okay." He paused. "I didn't know you were coming, Ma." What if he hadn't been home? He'd given her his cell number and remembered saying he lived in Los Altos. He just never expected a visit from her.

"Well," she harrumphed, "you shoulda known since you dumped Cleo like yesterday's garbage."

He closed his eyes a moment, a ripple of pain across his forehead. "I'll be there in about ten minutes."

It took five. He didn't want to keep Ma waiting. She was indeed on the corner, and he blocked the flow of traffic as she climbed into his car and settled herself with the seat belt, a plate of Saran-wrapped cookies on her lap.

He pulled away from the curb. "What are the cookies for, Ma?" He didn't know her name. She'd simply told him to call her Ma like Cleo did.

She harrumphed again. "Baked 'em for you and that friend of yours. But Cleo told me last night you weren't coming back. She said you had *differences*," she mimicked Cleo. "I figured she did something to piss you off and you dumped her."

"Cleo didn't piss me off," he corrected her. He liked Ma. She said it like it was, at least the facts according to Ma. A foot shorter than him, her white hair was permed and starched into tiny ringlets that didn't effectively manage to cover the thinning spot at the back of her head. She probably couldn't see it.

"I want the truth." She shook a crooked finger at him. "So I brought the cookies along to bribe you."

"Okay." He pulled into his drive wondering what version of the truth he'd give her. "Do you want some milk with your cookies?"

She snorted. "Milk gives me hot flashes."

She was long past the hot-flash stage, but no way was he going to say that. "I'll come round and get your door for you."

Ma stayed right where she was, then took his hand regally as he opened her door. "Coffee, then?" he suggested.

She peered up at him, one eye squinted against the sun. "Only if you make it hair-of-the-dog strong."

"Yup," he said. In the kitchen, he busied himself with the pot.

The island stood between them. "Nice house," Ma said, unwrapping the Saran at the table in his breakfast nook. She'd removed her coat and flung it over the back of a chair. Beneath she wore a pretty blue dress with tiny white flowers. She'd dressed up for him. Previously he'd seen her only in faded but clean housedresses.

"Thanks," he said as the coffee began to drip. "Cream and sugar?" he asked, retrieving a couple of mugs from the cabinet.

She snorted. Hair-of-the-dog obviously meant no diluting. "You been married before?"

"No."

She didn't ask why he hadn't, saying instead, "What do you need so much room and all that cookware for?"

The house had four bedrooms, three baths, living room, dining room, family room. He didn't bring his dates here, but in days of old, when he was a stockbroker, he'd held a lot of business parties. Now the living and dining rooms did little more than gather dust. He used one of the extra bedrooms as an office. But the kitchen he spent a lot of time in. He liked to cook and had every gadget known to man.

He'd never told Cleo he'd wanted to make a gourmet meal for her.

"I like to cook. And I guess I had dreams of a family at one point." If you didn't push hard enough, you didn't get what you wanted. He'd lived in the house more than fifteen years, but never stopped his climb to the top of the stock market long enough to find the right woman with whom to share the house.

The drip automatically stopped as he poured the first cup and put the pot back to continue filling.

"Well, you're not getting any younger," Ma quipped.

"No, I'm not," he admitted, setting the mug down in front of her. He'd pictured Cleo here, but those fantasies had come three years too late. "The cookies look chewy," he said to steer away the ache around his heart.

"Damn best," she agreed without an ounce of humility.

Enough for a second cup had dripped through, and he joined her at the table. The sun poured through the window, setting her hair to sparkling.

Sipping her coffee, she screwed her face up. "Perfect."

"So why are you really here, Ma?"

She pursed her lips, the skin wrinkling almost to her nose. "Here's the thing." She paused, bit into a cookie, washed it down with the coffee. "Cleo's got this whole trust issue going on."

"I know." Between three years of offhand comments and their brief relationship, he'd learned that.

"She's always waiting for the other shoe to drop, so to speak. Looking for that thing a man does that she can say *aha*"—she held up a finger—"I knew I shouldn't trust him."

Maybe that was Cleo's modus operandi, but in this case, she'd been right. He had a secret, a very big one.

"Most of the time, it's just crap stuff. She's never going to find perfection. Her expectations are way too high."

"Ma, she's got a daughter to think of. She's got to have high expectations."

Ma blew a raspberry. "That's bull. Heidi is an excuse to keep men away. She can just trot her kid out and tell some guy to go blow so Heidi won't get hurt when he leaves." She shook her head. "I've heard all her crap. She had a coupla really nice ones on the hook who would have been good for Heidi, but"—she rolled her eyes—"Cleo scared 'em off."

"You're not being fair." He felt uncomfortable hearing Cleo's personal business.

But Ma was on a roll. "Then she stops *dating*"—she finger-quoted—"but I'm no dummy. She's just not bringing them home. And what does that say? She's either ashamed of us or ashamed of them."

"Ma. You've got it all wrong. Cleo is cautious. She loves Heidi to death. She'd do anything for her."

Ma slapped the table. "Then she should bring a father home for her. Heidi wouldn't have had so many problems at public school if she'd had a male influence in her life."

She was being way too hard on Cleo. "She's done a hell of a job raising Heidi. With your help," he added.

"There's nothing that replaces having a daddy." She eyed him, then fluttered her eyelashes coquettishly. On Ma, it didn't have quite the right effect. In fact, it was kind of scary. "You were real good. Heidi listened to you. You spent quality time with her."

Yeah, for all of four days. Cleo had given Heidi a lifetime.

"I'm not the solution."

She grimaced. "Yeah. Because Cleo scared you off."

"She didn't scare me off. We just had—"

"*Differences.*" Ma cut him off, her voice dripping with

sarcasm. "Yeah, I know." She shook her head. "I've heard it all before."

It pissed him off that she made everything Cleo's fault. "Did you ever think that maybe Cleo was right, and the men she dated did turn out to be assholes? You know we're all on our best behavior until we get what we want."

She tipped her head. "That true for you, too? You were pulling a snow job on me and Heidi just so you could get in Cleo's pants, but you're really an asshole at heart?"

His heart thudded in his chest. "No."

"So tell me what *you*"—she pointed a bent finger—"did to screw it all up."

She was so quick to blame Cleo. He knew families had history, and an outsider understood only part of the story, but Cleo obviously hadn't told Ma the truth about him. He'd lied to Cleo. Maybe he didn't believe what he'd done for the past three years was amoral. He'd enjoyed it, brought sweetness into the lives of lonely women, but a hell of a lot of society would disagree with him.

Cleo had made a choice, but he was the one who hadn't been honest in the first place. He deserved what he got.

He would not let Ma go on disparaging her daughter.

"I'm not an asshole," he said. "But I do have a fault that Cleo couldn't live with."

Ma snorted. "Yeah. You're probably a serial killer or something." She sipped from her mug and grabbed another cookie.

He smiled, though he didn't feel it on the inside. "Actually, I sleep with women for money, and Cleo just didn't think that was the kind of man she wanted to have around her teenage daughter."

Ma spat out her coffee.

12

"NO WAY." MA LOOKED A LITTLE BUG-EYED.

"It's true." Admitting it to Cleo had broken something inside him. With Ma, he had no real stake. The lady could think of him whatever she wanted.

"How much money do you make?"

He laughed. Trust Ma. "Three to five thousand a date"—he seesawed his hand in the air—"give or take."

Ma gaped. "Holy shit."

This time when he smiled, he felt it. Somehow it was good to shock Ma. Maybe she'd begin appreciating Cleo a little more.

"How'd you get started?"

"I'd dated a few female courtesans myself."

"Courtesans? Like from the old days?"

"It's preferable to being called a whore." The word had such a negative connotation, while he considered what Isabel's agency provided a necessary service. In general, courtesans gave people their fantasies. Specifically, Walker empowered women.

To say that to Ma, however, sounded too much like justification.

"Aren't you afraid of being arrested?"

"We're very discreet. We only work with people recommended

to the agency, and we only accept *gifts*. Payment isn't required." Though of course it was *required*, just never stated in such terms.

"So you're tricky."

He grinned. "Exactly."

She started pestering him with questions. "How long have you been doing it?"

"About three years."

"What did you do before?"

"I was a stockbroker."

"Hah," she cackled, "so you lost your shirt and now you have to sell yourself."

"Actually, I got out at the height of the market."

"Why'd you do that?"

He patted his heart. "I wanted to make it to fifty."

"So if you're not doing it for the money . . ." She trailed off, spreading her hands.

He wasn't sure what he'd been expecting from Ma. Maybe a freak-out to rival Cleo's. He certainly hadn't anticipated her curiosity, but he satisfied it. "I like making women feel desirable and good about themselves."

Her face twisted. "Very admirable."

"I didn't say it was admirable. I simply enjoy it."

Sitting back in her chair, she crossed her arms over her bony chest. "What about protection?"

"Always."

She harrumphed, stared at him, her steely blue eyes working him over. "Well, at least you're honest about it."

He gave her a grim smile. "No. I wasn't honest. Cleo didn't know until last night."

She arched one scraggly eyebrow. "Did she see you with one of them?"

"She's always seen me with them."

"Heh. At the restaurant," she surmised. "She just didn't know what was going on."

"Correct."

She leaned forward and dropped her voice to an avid, greedy pitch. "Then last night, she got jealous while you were wining and dining one of them, and totally went ballistic, so you had to tell her."

"No. I haven't been on a date since Cleo brought me home to meet you and Heidi."

She made a noise in her throat. "She didn't *bring* you home. You showed up."

"I stand corrected."

"And I do realize you're trying very hard not to tell me exactly how Cleo figured it out last night."

"Some things aren't your business."

"None of it's my business." Ma laughed heartily, then broke into a cough he worried about. He noticed she hadn't asked to smoke in his house yet.

"Okay, so you're not going to tell me," she said. "But tell me this instead. How does a person get to be a courtesan with your so-called agency?"

"Recommendation. Then there's an interview process. Training."

Ma made a big round O of her lips. "Training," she whispered. "That sounds like fun."

He didn't tell her it was a psychology seminar on reading people's body language and interpreting nonverbal signals, all in the quest to figure out what a client needed if they weren't able to articulate their desires. Isabel's mission was to provide a client's perfect fantasy.

Tapping a finger on the table, Ma waited several beats. "How about you recommend Cleo for a job?"

Thank God he hadn't been drinking or he'd have spit it out just as Ma had done. "I don't think so."

"But she could pay for Heidi's tuition. And we could fix the bathroom. And she could get a new car. And she wouldn't have to work two jobs anymore."

"She'd never be home at night." Flabbergasted, it was the only excuse he could come up with.

"Oh yeah, right." Then she brightened. "But I bet there are plenty of men who want a little afternoon nookie."

He'd never met anyone like Ma. He expected her to freak, and instead she was offering up Cleo.

Though God help him, he had images of Cleo and him servicing a client's needs together. It was a heady fantasy.

"Ma," he said, "that is the dumbest thing I've ever heard. You know damn well she'd never do anything like that if she thought Heidi might figure it out."

The little lady sighed. "You're right. She's a hard case." Then she smiled. "But now that I know, I can make her see how what you do doesn't really matter."

"I've given up the life." He'd lost his taste for it. Not because it was wrong or immoral, but it was paltry compared to what he'd shared with Cleo. He wanted unparalleled sex like that, with the emotion, the feeling. As cliché as it sounded, she'd ruined him for other women.

Ma clapped her hands. "Then it's perfect. Since you're not a gigolo anymore, it's not a problem. I'll get her to see the light, and you can come back."

Ma didn't get it. Things were either black or they were white, no shade in between. Cleo saw all the shades of gray. "I would appreciate it if you didn't discuss this with Cleo."

She gaped. "Why not?"

"She's old enough to make up her own mind. And she's done that. If she changes it, she has my number."

"Shit. You give up too easy, boy." She cocked her head. "But you do care, right?"

His chest hurt, a slow burn beneath his ribs. He took too long to answer.

"My God, you really are in love with her."

She made it sound like some sort of anomaly. "Cleo's a very special woman," he said.

She huffed. "Well, I know that, but she usually doesn't let a man get close enough for long enough to figure it out."

Ah, but he'd gotten to know her over three years. She'd been burrowing deeper under his skin the whole time.

"You need to tell her," Ma declared.

"No. That's putting another burden on her. I'm not going to use love like some sort of bargaining chip." Besides, being in love with her didn't make a difference. He could not change the man he was. In fact, he wouldn't change. He might never take another client for Isabel, but he would always feel the things he'd done were good for the women he'd been with. He'd helped them. He wouldn't beg forgiveness for something he didn't believe was wrong. That would have been another lie.

"Wow," Ma said. "You're way too self-sacrificing."

He leaned forward, pointed his finger. "And don't try to be my fairy godmother, either."

She blew one of her raspberries. "You're no fun."

Probably not, but he wasn't about to let her harass Cleo.

"Did you tell Cleo all this stuff just like you told me?" She rolled her eyes and nodded her head as if she heard a question he hadn't asked. "Yeah, yeah, not about the love part, but everything else? Like how you make women feel good about themselves, and desirable, yadda yadda."

"No. It wouldn't have made a difference." Nor had Cleo given him the chance.

"You're an idiot." Ma shook her head slowly. "Come to think of it, you're both idiots. I wash my hands. Now, take me outside because I need a cigarette bad."

SATURDAY MORNING, CLEO SLEPT LATE AFTER TOSSING AND TURN-ing most of the night. When she came downstairs, she'd half expected Walker to be in the kitchen having coffee with Ma. Like he wasn't going to take no for answer.

Her stomach rolled over when he wasn't there. God. She actually missed him, not just a man around the house, but *him*.

The coffee in the pot was overcooked and a note from Ma lay on the kitchen table. She was out getting a few groceries. Cleo pulled open the tins, but couldn't find the cookies Ma had baked last night. Upset about Walker, maybe she'd thrown them out. Heidi wouldn't be home until the afternoon. A reprieve. But Cleo had to plan what she'd tell Heidi about Walker. Jeez. Things were so complicated.

Her cell phone rang just as a fresh pot of coffee finished brewing. Her heart raced. Damn if she wasn't hoping it was Walker. She picked up without even checking.

She really had to get over him. "Hello?"

"Yo, your car's ready."

It was Jimmy. Disappointment rumbled in her belly.

An hour later, after she'd rushed through a shower and jumped on the bus, she found him in his shop under a car body. "Hey, Jimmy," she said, bending to peer under.

His belly barely clearing the undercarriage, Jimmy rolled out flat on his back on a dolly. He grinned at her, his hands dirty and a streak of grease in his blond hair. "It's as good as new," he said. "Keys are on the counter, car's parked around the corner." He braced his feet to roll under the car again.

"Wait. I was wondering if it would be okay to do the install-ment thing like before."

"Your boyfriend took care of that the other day." He pushed off again, his head disappearing.

Her stomach started to squirm. She toed his leg. "What do you mean my boyfriend took care of it?"

Jimmy sighed, and spoke from under the car. "When I told him it'd be between five hundred and seven-fifty depending on how long it took, he said he'd give me the cash up front if I kept it to the five hundred." Something *kachunk*ed under the body. "And you made out, honey, because it took me longer. Still had to finish it up this morning."

Walker had paid for the car. Dammit. He hadn't asked; he'd just done it, pushing his way into her life, making decisions for her. Goddammit. She had an arrangement with Jimmy, and now he'd gotten screwed. She dreaded finding someone else to work on the car, someone who might bilk her, because really, what the hell did she know about cars? "I'll pay you the difference."

Jimmy rolled back out. This time grease smeared his cheek, and he stared her down—despite the fact that she was up—with a blue-eyed gaze. "Sweetheart, don't be stupid."

"I just—"

He cut her off. "Me and Walker worked it all out. I gambled and I lost, and I'm cool with it because it wasn't that much of a difference, and I'd still rather have the money up front. Capiche?"

"Yeah." Installments meant he had to wait for his money too long. "But I want you to know I really appreciate that you've let me make payments in the past."

"Cleo, I'm not getting on your case about paying me over a couple of months. Because you always pay me. I've had deadbeats who screw me over royally, like bouncing checks or cutting off a credit card payment. But I still like the money up front, so take the car and give Walker a big kiss, okay?" Then he slid back beneath the car's underbelly, discussion over.

Jimmy had always been sweet to her. Before her mom stopped driving, he'd fashioned a special plastic fitting to go over the gas cap because Ma, with her arthritis, had trouble undoing the factory-installed cap. He'd never quibbled about how Cleo had to pay him off. She'd always trusted him to tell her the truth about the car.

Yet she didn't trust Walker once she'd started having sex with him. That was what he'd accused her of the night the car broke down. She'd actually intended to let the tow truck driver take her home, a man she'd never met.

She didn't have a problem with men in general. She had a problem with men she'd had sex with.

She didn't like owing them, didn't like letting them think she needed them, didn't like giving them any kind of control. Maybe Ma was right, and she was blaming all the men she dated for the bad apples that had fallen into her life. Or maybe she just couldn't trust her own judgment anymore. Walker had some good traits. He'd saved her money on the car, not just by paying the labor up front, but by finding the part in the first place. He was smart, funny, caring, respectful, generous, well mannered, and sexy as all get-out.

He also slept with women for money. Honestly, no matter how much she liked him or how good he was to her, that was pretty much a fatal flaw. How she could overlook it?

But she still owed him five hundred bucks. God help her, despite what she *knew* was right, she actually wondered how many sexual favors it would take to pay it off.

13

"WHAT DO YOU MEAN, WALKER'S NOT COMING BACK?"

Cleo groaned inwardly. She and Heidi were crowding Ma's bathroom. It was just before five. Cleo had to shower, change, and grab a bite to eat before she headed to the restaurant for her Saturday night shift. Heidi had just returned from the sleepover and wanted to go to the movies with Viola, a childhood friend who lived three doors down.

God, she so did not need an argument with Heidi right now. So Cleo lied. She'd hate herself for that later. "He underestimated the amount of time it would take to do the bathroom, and he decided he can't make the commitment."

Heidi glared. A teenager's glare could rival that of a rabid dog. "That is bull, Mom, and you know it."

She should have reprimanded Heidi for talking back, but Cleo knew she was in the wrong. "All right. We had a fight. He's not coming back. End of story."

"That's so not fair, Mom."

Life had been hard before Walker; now it was harder after. She'd had one really good week. Didn't anyone realize that she missed him, too? But she'd made a decision. She had to do what was right. "Heidi, you barely knew him." Thank God it hadn't been long enough for Heidi to get attached. "You'll forget all about him in a week."

Heidi narrowed her eyes. Okay, wrong thing to say. Cleo just never knew what the right thing was.

"Why?" Heidi demanded.

Ma had asked the same thing. Cleo's excuses were flimsy. The truth was worse. "I don't want to talk about it."

"It was because of me, wasn't it?"

What? "You had nothing to do with it."

"You just don't want to tell me."

She could only stare dumbfounded at her daughter. "It was about Walker and me, not you."

"He said I hung around too much and that I was annoying him, and that's why he's not coming back."

"Don't be silly." Cleo's heart wrenched, and suddenly she wanted to tell Heidi the truth just so she wouldn't think it was her fault. Where on earth had she gotten such a notion?

Heidi's eyes shimmered. "Well, I know that's why you don't bring your dates home," she snapped. "Because you're ashamed of me, and you think I'll drive them away."

Cleo massaged a temple as she shook her head. "That's the silliest thing I've ever heard. The exact opposite is true. I don't bring dates home because they're not worthy of *you*."

"Yeah, right." Heidi sniffed. "Phil left because of me, and *you*"— she stabbed her finger at Cleo—"decided it wasn't worth bringing anyone else home."

Good God. Phil had left four years ago. Heidi had cried buckets over him. But Cleo had never told her daughter the things Phil said. Then again, she'd never been specific, and Heidi had made her own assumptions. She'd *needed* a reason. "He just wasn't in love with me."

Heidi pursed her lips and puffed out a breath. "I heard you two fighting."

Cleo's stomach dropped to the floor. "You heard what exactly?"

"I heard what Phil said. He didn't want me. He wanted his own kid."

Her heart broke for her daughter. Heidi had never said a word. "He was an asshole, Heidi." She reached, but Heidi stepped back.

"You've held it against me ever since." Her bottom lip trembled and though her eyes glistened, the teardrops didn't fall. She looked like the little girl Cleo missed so much.

"No, Heidi."

"It's true. I could never do anything right. You even yanked me out of public school because I wasn't good enough."

Cleo threw up her hands in defense. "Wait, wait, wait. Private school and my so-called boyfriends have nothing to do with each other. I just didn't like your friends there."

Heidi swiped at a tiny drop of moisture that tried to escape. "It started with Phil, and then you kept picking and picking. My friends weren't right. My grades weren't good enough. I didn't study hard enough."

Four years ago. No, no, everything had gone wrong with freshman year. They had been fine before that. Or had they? Maybe Heidi was right. Maybe she'd been picking on her daughter long before. Cleo put a hand over her mouth. God. She was a rotten mom, because honestly, she couldn't remember. Both she and Heidi had taken a long time to get over Phil. Then she'd started the second job at the restaurant. And please, please, please don't say she hadn't noticed something was wrong or that she'd suddenly become hypercritical.

"I'm sorry if you felt like I was picking. It was never your fault about Phil. And Walker's leaving isn't because of you, either."

"Then why?" Heidi whispered.

Cleo didn't know what to say. *Because I was fucking him, and then I found out he was fucking a bunch of women and getting paid for it.* God, no. She couldn't say that. It would kill her to say that, even if it was the truth. But it wasn't the whole truth. The problem wasn't Walker's morals; it was *her* jealousy. But what was she supposed to tell her daughter? A decent lie Heidi would believe just would not come to Cleo's lips.

"See, I was right." Heidi shoved her hair behind her ear. "You don't even know what to say." She stepped through the bathroom doorjamb. "Do I have permission to walk to Viola's instead of having you drive me?"

She should have argued, but Cleo admitted she was beaten. After all, it was only three houses away. "Yes, you can go."

She was the worst kind of mother. She'd let her daughter believe she wasn't good enough without even realizing what she was doing. She had no clue how to fix it.

CLEO LEANED AGAINST THE KITCHEN COUNTER. THE YOGURT TASTED sour. She knew it was her and not the yogurt. "How could she think I was ashamed of her?"

Ma shrugged as she ate her chicken pot pie at the dinner table. "Not too hard to understand. Boyfriend goes, you never bring another one home; ergo, you're ashamed of her."

"Has she talked to you about it?"

Her mother huffed. "If she had *talked*, you know I would have said something. She mumbles, and I don't understand half of it. In one ear and out the other."

Ma was no help. "I'm so tired," Cleo said, feeling her body slump against the counter and not being able to stop it.

"Maybe you should just let Walker come back." Ma waved her fork as if it were a magic wand. "Then Heidi would know he didn't go because of her."

"It's not that simple."

Ma ignored her. "Plus we'd get the bathroom fixed."

Cleo rinsed out the yogurt cup and tossed it in the recycle bin. "I'm not going to use him just to get the bathroom done."

"Why not? Men love it when women use them." Ma waggled her eyebrows. They needed plucking. "Especially if they get something out of it."

Sexual favors. Cleo already owed him. "Don't be ridiculous. I can't ask him to come back. There's a lot of stuff you just don't know and can't understand." And Cleo wasn't telling.

Ma played innocently with her chicken pot pie. "Oh, you mean like that he used to sleep with women for money?"

Cleo heard a roar in her ears that could only be her blood shooting up to the boiling point. "What?"

Ma smiled. "He told me."

Walker told her, but Cleo had to figure it out on her own? "My head hurts." A blinding ache jabbed abruptly at her temples.

"I went to see him this morning because you wouldn't talk."

"Ma." She gaped. "How *could* you?"

"It was easy. I took the bus to Los Altos because that's where he said he lived. Then I used a pay phone to have him come pick me up." She tipped her head and pressed her lips together a moment. "I suppose I could have just called him from here, but I figured that if I was already close by, he couldn't leave me stranded."

God, her mother was sneaky. How Ma got there wasn't what Cleo meant, but how could she dare go behind Cleo's back? What was the point in asking, though? Ma had always done what she wanted. "How'd you know his number?"

Ma shot her a *duh* look. "He gave me his cell phone number so I could tell him when it was convenient to come over. I mean"— she held up her hands—"I wouldn't want him showing up when I was naked in the shower or something."

Her mother was unbelievable. "I didn't need you ragging on him on my behalf."

"I was ragging on *my* behalf. It's awfully lonely watching soaps by yourself. He was company."

Her mother had *never* watched soaps. Okay, maybe *General Hospital* when they had the whole Luke and Laura thing going on. Cleo had been a baby at the time, but Ma still talked about it.

"All right," she cut off Ma's blathering, "aren't you shocked and horrified at what he does for a living?"

"It's not a *living*. He's rich from the stock market. He did it because he enjoyed making women feel good about themselves, attractive and desirable."

He'd certainly done that for Cleo. And he was rich? Well, she knew he was no slouch. "But Ma—"

"If he was still in the business, I'd think about paying him myself."

"Ma," she gasped. Okay, it was a horrible thought to even contemplate. "I can't believe you'd so blithely accept this. I mean, he spent so much time with Heidi, helping with her homework."

"Get over yourself," her mom snapped. "He was good to Heidi. He didn't molest her."

"I didn't mean that."

"He made her feel good about herself, too. Built her up, told her she was smart, never berated her if she got a problem wrong. So what if he did something in his private life that was a little different?"

"A little *different*?" Cleo shook her head. "I can't believe you're defending him."

"I'm not defending him. I'm saying I don't care about it, and I like him despite it. And if he's decided he's not going to do it anymore, then what's wrong with him coming around here to see us?"

"Because . . ." There was something wrong with it. There just was.

Ma put her fork down and turned serious. "Honey, I can truly understand that it would bother you if he was sleeping with a bunch of women, then coming home to you. I realize that would be tough."

Cleo couldn't take that.

"But it's over. He'd rather have you. Doesn't that mean anything?"

Cleo clenched her fists until her nails dug into her palms. "I don't know, Ma." She dropped her voice to a whisper. "I'm afraid of getting hurt." There. She'd admitted it.

"Everyone is."

"I'm afraid Heidi will get attached, and she'll get hurt, too."

"Life's a lot of risks, Cleo. But what if you're my age and your daughter's moved off to the wilds of Borneo with the man she loves and you think, What if I'd given Walker a chance and it worked and I wasn't alone for the rest of my life."

What if . . . God, she wanted a *what-if*. "But things with Heidi are so tenuous. I need to put all my energy into working on my relationship with her." Cleo glanced at her watch. She had to leave in five minutes or she'd be late.

"You and I had just as many problems when you were that age. We hated each other's guts. But it all worked out. Do you hate me now?"

"No, of course I don't." As much as she groused about the

smoking and Ma's irritating habits—Cleo had her own bad habits—she loved her mother.

"You and Heidi will get over it. And everyone eventually gets over a broken heart, too. But we never get over the regrets we have for the road not taken."

Did Ma have regrets? Yeah. Sure. Everyone did. "I'm going to be late," Cleo whispered, thinking about all the hours and evenings she was missing with Heidi because she had two jobs. She was sure she'd end up regretting the lost time.

"Just think about it, okay?"

"I'll think." She grabbed her purse, and was almost out the kitchen door before she turned. "Ma, have I picked too much on Heidi?"

Ma flapped a hand. "I'm not one to say how much is too much. I picked and picked and you went out and got yourself pregnant anyway."

One had nothing to do with the other. She'd been in love. And she'd been stupid.

Ma, however, was right about one thing. Cleo needed to think. About Heidi. About Walker. About the rest of her life and no regrets.

14

YOU'RE AN IDIOT.

Walker had to admit that Ma was a smart old bird. He *was* an idiot. He'd simply stepped into Cleo's life, decided what she needed, executed the plan, and expected her to fall right in line.

He honestly didn't know if it was right or wrong not to tell her about his life as one of Isabel's courtesans. But it *was* dumb. She was bound to ask him about those women eventually. Whether she could overlook his past or not, she deserved a better explanation than what he'd given her. She deserved to know that he had feelings for her.

So Walker drove up to Bella's for the end of Cleo's shift and planted his butt on the trunk of her car to wait. He was five minutes early; she was five minutes late coming out.

Damn if she didn't look gorgeous in the pool of lamplight she stopped in when she saw him. She'd undone the bun she wore for work, and her hair tumbled past her shoulders. The black slacks molded to her hips; the blouse emphasized her perfect breasts. Despite the coolness of the night, she hadn't put her jacket on.

He waited with his heart clogging his throat. Until Cleo glanced over her shoulder as if she thought they were being watched from a window and finally came to stand before him.

"I don't want to talk here," she said. "Take me for a drive."

At least she hadn't told him to get lost.

He opened his car door. She settled in silence. He flipped on the seat warmers, then took them out along Skyline instead of heading down the hill.

"Find a spot," she said, "so we can talk."

He knew a lot of spots, but none of them was for talking. Hell, he wasn't going to think about that. He found what she was looking for, pulling to a stop in a copse of trees hidden from the road. Shutting off the lights and engine, he plunged them into darkness.

"Ma said she came to see you."

He didn't even consider how to explain it away. "I told her about who I am and what I've done."

"Were you trying to get her on your side?"

Slowly, his eyes adjusting to the light of the moon, he could see her, not her expression, just the grim outline of her jaw. "I didn't want her to think any of this was your fault."

"Well, she's definitely on your side."

"Funny, she told me I was an idiot."

Cleo laughed, cut it off quickly. "Join the club."

Yeah, Ma was outspoken, but she was right. "There were a few things I didn't say last night."

"If you're going to explain why you were with those women and how it made them feel good about themselves and all, it's not necessary."

"That's—"

She held up her hand, painting a blank spot over her face. "It's not my business, really. I made it sound like I was judging you, and that wasn't my right."

"Cleo, I—"

She rode right over him. "Ma said you'd decided not to do it anymore, and that's not my right to ask for, either."

"Cleo, would you please shut up and let me say something?"

Her lips slapped shut. "Sorry."

"I love you."

She didn't say a word. He prayed for a full moon, but it was only a crescent.

Okay, he needed to give her more. He *owed* her more. Total honesty. "I can't undo who I am. I enjoyed it. I liked making women feel good." He wanted to touch her so badly his hand shook. "But I *loved* making you feel good."

He thought he heard a sigh of breath, the creak of the leather on the car seat as she shifted. But still, not a word.

"I want to start over with you. Pretend we're just meeting, that this is the first time. And you are my one and only." He'd beg if that would help. He just wasn't sure it would. "If you can accept what I've done in the past and know that it's over."

The dark moved as she put a hand over her mouth, made a noise he couldn't be sure of.

"I want to be with you, Cleo. And Heidi. And Ma." Then he simply rushed on because silence was deadly. "I've waited a long time for a family. I thought I'd lost my chance. But I want it with you."

He'd have thought he couldn't hear a thing over the pounding of his heart, but one whispered word came through. "Why?"

"Why what?"

She reached out, touched his mouth with the tips of her fingers. "Why would you love me? I've been a pain in the ass the whole time."

"You're sweet, kind, generous, loving, loyal."

"A Girl Scout?"

He laughed a little shakily. "Far from it, thank God."

*　*　*

CLEO HAD SEEN WALKER OUT THERE IN THE PARKING LOT AND HAD no clue what he wanted to say or why he'd been leaning on the back of her car. But her heart had tripped over itself.

Oh yeah, she'd done some thinking. That his way of life had been bad mostly because it made her feel as if she could never measure up. Heidi's well-being had been an excuse. Cleo had never been good enough for a man in her life. It was kind of hard to figure she'd be good enough now.

But she believed Walker. She believed he cared. She believed Ma, too, that sometimes the regret could be worse than the hurt. "I'm sorry about the awful things I said."

"They weren't so awful, just true."

Honestly, she couldn't remember exactly what she'd said last night. She only remembered the shock and pain and letdown.

Plus the fact that she'd judged him harshly. "I was jealous of all those women." She leaned closer, lowered her voice. "I always wondered about you, about them. You were the perfect date. I think I was probably jealous all along."

"You shouldn't have been. The greatest pleasure of the evening was seeing you."

"It's kind of a weird thing to think about. That women paid you." She wondered briefly what it would be like to receive money.

"It's powerful for women, enhancing how desirable they see themselves."

She shook her head. "But they're paying you. It's like saying they're not good enough."

"When men pay, we say the women are the sex objects, being used, and the men have all the power and thus the desirability." He cocked his head. "So isn't that true for women? In reality, when it's really good, it works both ways, a mutual exchange of power."

She'd never thought of it that way. Probably because men always had the power. Or maybe that was just her skewed way of thinking because she'd always been a dumpee instead of a dumper. She'd had no power at all. Yet Lord, how she'd craved it.

Walker reached for her hand, holding himself two inches away, and she realized he was asking permission. He'd stayed to his side of the car, waiting for her. Allowing her all the time she needed.

She laid her hand in his, and she was sure she heard him let out a long breath.

"That was the before," he said. "This is the after. I don't need power. I need you. Be my family, Cleo."

She didn't cry at the drop of a hat. When Phil left, she'd given herself one good hour and cut it off. But Walker made her eyes ache with unshed tears. "Heidi and me, we're a package, you know."

"I wouldn't have it any other way. She's as special as you are."

Oh God, she really was going to cry. "But she and I still have a bunch of problems to work out. Right now, she's not speaking to me."

"Isn't that part of growing up? The times you don't see eye to eye with your parents? It doesn't scare me away." He dropped his voice. "Let me help. Even if it's just to be there to hold you after another fight."

Except for Ma, no one had ever really been there for her. She wanted what Walker offered so badly, badly enough to risk her own heart. But could she risk Heidi's?

"This has to be for the long haul. Please don't come into our lives and walk out six months later. I can't let that happen to Heidi. She's more important than anything, more important than my own feelings."

Walker put his hand to her cheek, stroked his thumb over her skin. "Despite my name, I don't simply walk out. If I thought we couldn't make this work, I wouldn't have given up the life I had."

He was willing to change everything. For her. The momentousness of it terrified her. What if she was the one who couldn't live up to his sacrifice?

We never get over the regrets we have for the road not taken. Ma's words of wisdom.

"Love us, Walker," she whispered, her heart laid open to him.

"I do." He sealed it with a sweet kiss, their lips seeking.

When she could breathe again, she murmured against his mouth, "Now, about that five hundred dollars you paid Jimmy on my behalf."

She felt him smile in the car's dark interior. "I'm sure we can work it out."

"I have it all worked out," she said softly, putting her palm on his jeans.

"How?" It might be dark, but she was sure a sliver of light sparkled in his eyes.

"Well . . ." She stroked his cock, magnificently hard beneath his zipper. "Five hundred divided by fifty equals ten."

"And you said you sucked at math."

"Oh, I suck all right." She unbuckled his belt, broke the silence of the night with the rasp of his zipper, and burrowed a hand beneath the waistband of his briefs to all that hard, hot flesh. "And I'm much better at word problems," she said, smoothing a pearl of pre-come over his crown. "Like how many blow jobs at fifty dollars a pop will it take to pay off a five-hundred-dollar debt?"

"A million," he answered, lapsing into a groan as she palmed him from base to tip, then pulled him free of his jeans.

"Now who's bad at math?" She bent, sipped another bead of pre-come, then ran her tongue around the ridge of his crown. "The answer is ten."

"Fuck," he said on a mere breath of air, weaving his fingers through her hair and lightly pushing her head down. "That'll never be enough."

His come was so sweet, the feel of his flesh in her mouth like satin, his scent masculine and earthy.

"I'm going to have to charge a helluva lot more for the bathroom." Walker pumped his hips slowly, sliding deeper.

Cleo took him all the way to the back of her throat, flexing around him. Her hair was like silk in his fingers, her mouth warm, wet. She withdrew to suction his crown, and his balls tightened with need.

God, he could have this every day for the rest of his life, not just her mouth on him or the heat of her flesh, but the connection. It was there, mind to mind, heart to heart, flowing between them.

"Make me come, Cleo, love."

She took him deep, pumping him between her lips, and for one long moment, he gave her his essence, filling her with everything he was, shuddering for long, ecstatic moments as she soothed him with her mouth. When it was over, he hauled her up in his arms, felt the beat of her heart against his chest.

"Walker?" Her voice vibrated against his ear.

"Hmm?"

"You were right."

"About what?" His words slurred with contentment.

"Paying for sex is powerful."

Something eased in his chest. "And so is being paid for it," he murmured.

"I think I understand now."

God help him, he'd been waiting for that. Acceptance without judgment.

"I wonder what it would be like."

"What?" He was sure she would feel his heartbeat quicken against her breasts.

"To be a courtesan." She raised her gaze to his. "Maybe with you. Someday."

"Maybe someday." God, how he would love pleasuring her with another man, giving her the ultimate, two of everything.

"It's just a fantasy," she whispered.

"We all need our sexy fantasies." But his specialty was making fantasies come true.

She trailed a hand down his cheek. "I love you."

He closed his eyes to savor the words, the moment, as she snuggled closer, burrowing her nose into the crook of his neck.

Even courtesans had fantasies. She had just given him his.

NO SECOND CHANCES

PROLOGUE

Six months ago

HER BREATH CAUGHT HALFWAY INTO HER LUNGS.

Time had wrought changes, but she knew him instantly. At forty-eight, he was more handsome than she could have imagined. His jaw chiseled, his body bigger—six feet of hard muscle—his dark hair heavily salted with a gray that seemed to match the color of his eyes, a shade that had haunted her. The last time she'd seen him, he'd been a mere boy of eighteen compared to the man he'd become.

The memories she'd managed to bury slammed her chest so hard she was surprised she didn't crumple to her knees. Love, hate, joy, anger, ecstasy, pain, wonder, anguish, and fear. All the emotions that she'd thought were long gone, dead and buried. He was the best of her memories and the worst of them. He'd been a part of her hopes, then a piece of her nightmares.

If her muscles had cooperated, she would have run. Instead, she could only watch him cross the room. To her.

"Isabel." His smile was brilliant, devastating, but his silver gaze was guarded. "You've done well for yourself."

For a long time, she'd believed she would have another chance. Now, thirty years later, she knew there were no second chances.

1

ROYCE HARMON LAY IN THE DARK ON THE FRAGILE ANTIQUE SOFA in the front room of Isabel's Pacific Heights flat. It wasn't made for a man's six-foot frame, and if she saw him abusing it like this, Isabel would freak. But at three in the morning, she wasn't home to see him do it.

He'd arrived on a late Friday-evening flight, taken a taxi, let himself in with the key she'd given him. Now he waited. If he'd called ahead, would she have been there to greet him?

Royce stacked his hands beneath his head and stared out the picture window. During the day, one could see the streets sloping down to the water, Alcatraz, the bay dotted with sailboats. Right now, all he could see were stars, the heavens lit from below by the city's nighttime glow. Despite its legendary fog, the San Francisco sky was clear tonight, even in late October.

The three-bedroom flat was worth well into the millions even after the housing crisis. Isabel told him she'd inherited it. She'd never said from whom.

She cut off any discussion regarding the past. She refused any overtures about the future. As for the present, he was sure he wasn't the only man in her life. They'd made no commitment, never declared exclusivity, though he believed he was the only one with a key to her flat. No matter what time he arrived, whether she was home or out, he never found evidence of anyone else having been there, and she always seemed glad to see him.

He'd loved the seventeen-year-old girl she'd been with every last cell in his body. The woman she'd become? He couldn't say. He didn't know her. They fucked, but they weren't intimate. They didn't date. Occasionally they'd dine at restaurants down along the Peninsula or Marin or the East Bay, but never San Francisco. She chose out-of-the-way places and always asked for a table tucked in a dim corner. As if she were afraid of being recognized or seen with him.

All he knew about her was what he observed. She dressed expensively and elegantly. She had a BMW garaged beneath the building, but for the most part she used a limo service to get around town. Her jewels were real. She belonged to an exclusive club where she worked out daily. She never revealed what she did for a living, but when her cell phone rang, she always took the call in another room. She said she'd never married, so whom had she inherited from? And exactly what? Just the flat, or all the money, too?

Her secrets drove him crazy, but she wasn't telling, and if he couldn't live with that, the only alternative was to walk away. Royce couldn't do that. Thirty years ago, he'd made love to her with all his heart. He'd never truly reclaimed it. Bare-bones, their story was a stereotype. Her family was trailer trash, his, community pillars. He'd forced their love into hiding; she'd accused him of being ashamed. Maybe he was, but not of her, never her. Prosperity, Oklahoma, was like any other small town; the gossip was merciless. He'd refused to subject her to it. They'd fought regularly over the issue. One day those fights got the better of them. She'd run away. Two months later, he'd received an apology card from L.A. He couldn't argue with her reasons; everything she said was true. Their worlds were too disparate. Still, though he was about to start university, he'd boarded the first flight west. By the time he arrived in L.A., she'd already moved on. There were no more cards, no letters, no calls. If he'd been older, more savvy, he might have hired a private detective. But he wasn't. Royce was forced to move on, but he'd never forgotten. He'd married, raised a family, divorced, sent his girls off to college, expanded the family business, opened satellite offices, the last one in San Francisco.

Then six months ago, he'd seen her. A benefit at the symphony hall. His life had turned upside down. He still hadn't righted it.

In the quiet of the flat, the front door lock clicked.

Her high heels tip-tapped lightly from hardwood floor to Persian carpet to hardwood again as she strolled to the front window. She didn't turn to see him nor had he left his overnight bag in the hall, but taken it straight to the bedroom.

The starlight bathing her form showcased the slender lines of her body in a skintight costume, Wonder Woman or Supergirl or some other comic-book heroine.

She stretched like a cat kneading its paws, one arm straight up, fingers flexing, then the other, her hips swaying with each move as if she were dancing to music in her head. His cock rose to attention just as it did whenever she was near.

In the dark of the night, even when he was married, he'd jerked off to fantasies of her. He'd had her once, and despite the fumbling of virginity and youth, no other experience had ever compared.

Until he saw her again.

She unzipped the red boots, unsnapped the gold cloth belt shimmering at her waist, and wriggled out of the blue and red star-spangled bodysuit. She wore no bra or panties beneath. No lines to mar the costume.

Gloriously naked but for the golden Wonder Woman wristbands, she stood before the window. High on a San Francisco hill with only the darkness behind her, he doubted any peeper could have seen much, yet she wouldn't have cared. Raising her arms, she tugged off the costume tiara, tossed it carelessly, and pulled her hair from the knot on her head, letting the silky blonde tresses tumble down past her shoulders. She fluffed her hair. She was a sensual creature. She enjoyed touch. Her own, someone else's, even the stroke of the night air.

Royce couldn't stand another moment without touching her, too. As much as he enjoyed watching her, the smoothness of her skin was infinitely better. Rising, padding across the expensive carpet, he trailed a finger down her spine.

"You didn't tell me you were coming." She didn't startle or even turn. She knew the stillness of her house, had probably felt his breath disturbing it.

"I thought I'd surprise you."

"How long have you been waiting?"

Thirty years. "Since midnight."

She didn't apologize. "Ah well, now I'm here."

He bent to the curve of her neck, kissing the creamy skin. Another scent rose, the musk of come, salty male flesh, her own unique scent of arousal.

She'd been with a man. His stomach clenched, yet at the same time his cock surged and his balls filled to aching. He closed his eyes, breathed her in, and, in his mind, saw her stretched wide on a bed, fucking hard, coming hard.

He wanted her now, like this, in front of the window, for anyone to see. For everyone to know she was his.

Wrapping one arm beneath her breasts, he hauled her up against him and tunneled between her legs. "You're wet," he whispered.

"You're hard," she replied.

He rubbed, sliding in the moisture, and a fresh draft of her sweet sexual fragrance rose to his nose. Her scent intoxicated him; her wetness enflamed him. He hated that she'd been with someone else, yet it made him insane with lust.

"Those wristbands make me fucking hot." Bending at the knees, he rubbed his jeans and the bulge of his erection along the crease of her ass. "Put your hands on the table."

The long table beneath the window was thigh-high. Leaning down, she thrust her ass in the air. Royce went to his knees behind her and speared her with his tongue. She moaned. Her taste was sweet yet slightly acrid with the flavor of latex. She'd fucked with a condom, yet her ass cheeks were smeared with the scent of semen. He backed off to lick her flesh and a burst of come shot across his tongue. She hadn't showered it off.

He wanted to ask who, didn't dare to find out, wasn't sure he could bear it, and yet, the smell drove him mad with desire. The man had fucked her, withdrawn, ripped off the condom, and shot his load across her ass. He fucking hated it, yet he couldn't draw away from the taste and aroma of sex all over her. Fingering her clit, he took her with his tongue, drinking her juice, making her tremble.

"Royce, oh God."

Did she cry out her other lover's name with the same breathy lilt?

He licked and sucked, savored and owned, and tried to drive every thought of the other man from her mind.

"Fuck me, Royce, fuck me now." She begged and commanded.

He rose, fished the condom packet from his pocket. With Isabel, he made sure always to be prepared. No condom, no ride, but with a condom, she'd do it anywhere. He relished the risks they'd taken as much as she did. His favorite had been the top deck of the ferry, his long coat wrapped around them both. The risk made it fucking amazing.

She made it amazing now, the silk of her skin, the musk of sex rising off her, her sounds, the stars laid out before them. Rolling on the condom, he plunged deep, burying himself all the way to her womb. She cried out, her body tensing around him, holding him, and for the longest moment, they were silent, still, one being with two heartbeats. Royce covered her with his body. He wished now he'd removed his clothes, but there would be time enough for that later. He would have her more than once tonight, in the morning, all weekend. He had yet to get enough of her before he had to return home.

Reaching behind, she curled her fingers through his hair, pulled lightly. "Fuck me hard, Royce."

They didn't make love; they fucked. It was the only word she used. Yet deep in the core of him, he knew it was more, knew she felt it, too.

So he made love to her, driving deep with long, slow strokes until his mind stopped thinking and there was just sensation; the rasp of his jeans against his thighs, the ache in his balls, the throb rising in his cock, and her pussy contracting around him. He exploded inside her. At the last moment, as her orgasm dragged him into oblivion, he exercised one last vestige of control to pull out, tear off the condom, and spray her ass with his come, erasing the taste and scent of the other man. Now she was his.

Minutes later, he was naked on the Persian carpet with her ass pressed to his groin, her body plastered along his. He'd ditched the clothing in favor of feeling her every inch against him. Ruminating about all the ways he could say what he wanted, he realized there were none that wouldn't piss her off.

"That was a pleasant surprise," she murmured, holding his hand to her breast.

Had she snuggled like this with her other partner, the lazy post-coital moments?

"I need more than this." Oh yeah, that would piss her off.

"Sex doesn't get better than this, Royce."

His heart thumped against her shoulder blades. He knew that. "More time. More things besides sex. A stroll in Golden Gate Park. A cappuccino on Union Square. Shopping at Neiman Marcus. Dinner in Chinatown." *You all to myself, no sharing.*

"You're not here often enough for that. I don't want to waste a minute of time we could be fucking."

And *that* was a fucking excuse. She was avoiding. "We need to make some sort of commitment here."

She stilled in his arms. As he'd known she would. "Don't ruin what we already have, Royce."

"I'm ready for more."

"I'm not."

Fuck. He wasn't ready for an ultimatum, either. He'd already lost thirty years, half a goddamn lifetime. He couldn't see the rest ahead without her.

"Let's go to bed," she said.

It was on the tip of his tongue to ask how many men had slept in her bed. Yet just as he sensed he was the only one with a key to her flat, he believed he was the only one she allowed into her bed. For now he would take what he could get while he plotted how to breach her defenses. "All right."

She spoke before she moved. "I haven't been to the new Academy of Sciences in Golden Gate Park. Maybe you could take me sometime."

His breath left him too quickly, yet he closed his eyes to savor the small gift. There was a flicker of hope.

LYING ON HIS BACK, HE SNORED LIGHTLY. WHEN HE WAS GONE, SHE missed the sound. She missed his scent on the sheets. Sometimes after he left, she didn't let Neala change the linens right away. It was pathetic, but she liked to fall asleep smelling him.

She loved it when he surprised her with a visit. The sex was fantastic, and yes, she realized it was made better by the emotion between them. But her belly was also in knots of tension most of the time, too. Tonight, Royce's timing had sucked.

The prince had called a couple of weeks ago. His son had reached his majority, and it was time for his initiation. She'd long ago versed herself on the customs of the prince's small fiefdom. She didn't quite know why they were all princes and never kings even though they ruled, but that was the way it worked. The sons were virgins until eighteen; then they were initiated by a courtesan, a woman versed in the sexual arts. A courtesan in general, not necessarily one of Isabel's.

Her personal client list had dwindled over the last six months, but the prince was special. It never occurred to her to turn him down, though honestly she couldn't say she'd been dying to fulfill his request. Royce's return had changed things for her. She, however, was the most familiar with all the prince's customs, and he would accept no one else for his son's coming-of-age. There were rituals to be performed; everything had to be just so. The prince was there to make sure. A witness was required, an important part of the ceremony.

Yet she had to laugh. He'd wanted the ceremony "Americanized." Something typically American to start off the festivities. Like baseball and apple pie. Considering the time of year, a Halloween costume ball seemed like a perfect kickoff. Dressed in their ceremonial robes, the prince and his son fit right in.

Isabel curled against Royce's back, steeping herself in the feel of him. She tongued the nape of his neck, licking away the salt of his skin. She savored these moments where she stored his scent, his taste, his feel for the days and weeks when he was gone.

Tonight, she'd done her job to perfection. Both princes were pleased beyond their wildest imaginings.

In their fiefdom, it was considered bad form for a man to enter the marriage bed without first learning how to properly satisfy his wife. In addition to taking his virginity, her job had been to teach the young prince how to pleasure a woman. While it had been physically satisfying, it was nothing compared to the feel of Royce's cock inside her, his tongue on her, his fingers stroking her. Yes, Royce had certainly brought changes to her life. She no longer relished a new date or looked forward to a regular. None of them compared with what she felt when she was with Royce. The emotions added so much to the physical act.

She nuzzled Royce's hair. When he was young, his hair had been thick and dark, the texture of silk. Shot with gray, it was coarser now. His body was thicker, his muscles honed; his cock stayed harder longer. He was like fine wine, better with age.

She didn't think about all the years they'd missed, the things he'd had with another woman, like children. She ached thinking of him with sweet little dark-haired girls. She had only that one regret, but motherhood was never meant to be for her. Except for that one hole in her life, she loved who she was and what she was.

Even as she'd been dreading the day Royce finally asked for more. He wasn't going to let her hide him away for much longer. It was actually rather amusing—or karma—considering how he'd hidden their relationship from his family and the entire town of Prosperity when they were teens. One day soon, though, there would be a reckoning. She'd felt his increasing withdrawal when she refused to commit or even talk about the future.

There was a possibility he might be able to forgive her for the things she'd kept from him all those years ago. She might be able to make him understand why she'd done what she had, why she'd disappeared. But he wasn't going to forgive the secrets she was keeping from him now.

2

THE PHONE RANG, AND ISABEL IGNORED IT, STARING AT THE DOOR through which Walker Randall had just exited. Funny how things popped up at just the right time. Or the wrong time, depending on the perspective. It was too much to be mere coincidence. As if there were some grand design. Walker had found his special lady, and Isabel had Royce.

We're not people for deep relationships.

She'd always liked Walker. He was good to women, truly enjoyed them, admired them. She was sure he had depth in there somewhere, but for the most part he skated through life.

In truth, she was the same. Until Royce returned, she didn't have meaningful relationships with men. She had women friends, close ones. But really, did she go deep with them? For the most part, she listened, acted the sounding board, dispensed advice. She rarely asked for any, revealed very little. No one knew about Prosperity. Or Royce.

Then again, until Royce came back, she hadn't needed advice. Not for years. Not since she'd settled into Courtesans, found she loved it, found *herself*.

Whatever you decide now is what you'll be stuck with. Whether it's the lie or it's the truth.

That was what she'd told Walker. She knew from experience. She was stuck with her lie. Even if she wanted a real relationship—God, did she even know what that was?—the lie was all-encompassing. To maintain it, she had to give up Courtesans. Or tell Royce everything. Walker could probably fake it and be fine. For her, there was no way to avoid being outed. Eventually.

She should listen to her own advice. This wasn't like her. She'd become the frightened seventeen-year-old terrified of discovery. If anyone had found out . . . Of course, thirty years of experience had taught her that discovery was exactly what she'd needed back then. With discovery, her life would have been so different. But would it have been better? It was a rhetorical question that had no bearing. There was only now. She hadn't exactly lied to Royce. How can you be lying when you reveal absolutely nothing? She'd kept his questions at bay, frozen him out, afraid she'd actually have to tell a lie. Once she did, well, hell, where would the lying stop?

"It's going to end badly," she whispered aloud. The words seemed to fill the office, bouncing off the walls, until she wanted to cover her ears. Whether she told him the truth, lied, or continued saying nothing at all, they were living on borrowed time. Just as she had been thirty years ago.

This was not like her. Leaving him the first time had almost killed her, but she wasn't seventeen anymore. She was confident, strong, sure of herself. If she lost him again, well, hell, she'd lived through far worse. She was a survivor. She would survive this.

But oh God, how she'd miss him.

HE'D COME IN ON FRIDAY NIGHT INSTEAD OF MONDAY AS HE NOR-mally would. So he could see her. As it was, the San Francisco office was taking 25 percent of his time versus the normal 10 to 15 percent he usually dedicated to a start-up. Most men would call him pussy whipped. He'd spent the weekend loving her. She'd spent it fucking him.

Something had to give.

Monday afternoon, Royce took the bull by the horns and made a dinner reservation at Chez Louis, a popular restaurant two blocks from the office. When he'd called Isabel, he got her voice mail and left her the time and the place. He was not going to fucking hide in out-of-the-way places anymore.

"Would you care for a cocktail while you wait, sir?" The waiter was tall and thin with a long nose he looked down at Royce.

"Campari and soda and a champagne cocktail for the lady. She'll be here momentarily."

The man bustled away. Being a little before six, many of the tables were empty, the busboy wandering through to light the candles in the center of the white linen. Boasting fine continental cuisine, the ambience was elegant and dimly lit, the cloth napkins gold, the crystal glassware sparkling. Royce had been led to a booth. While intimate with high seat backs, it was not hidden in a back corner.

She was five minutes late. When he saw her, something hummed to life just below his skin. In heels, she was a couple of inches taller than the maitre d' guiding her. Classy yet sexy, she'd covered her red silk tank with a lacy see-through blouse over a midcalf pencil-thin skirt that forced a seductive wiggle into her walk. Heads turned. She outshone women ten years younger. His pulse thrummed along his veins, his physical responses to her immediate and overpowering.

She smiled as she slid into the booth, her lips a deep, seductive crimson like a movie star from the forties. The maitre d' flapped a napkin across her lap. Beneath the blouse and tank, her breasts were pert, mouthwatering.

She was beautiful yet maddeningly unapproachable. "Dinner at Louis's was a lovely idea," she said as if she hadn't been avoiding trendy nightspots for six months. When push came to shove, she'd acquiesced graciously.

The waiter arrived with their drinks, admiring politely without being sleazy as he set her champagne cocktail in front of her. She afforded him the same courteous smile she'd given the maitre d'. Isabel was always appreciative of those who served her.

The thought gave him an inward smile. Yeah, just as she appreciated how *he* served her. Sometimes he wondered if he touched her beyond the physical.

Alone again, she laced her fingers, leaning forward with her elbows on the table. "So, to what do I owe this pleasure? I didn't expect to see you until later tonight."

He usually ended up at her place by eight or eight thirty. He wasn't sure what hours she worked—sometimes she was already home; sometimes she arrived later; then there were times when she called him and said she wouldn't make it to the flat until close to midnight. There were always the questions he never asked. What was she doing? Who was she with? She never offered explanations.

"I was looking forward to some fine food and good conversation," he said.

Her gaze flickered. She recognized he had an agenda despite his innocuous statement. "When do you have to go back?"

He shrugged. "Tomorrow."

The bubbles fizzed in her glass as she sipped the champagne. "I assume you have some sort of . . ." She paused, perhaps searching for the right word. "Ultimatum?" She laid it out as a question.

"No." He didn't like ultimatums. When you made one, usually you were the loser. "But I want more, and you keep turning me down. We need to come to some sort of agreement on that. Or at least discuss it."

She picked up her menu, opened it, and he prepared himself for another avoidance tactic. Instead, she gave him the unexpected. "You're right. We're at a crossroads." She glanced at the waiter watching expectantly from across the room. "Let's order. Then we'll talk."

She gave the menu a cursory once-over, then snapped it shut, mind made up. A sense of foreboding crept along his skin, but he chose, ordered, waited until they were once again alone.

"My life is complicated," she said, meeting his gaze. Isabel had become direct, no mincing words, a prep for the old "things are complicated, we shouldn't get too involved" routine.

His thigh muscles tensed beneath the table. "It's only as complicated as we make it."

She held up her hand. "I'm not done yet."

"Go ahead." He was pissed suddenly. Fuck. He hated being helpless, yet she had the upper hand. She'd had it from the moment he'd seen her six months ago. He'd wanted her badly, like the proverbial hound dog sniffing after the sexy little poodle.

"I've decided you should know exactly what the complications are so you can determine your course of action." She made it sound like a fucking business venture.

"I'm all ears," he said, trying to keep the sarcasm out of his tone. But yeah, he was so goddamned pussy whipped. He could not let go.

She sat back, folded her arms beneath her breasts, tapping one elegantly polished nail against her lace-covered biceps. "I own an exclusive agency catering to the needs of rich, powerful men and women."

Jesus, she made it sound like an escort service, loosely defined, of course. "I understand that your business is important to you. I have no intention of interfering with that."

Isabel leaned forward once more, and, elbows on the table,

she clasped her hands and steepled her forefingers. "Royce, my agency's primary goal is satisfying our clients' fantasies." She waited a full three beats. "Their sexual fantasies."

THE ONLY MOVEMENT WAS THE TICK OF A MUSCLE ALONG ROYCE'S jaw, and the flutter of her heart against her breastbone.

"You mean, like . . ." His brow furrowed, his gaze roving her face, touching her almost intimately. "A whorehouse?"

Anyone else, Isabel would have laughed. With Royce it stung. "Courtesans, not whores," she said softly, but with an edge.

Silence stretched. Her skin itched under his gaze.

Then he shook his head, chuckled. "This is some sort of joke, right?"

She shook her head. She'd never told anyone before, never dated in the traditional sense. People came to her, referrals, clients, potential courtesans. She'd never had to explain.

Yet the explanation had never been this important. God, this was stupid. He wouldn't understand. He'd walk away. It would have been so much better to let him do that *before* he knew the truth about her rather than after.

She toughed it out despite the nervous sweat gathering between her breasts. "My agency is called Courtesans. I inherited it from the woman I worked for. She mentored me."

"The same person you inherited the apartment from?"

"Yes."

He gulped his Campari and soda as if his throat was suddenly parched. "That's a pretty damn lucrative business."

"Yes, it is." Her chest tightened; her eyes hurt. Stupid, stupid, stupid. She should have listened to Walker. The smart thing was not to tell.

"So you're like, what, the madam?"

Why not say it like it was? "Yes, I am. I meet with the clients, supervise the matches to an extent, interview new courtesans, and design our training programs."

He choked on the Campari. "Training programs?" he echoed.

He took something she was proud of and made it sound cheap and cheesy. "Our courtesans undergo a psychological intensive equipping them with all the tools necessary to ensure our clients' fantasy fulfillment."

He leaned forward, lowered his voice. "Don't they just fuck?"

His tone was worse than a physical punch. She'd been right; this could only end badly. But she would *not* let him make her feel ashamed. "No, that's not all we do. If it was, you could get it on any street corner."

"Oh, sorry." He put a hand to his chest. "I'm assuming a flat in Pacific Heights doesn't come off the earnings made on a street corner."

Carrying a large tray, their waiter weaved through the sparsely populated dining room. He slapped open a folding table, set the tray on it, then laid their plates before them with a flourish. "May I get you anything else?" He waved a hand. "Sir, another cocktail?"

Only ice cubes remained in Royce's glass. "No, thanks."

Isabel smiled, said she was fine, while inside, she trembled. She felt like she'd been nicked by a speeding train, everything fine on the outside while her insides were all jumbled around. She'd never get her heart back in the right place.

Royce picked up his knife and fork but didn't cut into his steak. "So tell me—"

She knew it was coming, wanted to close her eyes to hold it off.

"—are you just the madam or are you a courtesan as well?"

Her fingers felt frozen. The duck on her plate looked like a congealed mass. But she'd started the truth, he would get all of it, and she would not be ashamed. "Yes."

He looked at her, his gray eyes dark, hard, like slate.

Her ears started to ring. *Get up, run away.*

"Is that what you were doing on Friday night?"

Her throat hurt. But she did not—*would* not let even a micron of weakness show. "Yes."

His nostrils flared with a deep breath. "Who?"

Now that she'd started it, she would answer all his questions, as painful as that might be. "A prince," she said. "And his son."

3

EVEN AS ROYCE SAT SILENT AND IMMOBILIZED BEFORE HIS DINNER plate, something inside him howled in agony.

Isabel crossed her legs, leaning back against the booth, perfect and polished, as she pulverized his heart to dust.

"You slept with them both?" he repeated because he couldn't believe, couldn't wrap his hands around it.

"Technically, no. The prince only watched." There was a glint in her eye. He could swear she was laughing at him. Or that could simply be his frame of mind.

The questions tumbled through his brain so fast, he wasn't sure which to ask or even if he wanted to know. "Why?" It could have referred to many things.

She laid a hand on the table next to his, but didn't touch. "It might be easier if I told you everything instead of making you ask for details one by one," she said gently as if she were speaking to a mental patient or a plane crash survivor.

Christ, he didn't want details, and nothing would be easy, but at least he wouldn't have to force too many words past his aching throat. "Sure."

She closed her eyes far longer than it took to blink, and for the first time he considered that perhaps this was hard for her, too.

"I've been doing this a long time," she said, stopping for a sip of champagne. Their food was growing cold, but neither of them ate. "I never thought I'd see you again, so it didn't really matter." She puffed out a breath of air. "I didn't tell you in the beginning because I realized you would have a hard time understanding why I do what I do."

He made a noise. It might have been a chuckle, he wasn't sure, yet he managed to keep the sarcasm out of his voice. "That's an understatement."

She gave him a long, hard, penetrating look. His skin heated beneath it, and he was forced to drop his gaze.

"I like it. I don't expect you, a man, to understand, but becoming a courtesan gave me power when I had none. It gave me self-respect when I was at the bottom." Something unfathomable glittered in her eyes, and he wondered how far down the bottom had been. "I don't think about sex the way most people do. It's not immoral or sacred. It's something to be enjoyed." She held him with a level gaze. "I enjoy it even more when I get paid."

Her words were like a sharp stick in his eye.

"Until you came back into my life," she added softly.

He didn't want to think about what that meant. As if he was special and she wanted to give it all up for him. But of course, that was not what she meant, since she'd kept right on doing it while she fucked him. He couldn't breathe; his pulse pounded, his ire rising like a diver racing to the surface only to be hit by the bends.

He stuffed it down, barely, letting a question squeak past his paralyzed throat. "How long?"

"Almost since I left you." She interpreted his meaning correctly.

Aw Christ. He'd known deep in his gut that he'd somehow driven her to it.

"I was young. I couldn't get a job or find a place to stay. I sent you that letter from L.A. Then a friend told me I'd do better in

San Francisco." For the first time, she bent her head. "It wasn't better. I was on the street. I thought I'd die. Sometimes I wished I would die. Then Melora found me."

She said nothing that cast blame on him, but he wondered what her life would have been like if he hadn't kept her a secret, if he'd told his parents that either they accepted her or he was gone. With her. They wouldn't have fought that last time. She wouldn't have run away.

"Melora was my mentor. She saved me from the streets."

He couldn't help himself, the bitterness flowing in his words. "But she turned you into a—"

"I already was a whore, Royce," she said, oddly lacking in the bitterness he would have expected. "She turned me into a courtesan and showed me how I could have a good life, a life I enjoyed. A life I was in control of."

He breathed through the pain, through the confession. "But how can you be in control when you have to do whatever . . ." He couldn't finish.

"I do whatever *I* want. I make up the rules. No one looks down on me. No one disrespects me."

He winced. He'd loved her all those years ago. He'd sworn he didn't look down on her; it was just his parents. The reality was that if he'd truly valued her, he wouldn't have hesitated to take her home. "I drove you to this," he said, almost to himself, hearing the wonder in his voice.

She waved a hand dismissively. "Don't be stupid, Royce. I chose this, and I'm not sorry. I'd choose it again."

But would she have chosen it over him? He studied her, the proud bearing, self-confidence, elegance, and intelligence. She'd left before she graduated high school, but she'd turned herself into an articulate, cultured, competent woman.

"I like the person I've become," she said with no artifice. She truly believed it. "But I realize it's an adjustment for your moral fiber."

"My moral fiber," he echoed. He was ethical in business; he'd never cheated on his wife; he loved his daughters to distraction. Beyond that?

"Most people have a hard time not putting a judgment on what I do and who I am." She sat ramrod straight as if expecting *his* judgment.

"And you think I'm like most people."

She tipped her head. "Aren't you?"

Thirty years ago he hadn't stood up to his parents. Today he was his own man. He would expect either of his daughters to bring home the man she loved, asking for respect, receiving it. As long as the guy wasn't a criminal, a wife beater, or a drug addict.

But what if the guy sold himself for money?

"I am not judgmental," he said finally, acknowledging to himself that he sounded defensive. "I'm simply having trouble wrapping my mind around the concept."

She laughed. Her voice was huskier than he'd known all those years ago, but her laughter was no less musical. "Now, *that* is an understatement." She pushed her plate away untouched. "I'll tell you what. I'm going to leave you so you can think about all this, come to grips with it, and decide what you want to do about it. Sound fair?"

It wasn't fucking fair at all. She'd laid a whammy on him. "What do you expect me to decide?" He spread his hands. "Are you even considering giving it up?"

She gave him that unnervingly steady gaze again, her eyes a deep, enigmatic blue in the intimate restaurant lighting. "Melora left Courtesans to me. It's not just a business; it's a legacy. It's not just men and women who work for me or clients who come to me with needs; it's a relationship with people I care about. It's the life I've built for myself."

So no, she wasn't going to give it up. Fuck. "So you expect what from me?"

"I don't expect anything. You can either accept me as I am and we'll go on as before. Or you can walk away." She leaned forward, dropped her voice to that sweet, seductive pitch that sent him over the edge when he was buried deep inside her, and laid her hand over his for the first time since she'd blown his mind. "There is another choice. You can step fully into my life and let me show you how good it really is."

MAKING THAT OFFER HAD BEEN THE LAST THING ISABEL INTENDED. Yet it seemed the only way to demonstrate that she wasn't ashamed of what she was. She couldn't say how she'd made it through the whole ghastly conversation. She'd thought about laying bills on the table to cover the dinner she didn't eat, then decided against it because somehow it felt like adding insult to injury, as if she were blowing him off with a little money as a tip.

The grandfather clock struck midnight. Melora had shared her love of antique clocks and porcelain with Isabel. Yet Grandfather's chime was a portent of the end. Royce wasn't coming back.

She'd hoped, but hadn't expected.

For a moment she was seventeen again hitching a ride to California, leaving behind the boy she'd loved. She'd hated starting that last fight, but she'd told herself she'd had no choice. Yet something inside was torn and bleeding. If a bad thing had happened to her along the road, she wouldn't have cared all that much. The worst had already happened.

But she was *not* that girl. The person she'd become would have made different choices, stood up for herself. Then again, maybe all roads led to the here and now.

Makeup removed, face and body moisturized, Isabel crawled

between the sheets of the great four-poster bed. She loved the bed. Royce was the only man she'd ever shared it with, the only man she ever would share it with. She didn't bring her work home with her. And there would never be anyone in her life like Royce.

She'd slept with men without being paid by them in particular, but she'd always been paid for the act. She'd sometimes invited friends or other clients, like Simon Foster, who helped fulfill another patron's needs. But she always got paid in the end by someone. Money was power.

The only one who'd ever had her without paying was Royce.

Except . . . but she wouldn't think about that. She was the one who'd paid that price, and she'd wiped the memory from her mind a long time ago. She didn't even dream of it anymore.

She certainly wouldn't dream about it now. Instead she closed her eyes and burrowed into the pillow she'd pulled from the other side of the bed. Royce's pillow, his scent still lingering on it. He smelled like the outdoors, like trees and sunshine. He'd once tried to get her to hike with him. She'd laughed, claiming she'd ruin a nail, or something equally catastrophic. She was a city girl now, getting her workouts in a gym or a pool.

Now she wished she'd gone with him. Or to the Academy of Sciences as she'd suggested. It would have been a memory to keep. She'd stored the scent of his body, the taste of his come, the feel of his lips, but she needed more. Royce with the sun pouring down on his head, turning his hair to silver. The bunch of his calves as he hiked a path, the play of muscles as he climbed a steep trail.

She didn't realize she was crying until a drop of moisture slid from the bridge of her nose to the pillow. She never cried. She wiped away the teardrop. She'd lost him before. She'd survived. She would survive again. She'd still be able to dream of him.

Just as she would tonight. His hands on her, slightly rough with calluses. Yard work, he'd told her. She loved the feel of the hard ridges along her skin. His lips. Soft, moist, teasing her breasts. His tongue laving her nipple, his mouth sucking her inside, teeth biting, a sweet pleasure-pain. In her sleep, she rolled to her back, stretched, gave him greater access. Cool air caressed her as the covers fell away; hot hands stroked her; hair-roughened skin slid along hers until she felt his breath between her legs and opened for him.

"Oh God," she whispered as he teased her clit, brought it to life, made her throb. Shoving her fingers through his thick hair, she held on, arched into him, pushed against his mouth, begged for more.

Real hair, real skin, a real touch, all man. This was no died-and-gone-to-heaven dream. Royce lapped at her, sucked her, licked her, shoved two fingers high and deep inside her. She climaxed, her body gripping him. When she came off the cloud, she crawled down to wrap her arms and legs around him, trapping him against her.

"Was that one last fuck before you go?" she whispered, her whole body aching.

"I haven't fucked you yet," he murmured. "And I'm not leaving."

Her heart slowed to barely a living beat. She waited. The carriage clock ticked. The Westminster tocked.

"I can't accept and go on as we were." His fingers found the pulse at her throat. "But I can't walk away, either."

She squeezed her eyes shut.

"The only alternative is to share."

"I can share," she said, grabbing onto the desperation and holding it.

"You don't understand what I mean by *share*. Here's what I need." He gathered her hair in his hand, pulled her head back.

"We share each other's lives. You share mine, do what I do, see how I live."

Oh God, did he mean meet his daughters? Seeing them would quite literally tear a hole in her belly. Or did he mean go home? She could never go home. Prosperity *wasn't* home. The name was a lie, at least if you were born in a trailer park. Her mom was long dead, and there was nothing in Prosperity but bad memories. She would rather die than go back there.

"Company functions," he went on, "my pastimes, my work associates. See me as I am with them."

Her heart trembled. "And your family?"

"We do families when we know if we can fit into the other areas of our lives."

She held in the sigh of relief, but it was putting off the inevitable. "I can't go back to Prosperity."

"I'm not thinking about that yet." Then he brushed it aside. "We'll live your life, too, the parties or whatever you do, the sex you wanted to show me."

Oh God, how she'd love to show him pleasure, another woman to help her show him the heaven of two mouths devouring him. She wasn't jealous, not in the physical sense. The thought of giving him dual pleasures liquefied her. She was so very different from him.

Her throat dried up. "Are you sure you can do this without hating me later?"

He cupped her cheek. "No."

Her heart bled with the truth. But he hadn't walked away. He'd offered what she'd asked of him.

She couldn't be a coward now.

"I will take the risk with you," she said.

"And I will take the risk with you."

It sounded close to a vow.

4

SHE KNEW EVERYBODY WHO WAS ANYBODY. AT THE SYMPHONY, THE opera, a benefit for breast cancer, another for the fight against domestic violence. Isabel was the event's organizer, and the San Francisco elite were out in force.

Hell, no wonder she'd always sneaked him off to secluded places along the Peninsula. She couldn't move without someone greeting her. Yet no one, not one single person, referred to what she did for a living. Men didn't walk up and say, *Hey, how about a fuck later tonight.* She was treated with the utmost respect. She could have been a society matron instead of a . . . courtesan.

Though Royce did receive glances. The curious wondering who he was to her. He did his share of wondering, too. Had she slept with that distinguished gentleman holding her hand to his chest and laughing down at her? Had she sucked off the handsome kid— okay, he was probably thirty—squeezing her shoulder? Royce could never tell—was it that one, was it this one? It made him nuts, coiled like a snake in his gut.

The calls she used to take behind closed doors, she now performed in front of him. Christ. He hadn't thought much could shock him. But her clients were looking for threesomes, foursomes, men with men, BDSM, sex parties. Sometimes they wanted intricate scenarios played out, role playing, costuming. Hell, sometimes she even did a little psychological counseling.

Are you sure this is what you really want? Think about the emotional consequences.

Let's talk about how that makes you feel.

He never heard her make a date for herself. Yet he didn't have the guts to ask what she did when he was gone. The thought of her fucking someone else made him see through a haze of red. He wasn't ready to share. He knew she'd done multiples, that she wanted a threesome—or foursome—with him. He couldn't conceive of it. Yet.

But nor had he been able to leave her that night. He'd sat in the restaurant drinking boatloads of coffee. As bizarre and outlandish as it was, he'd been hard. As much as it twisted his guts, his breath had quickened imagining her lips wrapped around his cock while another man fucked her. He couldn't reconcile the two separate reactions.

As for introducing her to his life, he'd taken her to the branch Christmas function, brought her to holiday cocktail parties, a New Year's Eve celebration with his branch manager and his wife. He hadn't taken Isabel home, though he was sure his parents would have found her to be elegant and sophisticated. She couldn't be mistaken for Isabel from that dirty little trailer park that used to be on the outskirts of town.

But he hadn't asked her.

The night they'd agreed to try sharing their lives, she'd almost sounded terrified at the thought of returning to Prosperity. He'd used her reaction as an excuse for not asking. He was as terrified of introducing her to his daughters.

He felt trapped. They weren't any closer to a commitment. He wanted her away from San Francisco, from the life and people she knew. All to himself. No calls, no benefits, no men holding her hand ingratiatingly.

Breakfast, before he headed out to work and she went to the gym. The winter sun streamed through the bay window of her dining room, catching the crystal teardrops hanging from an antique cut-glass vase and shooting prisms of color across the lace tablecloth. She drank hot tea from a dainty bone china cup.

It was the start of a new year, time for a new tactic. Royce laid a plane ticket on the table. "I've booked a trip."

She tensed, setting the cup down on its saucer with a too-loud clink. "Oh?"

"This weekend. Palm Springs. Can you do it?" He hadn't wanted to give her much more than a day to think about it and come up with a reason why it wouldn't work. He already knew they had no other engagements scheduled, for once, thank God.

She sighed audibly, relief, he was sure, that he hadn't booked a trip home. "I can make it."

He raised one brow. "You won't bring your cell phone?"

She rolled her eyes. "It'll take a surgical procedure to remove it."

Royce laughed. "Then you better schedule the surgery right away." He felt his own measure of relief. He'd planned for more of a fight. "Do you have hiking boots?"

Her eyes widened as if he'd suggested a hundred-mile walk across the Mojave. "No. I've never hiked."

"Good God, woman, how is that possible with Yosemite and Tahoe, Big Basin and the Pinnacles all within a day's drive of you?" He'd taught his girls his love of the outdoors, many of their family vacations being hiking trips, though his wife had never gone. He'd thought of it as father-daughter bonding time.

"I've never been to Yosemite, and I don't even know where the Pinnacles are."

"Holy *hell*. You've been here thirty *years*."

She shrugged, gave him a saucy grin. "I've never done the touristy stuff."

She'd been fighting to survive. He refused to let the thought dampen his mood. "The Pinnacles are between Hollister and Soledad." About an hour and a half south of San Francisco. He'd checked the nearby state and national parks. Since finding Isabel, he hadn't ventured out to one yet. "I can't believe you've never gone to Yosemite, not even to see the redwoods."

She buttered half a piece of toast. "We've got redwoods right here in Muir Woods."

Which was up in Marin. "I bet you've never been there, either, have you?"

She shook her head, then let a smile grow on her lips. "My education is sorely lacking. You'll have to tutor me."

God, he wanted to. "We'll have to take you shopping and get the appropriate clothing." Tomorrow. Before the evening flight he'd booked. The idea buoyed his spirits. She was willing. He could introduce her to something he loved, like a present he could share.

"Dare I ask where and how far you're going to make me hike?"

"Slot canyons. Only four or five miles." He'd hiked slot canyons in Zion, and he'd done a little research on a place down in Palm Springs called the Painted Canyon.

The main idea had been taking Isabel out of San Francisco, away from her environment, giving her something entirely different.

Eyes wide again, she mouthed, "Four or five *miles*?"

He nodded. She was in shape, worked out daily. "Piece of cake."

"Right," she snorted. "Famous last words. What are slot canyons?"

"You'll see." His mind worked, planning the weekend. He'd booked a suite at one of the resorts, and a swank restaurant for a late dinner.

Elbow on the table, she leaned her chin on her fist. "If I do this hike, you have to do something for me."

His heart thrummed in his chest.

"A spa treatment afterward."

He guffawed. "I've never done a spa treatment in my life."

She raised one brow. "*I've* never hiked."

"Touché. All right, it's a deal."

"And," she added, her lids lowered seductively, "I think you're going to love this spa."

HIKING. SHE WAS INSANE. YET SHE WAS GIDDY WITH EXCITEMENT. She'd never been on a traditional vacation with a man, not even a weekender. When she went away, it was work, and she got paid for her work. This was new and exhilarating. While she was packing, Isabel had worn the boots around the flat to break them in. This was his life, his passion. He'd arranged and planned everything, his excitement at the excursion tangible.

She had always been the planner. It felt so damn good to have someone else do it for her. She'd told her assistant she was to be disturbed only in an emergency, defined as a close friend near death or the Dow Jones sinking below five thousand. Heh, it was a weekend, so at least that one wasn't going to happen.

Of course, she'd made an arrangement of her own. The spa. She would blow Royce away. She'd fantasized about introducing him to some of the slightly kinkier things she liked, but she remembered his words that night. When she'd asked if he was sure he wouldn't hate her later, he'd given her an honest *no*. So she'd hesitated. But the spa, a very special spa she knew of, might be the perfect way to test the waters.

They'd had a lovely evening flight, the resort was posh, and he'd woken her ungodly early to dress and drive out to the canyon. Of course, he'd needed a leisurely shower with a lot of sex first, hence the true reason for the ungodly hour.

"You look totally fuckable in those shorts," Royce said behind her as she stretched.

She loved it when he talked dirty. It had taken months to get him to open up to it. She'd adored shopping with him in the sporting goods store, bending over to tie the laces, trying on a million pairs of shorts for his approval. Making him hot and bothered.

"How are the boots?"

"Fine," she said. "I laced them tightly over the ankle like you said." She'd worn a thick pair of wool socks, too.

The morning was sunny but cool. The drive from Palm Springs had taken more than an hour, and it was now nine o'clock. Royce had assured her that once they got moving, they'd warm up, and by the time they made it through the canyons and up to the ridge, she'd be glad for the shorts rather than long pants.

"How's the pack feel?" He pushed it low on her hips, trailing his hands down over her ass. It was basically a large fanny pack with holders for two water bottles and room inside for sunscreen, a hat, lip balm, sunglasses, TP, a sliced apple, carrot sticks, and something Royce called *gorp*, a mixture of nuts, raisins, sunflower seeds, banana chips, and dried pineapple. If it got hot, she could shove her Windbreaker in there, too.

"Your legs have goose pimples." He crouched beside her, rubbing her calves to warm them.

"If you don't stop that," she warned, "we're never going to make it onto the trail."

"Spoilsport." He grinned up at her from beneath the brim of his hat. He looked so damn masculine in hiking shorts and mongo walking boots, his legs tanned, shoulders wide beneath his blue Windbreaker. She wanted to jump him.

They were still feeling their way through this whole "sharing their lives" thing. When she talked business in front of him, she felt self-conscious, and while they were out, she often likened it to being under his microscope, her every move analyzed, dissected, catalogued. But the sex between them? She couldn't get enough, and this weekend had given her the opening to introduce him to some alternatives for making it even more exciting.

He rose to tower his full six inches over her. Her stomach fluttered. Holding his hand out, he murmured, "Are you ready?"

God, she was ready, despite the fact that they'd spent most of the night rolling around in that big old bed at the resort, not to mention this morning's shower. Isabel was always ready.

"Sure." She laid her palm in his and let him lead.

She hadn't been on a sex date since their new agreement. He hadn't said she shouldn't or couldn't; it just seemed respectful of trying to grow their relationship.

"Much of the canyon is along the San Andreas Fault," he said, matching his longer stride to hers. The sandy canyon floor gave her legs an extra workout.

"It's beautiful." The canyon walls rose before them, the rock different shades of green, red, pink, giving rise to its name, the Painted Canyon. They'd taken a long, dusty dirt road into the park and had stopped the car at the mouth.

A quarter mile in, they came upon an arrow made of stones, pointing straight at a fissure in the canyon wall.

Royce consulted a hiking map. "That's where we go."

"We can't fit in there."

"That's why they're called slot canyons, because they're narrow. We'll fit."

Okay, maybe she'd bitten off more than she could chew, so to speak, but she wasn't going to tell him she had doubts. He led the way, climbing the rocks like stepping-stones. The higher he climbed, the more she realized the slope was not as steep as she'd first thought, and indeed, the rocks widened into a narrow canyon she hadn't discerned from the angle at the bottom.

"You okay?" he asked, glancing back.

"The view is certainly great." His butt in those snug hiking shorts.

"Watch the rocks, not my ass," he scolded, but she recognized the glint in his eye.

The air was fresh, clean, and she'd warmed up, with both the exertion and her dirty thoughts. The rock path, if you could call it that, zigged and zagged, always up, until suddenly Royce disappeared from view.

"Hey, where'd you go?" she called, her pulse racing.

"I'm here." His voice floated down from above.

She made it up the last rock, only to realize that the fissure they'd been climbing through now plunged down. Royce crouched near the head of a wooden ladder. "We have to get down there." He pointed to the bottom of another crevice, wide enough to stand in, but with the canyon walls rising on both sides. "You don't have claustrophobia, do you?"

She snorted. "Great time to ask." She stared down the six-foot ladder to the dusty bottom. "Where does it go?" She couldn't see how they'd get out once they climbed down.

"These mountains are riddled with wide fissures in the rock. There's ladders to the different levels, but eventually the narrow slot canyons lead up and out into the open. Then we hike to the ridge overlooking the Salton Sea."

"Have you been here before?"

"A hiking buddy of mine told me about the trail. It's well marked. We won't get lost." He held out the map, pointing to a dotted line across the topography.

"I'm not sure I'm in good enough shape to do this," she admitted. She was a gym rat. Climbing rocks was a whole different thing.

He stroked her cheek. "You'll do fine. It's not as bad as it looks."

Hah, he said he hadn't hiked this trail, so how did he know? But hell, she was no pussy. "All right."

"I'll go first, then hold the ladder for you." He scrambled down it like a monkey, then positioned the ladder tightly to the rock wall. "Your turn."

With his solid presence, it was easy. She climbed down practically into his arms. He nuzzled her hair. "Now, *that* was a view."

She elbowed him. "No funny business while we're hiking." But she was wet just from the warmth of his breath against her.

They were in the small cavern now, with only one way to go. Winding between the rocks, they turned a corner and found another ladder, this one heading up. A sliver of sky reached down between the rock walls, which were only about three feet apart. What she'd thought was a cavern was actually the bottom of yet another narrow canyon.

"You first. I'll hold the ladder," Royce said.

"You just want to look at my butt."

He put a hand to his chest in mock hurt. "I'm being chivalrous."

He set a booted foot on the bottom step and trailed a hand along her hip, her thigh, her calf, as she climbed. When she glanced back down to see him eyeing her ass, there was indeed a dark, sexy glint in his gaze. She shook her finger, and his wicked smile heated her.

At the top was another short, narrow plateau, another ladder at the end. From that vantage point, the slice of sky at the top was bright, a puffy white cloud floating over. The silence was soothing. She lived with noise, even in the flat, the sound of traffic from the street below, people, the creak of the old apartment building. She lived, breathed, walked city life. This was unique.

"Wow, this is cool," she called down.

"Thought you'd like it."

The air wasn't as cold as she'd have thought it would be without being in full sunlight. For a first hike, she was doing well, too. Granted, they were only half an hour into it, but she set a good pace, trailing her fingers along the rock on either side. The canyon was narrow, and in spots, as the path twisted and turned, she had to sidle through, her pack brushing the wall.

She glanced back. "Awesome." Nature's magic.

He reached out to run a hand down her hair. She'd worn it long, but tied in a ponytail to keep it out of the way.

Then she turned a corner in the rock, and sun streamed down into the narrows. "Oh my God." The light dazzled her, as if the heavens had opened up and God was looking down.

In the streamers of sunlight lay another ladder. She grabbed a rung to steady herself and leaned back to gaze into the sky. The warmth on her, the light palpable, it seemed a moment in time. "Oh Royce," she breathed. She recognized what he must feel on his hiking treks, the immensity of it. "I've never seen anything more beautiful."

"Neither have I." Just inside the circle of light, he stared at her, not the sky or the sun. Then he was on her, backing her up against the ladder, taking her with a deep, breath-stealing kiss.

5

SHE TASTED LIKE SUNLIGHT, HER SKIN WARMING EVEN AS THEY stood in the shaft of morning rays. Moaning, she fisted her hands in his Windbreaker and held him closer. God, he could never have enough of her, her scent fresh and sweet in his nostrils, the faint perfume of her sexual musk rising. He drove his tongue deep, tasted her, devoured her. Her breasts filled his hands, her nipples taut against his palms even through the layers of clothing.

Royce pushed her to the ladder, braced it with his hands as he rubbed his cock hard against her. She grabbed his hair, consumed his mouth with an equal fervor.

He couldn't say what drove him over the edge, watching the sway of her ass, the fall of sunlight on her blonde hair, or the fact that she'd stepped into his world without hesitation. Manicured nails, gym workouts, spa treatments—the city girl she'd become had willingly ventured into his country.

He wanted her here, now, in the bright outdoors. "Fuck me, baby," he murmured against her lips.

She dropped a hand to the hard bulge of his cock, squeezed, then tugged on his zipper. Reaching for the plastic lock of her pack, he unsnapped it, catching the nylon and dropping it gently to the canyon floor.

"Turn around," he demanded, a harsh rasp in his voice. "Hold on to the rung."

He hadn't planned this in particular, but with Isabel, he'd learned to be prepared for whenever and wherever the mood for sex struck her. This time it was all his doing, his need.

"Say you want me to fuck you." He hadn't gotten over the word, hadn't managed to turn it into *making love*. What they did was so much more than a mere fuck, but here, now, it was a primal word fitting the primeval place.

"I'll die if you don't fuck me, Royce. I want to remember it forever."

He covered his cock in the latex, then yanked down her shorts and panties. "Christ, you have a gorgeous ass."

"Touch me, Royce."

She gasped as he slid his hand between her legs and forward to the button of her clit. "Fuck, you're wet, baby."

"I've been wet since we started hiking."

He rubbed his cock between her legs, along her slick pussy, using the natural lube, teasing her at the same time.

"Fuck me, fuck me, fuck me, Royce," she chanted, wriggling her ass, widening her stance.

He plunged home, and she cried out, her voice rising along the canyon walls. The sun between the narrow canyon walls beat on him, blinded him. He drenched himself in her.

"Hard and fast. Please," she begged, pushing back on him, panting.

He held her hips, she clung to the ladder, and he took her all the way, thrusting deep. Her body milked him, contracting, working. No woman had ever felt to him the way she did, smooth, sweet silk wrapped tight around him.

"Work your clit, baby."

He loved watching her masturbate. Even when he wasn't touching her, when she was laid out on the bed for him, legs wide. He loved the sounds she made, the way her body undulated between his touch, her touch. Her fingers slipped over him as he plunged, caressed his balls, then back up to her clit. She had no inhibitions, no limits. He hated and loved it at the same time.

"Royce, oh God, Royce." He heard the rise in her voice, felt the squeeze of her pussy around him, the puff of her breath, all her little signals. She was close, so close.

In the distance, somewhere behind them, a woman's laugh echoed up through the narrows.

"Don't stop," she said, hearing it, too.

Somehow, impossibly, his cock got harder; his heart beat faster. Another voice joined the first, male, the two slightly closer now.

"Don't stop, don't stop," she chanted, caught up in the need.

His breath sawed. A drop of sweat fell into his eye. The sound of the voices and her pussy seemed to become one, and he needed it—fuck, he wanted it. The thought of the strangers coming upon them, seeing, watching. He shouted as her body clamped around him in orgasm, shooting him to climax, to the stars, to the sun so high above them.

THEY WERE DONE UP IN SHORT MINUTES, THE CONDOM STOWED IN a small trash bag, because far be it from Royce to litter the beauty of nature. Isabel's legs still felt wobbly, her heart pounded, her skin was flushed, and the voices were close, only three or four turns behind them, adult voices, thankfully, since she wasn't into giving kids an early education. Breathless and quaking with orgasmic aftermath, she snapped on the pack.

Royce grabbed her chin for a hard kiss. "Fuck, that was hot," he whispered, his gray eyes glittering like sterling. "Now, get your pretty little ass up the ladder."

She laughed. "Don't you want to see them?"

"I like the idea of keeping just ahead of them while they're dying to catch up and see who was making all that noise." He didn't seem to care that he'd shouted for all to hear.

"You're bad." She started climbing. She loved his attitude. Over the months they'd been together, he'd stepped beyond vanilla, taken delight in greater risks.

With this ladder, the narrow canyon walls gave way to open sky and softer, wider slopes covered with desert vegetation. Her body buzzing with all that sexual energy, she reached a fast clip, following the winding path until they hit another stone arrow like the one in the main canyon below. Laughter carried to them again as Royce consulted the map.

"Hurry," she whispered, laughing, "or they'll catch us."

"Both trails head to the ridge. That way"—the way of the arrow—"is longer but appears to be less steep, more switchbacks. This way"—which seemed to be a lot more climbing rocks than mere hiking—"is shorter, but harder."

She put her hand to his cock, squeezed, then grinned as he flexed in her palm. "The harder, the better."

By the end of the hike, Isabel wanted to take that back. Her muscles ached, the bottoms of her feet were tender, she had blisters, and she'd broken three nails scrambling over rocks. But by God, she'd made it. The five miles and the magnificent view of the Salton Sea from the ridge were worth every ache and pain, especially with the way Royce had taken her on the ladder, the voices growing closer, closer. It had been short and sweet, hard and fast, and oh so amazingly sexy.

"So, honey," she said sweetly, taking his arm in hers as they approached the car, "are you ready for your massage?"

She had such a delicious surprise in store for him. After what he'd given her, he deserved it.

* * *

HE'D HAD MASSAGES BEFORE, ESPECIALLY AFTER HE'D WORKED OUT or hiked too hard, or taken a tumble during a soccer game.

This wasn't a massage; it was an event, complete with a tray of fruit and champagne. They were shown to an anteroom, told to undress and pull on the fluffy robes provided.

"His and hers." He raised a brow.

"Don't worry." She laughed. "I've asked for a woman to massage you, not a man."

"Thank God." Though he wasn't a homophobe.

They relaxed in comfortable chairs, enjoyed the fruit and sparkling refreshment. Then she rose. "Come on, you're going to love this."

The room she pulled him into was tiled, with soft music playing, dim lighting, a light floral scent misting through the cubicle. A glass door to the left led to a wooden sauna room for after the massages.

"Take off your robe," she directed.

He hung it on the hook she indicated. Christ, he was already hard.

"Now lay on your stomach." She patted a long massage table. When he was prone on his belly, she laid a warm towel over him, covering his body from the small of his back to the tops of his thighs. He wondered if she was actually going to be his masseuse until she climbed onto the table next to his, stretched out, and draped herself with a towel.

"Now enjoy," she whispered, and pressed a buzzer next to her. "Close your eyes."

She was the queen of setting and seduction. The music lulled him as his muscles relaxed and he succumbed to the champagne he'd imbibed. It had been a good hike, steep climbs that made his muscles scream. Then there'd been her, the memory of her pussy, her lips, her taste, the contraction of her orgasm pushing him, driving him. Christ, it had been so fucking hot.

Hell, at least he was facedown so the masseuse wouldn't notice the state of his cock. It was crazy, but he could swear he smelled the musky scent of Isabel's come beneath the misting. He was vaguely aware of a door opening, then a woman's voice. "Hello, Mr. Harmon. I'm Sheila. I'll be taking care of you today."

Royce made a noise, cleared his throat, and glanced at her. He'd be damned if he'd let a woman touch him without even looking at her. A buxom blonde, Sheila was, laughingly, the epitome of the Swedish masseuse. "There, now," she said in a flat American tone, "doesn't that feel good?"

Well, hell yeah, it did. She had strong fingers, finding every knot in his neck, shoulder blades, and back, working them out.

"And Carlos is seeing to your lady friend's needs."

He cracked an eyelid. Isabel was receiving the same rubdown from a tall, handsome black man. She smiled at Royce.

His masseuse worked her way along each of his arms, a real deep-tissue massage that was almost painful at times, ending with his hand and fingers, then starting over again on the right side.

He had to admit it was luxurious. Isabel certainly knew how to pamper herself. She sighed, and he glanced up. With her arm stretched along the side of her head, her towel had slipped, revealing the plumped periphery of her breast. Moving over her back, curling down her side, Carlos's fingers dipped dangerously close to the luscious flesh. Royce's mouth watered.

Everything Isabel did was sexual, the way she moved, breathed, sighed, especially combined with the exotic feel of Sheila's fingers on him as he observed Isabel's sensual contentment.

The woman started on the soles of his feet. Hell, after five miles, he relished the deep rub. She worked his calves, first one, then the other, loosening places he hadn't realized had tightened up. She worked his thighs the same way.

Next to him, Isabel savored equal treatment.

Sheila's fingers slipped between his legs; a pinkie brushed his balls. He tensed.

And met Isabel's gaze. Her eyes slid over his body to the hands kneading his thigh. Her lips curved.

His thighs done, the woman's hands moved to his ass. Isabel watched as she squeezed each buttock, then dipped down over his cheeks. The towel slid, and a waft of air brushed his backside. Isabel raised a brow at him.

He knew what she wanted. He spread his legs slightly. Isabel's nostrils flared like a filly's as his masseuse's touch slid deeper between his legs, grazing a sensitive spot of flesh before caressing his nuts.

It was as if Isabel were commanding the hands that stroked him. His cock was hard, his balls filled to aching. He wanted her mouth on him, Isabel's. He wasn't a prude, but he'd never cheated on his wife, and the sex he'd had since the divorce had been sedate, comparatively. Until Isabel. She loved variety, in position, location, and he'd enjoyed her inventiveness. Yet he was well aware she held back for him, toned herself down.

Now she was escalating, subtly yes, but leading him nonetheless. As if this moment were a test to see how much he could handle. Before she fed him more.

His blood was hot. The dark fingers pushed Isabel's towel inevitably closer to the roundness of her buttock, revealing more of her creamy skin, inch by inch. Royce's cock twitched. She closed her eyes, knowing he was watching and getting harder and hotter with each new foray across her flesh.

In that moment, there was no jealousy, no time for it. The scented mist in the room, the firm fingers on his thighs, ass, balls, the rosy sexual hue of Isabel's skin as her arousal grew, the moan Carlos elicited from her, oh yeah, it was hot.

Sheila dug into his butt muscle, forcing his cock hard against the table, then slipped down and squeezed his balls. He couldn't control the groan that fell from his lips.

Isabel regarded him with eyes a deep, burning blue.

Royce felt the most extraordinary urge to climb off the table and fuck her senseless as Sheila and Carlos continued to stroke, caress, and massage them both. This was what Isabel wanted, to illicit crazy urges from him.

Facing Royce, Carlos's fingers climbed up her thighs, rubbing higher, higher, then disappearing beneath the edge of the towel, between Isabel's legs. Her eyelids drooped. Royce wondered if the man could feel how wet she was.

Because he knew she was creamy, he knew *her*, could smell her arousal as if he'd touched her and held his hand to his nostrils, steeping himself in her scent.

Christ, he was close to spontaneous combustion.

6

HIS EYES WERE DARK LIKE PEWTER, PENETRATING, HIS MUSCLES rigid with sexual tension. Isabel shivered watching him.

Royce was all male, and Sheila felt it. The masseuse's nipples were tight beads against her white smock. If Royce had rolled over in that moment, Isabel was sure Sheila would have taken his cock in her mouth and sucked him until he arched off the table and came down her throat.

Isabel's breath quickened with the image alone.

This was a special spa. With its expensive appointments, elegant décor, fresh fruit, healthy drink concoctions, expensive champagne, and talented therapists, it was no cheesy massage parlor. But the establishment offered a list of services that weren't posted. If you knew to ask and you had a good reference. Isabel had arranged many a client's stay here.

For today, she'd ordered a sensual his-and-hers massage. A tease. They were to play it by ear, and if Isabel wanted to up the stakes, she'd give them a signal. Sheila was definitely earning her commission. Royce's muscles bunched and flexed with every pass of her fingers. She stroked, rubbed, kneaded until his breath puffed through his nostrils. But he didn't turn over. He simply let his gaze burrow into Isabel.

Carlos squeezed her thigh, dipped down to lightly graze her pussy. She drew in a breath, savored the strokes of both Carlos's hand and Royce's dark eyes. Her insides were liquid. She could have come from the atmosphere alone; Royce's musky scent, Sheila's hard nipples, her own breathy exertions, and Carlos's cock hard along her thigh.

This was heaven. A relaxing massage accompanied by the rise of desire. The canyon fuck had been hot but fast. This was slow and luxurious. She loved watching her man being pleasured. She knew the taste and feel of his skin, the sounds he made, the hardness of his cock, the pulse of his veins when she held him in her mouth. But when she was savoring his body, she couldn't see.

It was so beautiful to watch.

Carlos hit a knot at the base of her spine, and she almost yelped. He worked it until it melted away.

God, she needed cock. Now.

Months ago, even weeks, she'd have turned her head without a second thought to take Carlos's very nice cock between her lips and suck him. That wouldn't do for today.

It was time for the second half of her surprise. "Carlos," she said, "prepare the sauna."

He gave her a handsome smile and opened the glass door, the heat from the room wafting over them. Pouring a carafe of water onto the coils, he sent a tower of steam whooshing into the air, turning the dry sauna into a steam room.

Isabel climbed off the table, towel still wrapped around her, and held her hand out to Royce. He rose, holding his towel tented over his cock, and folded his fingers around hers.

Leading him inside, she closed the door, and the heat and humidity enveloped them, as sensual as a touch. Condensation trickled down the glass. Putting her palm to his chest, she yanked off Royce's towel and tossed it onto the wooden bench behind them.

"Hey." A corner of his mouth lifted in either a smile or shock. "They can see us." He jutted his chin at the massage room outside.

"Yes, they can." She wriggled and let her own towel drop, her bare ass facing the door.

His mouth curved, and that was definitely a smile. "Dirty exhibitionist slut."

She laughed. "I resemble that." There were a lot of words in sexual play that were hot and sexy, not demeaning and degrading. It was all in the context. "Now sit." She backed him up and pushed him down onto the towel she'd thrown on the bench.

Isabel loved being in charge, which wasn't the same as being a dominatrix. Climbing on top, she straddled him, bracing herself with her hands on his shoulders.

"You made me crazy out there," she told him.

He raised one brow with a decidedly devilish cast even as he said most innocently, "Me?"

She leaned in, brushing his ear with her lips. "You squirmed. Even your flesh quivered."

"It did not."

"You wanted to roll over," she whispered, "and let her suck your cock, didn't you?"

He planted both hands on her cheeks and held her away. "I wanted to fuck you." He gave the word a deliciously guttural intonation.

The heat rose between them, their skin glistening, slippery. "You wanted to pull her smock off and suck her nipples."

"I wanted my cock buried in you while you sucked Carlos."

Oh God. This what she needed, the down-and-dirty images, his desire for the same over-the-top, sexy, nasty, filthy things she loved. Grabbing his ears, she pulled him close, clamped her lips on his, and kissed him hard. He opened his mouth, and she twisted against him, thrusting her tongue deep. He groaned, his cock surging. The coarse hair of his chest rubbed her nipples. She backed off long enough to say, "Pinch me."

He cupped her breast, squeezed her nipple hard between his thumb and forefinger. She almost shot off his lap, the sensation was so good, shooting straight down to her clit. She would have taken him right then, one second more of this passion, one moment less of coherent thought.

But there was something more she needed and wanted. More of the tease. More of his initiation into her way of life. Easing off his lap, holding his gaze, she slid to her knees before him.

The sight of him almost overpowered her intentions. "You have the most magnificent cock." He was perfection, her Adonis. He stole her breath. With all the men she'd taken in her life, he reigned supreme.

She gazed up into his beautiful face, her reflection shining in his silver eyes. She closed her fist around his cock, and, with her thumb, rubbed a drop of pre-come over his crown. He glanced up, past her, blinked, drawing in a deep breath, his cock flexing.

She knew without looking that Carlos and Sheila had followed her instructions to the letter, woman nestled back against man, framed in the glass door. Watching.

Any moment, Carlos would raise his hand to Sheila's nipple. Pinch her. Just as Royce had pleasured Isabel.

She was a voyeur and an exhibitionist. She'd done more things than Royce could begin to imagine. She wasn't ashamed of who she was, but neither was she the girl he used to know or the woman he wanted her to be.

But oh God, she could show him so many things.

ISABEL BENT TO HIS COCK, SLIDING HER LIPS DOWN THE LENGTH, engulfing him.

Royce put his hands to her head, holding her to him as she devoured his cock. God, the woman could suck. Her mouth was heaven. He tried not to think of how she'd become so good, the number of men who'd taught her. She knew his sensitive spots, had guessed them right from day one, their first fuck six months ago, the night he'd found her.

In many ways, she was the careful creation of other men. God, he wanted her to be *his* creation, but all he'd done was give her a beginning.

She grazed her teeth along his shaft. A shiver shot through him. He closed his eyes, his body involuntarily arching deeper into her mouth. When he opened his lids again, beyond her, through the glass door streaming with humidity, Carlos undid Sheila's smock. The man's eyes were obscured through the misted glass, but Royce was sure he looked directly at them. Petting the masseuse's trimmed pussy, he dipped, forced a knee between her legs, spread her, then played her with his fingers.

Royce groaned. It was Isabel's lips on him, the way she worked his balls with her pinkie, how she seemed to be touching every part of him. And it was them, Sheila spreading herself, laying her head back on Carlos's shoulder as he thrust his fingers up into her pussy.

Christ, it made his blood sizzle, his skin burn, his mind explode. As Isabel sucked him, his body pumped against her, driving deep. He let his head fall back against the sauna wall, the sweat dripping down his face, his chest, and gave himself up to the sensual sound of her mouth fucking him and the muted images of Carlos strumming Sheila's clit.

Isabel had laughingly called him vanilla, said she wanted to turn him into pistachio crème. He didn't know if he could do it, if he even wanted to, but for this moment, it was so damn fucking hot.

Suddenly, Carlos shoved Sheila up against the door, her palms flat against the glass. Yanking aside the woman's smock, he impaled her from behind. She opened her mouth in a cry, a moan.

Royce felt himself go mad with lust. Isabel was right. Watching was a high. He didn't know if he'd like it about himself later, but right now he didn't fucking care. Hauling her up by her forearms, he put his face to hers. "Fuck me. Do it now. I need it now."

The blue of her eyes as brilliant as a jewel, she reached inside a towel folded on the bench and withdrew a condom. Isabel, so prepared, everything planned, even her seduction.

"Let me do it," she whispered, holding him.

He could barely nod. The act was so expertly done, placing the condom just so, rolling it down his length. Even at such a simple task, her touch was erotic, unbearably exiting, and yet it took too damn long.

"Christ, woman, you make me fucking crazy." Pulling her over him, her body slippery with perspiration, his, hers, theirs, he spread her legs, covered his fingers in her juice. "God, you're wet, so fucking wet. I love that about you." He concentrated on the feel of her, the slickness of her pussy, the scent of her filling his head. "I touch you, and you're wet."

"I'm always ready for you."

As he was always ready for her. He stroked his cock along her cleft. She shivered.

How many men had made her tremble this way? How many men was she always wet and ready for?

"Fuck me, baby," he pleaded, closing his eyes to expunge the questions.

She kissed him then, her lips piquant with the flavor of his precome, salty, slightly sweet. She loved to kiss him after she'd sucked him, sharing the taste, the smell.

Then Royce had no time for thinking, only feeling, as she took him inside, her pussy closing around him, owning him. Her body was meant for loving, muscles deep inside contracting around him.

"God, baby, you're so good, so sweet." She crooned to him, words, sweet nothings.

Behind her, the door slammed in its frame. Carlos was in his element, pounding Sheila, her cries penetrating straight through the glass.

"Look at her," Isabel whispered. "Imagine you're fucking her, holding her breasts. Squeeze them, baby, pinch them."

She put his hands on her breasts as she rode him. "Pinch Sheila's nipples, baby honey."

Her nipples were tight, hard beads beneath his thumb and finger as he pinched until she moaned, writing on his cock. His hands slipped and slid over her breasts, her hips, her belly, her thighs, all that heat, the sweat, the glide of their bodies against each other.

"Ram your cock into her, sweetie. Fuck her from behind for me."

He fucked her, only her, wanted her, only her.

But he couldn't deny the heat burning in him as Carlos shouted his orgasm, the excitement rising as Sheila laid her face against the glass. He felt the woman's cries become a part of him, building the ache in his balls.

Yet it was Isabel who owned him.

"Make her scream for me," Isabel crooned, and the sound of her voice seduced him. Wrapping his arms around her, tight, binding her, he lifted, turned, laid her flat on the bench, and pounded his body against hers, steeping himself in the scent of her sweat, covering himself in it like a lion making his mark.

She arched, threw her head back, and shouted his name. He had no will, no control, and he wasn't sure it was a good thing. Yet her body simply dragged him with her into orgasm.

*   *   *

HE WAS STILL BURIED INSIDE HER, BUT SOMEHOW MANAGED TO turn her in his arms so the bench no longer dug into her flesh. She loved the slip-slide of his sweaty flesh against hers as he breathed. Their hearts beat together. She was wet, warm, cared for.

"Was it fun?" she whispered.

"Yes."

"As good as the slot canyon?"

He laughed softly, just a rumble against her breasts. "Do I have to choose?"

"No. That's the whole point. You can have both."

His answer was to hug her close.

She wasn't sure he believed her yet. She had other ways to prove it to him.

7

ISABEL SNUGGLED AGAINST HIM IN THE BACKSEAT OF THE CAR HE'D ordered to take them from the airport to her flat. She was a woman who loved her little luxuries, and she traveled in style. He'd made sure the limo had a bottle of champagne on ice. Royce had to admit he enjoyed having someone else battle Sunday traffic into the city, especially with a game at Candlestick, the 49ers' home stadium. The sun on the water was brilliant, blinding, gorgeous, but the day was a damn sight chillier than what they'd left behind in Palm Springs.

She rubbed her face against his shoulder like a contented feline. "Thank you for a wonderful trip."

"My pleasure." More than she could know. He stroked her arm. Every experience she gave him was precious, the hike through the canyon a gift.

She leaned forward for a sip of champagne, then toasted him. "And thank you for that exquisite massage at the spa yesterday."

He took the glass from her fingers, swallowed a generous mouthful. "You paid for that one, so I thank you."

Her lips pursed, slightly, almost imperceptibly, but he was aware of every nuance. He hadn't said what she wanted to hear. So he gave it to her. "It was hot."

She smiled, but her gaze was a shade off enthusiastic. She needed him to gush. He couldn't. The nasty little session had been excruciatingly hot, but in the mind-numbing heat of the sauna, condensation dripping down the glass door, blunting the edges of the image Carlos and Sheila made, it has also been fantasylike. Not quite real.

The reality was that he didn't know if he could sit back and watch her suck and fuck another man. He wasn't sure he could hack it even if he were part of the sucking and fucking himself. He'd never thought of himself as a possessive, jealous man, yet even as his dick hardened contemplating it, a hole tore open in his chest.

He never asked if she went on her so-called dates when he was back home or traveling. He didn't want to know.

"Would you like to try a little more of that kind of thing?" she asked finally.

There it was. He'd made his bed. He'd been the one to say they needed to share and explore each other's lives to see if they could make it work. Except that he wouldn't take her home to see his family—she sure as hell didn't want to go, either—and he hated the idea of letting another man touch her. So really, what the fuck were they sharing?

His head ached. Champagne did that to him sometimes. The car jerked and started in the traffic.

Yet he couldn't say no. He couldn't admit he was so far gone that the thought made him equal parts angry and turned on. After all, he'd asked for it. She'd told him who and what she was, what she wanted, and instead of climbing on a plane and getting the hell out when she'd given him the chance, he'd come slinking back like a tomcat, with what he'd told himself was a compromise.

He closed his eyes against the blinding sun on the water and tried to think of yesterday, the therapist's hands on her, stroking her. Royce had been achingly hard. Instead of being repelled, he'd wanted to fuck Isabel. He willed himself back to that moment. Sheila's fingers caressing his balls. The creamy skin of Isabel's breast. The towel slipping lower on the curve of her butt. Her scent. His mouth watered for a taste of her pussy.

"Yes," he whispered. "I want more." Mind over matter. She wanted him. She was with him. He was the only one she allowed in her bed and to whom she gave a key.

He could do this for her.

He only hoped he could handle the reality as much as he'd enjoyed yesterday's fantasy.

ISABEL DIDN'T WASTE A MOMENT SETTING HER PLANS FOR ROYCE IN motion. He would go mad for the things she could do for him. She knew the perfect couple.

"It's high tea," she told Noelle St. James. "You can't have coffee."

Noelle wrinkled her nose. "For a price, one can have anything one wants."

True enough. Being one of Isabel's premiere courtesans, Noelle knew the axiom well. While Isabel had chosen a breakfast tea—who cared if it was afternoon?—the waiter had agreed to bring Noelle strong, black coffee. The Rotunda, with its magnificent glass dome, topped Neiman Marcus overlooking Union Square. Posh with white tablecloths and silver tea service, the Rotunda prided itself on catering to its patrons' needs. Just as Courtesans did.

Noelle leaned forward, her dark eyes sparkling. At forty, she was an exotic creature with silky black hair cascading down her back and almond-shaped eyes that gave her a sultry, seductive gaze. She was slender and fine-boned despite her height of five-nine, and not for anybody did she give up her spiked heels.

They weren't just madam and courtesan. Noelle was one of her closest friends. She'd met Royce several times at various events Isabel had taken him to, and Noelle was the woman best qualified to help Isabel provide what Royce needed.

"So, you need a little pistachio crème." Noelle arched one perfect black brow.

Months ago, they'd had this conversation in reverse. Noelle had been looking for that something extra. Isabel had found it for her in the form of Dax Deacon. The two were now a couple even though Noelle still played courtesan to a select group of clients. Dax liked to watch. They had a perfect meeting of the minds.

Isabel wanted to show Royce the kinky lifestyle could work for them, too.

Or maybe she was trying to justify getting her own way, having her cake and eating it, too, et cetera, et cetera. Whatever.

"I need Royce to see that there are so many more delicious choices beyond vanilla."

Noelle spread her hands, her fingernails crimson. "Of course there are. What do you have in mind?"

The Rotunda was packed with ladies dressed to the nines sipping on Mumm champagne, tea, and savoring cakes and scones. The early-afternoon sun streamed down through the dome, gleaming in the patrons' hair, glittering in the glassware. Amid the buzz of chitchat, Isabel crossed her legs, put an elbow on the table, and leaned in. "You and I."

"You mean he wants a girlie show?" Noelle whispered.

Isabel laughed. "No, silly." She'd tried it, of course, for a hefty price. There wasn't much she hadn't done, but that particular thing wasn't to her taste. "I mean you and I pleasure Royce while Dax watches."

Their waiter chose to arrive at that moment, clearing his throat.

Noelle smiled, sharing a look with Isabel. It was sometimes

exciting to give a nice, discreet shock to a man. This one, tall, dark-haired, midthirties, ears a deep shade of red, had definitely gotten his shock. Yet he said not one untoward word. "Ladies," he murmured, clearing a space for Isabel's teapot, their two glasses of champagne, and Noelle's coffee. "Your treats will be out in a moment."

They smiled their thanks in unison. Isabel made it a point to always give her servers respect. After all, she was in a service business herself.

"Cheers." Noelle clinked flutes with her. "Do you want Dax to do you, too?"

"I know you don't like to share, sweetie."

Shrugging, Noelle flipped her hair over her shoulder. "I trust you; it's fine."

Noelle fully admitted she was jealous. She liked to be shared, but she wasn't so fond of doing the sharing herself. Which worked well for Dax, since his favorite sexual act was watching her. Not that he didn't get his own when they were once again alone. Their relationship was definitely on the outer edges, but Isabel had never seen Noelle so happy. After three failed marriages, she'd despaired of having a lasting, meaningful relationship. She'd become a courtesan instead. Until Isabel set her up with Dax, a match made in heaven if ever there was one.

"Thanks," Isabel said, touched that Noelle would make the gesture. "But let's not push Royce too far the first time."

Noelle put her elbow on the table, chin in hand, and stared off dreamily. "I have the most amazing fantasy."

"What?" Isabel encouraged her.

"I'll tie Dax to a chair and make believe he's forced to watch me do nasty things."

"Ooh," Isabel cooed. "So now you two are into a little dominance and submission."

"Not really." Noelle laughed, a tinkling sound that turned heads. "Can you imagine me dominating Dax?"

He was five years older, a sexy, hunky six foot four. No, she didn't see *anyone* dominating Dax. Unless he wanted it for a very special reason of his own. Or to please Noelle. The man would do anything for her.

Their high tea arrived on a triple-tiered platter. Finger sandwiches, cookies, tarts, petit fours, scones with clotted cream, lemon curd and preserves. "Anything else I can get you, ladies?" The waiter's gaze passed between them, lasting a few seconds too long.

"A tad more coffee," Noelle said. "So when?" she asked after his departure. She slathered cream on the scone and took a bite. "Oh God, to die for."

They watched their weight. Good health was everything. But one thing you learned as a courtesan was how to pamper yourself occasionally. Every woman deserved a treat, whether it was food, a massage, or a very special sexual fantasy fulfilled.

"Royce is in town for the rest of the week." Isabel laid a hand over Noelle's. "Thank you for doing this for me."

"Of course. We're friends. I love you, and I'd do anything for you." Then she winked. "Besides, Royce is"—she dropped her voice a couple of notches—"fucking hot."

Isabel laughed. "Yes, he is." Unlike Noelle, she wasn't jealous in the least, and she was dying to give Royce an evening he'd never forget. An evening that would have him coming back for more again and again.

Noelle picked out a finger sandwich. "Now, tell me everything you want to do."

Isabel revealed a fantasy so deliciously sexy it rivaled any treat on the table.

* * *

"NOELLE ST. JAMES?" ROYCE ECHOED. NOELLE. SHE BELONGED TO Dax Deacon. He'd met them. Several times. He knew their story. Noelle was a courtesan. Dax got off on watching her. And yeah, the woman was exceptionally attractive.

He was buried to the hilt inside Isabel, his balls aching, his thighs quaking as he held her against the wall. He'd hiked her floor-length satin evening dress to her hips and squeezed her delectable ass with shaking fingers.

Holy hell, he was about to explode, she made him so fucking crazy with her slutty dirty talk. Especially when they were inside a dark, empty ballroom with the thousand-dollars-a-plate benefit going on right next door.

"Yeah," she murmured before nipping his earlobe. "You need two mouths on you, Royce. You need to feel how good two tongues can be." She whispered mind-blowing images in his ear as he thrust inside her. "One of us licking your balls, the other sucking you."

While every man had dreamed of it, only Isabel would think of providing it.

"Tell me you want it," she urged.

"Christ." He plunged deep, pulled out, rammed into her again, grunting. "Fuck." He couldn't resist her. She was like no other, offering a man unbelievable fantasies. Yet he held back the one word she needed.

"I want you to have it," she panted as he fucked her hard, harder, his body punching her up against the wall.

All night, she'd touched and teased, whispered and seduced, until he couldn't stand it anymore. He'd had to have her. She'd known right where to take him. Isabel always knew.

"I need to give this to you." She shoved her fingers through her hair, pushed his head back, and kissed him hard.

He felt himself drowning in her, his orgasm building up from his balls, his cock ruling his brain, giving in, releasing in a great snap that slammed them both into the wall.

Every man would want this. Any man could need this. The scent of her intoxicated him; the feel of her claimed him. She was perfection, offering him the world. She made him want things he'd never thought he needed.

All he had to do was say yes to her.

"Fuck, yes, please." He couldn't have stopped himself if his very life depended on it. Yet he prayed she wouldn't ask him to let her do Dax Deacon after she'd given him to Noelle.

8

THEY STARTED WITH CHAMPAGNE COCKTAILS AND OYSTERS ROCKE-feller, then moved to the elegantly set dining table for Caesar salad, French onion soup, and a main course of Abalone Almondine.

For dessert, the women would feast on Royce.

Despite the innocuous chitchat and laughter, Royce understood that very well. His heart rate was up with anticipation and trepidation. It was a deadly combination, the push-me-pull-me of fear and desire, the one forcing the other higher.

He laid his napkin by his plate. "That was perfection. You're a marvelous cook."

Noelle laughed, a smoky, sultry sound like a Diana Krall melody. "You're so sweet, but Dax"—she petted the man's hand—"he hires the most marvelous caterer when we entertain."

Of course. "Then my compliments to the chef, whoever he or she may be." He lifted his glass of Far Niente chardonnay, a lush wine with an extraordinary spicy oak aroma. Expensive, of course.

Royce had been raised in a well-to-do family, but nothing like this. They'd entered Dax's estate through an electric gate along a drive bordered with bushes that would be magnificent with blooms in the spring. A vaguely Frank Lloyd Wright style with floor-to-ceiling windows in living and dining room, the house overlooked the churning ocean just outside the Golden Gate. A dark and stormy night—like the proverbial Gothic novel—the waves crashed at the base of the cliff. On a summer day, you'd see the sailboats covering every square inch of white-crested ocean. Although, come to think of it, he wasn't sure many ventured beyond the bridge, preferring to sail the bay waters instead. Now, a midwinter night, there was only darkness, the storm obscuring the lights, if any, along the opposite shore. He could see nothing, and no one was out there to see them.

Noelle laid her fingertips on the table and rose. With three-inch heels, she was a magnificent Amazon, sleek black hair, creamy skin, dark, mysterious eyes.

It was no wonder Dax could barely look anywhere else but at her. He'd added his two cents to the conversation, but for the most part, the man observed. Six-four at least, Dax Deacon was more than a match for Noelle in height, but he was as blond as she was dark. Despite the civilized tuxedo, he watched her like a Viking warrior with his eye on the war prize.

Royce wondered how Dax could share. It didn't fit the intense gaze. Yet Isabel claimed he got off on watching Noelle. No matter what she did or whom she did it with, Noelle St. James somehow involved him, calling him, having her date call him; sometimes Dax even went along to observe.

It was a freaking odd relationship. Yet somehow it seemed to work for them. Besides, who was Royce to judge? He was dating the madam.

"I think we should get a little more comfortable, don't you, Isabel?" Noelle winked at Dax. The only answer was a slight twitch along his jaw.

Wearing a flowing skirt and camisole of some gauzy tie-dyed material, Noelle slid her blue and lime green scarf from her throat. The bright plumage did her coloring justice.

Yet to Royce's mind, Isabel eclipsed her in simple black velvet and pearls.

"Yes, quite," Isabel said, rising from the table, trailing her fingers along the collar of Royce's white dress shirt as she headed to the living room, wineglass in hand. "You look so starched in that suit jacket and tie, Royce. Maybe you should take it off." Two steps down, she wandered across the thick carpeting, walking right out of her high-heeled shoes.

He could feel his breath, his heart, his blood in his veins, his mind cataloguing every nuance of the rise in his desire. Their scents combined in an intoxicating blend of sweet, fruity, musky, aroused.

He followed her as if she were a siren, the choice gone as he left his jacket tossed over his chair, his tie loosened.

"Oh, you can do better than that," she whispered, fingering his shirt buttons. She slid one after another after another with long, coral-colored nails. She pulled his tie, tossed it on the dining room steps, then trailed a finger down the center of his chest, finally laying her palm against his heart.

Royce swallowed, the tempo of his pulse giving away his emotions.

She smiled, went up on tiptoes, whispered against his ear. "I'll make this so good for you, baby."

She would. He had no doubt. Physically, she would give him a night like no other he'd ever had. But what about the morning?

It wasn't a typical guy thought. But then, Isabel was no typical woman.

"So, what should we do with old Dax here?" Noelle mused.

Royce turned slightly, bringing Isabel flush to his side, his hand on her nape at the base of her hair knot.

Up the two steps, onstage, Noelle circled the table, trailing her green and blue scarf along the cream carpet. She stopped beside

Dax's chair, legs spread, high heels planted. His back to them, he tipped his head to gaze up at her.

"Stand up," she ordered in little more than a whisper.

He rose. The air crackled between them. Royce felt like a voyeur, the sensation incredibly hot. Beneath his touch, Isabel stirred, drew in a breath. She felt it, too. Like standing on the precipice outside the living room window, the ocean beating and churning below.

Noelle closed the gap between them, her breasts brushing Dax's tuxedo jacket. "Turn the seat around to face the living room."

Dax flipped his chair's position without taking his gaze off her.

"Sit down, hands hanging at your sides."

The tall man did as ordered. Even several feet away, Royce could discern the blazing heat in his blue eyes. The tuxedo jacket didn't manage to hide the bulge in his pants.

She straddled him, her multicolored skirt draping his legs, and Royce felt the special communion between them.

"You want this," he thought he heard her say.

"Fuck yes," Dax murmured.

Royce felt an answering flicker in his cock. Fuck yes, he wanted it, too, despite what came in the morning. He laid his arm across Isabel's shoulders, tightened the grip, hauling her as close as he could get her. She shivered against his side.

This was what she'd always wanted for him.

Noelle slipped the end of her scarf through the slats of the chair, then around Dax's wrist. Tying it off, she wrapped the length over his chest and secured his other hand.

"You can't move."

He shook his head, his lips curved. Royce was sure he could wriggle out of the knots, but he wouldn't try.

Cupping his cheeks, Noelle kissed him long, deep, then finally backed off to survey her handiwork. "He looks so pretty in blue and green, doesn't he, Isabel?" She tossed her long hair over her shoulder.

"Delicious," Isabel murmured, but when he gazed down at her, Royce found her eyes on him, the blue as blazingly hot as Dax's.

Noelle turned her back on Dax, skipping down the two steps. "So what are we going to do to your honey? Make him perform a sexy striptease for us?" Her eyes sparkled like stars in a clear night sky.

He'd have thought they would choreograph the whole event ahead of time, but Isabel shook her head. "We'll strip him down together."

Clinging to his side, she followed the arrow of hair with her finger down to his navel. Goose bumps trailed his skin in her wake. "Help me," she urged Noelle.

Wrapping her hand around his biceps, Noelle did the same, her touch slightly cooler than Isabel's. Together they traced the line of his belt.

There was a certain symmetry to their movements, one on either side of him. He felt a moment's discomfort facing a man tied to a chair as they peeled off his shirt like gift wrap.

But Dax's gaze was for his lady, focused, intent, like an arc of electricity straight to her. Yet, deep in the game now, Noelle ignored him.

It was the weirdest goddamn thing.

Then Isabel was unbuckling his belt, and his focus fell from the abstract to the down-and-dirty.

"You're already hard." Her pinkie grazed his crown through his slacks.

"Fuck yes," he echoed Dax.

She laughed, her breath caressing his ear, and his cock throbbed at the sound. "Unzip him," she told Noelle.

"My pleasure." Her voice bore a huskier note than before.

The zipper slid down, teasing his flesh. He'd gone commando. Somehow it had seemed expected.

"Ooh." Noelle let out a sigh. "He's magnificent." She glanced at Dax, her eyes crinkling. "But don't worry, sweetie, you are, too."

Isabel was the first to touch him, stroking down into the placket of his pants. She nuzzled his ear. "He's so hard. I can feel blood pumping through his cock."

"Let me feel." Noelle laid her hand on him, too.

He stiffened. Not his cock, but his body, as if he were suddenly wired with tension. Their hands were both soft, well cared for, silky, Isabel's a tad warmer, as if her blood burned slightly hotter.

"Oh my," Noelle said, squeezing his balls, pressing her full length against him.

His heart raced. It wasn't necessarily all good.

"Shoes," Isabel said, once again nuzzling his ear, her warmth permeating him.

In tandem, they crouched, untying his shoelaces, lifting one foot, then the other, to remove shoes and socks, their two heads bent to the task, light and dark, both sexy, but . . .

He couldn't say whether it was a movement or a sound, but he glanced up to find Dax's concentration on him now. There was something in his regard. An empathy perhaps. *Relax. Enjoy. Take it for what it's worth.*

Isabel tugged on his pant leg, pulling his suit pants off his hips. He touched her hair, knotted in her usual elegance.

Relax. Enjoy.

In that moment, he let it all go, pulling on her hair, setting it free to tumble over her shoulders, and with it, he let his inhibitions fall away, too. For now. Until the morning.

"Suck me, baby," he whispered just for her. "Do it together."

Something shone bright in her gaze, and he knew he'd given her what she needed.

* * *

GOD, HE WAS SO DELICIOUSLY SEXY. DAX WAS HOT, SURE, BUT ROYCE was over-the-top. Isabel couldn't get enough of him. No man had held her interest this long unless he was paying her.

"Come to Mama," she crooned to his cock as Noelle pulled on his other pant leg and his slacks slid down his thighs. He bobbed close to her lips. Her mouth watered. But she didn't suck him in, teasing herself a little longer.

Then they had him out of his pants, clothes strewn everywhere, and God, he was magnificent, just as Noelle said. His cock was long, thick. A vein pulsed, and a tiny drop of pre-come beaded on the tip. He'd trimmed his pubic hair and shaved his balls smooth.

God, how she loved a man's smooth balls in her mouth.

"Now, that is a pretty picture." Noelle sat back, legs beneath her, hands on her thighs. Dax was tied to the chair decked out in full tuxedo, and Noelle had removed nothing but her scarf. Settling back on her calves next to Noelle, Isabel herself hadn't even taken off her dress. Yet she'd forced Royce to stand there before them in all his glory.

God, she was proud of him, wanted to show him off, wanted *him* to recognize how others saw him.

You're beautiful just the way you are, baby.

Why now, she couldn't say, yet his long-ago words echoed in her head.

But my folks just aren't going to understand.

Was that a piece of why she'd done this? To force him into her world the way he'd never let her into his? No. That last fight had a purpose all its own that had nothing to do with Royce and everything to do with her need to get out of Prosperity.

So this? This was a gift, not payback.

"You are so beautiful," she whispered with all the reverence she felt, gazing up at him with her heart in her eyes, hoping he could see. "Touch him, Noelle. Wrap your fingers around his cock."

Her cheeks burned as Noelle slowly reached out. Her body heated from the outside in.

Royce's eyes shimmered like quicksilver. Then his lids closed, and he tipped his head back, exhaling sharply as Noelle curled her fingers around his shaft and stroked his balls with her thumb.

Noelle was good. Men burned for her. And she loved sex. She was a courtesan by choice, not necessity. She wasn't capable of monogamy, yet she had dreamed of love. Then Isabel had found Dax for her. The perfect man for a promiscuous woman.

Together she and Noelle would make Royce feel better than any one woman alone could, even Isabel herself.

She rose. Her heart drumrolled beneath her breast. Shoving her fingers through his hair, she pulled him down, mouth to mouth, eye to eye.

"Suck him, Noelle."

His eyes smoldered like hot coals. Then she kissed him, claimed him, even as she gave him to another woman.

9

SHE CONSUMED HIM WITH HER KISS, TASTING, DRINKING HIM, THEN pouring herself into him. Royce couldn't find air to breathe, but he wrapped one arm around her, anchoring her to him.

Christ, the feeling. The hot sweetness of her kiss. Her lips beneath his, her tongue driving him mad.

And the silky warm depths of another mouth on his cock. Jesus. Never in his life. Not like this.

Noelle licked his slit. His cock pulsed, feeding her a drop of pre-come. In so many ways, it was betrayal, and yet . . . so fucking hot his hips simply surged, pushing deeper into her mouth.

He groaned into Isabel's kiss. She backed off, whispering against his lips. "It's so good, baby, isn't it?"

He blinked, swallowed, beyond words, almost beyond thought.

She stepped back, leaving him bereft without her touch. But Christ, the woman on her knees pulled at his cock, sucking him deep, taking him, the sensations beyond a mere blow job. Because of Isabel's gaze on him, her words pushing him.

"That's so hot, baby," she crooned, "so sweet, so good."

His legs trembled. Spots swam before his eyes. He'd never risen to climax so fast, only managing to tamp down the explosion with his last micron of willpower.

Isabel reached behind, slowly pulling her zipper. Then she wriggled, letting the sleeves fall down her arms, and pushed the fabric over her hips until it pooled at her feet. No panties, no bra, just smooth, creamy flesh, dusky nipples, and barely there bush. She kicked the dress aside to stand before him in a choker of pearls, garter belt, and black stockings.

His heart stopped.

"Don't let him come yet, Noelle, you naughty girl."

The sultry, dark-haired minx slid back. The pressure in his balls and behind his eyelids eased. He could breathe again.

Her mouth shiny, lipstick undisturbed, Noelle tipped her head over her shoulder. "He tastes good, sweetie."

Dax made a noise, a grunt—who the hell could be sure?

Royce had damn near forgotten he was there. He wasn't particularly modest. He'd shared a number of locker rooms. This was different, close to terrifying, yet hotter than a desert sun.

His breath sawed in his throat.

Noelle set her sultry gaze on Isabel. "Let's suck him together."

"Yes." Isabel smiled, trailed a finger over his cheek, down his arm, grabbed his hand.

Christ if her touch didn't make him shiver all over. He followed her as if she were the Pied Piper. Or he was a lamb to the slaughter. Hard to tell with these two.

A fireplace on one end, the bank of windows adjacent, he had the sense the living room furniture had been rearranged for just this show. Coffee table absent, the sofa, love seat, and chairs formed a U facing Dax, the back of the U being the long couch. Isabel planted a palm on his chest and shoved him down onto the soft, expensive leather.

Hell, he wasn't all milquetoast. Snagging her with an arm around her waist, he pulled her down, tweaking her nipple between his thumb and finger.

"Two can play," he said, pinching her hard the way she liked. Her moan strummed his cock. The silk of her stocking caressed his thigh as she arched into him, offering her breast. He licked her, sucked, bit lightly. The musky scent of her desire filled his head. Then she opened her eyes, gazed down at him. "We're going to suck you so well, you won't even remember your own name."

He had no doubt they could do it. He smoothed a hand down to squeeze her ass cheek. "Then I'm going to fuck the hell out of you until you scream."

She dropped a kiss on his lips. "Oh yeah." She slid off his lap down to the floor beside him. Capturing his gaze, she slipped the pad of her finger around his cockhead, coating herself with pre-come, then lifted her hand to her mouth and rubbed him all over her lips.

At the tender of age of eighteen, thinking he was a man of the world, he could never have imagined the things she would do to him, the places she'd take him to, the emotions she would make him feel.

"Hold him for me, Noelle."

As if they'd done this a thousand times, Noelle dropped to the carpet by his other knee. Careful to keep the view clear for her bound man, she closed her fingers around Royce's cock and ceremonially offered him to Isabel.

God, her mouth. Warm. Wet. Her tongue all over him, sucking his crown, licking his slit. Then she pumped him between her lips. Fingers massaged his shaved balls, then lips caressed him, sucked his sac into yet another warm, wet, willing mouth.

"Oh fuck." Head falling back to the sofa, his cock surged. He fisted his hand in Isabel's hair. "That's so fucking good."

She murmured something, vibrating against his cock. She was right, so fucking right about how good it could be.

Then they were licking him together, two tongues on his shaft, caressing his crown, touching each other in a brief sexy kiss, and back down again. Fingers, mouths, hands, tongues, all over him. They pinched his nipples in tandem, shooting electricity to the tip of his cock.

"Fuck, fuck, fuck," he whispered without an ounce of control, just starbursts behind his lids.

Isabel slid back to the tip of his shaft, breathing warm air on his crown. "Don't come yet, baby," she murmured to his cock.

His legs began to quiver, his mind screaming. *Hold off, hold off.*

Noelle blew her lips against his balls, the vibrations shooting straight to the slit of his dick. Nothing else seemed to exist but his cock, balls, and their mouths pleasuring him to death.

He opened his eyes, had to or he'd explode. But holy hell, the sight of them, dark versus light, down on their knees, moist lips all over him . . .

"Noelle." Dax broke the spell. "Fuck him for me. Now." He might have been bound, but he was the master.

"Oh yeah, baby, fuck her for me." The final seduction was Isabel's lips against his, her words filling his mouth. "I need to see what it's like, how beautiful your cock is entering her. The expression on her face. Because that's how I must look. Let me share it, baby."

At that moment, Royce didn't care who fucked him as long as a warm pussy engulfed his cock. This was where Isabel wanted him, so caught up in the action he was willing to do anything, needed it, past the point of being about something *she* chose for him. He wanted it for himself.

She pushed his shoulder, helping him to lie flat on the wide sofa. Noelle grabbed a condom from a small bowl at the foot of the couch. Together they knelt by his side, Isabel's warm fingers on his cock as Noelle rolled on the condom. Another ritual. Then she stood above them, lifted her camisole over her head, black hair floating down to cover a gorgeous pair of breasts, and stepped out of her skirt.

Dax groaned. She was worthy of the guttural sound, a slice of perfection. Isabel, however, was the whole pie. She sucked his cock, lubricating the condom, then held him aloft as Noelle laid one knee by his side along the sofa and straddled him.

Her pussy glistened. She was wet and ready, lowering herself until his head breached her, Isabel's coral-tipped thumb almost touching her clit as she held his cock. Her grip was tight, Noelle's pussy hot and slippery on his crown.

Isabel breathed deep, then parted her lips, letting out a sigh of satisfaction. "God, that is so beautiful. Look how much she loves it."

Isabel's fingers on him were like a cock ring, keeping his orgasm at bay despite how powerful the sensations were. He didn't gaze at Noelle. It was Isabel's face he needed. As she'd sucked his cock, rubbed her face all over him, she'd removed all vestiges of makeup from her cheeks. Yet she shone. The dark smudge of mascara beneath her eyes transformed her into Cleopatra, a queen. He was hers to command.

He raised his hips, penetrating deeper into Noelle's plump, aroused pussy.

"Oh God, yes." She closed her eyes, tipped her head back, and began to ride slowly. "Oh Dax, can you see it? Watch him fuck me."

"It's goddamn beautiful," Dax answered, his voice deeper, huskier.

Isabel pushed her hand through Royce's hair, then leaned over to claim his mouth. Noelle had his cock, but Isabel owned him. He drowned in her kiss, in the feel of her mouth on him, her lips, her tongue, even as his cock was enveloped in another woman's body. Their touch was everywhere, inside and out.

"Lick me, baby," she whispered against his mouth.

God, yes. He was beyond saying the words, his body pulsing, throbbing, driving into Noelle without conscious effort, just a machine for their use.

Until Isabel climbed over his face, cupped a hand beneath his head, held him to her, and her flavor burst against his lips. Luscious, fragrant with arousal, he tongued her hot, sweet cunt, licked the hard bud of her clit, buried his face in her. So wet, covering him, soaking him in her juice. She moaned and rode his mouth as Noelle rode his cock. He cupped her ass, held her to him, licking, sucking, penetrating, driving her as high and out of control as she did him.

Crying out, Isabel pinched her own nipples, head falling back, hair brushing her shoulders. Noelle gripped her waist from behind, and together they gave Royce the best of both worlds.

ISABEL'S HEART GALLOPED IN HER CHEST. SO MANY TIMES, SO MANY men, all the things she'd done, but nothing had ever been like this. Because no man had ever been Royce. She'd tried to fantasize, imagine him when she'd closed her eyes. His hair was soft yet coarse against her thighs, the dark locks versus the gray strands. His lips were mobile, warm, his tongue diving deep inside her. She was on sensory overload, Noelle's breath on her shoulders, her back, sensual, their bodies brushing, rubbing, stroking. And Royce's mouth pushing her closer to mindlessness. There was only sensation without thought, heat building, then punching down to her clit, shooting out, and she doubled over him, squeezed her lids shut, her body wracked with contractions.

She opened her eyes. "Oh God," slipped out on a mere breath. His face buried between her legs, so beautiful, eyes shining with a silver light that pierced her.

Even as his cock lay buried in Noelle's pussy, she was the only woman in the world for him. Somehow he still made it all about her.

"He so loves this," Noelle whispered from afar as Isabel drifted down from the heavens, Royce's lips still playing her, his gaze still holding her.

There was only one *he* who elicited that breathy quality in Noelle's voice. Her body rolling lightly to the rhythm of Royce's tongue, Isabel tilted her head. Dax's handsome face was carved in stark lines, his nostrils flared, his eyes the dark of the stormy ocean outside.

Who Noelle had sex with didn't matter; there was a bond that stretched between them, connected them, made them a part of each other.

God, it was so what she needed with Royce, what she'd needed to give him with this night.

Noelle kissed her nape, her voice dipping low. "I need my baby."

"Take him," Isabel murmured in kind.

Rising, Noelle slipped off, padding across the carpet. Isabel slid down Royce's body until her breasts grazed his nipples. He sucked in a breath.

"My turn," she whispered, stroking his jaw with her finger. She licked his lips, tasting herself.

"Fuck me." He pushed the hair back from her face. "I need you." The words, his voice, the husky note, God, how he touched her deep inside.

"I need you, too." Reaching between his legs, she rolled off the used condom. For the briefest moment, she thought of taking him bareback. How sweet, how perfect, flesh to flesh. It had been so long she had no idea what it felt like. But she'd been with too many; condoms, yes, she couldn't risk him.

She left him long enough to set aside the old—Noelle had thought of everything—and grab another from the bowl.

On the stairs, Noelle knelt in supplication before Dax, unzipping him, worshipping his cock. His heavy groan filled the room.

Isabel laid the condom on the tip of Royce's cock. "Thank you."

"For what?" He stroked a hand through her hair.

"This." For feeding her needs. She bent her head to him, using her lips down his shaft to roll on the condom. His skin bore the scent of Noelle's lotion and the musk of her juice, and despite the condom, a slight feminine flavor much like her own lingered on him.

She raised her head. "For entering my world." Crawling up his body, she pressed her mound to his cock, rubbed her breasts against the hair-roughened skin of his chest, caressed his lip with her thumb. "For coming back."

For a moment, she thought his breath had stopped. Then he exhaled, bathing her lips in warmth, and, in one smooth motion, rolled her beneath him.

"Don't thank me." Elbows braced beside her, he cupped her cheek, kissed her gently even as he opened her legs with a knee between them and unerringly slid home, quick, hard, deep.

She cried out. There was always that moment of pleasure and pain, when her body stretched, accommodated, accepted, filled. With Royce it was the moment she felt complete, a metaphor for the things he'd done for her, accepting the woman she'd become.

"Okay?" he whispered, holding still except for the beat of his cock inside her as if it were her own pulse.

"Okay." Oh God. So much more than okay. She raised her legs

to his waist, wrapped her arms around his shoulders, tugged his face to her neck. "Fuck me. Please."

He moved inside her, and it was elemental. A communion beyond anything they'd shared before.

As the sounds of Noelle taking Dax to heaven echoed in the room, Isabel held in her ecstasy. No moans, no cries.

Instead she put her lips to Royce's and whispered, "I love you."

10

I LOVE YOU.

He wasn't sure Isabel knew she'd never said those words to him before. At least not in thirty years.

Even after almost twenty-four hours, he could still hear her voice. It held the power to steal his breath at the oddest moments, on a conference call with a Portland customer, in an afternoon meeting before he packed up his laptop for the Friday night flight out.

Royce lifted her fingers to his lips. "You didn't have to walk me in."

"I wanted to."

Yet she had never done so before, and now she had the driver out there circling the airport like a buzzard, waiting as she said her good-byes at the security line.

The terminal was Friday evening madness, business travelers trying to make it home in time for the weekend with the family. Noise, people bumping into them; someone had run over his foot with a suitcase. Since the girls were away at college, he'd often stayed the weekend with Isabel, but Julie, his eldest, had a recital Saturday night. Though he and Isabel had things to discuss after last night with Noelle and Dax, he hadn't considered missing his daughter's concert.

"I've got to fly to Cincinnati on Monday, so I won't make it back until next weekend." Which freaking pissed him off because he didn't want to rehash last night over the phone. It required a sit-down.

"I'll miss you." She clung to his arm. Wearing a blue power suit, her eyes were dark as sapphires.

"I'm gonna miss you, too." He couldn't resist tunneling his hand beneath her hair. She'd worn it down. For him, he thought, though she hadn't said that. He pulled her up to meet his lips, the kiss sweet, gentle, yet powerful enough to make his heart skip several beats. Christ, she did things to him even with a simple kiss.

Things were different after last night. *She* was different. Softer somehow. Her gaze touched him with a wealth of meaning, as if what they'd done had taken their relationship to a new level. A higher level for her.

Royce wished he could believe the same thing.

She traced her thumb along the five-o'clock shadow on his chin. "Call me when you get there." *So I know you're safe.* Her final words might have been unsaid, but he heard them just the same.

Yeah, things were different. His orgasm had been cataclysmic, and as he'd come down off the high with her in his arms, he'd forgotten they weren't alone. His mind erased that he'd fucked another woman before Isabel took him. Even now, he wasn't sure whether the climax had been so mind-blowing because of all the things she and Noelle had done to him. Or because of her words.

I love you.

He hadn't said them back.

She wiped a smudge of her lipstick from his mouth, though oddly, her lips were still in perfect condition. "That security line's a nightmare. You better go before you're late for your flight." She straightened his tie, smoothed her fingers down his lapel, laid her palm over his heart. It was so . . . wifely.

I love you.

Why couldn't he say the words?

"Okay, yeah, gotta go." He didn't want to leave. Pulling her in again for one last kiss, he felt like an eighteen-year-old going off to college and leaving his high school sweetheart behind. The gut-twisting moment when you're terrified everything will be changed when you see her again.

The same feeling he'd had thirty years ago.

HER BELLY ACHED LIKE WITHDRAWALS. HE'D BEEN GONE FIVE DAYS. In the past few months, they'd been apart longer than that. But that was before. Somehow she'd separated their relationship into the time before Noelle and Dax . . . and the time after.

He hadn't asked her to go to his daughter's recital. Of course, she wouldn't have gone anyway. But sometimes she thought about his kids. She imagined him with a baby in his arms. He was a good father. She was afraid she would have been a bad mother. It was better he never asked her to meet them.

But that night, God, that night with Noelle, he'd finally accepted her. It changed everything between them.

Isabel put the finishing touches on her makeup. Her heart wasn't in it tonight. She'd made the date before Palm Springs. Another *before.* In fact, she hadn't been on a date since she'd initiated the prince. But, as mayor of a major East Coast city, her client considered himself American royalty and requested her because she was the top tier. In his mind, that made her the best, the most desirable.

She didn't generally like to be dictated to, but with all practicality, his money was hard to say no to. It was also a business matter. He brought her a lot of clients. Pissing him off wasn't wise.

She'd always enjoyed the sex and the affirmation. But now, Royce accepted her. Now it wouldn't be the same without him. There wouldn't be that special connection. Like what Dax and Noelle shared.

She *needed* the connection. Funny, all those months ago she'd told Noelle how dangerous it was to be so dependent on one man. Now she craved it.

It was time to give up her clients. She didn't need them anymore. She had Royce. If they needed an extra kick, she'd find someone to join them. Tonight, she'd tell the mayor it would be the last time with her. He'd have to choose a new girl.

HE SHOULD HAVE CALLED, TOLD HER HE WAS COMING. HE'D CUT HIS Cincinnati trip short, crammed everything he'd needed to accomplish into three days instead of the five he'd planned on.

He should have learned not to surprise her.

Fuck. Where was she?

Royce sat on her fragile living room sofa. It was after midnight, and the night sky was damp with fog, seemingly devoid of stars. He'd been in the same position before, waiting for her. He closed his eyes against the clench in his gut.

Maybe she was out with girlfriends.

Except that he didn't believe Isabel had girlfriends in the traditional sense. If she was out with friends, well, hell, that probably meant she was having sex with them.

Fuck.

She'd never said she wouldn't *date*. She'd never said she wouldn't fuck some other guy when he was gone. Or maybe two or three or four—hell, how about a whole fucking gang bang?

He rose, paced, his stride eating up her Persian carpet, back and forth, back and forth, in front of the picture window.

Until headlights slashed across the road below. He stood on the edge looking out. A black Town Car, one of her preferences. The suited driver climbed out, rounded the hood, opened the door, and held out a hand. A vision in gold lamé stepped out.

Royce backed away from the window. Not that she could see him three floors above in her darkened window. Not that he cared if she saw. *He* was the one who didn't want to fucking see.

He remembered lying on that same goddamn sofa all those months ago. Waiting for her. Wondering if he was actually in love with her. The question had changed. Because yes, he was definitely goddamn in love with her. But did he love the woman she'd become? Or the woman he wanted her to be?

The only thing he was totally sure of was that he couldn't abide her so-called dates. He wasn't built like Dax Deacon where he got off on her calling him to relay every dirty detail. He didn't want to be tied to a fucking chair watching some other man enjoy her. He'd come far enough that he could actually contemplate sharing her, but he had to be involved, touching, kissing, something. That was his limit. But she had none. He hated to think how she paid for the car and the flat, her clothes, her jewelry, even the food she ate.

He was so fucking jealous he couldn't think straight, and he was afraid of what would come out of his mouth when she walked in that door. He wasn't sure he could contain the emotions roiling inside him. If he wasn't very, very careful, he'd set fire to the bridge they'd built between them.

He flopped heavily onto the sofa, its delicate frame creaking, straining, and dropped his head into his hands. He knew he had it good. What other woman in the world would actually let her man fuck another woman, enjoy it, participate in it, give him that kind of ultimate freedom? Yet he wanted *her* over that freedom.

He couldn't go on this way. He didn't know how to change it without losing her. Yet if he didn't do something, he'd lose himself.

The lock clicked loudly through the flat. Then her heels tapped on the hardwood. Until she stopped at the edge of the carpet. His briefcase and bag sat in the hall where he'd dropped them the moment he'd entered the cold, dark, silent apartment.

"You didn't tell me you were coming," she said, her tone neutral.

"I wasn't sure I'd make it out." Leaning over, he flipped on a standing lamp. "It was starting to snow in Cincinnati." Yet he would have camped out all night at the airport waiting if he'd had to.

Why hadn't he called, at least about his intentions? Because he'd wanted to catch her at something?

She shifted on her feet, stepping out of the shoes, then padded across the carpet. "Well, I'm so glad you came." She leaned down for a kiss, her fingers sweet and warm on his cheek.

Not a hair was out of place, her gold dress sparkled, and her lipstick was perfect, her breath minty fresh. Yet the scent of sex clung to her, making him both hard and angry.

She came down on the sofa beside him, one knee hooked beneath her, and laid an arm along the back. "Well, then, this is an extra unexpected pleasure."

He thought a spark of wariness passed through her gaze. A wave of near rage swept through him, and he wanted to rip off her dress, tear her panties, spread her legs, and fuck her, mark her with his scent, show her exactly who she belonged to. His cock throbbed with the need.

He could feel his breath rasp harshly in his throat, an ache in his eyeballs, his heart rapping against his ribs, and the rush of blood through his eardrums.

Christ, he loved her. But she tore his guts out.

Her chest rose, her breath suddenly rapid. "What's wrong?"

As if someone or something else had taken over his body, he saw a hand rise to the thigh-high slit in her dress. The material gave way with a loud rip, the tear reaching all the way to her navel.

Her trimmed pussy was bare. No stockings, no panties, just all that pink flesh. He scented her again, not just sex, but her own pure, sweet arousal. Had he made her wet? Or was it residual from fucking some other asshole?

"Condom," she whispered, going for her purse.

"Fuck the condom." He didn't even unbuckle, simply tore at his zipper and pulled his cock from his briefs. Yet instead of spreading her legs, he rose over her, fisted his hand in her hair, and shoved his cock between her parted lips.

She made a noise, held him off with a hand on his hip, until finally, she opened, took him deep. Her moan vibrated along his cock.

Christ, he wanted her mouth filled. He didn't want her words, didn't want to hear her say she loved him after she'd been out fucking some fat cat with cash bulging his pockets. He needed his own words. "Suck me. Christ, I need your mouth on me. Make me come. Drain me." *Be mine, only mine.*

Yet he wouldn't say he loved her, wouldn't give her the power.

He pushed her back against the sofa arm, fucked her mouth, pumping hard, fast, deep. She took everything he had to give, spread her legs, and added her own pleasure to the mix. The orgasm built in his balls, behind his eyelids, in his throat, choking off the words he would have said. Her mouth was so good, so warm and wet, so willing, so fucking expert. She worked him, worked herself, and he was no longer the one in control, no longer taking her but the one being taken. He clamped fingers hard on the back of the sofa, his joints aching, his eyes squeezed shut so that there was nothing but stars behind his lids and the feel and scent of her in his head.

He shot his load hard, deep, his gut contracting, his mind spiraling to another dimension where someone who sounded like him shouted out words he never would have given her tonight.

"Fuck, fuck, fuck. God, I love you. I so fucking love you."

11

"NOW, *THAT* WAS HOT," SHE MURMURED AGAINST HIS HEATED SKIN. Pinned beneath him on the sofa, Isabel nuzzled his neck, rubbed herself on him, imprinting him.

He loved her. That was what he'd shouted. She tucked the words close to her heart and tightened her grip on him.

Yet something was wrong. *Very* wrong.

She shouldn't have gone out tonight. Somewhere along the way, it had felt like cheating, all her reasons for doing it mere justifications. Finding Royce sitting in the dark flat had been like getting caught at it. Despite that they'd made no promises in that direction.

He sat up. Suddenly. Leaving her cold. Isabel shivered.

Stuffing his cock back in his pants and zipping up, he didn't even look at her, just waved a hand vaguely in the air. "Sorry about the dress."

She straightened on the couch, pulled the dress down, but the tear left her pussy exposed with no way to cover it. "That's okay. It was hot and worth it." Yet there was a lump in her throat she couldn't swallow past.

He rubbed an eye, then smoothed his hair. Finally, he leaned forward, elbows on his knees. "Look, this isn't working for me."

It took her five seconds to breathe again. She didn't have time to formulate an answer.

He clasped his hands between his legs. "I want something normal. Where you come home with me for holidays; I introduce you to my parents, my girls."

Her heart rolled over and over in her chest, tumbling down to the very pit of her stomach. She'd waited thirty years to hear that. But he was thirty years too late. "Royce."

"And not as a courtesan," he added without letting her finish.

"That's okay. We don't have to tell them about that."

He turned, eyed her with a dark gaze. "That's not what I mean."

Something trembled deep inside. She knew what was coming, and she knew they'd never survive it. "Don't say it."

He rose, paced to the window. "I will fucking say it. I want you to stop. Give it up. The whole thing. Be with *me*." He stabbed a finger at his chest.

She closed her eyes. He didn't understand. She'd tried to explain, but he hadn't gotten it. "I can never give it up. Courtesans kept me alive. I made a promise to Melora to take care of her girls." All the girls like her who needed to rebuild themselves from the ground up. Without Melora and Courtesans, Isabel would have died. Literally. Courtesans was her legacy. Courtesans was her *life*.

"Women like Noelle?" He swept out a hand. "She doesn't need you."

"You don't know her. You don't know her story." Noelle hadn't come from the streets like Isabel did, but she'd been damaged nonetheless. Plenty of her courtesans had come from far more horrifying backgrounds, too. They needed her.

She wasn't about to debate the worthiness of her legacy. Only one thing mattered. She rose from the couch, didn't bother to hold her dress together, the dress *he* had torn. "It's not your family's business what I do for a living. You don't have to tell them."

He pressed his lips together. "They'll find out. You've got satellite offices in all the major cities."

And abroad. She was proud of it, but her pride wasn't the issue. His lack of it was. "Let's face it, Royce. You're ashamed of me."

"I'm not."

He wouldn't face the truth. She remembered it all too clearly. "You were ashamed of me thirty years ago and hid me from your parents. Now you want to hide me from your daughters." But was that the complete truth? She'd never asked to see photos, never asked his children's names, closed her ears when he said them. She'd never really let him talk about them.

Heat suffused Royce's face, his skin reddening. "You were the one who cut and run when we were teenagers."

Her temples throbbed. She was a woman now, self-confident, sure. Yet he so easily thrust her back to those years, to being that girl, all the doubts, all the anger. "My leaving had nothing to do with your family. I would have stayed. I would have fought—" She stopped. The real reason she'd left wasn't pertinent. She might have engineered that last argument, but she'd used an issue that was already between them.

"You didn't stay; you didn't fight. I was wrong, too, but you didn't give me a chance to fix anything. You sent me a goddamn letter from L.A., then disappeared again."

She closed her eyes. What was the point? They were too different then, too different now. It was wrong to make it all his fault. His parents had been an excuse so she didn't have to tell him the truth.

She didn't realize how long she'd stood there with her eyes closed until the ticking of the grandfather clock penetrated the silence.

"Why did you really leave?"

She'd waited too long, given him time to think. "I was tired of fighting." She turned, crossed the carpet, picked up her shoes.

"You're lying."

She stood there, her back to him, chill bumps rising on her skin. The heating was still set at sixty-two. She hadn't turned it up when she came in; neither had he. He'd warmed her so fast, she hadn't needed it.

She knew why she hadn't told him back then. But why keep on lying about it? He hadn't accepted her when she was seventeen, and despite what she'd let herself believe this past week, he didn't accept her now. He never would. So what fucking difference did it make if she told him the truth?

She turned to him. The standing lamp lit his face, and behind him the city was aglow with lights. Maybe she even owed him the truth. He could let go of his guilt. Maybe she could let go of hers.

"I left because I was pregnant."

Not a single muscle twitched on his face nor in his entire body.

Every inch of her skin turned icy. She didn't think about that time except the passing regret that it had been her one and only chance to feel a living being inside her. Though of course she hadn't felt that way until years later, when she'd realized the chance would never come again.

He breathed, a long inhale, an equally long exhale. "We used a condom."

"Yes, we did." She prayed he wouldn't ask. But there were times in her life when God had left her to her own devices. This was one of them.

"Then I don't understand how."

He wasn't a stupid man. He hadn't been a stupid boy. He'd just been so trusting. "It wasn't yours."

* * *

HER FLAT WAS SUDDENLY SO SMALL, THE WALLS CLOSED IN ON HIM. There were certain things that he believed in. They gave him a foundation to stand on. He believed in his daughters, that they loved him as much as he loved them. That if ever he had to, he would lay his life down for them. That if he worked hard, life would reward him. That at seventeen, Isabel had loved him and only him.

If you took away a cornerstone of the foundation, the whole thing crumbled.

"Who?" His voice croaked. Someone he knew? A friend? One of the guys on the team?

"Harley." She didn't blink, didn't move, didn't change one inflection.

He couldn't think. "Who the hell was Harley?" She said it as if he were supposed to know.

They stood five feet from each other on opposite ends of the world.

"My mother's husband."

Everything fell out of the bottom of his world, straight down through the three floors beneath him, and he dropped right into the hole. "You slept with your stepfather?"

Her blue eyes turned glacial, her gaze covering him with a layer of frost that chilled his bones.

Then she turned, padded down the hardwood hall, her bare feet not making a sound. Then he heard what he'd said, recognized the accusation.

"It doesn't make sense," he whispered to the empty room. His voice echoed, bouncing off the wall right back at him.

"It makes perfect sense." Her voice floated down the hallway to him. "I snuck out. To be with you. He caught me climbing back in the window."

He couldn't see her at the end of the darkness, the words quiet, yet they reverberated from one wall to the next to the next.

"He said I smelled like sex."

Royce covered his ears. He heard his own thoughts. Tonight. How much he'd hated the scent yet how it crazed him with lust. Just before he tore her dress and shoved his cock in her mouth.

He couldn't remember moving, yet he was at the open door of her bedroom. By her closet, she shrugged out of the ruined dress, kicked it, then pulled on her robe, a thick terry cloth.

"He raped you after we . . ." He couldn't even finish the thought. It tore a layer of flesh from his bones, exposed his heart. "Why didn't you tell me?"

She tipped her head and smiled. It was as cold as her eyes. "What would you have done?"

"I don't know. Beat the shit out of him. Taken care of you."

She laughed. "Right. You wouldn't tell your parents about me even before that. So, like, I was supposed to think you'd suddenly say, *Hey, Mom and Dad, here's my white trash girlfriend Isabel who's pregnant with her stepdaddy's kid*?" She chuckled, shook her head. "Give me a break."

This was the woman she'd become. Cold. Brittle. Emotionless. He'd had a hand in it. They'd made love that one glorious time. Then everything had gone to hell. Now he knew why she hadn't let him touch her again. She was right. Her running away had had nothing to do with him hiding her from his parents. And everything to do with it. Because if he'd acknowledged her publicly, she would have believed in him enough to come to him with the truth about Harley.

"I'm sorry."

She came to him then, put her hand to his cheek. Her touch had always been so warm. Now it was cold. So was her gaze. "Poor Royce. Don't let it bother you. It was a long time ago, and it wasn't your fault."

"But the baby," he whispered.

She *tsk*ed. "Lost it." She raised one brow. "I never even showed. Didn't need to run away after all."

She spoke as if she felt nothing about it. Maybe she no longer did. For her, it had been over for thirty years, whereas for him, it was the here and now.

She turned, headed to the bathroom, her robe flying out behind her. "It's late. I have to take off my makeup." Stopping, one hand on the jamb, she looked back at him. "It's probably better if you get a hotel tonight. I'm not up to company." She disappeared inside her white-tiled bathroom. Then her voice floated out through the doorway. "And you can leave the key on the hall table."

HIS DRESS SHOES ECHOED ON THE HARDWOOD LIKE DRUMBEATS. IN the quiet of the night, she heard the front door close, a sound she would have missed in the daytime.

Isabel stared at herself in the mirror. Her cheeks were alabaster. Her heart was hard. She would never be warm again. Leaning over the claw-foot tub, she turned on the water, running it hot until steam began to rise, clouding the room. She closed the bathroom door. In the cool air, the steam condensed on the mirror until she could no longer see herself.

She let the robe fall, then stepped into the near-scalding water, her skin turning pink like a boiled lobster. She still couldn't get warm. She curled in on herself, hugging her arms to her belly, her forehead resting on her bent knees.

Honestly, she hadn't thought the whole thing bothered her anymore. She didn't think it could still hurt like this. Harley had dumped her mom two years after Isabel ran away. It was Melora who'd said she needed to contact her mother, close the circle. By the time she realized Melora was right, her mom was dead. Cirrhosis of the liver. Isabel closed the circle on her own and forgave her mom for marrying an asshole—two assholes if you counted Isabel's father, who'd run out when she was a toddler. It was a hell of a lot easier to forgive the dead than it was the living. She didn't mourn the baby, because really, what the hell kind of life would the poor thing have had? Maybe if she'd had prenatal care, a meal at least once a day, it wouldn't have died, but on the streets, those things were hard to come by if you didn't have a pimp to take care of you. Melora had found her bleeding in an alley. Now she mourned that she never got another chance.

Because maybe she would have been a better mother than her own had been. Maybe she would have been like Melora. Especially if she'd had a man like Royce to help her raise the child.

She cranked off the taps. Her skin pink below the water level, white above, she nevertheless began to feel the heat penetrating.

Though she'd hoped, she hadn't expected Royce would understand. His first question was a horrified *You slept with your stepfather?* It would have been all those years ago, too.

She *was* white trash. Of course she would have slept with her stepfather and had his kid. That was what all the girls in her trailer park did. Everybody knew that.

What they didn't know was how she'd locked her door every night after that, praying he couldn't get in again, and knowing that one day soon he would.

The worst was that for a very short time, she thought about telling Royce it was his child, letting him shoulder the responsibility. That was when she'd known she had to get out.

Sliding beneath the water, she soaked her hair. It was better that he was gone. She'd been fine before. She'd be fine again. She was strong. She loved her life.

And she would never let a man look at her again like she was dirt.

12

HE HADN'T CALLED; SHE'D GOTTEN THROUGH THE WEEKEND ANY-way. Life was fine. Really, life was good.

Swear it. Now she just had to get rid of this ache that was like a persistent cough. It attacked when you were least prepared, as-sailing you until your eyes watered.

She had other things to take care of.

Like Simon Foster, one of her very special clients, who needed something to dazzle a lady. Simon was an animal in bed. At fifty, he had the stamina of a man fifteen years younger. He was always up for anything she suggested, and she'd never hesitated to ask for his help with a client if she thought he fit the bill. The times she'd seen him in the last few months, he'd reminded her of Royce: the looks, the hair, the body.

Damn. *Everything* reminded her of Royce. Even a simple phone call from an old friend.

She'd never thought Simon, of all men, would succumb to the mythical lure of *the one*.

"I'd like to arrange this ASAP," he said. "The sooner, the better."

"Ooh. Desperate to impress, are we, darling?" It boggled her mind.

"You have no idea."

"Then I simply can't fail you, can I?" She *wouldn't* fail him.

While always invested in making sure his partner received the ultimate in pleasure, Simon had never been emotionally invested. He was like her, not meant for deep relationships. Royce's walking out was affirmation of that. All right, she'd suggested he leave. But he didn't have to do what she told him.

God, she sounded like such a bitch. Justifying herself. She hated it.

"Simon, if she's the one, I hope this works for you."

"She *is* the one."

Isabel held on to the phone long after he'd disconnected. First Walker Randall had met someone, now Simon. Was it contagious? She'd have thought them both immune. Or too old to change their ways. Especially Simon. For God's sake, Simon was too lusty for one woman. But then, he'd called to have Isabel arrange a third for his little party with *the one*. Perhaps he hadn't changed at all.

Except for that tone in his voice, a gentleness she'd never heard before, and yes, an edge of desperation, too. Whoever the woman was, she was special to him.

Walker had given up being a courtesan. What would Simon give up for his lady?

That ache started in Isabel's chest again.

What would she give up for Royce?

Her own hard edges smacked her in the face. When she thought about it, really allowed a little self-examination, she was forced to admit she hadn't given up a thing for Royce. She'd asked for acceptance, received it in abundance . . . and given nothing in return. Not even honesty. She'd always held things back. Since she hadn't said she wouldn't date and he hadn't asked her not to date, well, then, dating her clients was fine. Yet Royce had done everything she asked, including Noelle. Because *she* wanted it. Isabel had refused talk of the future, didn't show enough caring or concern to even ask about his girls, their colleges, majors, hopes, dreams. That bothered her, how she'd cut out such an important part of his life. Then suddenly, when he'd had a little trouble accepting a past that she'd lived with for thirty years, she'd thrown him out.

Simon, Walker, and Royce weren't the ones who couldn't change for a chance at love and happiness. *She* was. She was afraid to change. After all these years of thinking she was so strong and self-confident, Isabel had to admit she was a coward. She claimed she wasn't ready for a deep relationship, but the truth was that it terrified her. After all these years, she was still afraid of getting hurt again.

The phone was still in her hand. She dialed her travel agent. It was time to go to Royce instead of always making him come to her. It was time to return to the place she'd been running from for thirty years. It was time to go home.

PROSPERITY WAS LITTLE MORE THAN A DUST SPECK ON A LONG, flat stretch of highway an hour and a half north of Oklahoma City. Thirty years ago, when Isabel left, it had been less than a dust speck. The town square had been spruced up, old-fashioned benches of wood and wrought-iron curlicues, streetlamps with an antique look, planter boxes along the sidewalk, and parking meters. Downtown Prosperity was middle America whitewashed and painted with a bright facade. She'd taken a red-eye flight, and the morning was still early, a bit before eight. It was breath-in-the-air cold, but dry, whatever snow they'd had now dirty piles of hardened slush along the highway. A street sweeper ambled down the empty curb, and business owners, bundled up against the wind chill in mufflers, gloves, and hats pulled so low only their eyes were visible, cleaned yesterday's dirt from the sidewalks. She didn't recognize the names of the shops or the people. She hadn't expected to.

Royce's manufacturing plant was on the other side of town. She'd looked up the address to find out if it was still where she remembered and called the main number yesterday to be sure he wasn't traveling this week.

Maybe she should have had the courage to actually call *him*.

The route took her past her old street. The trailer park was gone, replaced with small starter homes. Oddly, her belly crimped. She should have been glad she didn't have to see the dump. Vindicated, as if she'd outlasted it, something. Yet the fact that it was gone was more of a reminder of *everything* that was gone. Maybe you couldn't get anything back. Just as she'd thought that first night all those months ago when she'd seen Royce in San Francisco, maybe there were no second chances.

Isabel curled her fingers around the steering wheel, holding it tight until her knuckles turned white.

When Royce left her key on the hall table, perhaps that was all there was.

TRACY, HIS SECRETARY, HELD THE DOOR OF HIS OFFICE CLOSED. "There's some lady out there who wants to talk to you," she stage-whispered, which totally negated the whispering.

Royce pushed his keyboard away and sat back in his chair. "Who is she?"

"I don't know," she once again whispered. Tracy had lived in Prosperity all her life, raised a family, and when the kids went off to college ten years ago and never returned, she came to work for him. She wasn't a Fortune 500 executive admin, but usually she was competent.

"Did you ask her?"

Tracy raised her eyebrows to the bottom of her gray bangs. "She won't give me a last name. Just tell him Isabel would like to see him," she mimicked.

His ears began to buzz with the rush of his blood.

She'd come home. For him.

"Send her in."

Tracy cocked her head as if she expected him to tell her who the woman was. When he didn't, she opened the door, then swept out a hand indicating entry.

Isabel wore tight jeans, fur-lined boots, and a thick Scandinavian sweater under a suede jacket long enough to cover her butt.

"I've never seen you in jeans." It was the most inane greeting, but he was afraid of saying too much in case he actually started to beg.

She closed the door. "It's cold here. Jeans seemed appropriate."

Obviously she remembered the ass-numbing winters. "Have a seat." *Tell me what you want. Please.*

After taking the chair opposite, she hugged the suede coat tighter as if he kept his office too cool. "I'll make this brief."

He realized her businesslike manner was nerves. He'd never seen her nervous, either, not this woman. "I have time." He glanced at his watch. "No meetings until ten."

"Oh." She rolled her lips, smoothing her lipstick. Then she crossed her legs the opposite direction. "All right. I was wrong. I had a date on Wednesday night, and I shouldn't have done that. Not after what we'd shared."

His fingers tingled with pins and needles as if they'd been asleep.

"Instead of dealing with the issue, I just accused you of being ashamed of me."

"What I said came across that way."

She waved a hand at him. "Look, what I do is not your normal run-of-the-mill job. You can't tell your friends or your family. I understand that." She leaned forward, put her fingertips on the desk. "But I'm not here to tell you that I'm going to give up Courtesans."

A fist closed around his lungs and squeezed all the breath out.

"But we can make this work. I don't have to take clients."

She didn't have to sleep with other men. A chip of ice broke off his heart. "You claimed you can never be vanilla again."

She sat back, wrapping the coat tight again, as if he'd actually caused the chill in the room. "I loved what we did with Noelle and Dax. I'm not saying I don't want to do stuff like that. But only with you." Then she shrugged. "But I don't need it the way I *need* you."

Warmth stole across his skin. He realized he hadn't been warm since he left her, and it had nothing to do with Oklahoma in January. "I need you," he whispered.

She dropped her voice, too. "I just can't stop managing Courtesans. I don't know how to let that go. Melora saved me." She swallowed, her eyes moist with emotion. "I told you that I was out on the streets, that she found me. But I didn't tell you I was hemorrhaging. I knew I'd lost the baby, but it just wouldn't stop bleeding. Melora, she came to the ugliest, seediest parts of town to find us, girls in trouble, to help us. She took me to the hospital. Then she took me into her home, her life. She made me who I am. And she passed everything on to me." She held him, her gaze steady. "Someday, I need to pass it on, too."

He closed his eyes a moment, thinking of her alone, bleeding. Trembling with emotion, he could feel her terror and bewilderment. He'd wanted to hate her for running away without telling him, for the years of guilt she'd left him with, for cutting him out, not trusting that he'd believe in her. For the guilt he felt even now.

Yet overriding it all was horror for what she'd endured, her step-father's touch, the months she'd spent alone. And admiration for the woman she'd become. On the plane trip home, he'd actually experienced the wonder of imagining her rounded with child. *His* child. In the end, though, with all his musings, guilt, and anger, he realized the pointlessness of it all. If she'd stayed, he wouldn't have his girls, and he couldn't trade them for a life with her any more than she could give up Courtesans.

"Please tell me how we can work this out," she said softly.

The here and now. That was what they had. "I can take anything except thinking about you fucking another man while I'm out of town."

Her eyes seemed to get bluer as she gazed at him. "I don't need that."

"Yes, you do." He rose, skirted the desk, tipped her chin with his finger. "Tell me how long you'd last without touching another man."

She clasped his hand, held his palm to her cheek. "The question is how long I'd last without touching *you*. I've loved you since the first time I saw you play football in high school. When I knew I was going to have a baby and it wasn't yours and I thought you'd never be able to forget or get over it, I wanted to die." She closed her eyes briefly. "But you came back. I've had thirty years to get other men out of my system. Now there's only you." She dropped her voice to less than a whisper, a mere feathering of words across her lips. "You're the one, Royce. You always were."

Royce went down on his knee beside her. "Here's how we can work it out." He kissed her fingertips. "Courtesans is your business. My family doesn't need to know what you do. With the girls at college, I can just as easily make my base in San Francisco. But you will meet them. You will meet my parents. I'm not going to hide you as if I'm ashamed of you."

Royce wiped a tear from beneath her eye with his thumb. "Hey, you never cry."

"You've just never seen me." Isabel couldn't help it. She wasn't a crier, but then, she'd never before gotten everything in the world that she desired. "I want to meet your girls. I can only imagine they must be the most perfect little creatures with you as their dad."

He laughed. "They're not little, and they're not perfect. But you're going to love them."

She put a hand to his cheek. "I love you."

"I never stopped loving you," he said. "Both of us need to let go of the past. It's only important because it made us who we are. This is a new beginning that's not rooted in what we had. No expectations."

She had no words. Instead she kissed him until her heart wanted to burst. God, how she'd missed his kiss.

Royce pulled back. "I've been thinking"—he rubbed his nose to hers, then put his lips to her ear—"that what we did with Noelle and Dax was pretty damn fun."

She pulled back to look at him. "It was?"

His eyes sparked. "Fuck yes."

She laughed, the first laugh she'd truly felt in days. He sounded so like Dax that night. "And?"

"We shouldn't limit our options."

She smiled at him, trailing her thumb along his bottom lip. "Where you're concerned, I have no limits."

ABOUT THE AUTHOR

Jasmine Haynes has been penning stories for as long as she's been able to write. With a bachelor's degree in accounting from Cal Poly San Luis Obispo, she's worked in the high-tech Silicon Valley for the last twenty years and hasn't met a boring accountant yet! Well, maybe a few. She and her husband live with Star, the mighty moose-hunting dog (if she weren't afraid of her own shadow) plus numerous wild cats (who have discovered that food from a bowl is easier than slaying gophers for their dinner). Jasmine's pastimes, when not writing her heart out, are speed-walking in the Redwoods, watching classic movies, and brainstorming with writer friends in coffee shops. Jasmine also writes as Jennifer Skully and JB Skully. Please visit her at www.jasminehaynes.com and www.jasminehaynes.blogspot.com. She loves to hear from readers.